The White Company

The White Company

Sir Arthur Conan Doyle

MINT EDITIONS

The White Company was first published in 1891.

This edition published by Mint Editions 2020.

ISBN 9781513267371 | E-ISBN 9781513272375

Published by Mint Editions®

minteditionbooks.com

Publishing Director: Jennifer Newens
Design & Production: Rachel Lopez Metzger
Typesetting: Westchester Publishing Services

Contents

I

How the Black Sheep Came Forth from the Fold

The great bell of Beaulieu was ringing. Far away through the forest might be heard its musical clangor and swell. Peat-cutters on Blackdown and fishers upon the Exe heard the distant throbbing rising and falling upon the sultry summer air. It was a common sound in those parts—as common as the chatter of the jays and the booming of the bittern. Yet the fishers and the peasants raised their heads and looked questions at each other, for the angelus had already gone and vespers was still far off. Why should the great bell of Beaulieu toll when the shadows were neither short nor long?

All round the Abbey the monks were trooping in. Under the long green-paved avenues of gnarled oaks and of lichened beeches the white-robed brothers gathered to the sound. From the vine-yard and the vine-press, from the bouvary or ox-farm, from the marl-pits and salterns, even from the distant iron-works of Sowley and the outlying grange of St. Leonard's, they had all turned their steps homewards. It had been no sudden call. A swift messenger had the night before sped round to the outlying dependencies of the Abbey, and had left the summons for every monk to be back in the cloisters by the third hour after noontide. So urgent a message had not been issued within the memory of old lay-brother Athanasius, who had cleaned the Abbey knocker since the year after the Battle of Bannockburn.

A stranger who knew nothing either of the Abbey or of its immense resources might have gathered from the appearance of the brothers some conception of the varied duties which they were called upon to perform, and of the busy, wide-spread life which centred in the old monastery. As they swept gravely in by twos and by threes, with bended heads and muttering lips there were few who did not bear upon them some signs of their daily toil. Here were two with wrists and sleeves all spotted with the ruddy grape juice. There again was a bearded brother with a broad-headed axe and a bundle of faggots upon his shoulders, while beside him walked another with the shears under his arm and the white wool still clinging to his whiter gown. A long, straggling troop bore spades and mattocks while the two rearmost of all staggered along under a huge basket o' fresh-caught carp, for the morrow was Friday, and there were fifty platters to be filled and as many sturdy trenchermen behind them. Of all the throng there was scarce one who was not labor-stained and weary, for Abbot Berghersh was a hard man to himself and to others.

Meanwhile, in the broad and lofty chamber set apart for occasions of import, the Abbot himself was pacing impatiently backwards and forwards, with his long white nervous hands clasped in front of him. His thin, thought-worn features and sunken, haggard cheeks bespoke one who had indeed beaten down that inner foe whom every man must face, but had none the less suffered sorely in the contest. In crushing his passions he had well-nigh crushed himself. Yet, frail as was his person there gleamed out ever and anon from under his drooping brows a flash of fierce energy, which recalled to men's minds that he came of a fighting stock, and that even now his twin-brother, Sir Bartholomew Berghersh, was one of the most famous of those stern warriors who had planted the Cross of St. George before the gates of Paris. With lips compressed and clouded brow, he strode up and down the oaken floor, the very genius and impersonation of asceticism, while the great bell still thundered and clanged above his head. At last the uproar died away in three last, measured throbs, and ere their echo had ceased the Abbot struck a small gong which summoned a lay-brother to his presence.

"Have the brethren come?" he asked, in the Anglo-French dialect used in religious houses.

"They are here," the other answered, with his eyes cast down and his hands crossed upon his chest.

"All?"

"Two and thirty of the seniors and fifteen of the novices, most holy father. Brother Mark of the Spicarium is sore smitten with a fever and could not come. He said that—"

"It boots not what he said. Fever or no, he should have come at my call. His spirit must be chastened, as must that of many more in this Abbey. You yourself, brother Francis, have twice raised your voice, so it hath come to my ears, when the reader in the refectory hath been dealing with the lives of God's most blessed saints. What hast thou to say?"

The lay-brother stood meek and silent, with his arms still crossed in front of him.

"One thousand Aves and as many Credos, said standing with arms outstretched before the shrine of the Virgin, may help thee to remember that the Creator hath given us two ears and but one mouth, as a token that there is twice the work for the one as for the other. Where is the master of the novices?"

"He is without, most holy father."

"Send him hither."

The sandalled feet clattered over the wooden floor, and the iron-bound door creaked upon its hinges. In a few moments it opened again to admit a short square monk with a heavy, composed face and an authoritative manner.

"You have sent for me, holy father?"

"Yes, brother Jerome, I wish that this matter be disposed of with as little scandal as may be, and yet it is needful that the example should be a public one." The Abbot spoke in Latin now, as a language which was more fitted by its age and solemnity to convey the thoughts of two high dignitaries of the order.

"It would, perchance, be best that the novices be not admitted," suggested the master. "This mention of a woman may turn their minds from their pious meditations to worldly and evil thoughts."

"Woman! woman!" groaned the Abbot. "Well has the holy Chrysostom termed them *radix malorum*. From Eve downwards, what good hath come from any of them? Who brings the plaint?"

"It is brother Ambrose."

"A holy and devout young man."

"A light and a pattern to every novice."

"Let the matter be brought to an issue then according to our old-time monastic habit. Bid the chancellor and the sub-chancellor lead in the brothers according to age, together with brother John, the accused, and brother Ambrose, the accuser."

"And the novices?"

"Let them bide in the north alley of the cloisters. Stay! Bid the sub-chancellor send out to them Thomas the lector to read unto them from the 'Gesta beati Benedicti.' It may save them from foolish and pernicious babbling."

The Abbot was left to himself once more, and bent his thin gray face over his illuminated breviary. So he remained while the senior monks filed slowly and sedately into the chamber seating themselves upon the long oaken benches which lined the wall on either side. At the further end, in two high chairs as large as that of the Abbot, though hardly as elaborately carved, sat the master of the novices and the chancellor, the latter a broad and portly priest, with dark mirthful eyes and a thick outgrowth of crisp black hair all round his tonsured head. Between them stood a lean, white-faced brother who appeared to be ill at ease, shifting his feet from side to side and tapping his chin nervously with the long parchment roll which he held in his hand. The Abbot, from his point of vantage, looked down on the two long lines of faces, placid and sun-browned for the most part, with the large bovine eyes and unlined features which told of their easy, unchanging existence. Then he turned his eager fiery gaze upon the pale-faced monk who faced him.

"This plaint is thine, as I learn, brother Ambrose," said he. "May the holy Benedict, patron of our house, be present this day and aid us in our findings! How many counts are there?"

"Three, most holy father," the brother answered in a low and quavering voice.

"Have you set them forth according to rule?"

"They are here set down, most holy father, upon a cantle of sheep-skin."

"Let the sheep-skin be handed to the chancellor. Bring in brother John, and let him hear the plaints which have been urged against him."

At this order a lay-brother swung open the door, and two other lay-brothers entered leading between them a young novice of the order. He was a man of huge stature, dark-eyed and red-headed, with a peculiar half-humorous, half-defiant expression upon his bold, well-marked features. His cowl was thrown back upon his shoulders, and his gown, unfastened at the top, disclosed a round, sinewy neck, ruddy and corded like the bark of the fir. Thick, muscular arms, covered with a reddish down, protruded from the wide sleeves of his habit, while his white shirt, looped up upon one side, gave a glimpse of a huge knotty leg, scarred and torn with the scratches of brambles. With a bow to the Abbot, which had in it perhaps more pleasantry than reverence, the novice strode across to the carved prie-dieu which had been set apart for him, and stood silent and erect with his hand upon the gold bell which was used in the private orisons of the Abbot's own household. His dark eyes glanced rapidly over the assembly, and finally settled with a grim and menacing twinkle upon the face of his accuser.

The chancellor rose, and having slowly unrolled the parchment-scroll, proceeded to read it out in a thick and pompous voice, while a subdued rustle and movement among the brothers bespoke the interest with which they followed the proceedings.

"Charges brought upon the second Thursday after the Feast of the Assumption, in the year of our Lord thirteen hundred and sixty-six, against brother John, formerly known as Hordle John, or John of Hordle, but now a novice in the holy monastic order of the Cistercians. Read upon the same day at the Abbey of Beaulieu in the presence of the most reverend Abbot Berghersh and of the assembled order.

"The charges against the said brother John are the following, namely, to wit:

"First, that on the above-mentioned Feast of the Assumption, small beer having been served to the novices in the proportion of one quart to each four, the said brother John did drain the pot at one draught to the detriment of brother Paul, brother Porphyry and brother Ambrose, who could scarce eat their none-meat of salted stock-fish on account of their exceeding dryness."

At this solemn indictment the novice raised his hand and twitched his lip, while even the placid senior brothers glanced across at each other and coughed to cover their amusement. The Abbot alone sat gray and immutable, with a drawn face and a brooding eye.

"Item, that having been told by the master of the novices that he should restrict his food for two days to a single three-pound loaf of bran and beans, for the greater honoring and glorifying of St. Monica, mother of the holy Augustine, he was heard by brother Ambrose and others to say that he wished twenty thousand devils would fly away with the said Monica, mother of the holy Augustine, or any other saint who came between a man and his meat. Item, that upon brother Ambrose reproving him for this blasphemous wish, he did hold the said brother face downwards over the piscatorium or fish-pond for a space during which the said brother was able to repeat a pater and four aves for the better fortifying of his soul against impending death."

There was a buzz and murmur among the white-frocked brethren at this grave charge; but the Abbot held up his long quivering hand. "What then?" said he.

"Item, that between nones and vespers on the feast of James the Less the said brother John was observed upon the Brockenhurst road, near the spot which is known as Hatchett's Pond in converse with a person of the other sex, being a maiden of the name of Mary Sowley, the daughter of the King's verderer. Item, that after sundry japes and jokes the said brother John did lift up the said Mary Sowley and did take, carry, and convey her across a stream, to the infinite relish of the devil and the exceeding detriment of his own soul, which scandalous and wilful falling away was witnessed by three members of our order."

A dead silence throughout the room, with a rolling of heads and upturning of eyes, bespoke the pious horror of the community.

The Abbot drew his gray brows low over his fiercely questioning eyes.

"Who can vouch for this thing?" he asked.

"That can I," answered the accuser. "So too can brother Porphyry, who was with me, and brother Mark of the Spicarium, who hath been so much stirred and inwardly troubled by the sight that he now lies in a fever through it."

"And the woman?" asked the Abbot. "Did she not break into lamentation and woe that a brother should so demean himself?"

"Nay, she smiled sweetly upon him and thanked him. I can vouch it and so can brother Porphyry."

"Canst thou?" cried the Abbot, in a high, tempestuous tone. "Canst thou so? Hast forgotten that the five-and-thirtieth rule of the order is that in the presence of a woman the face should be ever averted and the eyes cast down? Hast forgot it, I say? If your eyes were upon your sandals, how came ye to see this smile of which ye prate? A week in your cells, false brethren, a week of rye-bread and lentils, with double lauds and double matins, may help ye to remembrance of the laws under which ye live."

At this sudden outflame of wrath the two witnesses sank their faces on to their chests, and sat as men crushed. The Abbot turned his angry eyes away from them and bent them upon the accused, who met his searching gaze with a firm and composed face.

"What hast thou to say, brother John, upon these weighty things which are urged against you?"

"Little enough, good father, little enough," said the novice, speaking English with a broad West Saxon drawl. The brothers, who were English to a man, pricked up their ears at the sound of the homely and yet unfamiliar speech; but the Abbot flushed red with anger, and struck his hand upon the oaken arm of his chair.

"What talk is this?" he cried. "Is this a tongue to be used within the walls of an old and well-famed monastery? But grace and learning have ever gone hand in hand, and when one is lost it is needless to look for the other."

"I know not about that," said brother John. "I know only that the words come kindly to my mouth, for it was the speech of my fathers before me. Under your favor, I shall either use it now or hold my peace."

The Abbot patted his foot and nodded his head, as one who passes a point but does not forget it.

"For the matter of the ale," continued brother John, "I had come in hot from the fields and had scarce got the taste of the thing before mine eye lit upon the bottom of the pot. It may be, too, that I spoke somewhat shortly concerning the bran and the beans, the same being poor provender and unfitted for a man of my inches. It is true also that I did lay my hands upon this jack-fool of a brother Ambrose, though, as you can see, I did him little scathe. As regards the maid, too, it is true that I did heft her over the stream, she having on her hosen and shoon, whilst I had but my wooden sandals, which could take no hurt from the water. I should have thought shame upon my manhood, as well as my monkhood, if I had held back my hand from her." He glanced around as he spoke with the half-amused look which he had worn during the whole proceedings.

"There is no need to go further," said the Abbot. "He has confessed to all. It only remains for me to portion out the punishment which is due to his evil conduct."

He rose, and the two long lines of brothers followed his example, looking sideways with scared faces at the angry prelate.

"John of Hordle," he thundered, "you have shown yourself during the two months of your novitiate to be a recreant monk, and one who is unworthy to wear the white garb which is the outer symbol of the spotless spirit. That dress shall therefore be stripped from thee, and thou shalt be cast into the outer world without benefit of clerkship, and without lot or part in the graces and blessings of those who dwell under the care of the Blessed Benedict. Thou shalt come back neither to Beaulieu nor to any of the granges of Beaulieu, and thy name shall be struck off the scrolls of the order."

The sentence appeared a terrible one to the older monks, who had become so used to the safe and regular life of the Abbey that they would have been as helpless as children in the outer world. From their pious oasis they looked dreamily out at the desert of life, a place full of stormings and strivings—comfortless, restless, and overshadowed by evil. The young novice, however, appeared to have other thoughts, for his eyes sparkled and his smile broadened. It needed but that to add fresh fuel to the fiery mood of the prelate.

"So much for thy spiritual punishment," he cried. "But it is to thy grosser feelings that we must turn in such natures as thine, and as thou art no longer under the shield of holy church there is the less difficulty. Ho there! lay-brothers—Francis, Naomi, Joseph—seize him and bind his arms! Drag him forth, and let the foresters and the porters scourge him from the precincts!"

As these three brothers advanced towards him to carry out the Abbot's direction, the smile faded from the novice's face, and he glanced right and left with his fierce brown eyes, like a bull at a baiting. Then, with a sudden deep-chested shout, he tore up the heavy oaken prie-dieu and poised it to strike, taking two steps backward the while, that none might take him at a vantage.

"By the black rood of Waltham!" he roared, "if any knave among you lays a finger-end upon the edge of my gown, I will crush his skull like a filbert!" With his thick knotted arms, his thundering voice, and his bristle of red hair, there was something so repellent in the man that the three brothers flew back at the very glare of him; and the two rows of white monks strained away from him like poplars in a tempest. The Abbot only sprang forward with shining eyes; but the chancellor and the master hung upon either arm and wrested him back out of danger's way.

"He is possessed of a devil!" they shouted. "Run, brother Ambrose, brother Joachim! Call Hugh of the Mill, and Woodman Wat, and Raoul with his arbalest and bolts. Tell them that we are in fear of our lives! Run, run! for the love of the Virgin!"

But the novice was a strategist as well as a man of action. Springing forward, he hurled his unwieldy weapon at brother Ambrose, and, as desk and monk clattered on to the floor together, he sprang through the open door and down the winding stair. Sleepy old brother Athanasius, at the porter's cell, had a fleeting vision of twinkling feet and flying skirts; but before he had time to rub his eyes the recreant had passed the lodge, and was speeding as fast as his sandals could patter along the Lyndhurst Road.

II

How Alleyne Edricson Came Out into the World

Never had the peaceful atmosphere of the old Cistercian house been so rudely ruffled. Never had there been insurrection so sudden, so short, and so successful. Yet the Abbot Berghersh was a man of too firm a grain to allow one bold outbreak to imperil the settled order of his great household. In a few hot and bitter words, he compared their false brother's exit to the expulsion of our first parents from the garden, and more than hinted that unless a reformation occurred some others of the community might find themselves in the same evil and perilous case. Having thus pointed the moral and reduced his flock to a fitting state of docility, he dismissed them once more to their labors and withdrew himself to his own private chamber, there to seek spiritual aid in the discharge of the duties of his high office.

The Abbot was still on his knees, when a gentle tapping at the door of his cell broke in upon his orisons.

Rising in no very good humor at the interruption, he gave the word to enter; but his look of impatience softened down into a pleasant and paternal smile as his eyes fell upon his visitor.

He was a thin-faced, yellow-haired youth, rather above the middle size, comely and well shapen, with straight, lithe figure and eager, boyish features. His clear, pensive gray eyes, and quick, delicate expression, spoke of a nature which had unfolded far from the boisterous joys and sorrows of the world. Yet there was a set of the mouth and a prominence of the chin which relieved him of any trace of effeminacy. Impulsive he might be, enthusiastic, sensitive, with something sympathetic and adaptive in his disposition; but an observer of nature's tokens would have confidently pledged himself that there was native firmness and strength underlying his gentle, monk-bred ways.

The youth was not clad in monastic garb, but in lay attire, though his jerkin, cloak and hose were all of a sombre hue, as befitted one who dwelt in sacred precincts. A broad leather strap hanging from his shoulder supported a scrip or satchel such as travellers were wont to carry. In one hand he grasped a thick staff pointed and shod with metal, while in the other he held his coif or bonnet, which bore in its front a broad pewter medal stamped with the image of Our Lady of Rocamadour.

"Art ready, then, fair son?" said the Abbot. "This is indeed a day of comings and of goings. It is strange that in one twelve hours the Abbey should have cast off its foulest weed and should now lose what we are fain to look upon as our choicest blossom."

"You speak too kindly, father," the youth answered. "If I had my will I should never go forth, but should end my days here in Beaulieu. It hath been my home as far back as my mind can carry me, and it is a sore thing for me to have to leave it."

"Life brings many a cross," said the Abbot gently. "Who is without them? Your going forth is a grief to us as well as to yourself. But there is no help. I had given my foreword and sacred promise to your father, Edric the Franklin, that at the age of twenty you should be sent out into the world to see for yourself how you liked the savor of it. Seat thee upon the settle, Alleyne, for you may need rest ere long."

The youth sat down as directed, but reluctantly and with diffidence. The Abbot stood by the narrow window, and his long black shadow fell slantwise across the rush-strewn floor.

"Twenty years ago," he said, "your father, the Franklin of Minstead, died, leaving to the Abbey three hides of rich land in the hundred of Malwood, and leaving to us also his infant son on condition that we should rear him until he came to man's estate. This he did partly because your mother was dead, and partly because your elder brother, now Socman of Minstead, had already given sign of that fierce and rude nature which would make him no fit companion for you. It was his desire and request, however, that you should not remain in the cloisters, but should at a ripe age return into the world."

"But, father," interrupted the young man, "it is surely true that I am already advanced several degrees in clerkship?"

"Yes, fair son, but not so far as to bar you from the garb you now wear or the life which you must now lead. You have been porter?"

"Yes, father."

"Exorcist?"

"Yes, father."

"Reader?"

"Yes, father."

"Acolyte?"

"Yes, father."

"But have sworn no vow of constancy or chastity?"

"No, father."

"Then you are free to follow a worldly life. But let me hear, ere you start, what gifts you take away with you from Beaulieu? Some I already know. There is the playing of the citole and the rebeck. Our choir will be dumb without you. You carve too?"

The youth's pale face flushed with the pride of the skilled workman. "Yes, holy father," he answered. "Thanks to good brother Bartholomew, I carve in wood and in ivory, and can do something also in silver and in bronze. From brother Francis I have learned to paint on vellum, on glass, and on metal, with a knowledge of those pigments and essences which can preserve the color against damp or a biting air. Brother Luke hath given me some skill in damask work, and in the enamelling of shrines, tabernacles, diptychs and triptychs. For the rest, I know a little of the making of covers, the cutting of precious stones, and the fashioning of instruments."

"A goodly list, truly," cried the superior with a smile. "What clerk of Cambrig or of Oxenford could say as much? But of thy reading—hast not so much to show there, I fear?"

"No, father, it hath been slight enough. Yet, thanks to our good chancellor, I am not wholly unlettered. I have read Ockham, Bradwardine, and other of the schoolmen, together with the learned Duns Scotus and the book of the holy Aquinas."

"But of the things of this world, what have you gathered from your reading? From this high window you may catch a glimpse over the wooden point and the smoke of Bucklershard of the mouth of the Exe, and the shining sea. Now, I pray you, Alleyne, if a man were to take a ship and spread sail across yonder waters, where might he hope to arrive?"

The youth pondered, and drew a plan amongst the rushes with the point of his staff. "Holy father," said he, "he would come upon those parts of France which are held by the King's Majesty. But if he trended to the south he might reach Spain and the Barbary States. To his north would be Flanders and the country of the Eastlanders and of the Muscovites."

"True. And how if, after reaching the King's possessions, he still journeyed on to the eastward?"

"He would then come upon that part of France which is still in dispute, and he might hope to reach the famous city of Avignon, where dwells our blessed father, the prop of Christendom."

"And then?"

"Then he would pass through the land of the Almains and the great Roman Empire, and so to the country of the Huns and of the Lithuanian pagans, beyond which lies the great city of Constantine and the kingdom of the unclean followers of Mahmoud."

"And beyond that, fair son?"

"Beyond that is Jerusalem and the Holy Land, and the great river which hath its source in the Garden of Eden."

"And then?"

"Nay, good father, I cannot tell. Methinks the end of the world is not far from there."

"Then we can still find something to teach thee, Alleyne," said the Abbot complaisantly. "Know that many strange nations lie betwixt there and the end of the world. There is the country of the Amazons, and the country of the dwarfs, and the country of the fair but evil women who slay with beholding, like the basilisk. Beyond that again is the kingdom of Prester John and of the great Cham. These things I know for very sooth, for I had them from that pious Christian and valiant knight, Sir John de Mandeville, who stopped twice at Beaulieu on his way to and from Southampton, and discoursed to us concerning what he had seen from the reader's desk in the refectory, until there was many a good brother who got neither bit nor sup, so stricken were they by his strange tales."

"I would fain know, father," asked the young man, "what there may be at the end of the world?"

"There are some things," replied the Abbot gravely, "into which it was never intended that we should inquire. But you have a long road before you. Whither will you first turn?"

"To my brother's at Minstead. If he be indeed an ungodly and violent man, there is the more need that I should seek him out and see whether I cannot turn him to better ways."

The Abbot shook his head. "The Socman of Minstead hath earned an evil name over the country side," he said. "If you must go to him, see at least that he doth not turn you from the narrow path upon which you have learned to tread. But you are in God's keeping, and Godward should you ever look in danger and in trouble. Above all, shun the snares of women, for they are ever set for the foolish feet of the young. Kneel down, my child, and take an old man's blessing."

Alleyne Edricson bent his head while the Abbot poured out his heartfelt supplication that Heaven would watch over this young soul, now going forth into the darkness and danger of the world. It was no mere form for either of them. To them the outside life of mankind did indeed seem to be one of violence and of sin, beset with physical and still more with spiritual danger. Heaven, too, was very near to them in those days. God's direct agency was to be seen in the thunder and the rainbow, the whirlwind and the lightning. To the believer, clouds of angels and confessors, and martyrs, armies of the sainted and the saved, were ever stooping over their struggling brethren upon earth, raising, encouraging, and supporting them. It was then with a lighter heart and a stouter courage that the young man turned from the Abbot's room, while the latter, following him to the stair-head, finally commended him to the protection of the holy Julian, patron of travellers.

Underneath, in the porch of the Abbey, the monks had gathered to give him a last God-speed. Many had brought some parting token by which he should remember them. There was brother Bartholomew with a crucifix of rare carved ivory, and brother Luke with a white-backed psalter adorned with golden bees, and brother Francis with the "Slaying of the Innocents" most daintily set forth upon vellum. All these were duly packed away deep in the traveller's scrip, and above them old pippin-faced brother Athanasius had placed a parcel of simnel bread and rammel cheese, with a small flask of the famous blue-sealed Abbey wine. So, amid hand-shakings and laughings and blessings, Alleyne Edricson turned his back upon Beaulieu.

At the turn of the road he stopped and gazed back. There was the wide-spread building which he knew so well, the Abbot's house, the long church, the cloisters with their line of arches, all bathed and mellowed in the evening sun. There too was the broad sweep of the river Exe, the old stone well, the canopied niche of the Virgin, and in the centre of all the cluster of white-robed figures who waved their hands to him. A sudden mist swam up before the young man's eyes, and he turned away upon his journey with a heavy heart and a choking throat.

III

How Hordle John Cozened the Fuller of Lymington

It is not, however, in the nature of things that a lad of twenty, with young life glowing in his veins and all the wide world before him, should spend his first hours of freedom in mourning for what he had left. Long ere Alleyne was out of sound of the Beaulieu bells he was striding sturdily along, swinging his staff and whistling as merrily as the birds in the thicket. It was an evening to raise a man's heart. The sun shining slantwise through the trees threw delicate traceries across the road, with bars of golden light between. Away in the distance before and behind, the green boughs, now turning in places to a coppery redness, shot their broad arches across the track. The still summer air was heavy with the resinous smell of the great forest. Here and there a tawny brook prattled out from among the underwood and lost itself again in the ferns and brambles upon the further side. Save the dull piping of insects and the sough of the leaves, there was silence everywhere—the sweet restful silence of nature.

And yet there was no want of life—the whole wide wood was full of it. Now it was a lithe, furtive stoat which shot across the path upon some fell errand of its own; then it was a wild cat which squatted upon the outlying branch of an oak and peeped at the traveller with a yellow and dubious eye. Once it was a wild sow which scuttled out of the bracken, with two young sounders at her heels, and once a lordly red staggard walked daintily out from among the tree trunks, and looked around him with the fearless gaze of one who lived under the King's own high protection. Alleyne gave his staff a merry flourish, however, and the red deer bethought him that the King was far off, so streaked away from whence he came.

The youth had now journeyed considerably beyond the furthest domains of the Abbey. He was the more surprised therefore when, on coming round a turn in the path, he perceived a man clad in the familiar garb of the order, and seated in a clump of heather by the roadside. Alleyne had known every brother well, but this was a face which was new to him—a face which was very red and puffed, working this way and that, as though the man were sore perplexed in his mind. Once he shook both hands furiously in the air, and twice he sprang from his seat and hurried down the road. When he rose, however, Alleyne observed that his robe was much too long and loose for him in every direction, trailing upon the ground and bagging about his ankles, so that even with trussed-up skirts he could make little progress. He ran once, but the long gown clogged him so that he slowed down into a shambling walk, and finally plumped into the heather once more.

"Young friend," said he, when Alleyne was abreast of him, "I fear from thy garb that thou canst know little of the Abbey of Beaulieu."

"Then you are in error, friend," the clerk answered, "for I have spent all my days within its walls."

"Hast so indeed?" cried he. "Then perhaps canst tell me the name of a great loathly lump of a brother wi' freckled face an' a hand like a spade. His eyes were black an' his hair was red an' his voice like the parish bull. I trow that there cannot be two alike in the same cloisters."

"That surely can be no other than brother John," said Alleyne. "I trust he has done you no wrong, that you should be so hot against him."

"Wrong, quotha?" cried the other, jumping out of the heather. "Wrong! why he hath stolen every plack of clothing off my back, if that be a wrong, and hath left me here in this sorry frock of white falding, so that I have shame to go back to my wife, lest she think that I have donned her old kirtle. Harrow and alas that ever I should have met him!"

"But how came this?" asked the young clerk, who could scarce keep from laughter at the sight of the hot little man so swathed in the great white cloak.

"It came in this way," he said, sitting down once more: "I was passing this way, hoping to reach Lymington ere nightfall when I came on this red-headed knave seated even where we are sitting now. I uncovered and louted as I passed thinking that he might be a holy man at his orisons, but he called to me and asked me if I had heard speak of the new indulgence in favor of the Cistercians. 'Not I,' I answered. 'Then the worse for thy soul!' said he; and with that he broke into a long tale how that on account of the virtues of the Abbot Berghersh it had been decreed by the Pope that whoever should wear the habit of a monk of Beaulieu for as long as he might say the seven psalms of David should be assured of the kingdom of Heaven. When I heard this I prayed him on my knees that he would give me the use of his gown, which after many contentions he at last agreed to do, on my paying him three marks towards the regilding of the image of Laurence the martyr. Having stripped his robe, I had no choice but to let him have the wearing of my good leathern jerkin and hose, for, as he said, it was chilling to the blood and unseemly to the eye to stand frockless whilst I made my orisons. He had scarce got them on, and it was a sore labor, seeing that my inches will scarce match my girth—he had scarce got them on, I say, and I not yet at the end of the second psalm, when he bade me do honor to my new dress, and with that set off down the road as fast as feet would carry him. For myself, I could no more run than if I had been sown in a sack; so here I sit, and here I am like to sit, before I set eyes upon my clothes again."

"Nay, friend, take it not so sadly," said Alleyne, clapping the disconsolate one upon the shoulder. "Canst change thy robe for a jerkin once more at the Abbey, unless perchance you have a friend near at hand."

"That have I," he answered, "and close; but I care not to go nigh him in this plight, for his wife hath a gibing tongue, and will spread the tale until I could not show my face in any market from Fordingbridge to Southampton. But if you, fair sir, out of your kind charity would be pleased to go a matter of two bow-shots out of your way, you would do me such a service as I could scarce repay."

"With all my heart," said Alleyne readily.

"Then take this pathway on the left, I pray thee, and then the deer-track which passes on the right. You will then see under a great beech-tree the hut of a charcoal-burner. Give him my name, good sir, the name of Peter the fuller, of Lymington, and ask him for a change of raiment, that I may pursue my journey without delay. There are reasons why he would be loth to refuse me."

Alleyne started off along the path indicated, and soon found the log-hut where the burner dwelt. He was away faggot-cutting in the forest, but his wife, a ruddy bustling dame, found the needful garments and tied them into a bundle. While she busied herself in finding and folding them, Alleyne Edricson stood by the open door looking in at her with much interest and some distrust, for he had never been so nigh to a woman before. She had round red arms, a dress of some sober woollen stuff, and a brass brooch the size of a cheese-cake stuck in the front of it.

"Peter the fuller!" she kept repeating. "Marry come up! if I were Peter the fuller's wife I would teach him better than to give his clothes to the first knave who asks for them. But he was always a poor, fond, silly creature, was Peter, though we are beholden to him for helping to bury our second son Wat, who was a 'prentice to him at Lymington in the year of the Black Death. But who are you, young sir?"

"I am a clerk on my road from Beaulieu to Minstead."

"Aye, indeed! Hast been brought up at the Abbey then. I could read it from thy reddened cheek and downcast eye. Hast learned from the monks, I trow, to fear a woman as thou wouldst a lazar-house. Out upon them! that they should dishonor their own mothers by such teaching. A pretty world it would be with all the women out of it."

"Heaven forfend that such a thing should come to pass!" said Alleyne.

"Amen and amen! But thou art a pretty lad, and the prettier for thy modest ways. It is easy to see from thy cheek that thou hast not spent thy days in the rain and the heat and the wind, as my poor Wat hath been forced to do."

"I have indeed seen little of life, good dame."

"Wilt find nothing in it to pay for the loss of thy own freshness. Here are the clothes, and Peter can leave them when next he comes this way. Holy Virgin! see the dust upon thy doublet! It were easy to see that there is no woman to tend to thee. So!—that is better. Now buss me, boy."

Alleyne stooped and kissed her, for the kiss was the common salutation of the age, and, as Erasmus long afterwards remarked, more used in England than in any other country. Yet it sent the blood to his temples again, and he wondered, as he turned away, what the Abbot Berghersh would have answered to so frank an invitation. He was still tingling from this new experience when he came out upon the high-road and saw a sight which drove all other thoughts from his mind.

Some way down from where he had left him the unfortunate Peter was stamping and raving tenfold worse than before. Now, however, instead of the great white cloak, he had no clothes on at all, save a short woollen shirt and a pair of leather shoes. Far down the road a long-legged figure was running, with a bundle under one arm and the other hand to his side, like a man who laughs until he is sore.

"See him!" yelled Peter. "Look to him! You shall be my witness. He shall see Winchester jail for this. See where he goes with my cloak under his arm!"

"Who then?" cried Alleyne.

"Who but that cursed brother John. He hath not left me clothes enough to make a gallybagger. The double thief hath cozened me out of my gown."

"Stay though, my friend, it was his gown," objected Alleyne.

"It boots not. He hath them all—gown, jerkin, hosen and all. Gramercy to him that he left me the shirt and the shoon. I doubt not that he will be back for them anon."

"But how came this?" asked Alleyne, open-eyed with astonishment.

"Are those the clothes? For dear charity's sake give them to me. Not the Pope himself shall have these from me, though he sent the whole college of cardinals to ask it. How came it? Why, you had scarce gone ere this loathly John came running back again, and, when I oped mouth to reproach him, he asked me whether it was indeed likely that a man of prayer would leave his own godly raiment in order to take a layman's jerkin. He had, he said, but gone for a while that I might be the freer for my devotions. On this I plucked off the gown, and he with much show of haste did begin to undo his points; but when I threw his frock down he clipped it up and ran off all untrussed, leaving me in this sorry plight. He laughed so the while, like a great croaking frog, that I might have caught him had my breath not been as short as his legs were long."

The young man listened to this tale of wrong with all the seriousness that he could maintain; but at the sight of the pursy red-faced man and the dignity with which he bore him, the laughter came so thick upon him that he had to lean up against a tree-trunk. The fuller looked sadly and gravely at him; but finding that he still laughed, he bowed with much mock politeness and stalked onwards in his borrowed clothes. Alleyne watched him until he was small in the distance, and then, wiping the tears from his eyes, he set off briskly once more upon his journey.

IV

How the Bailiff of Southampton Slew the Two Masterless Men

The road along which he travelled was scarce as populous as most other roads in the kingdom, and far less so than those which lie between the larger towns. Yet from time to time Alleyne met other wayfarers, and more than once was overtaken by strings of pack mules and horsemen journeying in the same direction as himself. Once a begging friar came limping along in a brown habit, imploring in a most dolorous voice to give him a single groat to buy bread wherewith to save himself from impending death. Alleyne passed him swiftly by, for he had learned from the monks to have no love for the wandering friars, and, besides, there was a great half-gnawed mutton bone sticking out of his pouch to prove him a liar. Swiftly as he went, however, he could not escape the curse of the four blessed evangelists which the mendicant howled behind him. So dreadful are his execrations that the frightened lad thrust his fingers into his ear-holes, and ran until the fellow was but a brown smirch upon the yellow road.

Further on, at the edge of the woodland, he came upon a chapman and his wife, who sat upon a fallen tree. He had put his pack down as a table, and the two of them were devouring a great pasty, and washing it down with some drink from a stone jar. The chapman broke a rough jest as he passed, and the woman called shrilly to Alleyne to come and join them, on which the man, turning suddenly from mirth to wrath, began to belabor her with his cudgel. Alleyne hastened on, lest he make more mischief, and his heart was heavy as lead within him. Look where he would, he seemed to see nothing but injustice and violence and the hardness of man to man.

But even as he brooded sadly over it and pined for the sweet peace of the Abbey, he came on an open space dotted with holly bushes, where was the strangest sight that he had yet chanced upon. Near to the pathway lay a long clump of greenery, and from behind this there stuck straight up into the air four human legs clad in parti-colored hosen, yellow and black. Strangest of all was when a brisk tune struck suddenly up and the four legs began to kick and twitter in time to the music. Walking on tiptoe round the bushes, he stood in amazement to see two men bounding about on their heads, while they played, the one a viol and the other a pipe, as merrily and as truly as though they were seated in a choir. Alleyne crossed himself as he gazed at this unnatural sight, and could scarce hold his ground with a steady face, when the two dancers, catching sight of him, came bouncing in his direction. A spear's length from him, they each threw a somersault into the air, and came down upon their feet with smirking faces and their hands over their hearts.

"A guerdon—a guerdon, my knight of the staring eyes!" cried one.

"A gift, my prince!" shouted the other. "Any trifle will serve—a purse of gold, or even a jewelled goblet."

Alleyne thought of what he had read of demoniac possession—the jumpings, the twitchings, the wild talk. It was in his mind to repeat over the exorcism proper to such attacks; but the two burst out a-laughing at his scared face, and turning on to their heads once more, clapped their heels in derision.

"Hast never seen tumblers before?" asked the elder, a black-browed, swarthy man, as brown and supple as a hazel twig. "Why shrink from us, then, as though we were the spawn of the Evil One?"

"Why shrink, my honey-bird? Why so afeard, my sweet cinnamon?" exclaimed the other, a loose-jointed lanky youth with a dancing, roguish eye.

"Truly, sirs, it is a new sight to me," the clerk answered. "When I saw your four legs above the bush I could scarce credit my own eyes. Why is it that you do this thing?"

"A dry question to answer," cried the younger, coming back on to his feet. "A most husky question, my fair bird! But how? A flask, a flask!—by all that is wonderful!" He shot out his hand as he spoke, and plucking Alleyne's bottle out of his scrip, he deftly knocked the neck off, and poured the half of it down his throat. The rest he handed to his comrade, who drank the wine, and then, to the clerk's increasing amazement, made a show of swallowing the bottle, with such skill that Alleyne seemed to see it vanish down his throat. A moment later, however, he flung it over his head, and caught it bottom downwards upon the calf of his left leg.

"We thank you for the wine, kind sir," said he, "and for the ready courtesy wherewith you offered it. Touching your question, we may tell you that we are strollers and jugglers, who, having performed with much applause at Winchester fair, are now on our way to the great Michaelmas market at Ringwood. As our art is a very fine and delicate one, however, we cannot let a day go by without exercising ourselves in it, to which end we choose some quiet and sheltered spot where we may break our journey. Here you find us; and we cannot wonder that you, who are new to tumbling, should be astounded, since many great barons, earls, marshals and knights, who have wandered as far as the Holy Land, are of one mind in saying that they have never seen a more noble or gracious performance. If you will be pleased to sit upon that stump, we will now continue our exercise."

Alleyne sat down willingly as directed with two great bundles on either side of him which contained the strollers' dresses—doublets of flame-colored silk and girdles of leather, spangled with brass and tin. The jugglers were on their heads once more, bounding about with rigid necks, playing the while in perfect time and tune. It chanced that out of one of the bundles there stuck the end of what the clerk saw to be a cittern, so drawing it forth, he tuned it up and twanged a harmony to the merry lilt which the dancers played. On that they dropped their own instruments, and putting their hands to the ground they hopped about faster and faster, ever shouting to him to play more briskly, until at last for very weariness all three had to stop.

"Well played, sweet poppet!" cried the younger. "Hast a rare touch on the strings."

"How knew you the tune?" asked the other.

"I knew it not. I did but follow the notes I heard."

Both opened their eyes at this, and stared at Alleyne with as much amazement as he had shown at them.

"You have a fine trick of ear then," said one. "We have long wished to meet such a man. Wilt join us and jog on to Ringwood? Thy duties shall be light, and thou shalt have two-pence a day and meat for supper every night."

"With as much beer as you can put away," said the other, "and a flask of Gascon wine on Sabbaths."

"Nay, it may not be. I have other work to do. I have tarried with you over long," quoth Alleyne, and resolutely set forth upon his journey once more. They ran behind him some little way, offering him first fourpence and then sixpence a day, but he only smiled and shook his head, until at last they fell away from him. Looking back, he saw that the smaller had mounted on the younger's shoulders, and that they stood so, some ten feet high, waving their adieus to him. He waved back to them, and then hastened on, the lighter of heart for having fallen in with these strange men of pleasure.

Alleyne had gone no great distance for all the many small passages that had befallen him. Yet to him, used as he was to a life of such quiet that the failure of a brewing or the altering of an anthem had seemed to be of the deepest import, the quick changing play of the lights and shadows of life was strangely startling and interesting. A gulf seemed to divide this brisk uncertain existence from the old steady round of work and of prayer which he had left behind him. The few hours that had passed since he saw the Abbey tower stretched out in his memory until they outgrew whole months of the stagnant life of the cloister. As he walked and munched the soft bread from his scrip, it seemed strange to him to feel that it was still warm from the ovens of Beaulieu.

When he passed Penerley, where were three cottages and a barn, he reached the edge of the tree country, and found the great barren heath of Blackdown stretching in front of him, all pink with heather and bronzed with the fading ferns. On the left the woods were still thick, but the road edged away from them and wound over the open. The sun lay low in the west upon a purple cloud, whence it threw a mild, chastening light over the wild moorland and glittered on the fringe of forest turning the withered leaves into flakes of dead gold, the brighter for the black depths behind them. To the seeing eye decay is as fair as growth, and death as life. The thought stole into Alleyne's heart as he looked upon the autumnal country side and marvelled at its beauty. He had little time to dwell upon it however, for there were still six good miles between him and the nearest inn. He sat down by the roadside to partake of his bread and cheese, and then with a lighter scrip he hastened upon his way.

There appeared to be more wayfarers on the down than in the forest. First he passed two Dominicans in their long black dresses, who swept by him with downcast looks and pattering lips, without so much as a glance at him. Then there came a gray friar, or minorite, with a good paunch upon him, walking slowly and looking about him with the air of a man who was at peace with himself and with all men. He stopped Alleyne to ask him whether it was not true that there was a hostel somewhere in those parts which was especially famous for the stewing of eels. The clerk having made answer that he had heard the eels of Sowley well spoken of, the friar sucked in his lips and hurried forward. Close at his heels came three laborers walking abreast, with spade and mattock over their shoulders. They sang some rude chorus right tunefully as they walked, but their English was so coarse and rough that to the ears of a cloister-bred man it sounded like a foreign and barbarous tongue. One of them carried a young bittern which they had caught upon the moor, and they offered it to Alleyne for a silver groat. Very glad he was to get safely past them, for, with their bristling red beards and their fierce blue eyes, they were uneasy men to bargain with upon a lonely moor.

Yet it is not always the burliest and the wildest who are the most to be dreaded. The workers looked hungrily at him, and then jogged onwards upon their way in slow, lumbering Saxon style. A worse man to deal with was a wooden-legged cripple who came hobbling down the path, so weak and so old to all appearance that a child need not stand in fear of him. Yet when Alleyne had passed him, of a sudden, out of pure devilment, he screamed out a curse at him, and sent a jagged flint stone hurtling past his ear. So horrid was the causeless rage of the crooked creature, that the clerk came over a cold thrill, and took to his heels until he was out of shot from stone or word. It seemed to him that in this country of England there was no protection for a man save that which lay in the strength of his own arm and the speed of his own foot. In the cloisters he had heard vague talk of the law—the mighty law which was higher than prelate or baron, yet no sign could he see of it. What was the benefit of a law written fair upon parchment, he wondered, if there were no officers to enforce it. As it fell out, however, he had that very evening, ere the sun had set, a chance of seeing how stern was the grip of the English law when it did happen to seize the offender.

A mile or so out upon the moor the road takes a very sudden dip into a hollow, with a peat-colored stream running swiftly down the centre of it. To the right of this stood, and stands to this day, an ancient barrow, or burying mound, covered deeply in a bristle of heather and bracken. Alleyne was plodding down the slope upon one side, when he saw an old dame coming towards him upon the other, limping with weariness and leaning heavily upon a stick. When she reached the edge of the stream she stood helpless, looking to right and to left for some ford. Where the path ran down a great stone had been fixed in the centre of the brook, but it was too far from the bank for her aged and uncertain feet. Twice she thrust forward at it, and twice she drew back, until at last, giving up in despair, she sat herself down by the brink and wrung her hands wearily. There she still sat when Alleyne reached the crossing.

"Come, mother," quoth he, "it is not so very perilous a passage."

"Alas! good youth," she answered, "I have a humor in the eyes, and though I can see that there is a stone there I can by no means be sure as to where it lies."

"That is easily amended," said he cheerily, and picking her lightly up, for she was much worn with time, he passed across with her. He could not but observe, however, that as he placed her down her knees seemed to fail her, and she could scarcely prop herself up with her staff.

"You are weak, mother," said he. "Hast journeyed far, I wot."

"From Wiltshire, friend," said she, in a quavering voice; "three days have I been on the road. I go to my son, who is one of the King's regarders at Brockenhurst. He has ever said that he would care for me in mine old age."

"And rightly too, mother, since you cared for him in his youth. But when have you broken fast?"

"At Lyndenhurst; but alas! my money is at an end, and I could but get a dish of bran-porridge from the nunnery. Yet I trust that I may be able to reach Brockenhurst to-night, where I may have all that heart can desire; for oh! sir, but my son is a fine man, with a kindly heart of his own, and it is as good as food to me to think that he should have a doublet of Lincoln green to his back and be the King's own paid man."

"It is a long road yet to Brockenhurst," said Alleyne; "but here is such bread and cheese as I have left, and here, too, is a penny which may help you to supper. May God be with you!"

"May God be with you, young man!" she cried. "May He make your heart as glad as you have made mine!" She turned away, still mumbling blessings, and Alleyne saw her short figure and her long shadow stumbling slowly up the slope.

He was moving away himself, when his eyes lit upon a strange sight, and one which sent a tingling through his skin. Out of the tangled scrub on the old overgrown barrow two human faces were looking out at him; the sinking sun glimmered full upon them, showing up every line and feature. The one was an oldish man with a thin beard, a crooked nose, and a broad red smudge from a birth-mark over his temple; the other was a negro, a thing rarely met in England at that day, and rarer still in the quiet southland parts. Alleyne had read of such folk, but had never seen one before, and could scarce take his eyes from the fellow's broad pouting lip and shining teeth. Even as he gazed, however, the two came writhing out from among the heather, and came down towards him with such a guilty, slinking carriage, that the clerk felt that there was no good in them, and hastened onwards upon his way.

He had not gained the crown of the slope, when he heard a sudden scuffle behind him and a feeble voice bleating for help. Looking round, there was the old dame down upon the roadway, with her red whimple flying on the breeze, while the two rogues, black and white, stooped over her, wresting away from her the penny and such other poor trifles as were worth the taking. At the sight of her thin limbs struggling in weak resistance, such a glow of fierce anger passed over Alleyne as set his head in a whirl. Dropping his scrip, he bounded over the stream once more, and made for the two villains, with his staff whirled over his shoulder and his gray eyes blazing with fury.

The robbers, however, were not disposed to leave their victim until they had worked their wicked will upon her. The black man, with the woman's crimson scarf tied round his swarthy head, stood forward in the centre of the path, with a long dull-colored knife in his hand, while the other, waving a ragged cudgel, cursed at Alleyne and dared him to come on. His blood was fairly aflame, however, and he needed no such challenge. Dashing at the black man, he smote at him with such good will that the other let his knife tinkle into the roadway, and hopped howling to a safer distance. The second rogue, however, made of sterner stuff, rushed in upon the clerk, and clipped him round the waist with a grip like a bear, shouting the while to his comrade to come round and stab him in the back. At this the negro took heart of grace, and picking up his dagger again he came stealing with prowling step and murderous eye, while the two swayed backwards and forwards, staggering this way and that. In the very midst of the scuffle, however, whilst Alleyne braced himself to feel the cold blade between his shoulders, there came a sudden scurry of hoofs, and the black man yelled with terror and ran for his life through the heather. The man with the birth-mark, too, struggled to break away, and Alleyne heard his teeth chatter and felt his limbs grow limp to his hand. At this sign of coming aid the clerk held on the tighter, and at last was able to pin his man down and glanced behind him to see where all the noise was coming from.

Down the slanting road there was riding a big, burly man, clad in a tunic of purple velvet and driving a great black horse as hard as it could gallop. He leaned well over its neck as he rode, and made a heaving with his shoulders at every bound as though he were lifting the steed instead of it carrying him. In the rapid glance Alleyne saw that he had white doeskin gloves, a curling white feather in his flat velvet cap, and a broad gold, embroidered baldric across his bosom. Behind him rode six others, two and two, clad in sober brown jerkins, with the long yellow staves of their bows thrusting out from behind their right shoulders. Down the hill they thundered, over the brook and up to the scene of the contest.

"Here is one!" said the leader, springing down from his reeking horse, and seizing the white rogue by the edge of his jerkin. "This is one of them. I know him by that devil's touch upon his brow. Where are your cords, Peterkin? So! Bind him hand and foot. His last hour has come. And you, young man, who may you be?"

"I am a clerk, sir, travelling from Beaulieu."

"A clerk!" cried the other. "Art from Oxenford or from Cambridge? Hast thou a letter from the chancellor of thy college giving thee a permit to beg? Let me see thy letter." He had a stern, square face, with bushy side whiskers and a very questioning eye.

"I am from Beaulieu Abbey, and I have no need to beg," said Alleyne, who was all of a tremble now that the ruffle was over.

"The better for thee," the other answered. "Dost know who I am?"

"No, sir, I do not."

"I am the law!"—nodding his head solemnly. "I am the law of England and the mouthpiece of his most gracious and royal majesty, Edward the Third."

Alleyne louted low to the King's representative. "Truly you came in good time, honored sir," said he. "A moment later and they would have slain me."

"But there should be another one," cried the man in the purple coat. "There should be a black man. A shipman with St. Anthony's fire, and a black man who had served him as cook—those are the pair that we are in chase of."

"The black man fled over to that side," said Alleyne, pointing towards the barrow.

"He could not have gone far, sir bailiff," cried one of the archers, unslinging his bow. "He is in hiding somewhere, for he knew well, black paynim as he is, that our horses' four legs could outstrip his two."

"Then we shall have him," said the other. "It shall never be said, whilst I am bailiff of Southampton, that any waster, riever, draw-latch or murtherer came scathless away from me and my posse. Leave that rogue lying. Now stretch out in line, my merry ones, with arrow on string, and I shall show you such sport as only the King can give. You on the left, Howett, and Thomas of Redbridge upon the right. So! Beat high and low among the heather, and a pot of wine to the lucky marksman."

As it chanced, however, the searchers had not far to seek. The negro had burrowed down into his hiding-place upon the barrow, where he might have lain snug enough, had it not been for the red gear upon his head. As he raised himself to look over the bracken at his enemies, the staring color caught the eye of the bailiff, who broke into a long screeching whoop and spurred forward sword in hand. Seeing himself discovered, the man rushed out from his hiding-place, and bounded at the top of his speed down the line of archers, keeping a good hundred paces to the front of them. The two who were on either side of Alleyne bent their bows as calmly as though they were shooting at the popinjay at the village fair.

"Seven yards windage, Hal," said one, whose hair was streaked with gray.

"Five," replied the other, letting loose his string. Alleyne gave a gulp in his throat, for the yellow streak seemed to pass through the man; but he still ran forward.

"Seven, you jack-fool," growled the first speaker, and his bow twanged like a harp-string. The black man sprang high up into the air, and shot out both his arms and his legs, coming down all a-sprawl among the heather. "Right under the blade bone!" quoth the archer, sauntering forward for his arrow.

"The old hound is the best when all is said," quoth the bailiff of Southampton, as they made back for the roadway. "That means a quart of the best malmsey in Southampton this very night, Matthew Atwood. Art sure that he is dead?"

"Dead as Pontius Pilate, worshipful sir."

"It is well. Now, as to the other knave. There are trees and to spare over yonder, but we have scarce leisure to make for them. Draw thy sword, Thomas of Redbridge, and hew me his head from his shoulders."

"A boon, gracious sir, a boon!" cried the condemned man.

"What then?" asked the bailiff.

"I will confess to my crime. It was indeed I and the black cook, both from the ship 'La Rose de Gloire,' of Southampton, who did set upon the Flanders merchant and rob him of his spicery and his mercery, for which, as we well know, you hold a warrant against us."

"There is little merit in this confession," quoth the bailiff sternly. "Thou hast done evil within my bailiwick, and must die."

"But, sir," urged Alleyne, who was white to the lips at these bloody doings, "he hath not yet come to trial."

"Young clerk," said the bailiff, "you speak of that of which you know nothing. It is true that he hath not come to trial, but the trial hath come to him. He hath fled the law and is beyond its pale. Touch not that which is no concern of thine. But what is this boon, rogue, which you would crave?"

"I have in my shoe, most worshipful sir, a strip of wood which belonged once to the bark wherein the blessed Paul was dashed up against the island of Melita. I bought it for two rose nobles from a shipman who came from the Levant. The boon I crave is that you will place it in my hands and let me die still grasping it. In this manner, not only shall my own eternal salvation be secured, but thine also, for I shall never cease to intercede for thee."

At the command of the bailiff they plucked off the fellow's shoe, and there sure enough at the side of the instep, wrapped in a piece of fine sendall, lay a long, dark splinter of wood. The archers doffed caps at the sight of it, and the bailiff crossed himself devoutly as he handed it to the robber.

"If it should chance," he said, "that through the surpassing merits of the blessed Paul your sin-stained soul should gain a way into paradise, I trust that you will not forget that intercession which you have promised. Bear in mind too, that it is Herward the bailiff for whom you pray, and not Herward the sheriff, who is my uncle's son. Now, Thomas, I pray you dispatch, for we have a long ride before us and sun has already set."

Alleyne gazed upon the scene—the portly velvet-clad official, the knot of hard-faced archers with their hands to the bridles of their horses, the thief with his arms trussed back and his doublet turned down upon his shoulders. By the side of the track the old dame was standing, fastening her red whimple once more round her head. Even as he looked one of the archers drew his sword with a sharp whirr of steel and stept up to the lost man. The clerk hurried away in horror; but, ere he had gone many paces, he heard a sudden, sullen thump, with a choking, whistling sound at the end of it. A minute later the bailiff and four of his men rode past him on their journey back to Southampton, the other two having been chosen as grave-diggers. As they passed Alleyne saw that one of the men was wiping his sword-blade upon the mane of his horse. A deadly sickness came over him at the sight, and sitting down by the wayside he burst out weeping, with his nerves all in a jangle. It was a terrible world thought he, and it was hard to know which were the most to be dreaded, the knaves or the men of the law.

V

How a Strange Company Gathered at the "Pied Merlin"

The night had already fallen, and the moon was shining between the rifts of ragged, drifting clouds, before Alleyne Edricson, footsore and weary from the unwonted exercise, found himself in front of the forest inn which stood upon the outskirts of Lyndhurst. The building was long and low, standing back a little from the road, with two flambeaux blazing on either side of the door as a welcome to the traveller. From one window there thrust forth a long pole with a bunch of greenery tied to the end of it—a sign that liquor was to be sold within. As Alleyne walked up to it he perceived that it was rudely fashioned out of beams of wood, with twinkling lights all over where the glow from within shone through the chinks. The roof was poor and thatched; but in strange contrast to it there ran all along under the eaves a line of wooden shields, most gorgeously painted with chevron, bend, and saltire, and every heraldic device. By the door a horse stood tethered, the ruddy glow beating strongly upon his brown head and patient eyes, while his body stood back in the shadow.

Alleyne stood still in the roadway for a few minutes reflecting upon what he should do. It was, he knew, only a few miles further to Minstead, where his brother dwelt. On the other hand, he had never seen this brother since childhood, and the reports which had come to his ears concerning him were seldom to his advantage. By all accounts he was a hard and a bitter man.

It might be an evil start to come to his door so late and claim the shelter of his roof. Better to sleep here at this inn, and then travel on to Minstead in the morning. If his brother would take him in, well and good.

He would bide with him for a time and do what he might to serve him. If, on the other hand, he should have hardened his heart against him, he could only go on his way and do the best he might by his skill as a craftsman and a scrivener. At the end of a year he would be free to return to the cloisters, for such had been his father's bequest. A monkish upbringing, one year in the world after the age of twenty, and then a free selection one way or the other—it was a strange course which had been marked out for him. Such as it was, however, he had no choice but to follow it, and if he were to begin by making a friend of his brother he had best wait until morning before he knocked at his dwelling.

The rude plank door was ajar, but as Alleyne approached it there came from within such a gust of rough laughter and clatter of tongues that he stood irresolute upon the threshold. Summoning courage, however, and reflecting that it was a public dwelling, in which he had as much right as any other man, he pushed it open and stepped into the common room.

Though it was an autumn evening and somewhat warm, a huge fire of heaped billets of wood crackled and sparkled in a broad, open grate, some of the smoke escaping up a rude chimney, but the greater part rolling out into the room, so that the air was thick with it, and a man coming from without could scarce catch his breath. On this fire a great cauldron bubbled and simmered, giving forth a rich and promising smell. Seated round it were a dozen or so folk, of all ages and conditions, who set up such a shout as Alleyne entered that he stood peering at them through the smoke, uncertain what this riotous greeting might portend.

"A rouse! A rouse!" cried one rough looking fellow in a tattered jerkin. "One more round of mead or ale and the score to the last comer."

"'Tis the law of the 'Pied Merlin,'" shouted another. "Ho there, Dame Eliza! Here is fresh custom come to the house, and not a drain for the company."

"I will take your orders, gentles; I will assuredly take your orders," the landlady answered, bustling in with her hands full of leathern drinking-cups. "What is it that you drink, then? Beer for the lads of the forest, mead for the gleeman, strong waters for the tinker, and wine for the rest. It is an old custom of the house, young sir. It has been the use at the 'Pied Merlin' this many a year back that the company should drink to the health of the last comer. Is it your pleasure to humor it?"

"Why, good dame," said Alleyne, "I would not offend the customs of your house, but it is only sooth when I say that my purse is a thin one. As far as two pence will go, however, I shall be right glad to do my part."

"Plainly said and bravely spoken, my suckling friar," roared a deep voice, and a heavy hand fell upon Alleyne's shoulder. Looking up, he saw beside him his former cloister companion the renegade monk, Hordle John.

"By the thorn of Glastonbury! ill days are coming upon Beaulieu," said he. "Here they have got rid in one day of the only two men within their walls—for I have had mine eyes upon thee, youngster, and I know that for all thy baby-face there is the making of a man in thee. Then there is the Abbot, too. I am no friend of his, nor he of mine; but he has warm blood in his veins. He is the only man left among them. The others, what are they?"

"They are holy men," Alleyne answered gravely.

"Holy men? Holy cabbages! Holy bean-pods! What do they do but live and suck in sustenance and grow fat? If that be holiness, I could show you hogs in this forest who are fit to head the calendar. Think you it was for such a life that this good arm was fixed upon my shoulder, or that head placed upon your neck? There is work in the world, man, and it is not by hiding behind stone walls that we shall do it."

"Why, then, did you join the brothers?" asked Alleyne.

"A fair enough question; but it is as fairly answered. I joined them because Margery Alspaye, of Bolder, married Crooked Thomas of Ringwood, and left a certain John of Hordle in the cold, for that he was a ranting, roving blade who was not to be trusted in wedlock. That was why, being fond and hot-headed, I left the world; and that is why, having had time to take thought, I am right glad to find myself back in it once more. Ill betide the day that ever I took off my yeoman's jerkin to put on the white gown!"

Whilst he was speaking the landlady came in again, bearing a broad platter, upon which stood all the beakers and flagons charged to the brim with the brown ale or the ruby wine. Behind her came a maid with a high pile of wooden plates, and a great sheaf of spoons, one of which she handed round to each of the travellers. Two of the company, who were dressed in the weather-stained green doublet of foresters, lifted the big pot off the fire, and a third, with a huge pewter ladle, served out a portion of steaming collops to each guest. Alleyne bore his share and his ale-mug away with him to a retired trestle in the corner, where he could sup in peace and watch the strange scene, which was so different to those silent and well-ordered meals to which he was accustomed.

The room was not unlike a stable. The low ceiling, smoke-blackened and dingy, was pierced by several square trap-doors with rough-hewn ladders leading up to them. The walls of bare unpainted planks were studded here and there with great wooden pins, placed at irregular intervals and heights, from which hung over-tunics, wallets, whips, bridles, and saddles. Over the fireplace were suspended six or seven shields of wood, with coats-of-arms rudely daubed upon them, which showed by their varying degrees of smokiness and dirt that they had been placed there at different periods. There was no furniture, save a single long dresser covered with coarse crockery, and a number of wooden benches and trestles, the legs of which sank deeply into the soft clay floor, while the only light, save that of the fire, was furnished by three torches stuck in sockets on the wall, which flickered and crackled, giving forth a strong resinous odor. All this was novel and strange to the cloister-bred youth; but most interesting of all was the motley circle of guests who sat eating their collops round the blaze. They were a humble group of wayfarers, such as might have been found that night in any inn through the length and breadth of England; but to him they represented that vague world against which he had been so frequently and so earnestly warned. It did not seem to him from what he could see of it to be such a very wicked place after all.

Three or four of the men round the fire were evidently underkeepers and verderers from the forest, sunburned and bearded, with the quick restless eye and lithe movements of the deer among which they lived. Close to the corner of the chimney sat a middle-aged gleeman, clad in a faded garb of Norwich cloth, the tunic of which was so outgrown that it did not fasten at the neck and at the waist. His face was swollen and coarse, and his watery protruding eyes spoke of a life which never wandered very far from the wine-pot. A gilt harp, blotched with many stains and with two of its strings missing, was tucked under one of his arms, while with the other he scooped greedily at his platter. Next to him sat two other men of about the same age, one with a trimming of fur to his coat, which gave him a dignity which was evidently dearer to him than his comfort, for he still drew it round him in spite of the hot glare of the faggots. The other, clad in a dirty russet suit with a long sweeping doublet, had a cunning, foxy face with keen, twinkling eyes and a peaky beard. Next to him sat Hordle John, and beside him three other rough unkempt fellows with tangled beards and matted hair—free laborers from the adjoining farms, where small patches of freehold property had been suffered to remain scattered about in the heart of the royal demesne. The company was completed by a peasant in a rude dress of undyed sheepskin, with the old-fashioned galligaskins about his legs, and a gayly dressed young man with striped cloak jagged at the edges and parti-colored hosen, who looked about him with high disdain upon his face, and held a blue smelling-flask to his nose with one hand, while he brandished a busy spoon with the other. In the corner a very fat man was lying all a-sprawl upon a truss, snoring stertorously, and evidently in the last stage of drunkenness.

"That is Wat the limner," quoth the landlady, sitting down beside Alleyne, and pointing with the ladle to the sleeping man. "That is he who paints the signs and the tokens. Alack and alas that ever I should have been fool enough to trust him! Now, young man, what manner of a bird would you suppose a pied merlin to be—that being the proper sign of my hostel?"

"Why," said Alleyne, "a merlin is a bird of the same form as an eagle or a falcon. I can well remember that learned brother Bartholomew, who is deep in all the secrets of nature, pointed one out to me as we walked together near Vinney Ridge."

"A falcon or an eagle, quotha? And pied, that is of two several colors. So any man would say except this barrel of lies. He came to me, look you, saying that if I would furnish him with a gallon of ale, wherewith to strengthen himself as he worked, and also the pigments and a board, he would paint for me a noble pied merlin which I might hang along with the blazonry over my door. I, poor simple fool, gave him the ale and all that he craved, leaving him alone too, because he said that a man's mind must be left untroubled when he had great work to do. When I came back the gallon jar was empty, and he lay as you see him, with the board in front of him with this sorry device." She raised up a panel which was leaning against the wall, and showed a rude painting of a scraggy and angular fowl, with very long legs and a spotted body.

"Was that," she asked, "like the bird which thou hast seen?"

Alleyne shook his head, smiling.

"No, nor any other bird that ever wagged a feather. It is most like a plucked pullet which has died of the spotted fever. And scarlet too! What would the gentles Sir Nicholas Boarhunte, or Sir Bernard Brocas, of Roche Court, say if they saw such a thing—or, perhaps, even the King's own Majesty himself, who often has ridden past this way, and who loves his falcons as he loves his sons? It would be the downfall of my house."

"The matter is not past mending," said Alleyne. "I pray you, good dame, to give me those three pigment-pots and the brush, and I shall try whether I cannot better this painting."

Dame Eliza looked doubtfully at him, as though fearing some other stratagem, but, as he made no demand for ale, she finally brought the paints, and watched him as he smeared on his background, talking the while about the folk round the fire.

"The four forest lads must be jogging soon," she said. "They bide at Emery Down, a mile or more from here. Yeomen prickers they are, who tend to the King's hunt. The gleeman is called Floyting Will. He comes from the north country, but for many years he hath gone the round of the forest from Southampton to Christchurch. He drinks much and pays little but it would make your ribs crackle to hear him sing the 'Jest of Hendy Tobias.' Mayhap he will sing it when the ale has warmed him."

"Who are those next to him?" asked Alleyne, much interested. "He of the fur mantle has a wise and reverent face."

"He is a seller of pills and salves, very learned in humors, and rheums, and fluxes, and all manner of ailments. He wears, as you perceive, the vernicle of Sainted Luke, the first physician, upon his sleeve. May good St. Thomas of Kent grant that it may be long before either I or mine need his help! He is here to-night for herbergage, as are the others except the foresters. His neighbor is a tooth-drawer. That bag at his girdle is full of the teeth that he drew at Winchester fair. I warrant that there are more sound ones than sorry, for he is quick at his work and a trifle dim in the eye. The lusty man next him with the red head I have not seen before. The four on this side are all workers, three of them in the service of the bailiff of Sir Baldwin Redvers, and the other, he with the sheepskin, is, as I hear, a villein from the midlands who hath run from his master. His year and day are well-nigh up, when he will be a free man."

"And the other?" asked Alleyne in a whisper. "He is surely some very great man, for he looks as though he scorned those who were about him."

The landlady looked at him in a motherly way and shook her head. "You have had no great truck with the world," she said, "or you would have learned that it is the small men and not the great who hold their noses in the air. Look at those shields upon my wall and under my eaves. Each of them is the device of some noble lord or gallant knight who hath slept under my roof at one time or another. Yet milder men or easier to please I have never seen: eating my bacon and drinking my wine with a merry face, and paying my score with some courteous word or jest which was dearer to me than my profit. Those are the true gentles. But your chapman or your bearward will swear that there is a lime in the wine, and water in the ale, and fling off at the last with a curse instead of a blessing. This youth is a scholar from Cambrig, where men are wont to be blown out by a little knowledge, and lose the use of their hands in learning the laws of the Romans. But I must away to lay down the beds. So may the saints keep you and prosper you in your undertaking!"

Thus left to himself, Alleyne drew his panel of wood where the light of one of the torches would strike full upon it, and worked away with all the pleasure of the trained craftsman, listening the while to the talk which went on round the fire. The peasant in the sheepskins, who had sat glum and silent all evening, had been so heated by his flagon of ale that he was talking loudly and angrily with clenched hands and flashing eyes.

"Sir Humphrey Tennant of Ashby may till his own fields for me," he cried. "The castle has thrown its shadow upon the cottage over long. For three hundred years my folk have swinked and sweated, day in and day out, to keep the wine on the lord's table and the harness on the lord's back. Let him take off his plates and delve himself, if delving must be done."

"A proper spirit, my fair son!" said one of the free laborers. "I would that all men were of thy way of thinking."

"He would have sold me with his acres," the other cried, in a voice which was hoarse with passion. "'The man, the woman and their litter'—so ran the words of the dotard bailiff. Never a bullock on the farm was sold more lightly. Ha! he may wake some black night to find the flames licking about his ears—for fire is a good friend to the poor man, and I have seen a smoking heap of ashes where over night there stood just such another castlewick as Ashby."

"This is a lad of mettle!" shouted another of the laborers. "He dares to give tongue to what all men think. Are we not all from Adam's loins, all with flesh and blood, and with the same mouth that must needs have food and drink? Where all this difference then between the ermine cloak and the leathern tunic, if what they cover is the same?"

"Aye, Jenkin," said another, "our foeman is under the stole and the vestment as much as under the helmet and plate of proof. We have as much to fear from the tonsure as from the hauberk. Strike at the noble and the priest shrieks, strike at priest and the noble lays his hand upon glaive. They are twin thieves who live upon our labor."

"It would take a clever man to live upon thy labor, Hugh," remarked one of the foresters, "seeing that the half of thy time is spent in swilling mead at the 'Pied Merlin.'"

"Better that than stealing the deer that thou art placed to guard, like some folk I know."

"If you dare open that swine's mouth against me," shouted the woodman, "I'll crop your ears for you before the hangman has the doing of it, thou long-jawed lackbrain."

"Nay, gentles, gentles!" cried Dame Eliza, in a singsong heedless voice, which showed that such bickerings were nightly things among her guests. "No brawling or brabbling, gentles! Take heed to the good name of the house."

"Besides, if it comes to the cropping of ears, there are other folk who may say their say," quoth the third laborer. "We are all freemen, and I trow that a yeoman's cudgel is as good as a forester's knife. By St. Anselm! it would be an evil day if we had to bend to our master's servants as well as to our masters."

"No man is my master save the King," the woodman answered. "Who is there, save a false traitor, who would refuse to serve the English king?"

"I know not about the English king," said the man Jenkin. "What sort of English king is it who cannot lay his tongue to a word of English? You mind last year when he came down to Malwood, with his inner marshal and his outer marshal, his justiciar, his seneschal, and his four and twenty guardsmen. One noontide I was by Franklin Swinton's gate, when up he rides with a yeoman pricker at his heels. 'Ouvre,' he cried, 'ouvre,' or some such word, making signs for me to open the gate; and then 'Merci,' as though he were adrad of me. And you talk of an English king?"

"I do not marvel at it," cried the Cambrig scholar, speaking in the high drawling voice which was common among his class. "It is not a tongue for men of sweet birth and delicate upbringing. It is a foul, snorting, snarling manner of speech. For myself, I swear by the learned Polycarp that I have most ease with Hebrew, and after that perchance with Arabian."

"I will not hear a word said against old King Ned," cried Hordle John in a voice like a bull. "What if he is fond of a bright eye and a saucy face. I know one of his subjects who could match him at that. If he cannot speak like an Englishman I trow that he can fight like an Englishman, and he was hammering at the gates of Paris while ale-house topers were grutching and grumbling at home."

This loud speech, coming from a man of so formidable an appearance, somewhat daunted the disloyal party, and they fell into a sullen silence, which enabled Alleyne to hear something of the talk which was going on in the further corner between the physician, the tooth-drawer and the gleeman.

"A raw rat," the man of drugs was saying, "that is what it is ever my use to order for the plague—a raw rat with its paunch cut open."

"Might it not be broiled, most learned sir?" asked the tooth-drawer. "A raw rat sounds a most sorry and cheerless dish."

"Not to be eaten," cried the physician, in high disdain. "Why should any man eat such a thing?"

"Why indeed?" asked the gleeman, taking a long drain at his tankard.

"It is to be placed on the sore or swelling. For the rat, mark you, being a foul-living creature, hath a natural drawing or affinity for all foul things, so that the noxious humors pass from the man into the unclean beast."

"Would that cure the black death, master?" asked Jenkin.

"Aye, truly would it, my fair son."

"Then I am right glad that there were none who knew of it. The black death is the best friend that ever the common folk had in England."

"How that then?" asked Hordle John.

"Why, friend, it is easy to see that you have not worked with your hands or you would not need to ask. When half the folk in the country were dead it was then that the other half could pick and choose who they would work for, and for what wage. That is why I say that the murrain was the best friend that the borel folk ever had."

"True, Jenkin," said another workman; "but it is not all good that is brought by it either. We well know that through it corn-land has been turned into pasture, so that flocks of sheep with perchance a single shepherd wander now where once a hundred men had work and wage."

"There is no great harm in that," remarked the tooth-drawer, "for the sheep give many folk their living. There is not only the herd, but the shearer and brander, and then the dresser, the curer, the dyer, the fuller, the webster, the merchant, and a score of others."

"If it come to that." said one of the foresters, "the tough meat of them will wear folks teeth out, and there is a trade for the man who can draw them."

A general laugh followed this sally at the dentist's expense, in the midst of which the gleeman placed his battered harp upon his knee, and began to pick out a melody upon the frayed strings.

"Elbow room for Floyting Will!" cried the woodmen. "Twang us a merry lilt."

"Aye, aye, the 'Lasses of Lancaster,'" one suggested.

"Or 'St. Simeon and the Devil.'"

"Or the 'Jest of Hendy Tobias.'"

To all these suggestions the jongleur made no response, but sat with his eye fixed abstractedly upon the ceiling, as one who calls words to his mind. Then, with a sudden sweep across the strings, he broke out into a song so gross and so foul that ere he had finished a verse the pure-minded lad sprang to his feet with the blood tingling in his face.

"How can you sing such things?" he cried. "You, too, an old man who should be an example to others."

The wayfarers all gazed in the utmost astonishment at the interruption.

"By the holy Dicon of Hampole! our silent clerk has found his tongue," said one of the woodmen. "What is amiss with the song then? How has it offended your babyship?"

"A milder and better mannered song hath never been heard within these walls," cried another. "What sort of talk is this for a public inn?"

"Shall it be a litany, my good clerk?" shouted a third; "or would a hymn be good enough to serve?"

The jongleur had put down his harp in high dudgeon. "Am I to be preached to by a child?" he cried, staring across at Alleyne with an inflamed and angry countenance. "Is a hairless infant to raise his tongue against me, when I have sung in every fair from Tweed to Trent, and have twice been named aloud by the High Court of the Minstrels at Beverley? I shall sing no more to-night."

"Nay, but you will so," said one of the laborers. "Hi, Dame Eliza, bring a stoup of your best to Will to clear his throat. Go forward with thy song, and if our girl-faced clerk does not love it he can take to the road and go whence he came."

"Nay, but not too fast," broke in Hordle John. "There are two words in this matter. It may be that my little comrade has been over quick in reproof, he having gone early into the cloisters and seen little of the rough ways and words of the world. Yet there is truth in what he says, for, as you know well, the song was not of the cleanest. I shall stand by him, therefore, and he shall neither be put out on the road, nor shall his ears be offended indoors."

"Indeed, your high and mighty grace," sneered one of the yeomen, "have you in sooth so ordained?"

"By the Virgin!" said a second, "I think that you may both chance to find yourselves upon the road before long."

"And so belabored as to be scarce able to crawl along it," cried a third.

"Nay, I shall go! I shall go!" said Alleyne hurriedly, as Hordle John began to slowly roll up his sleeve, and bare an arm like a leg of mutton. "I would not have you brawl about me."

"Hush! lad," he whispered, "I count them not a fly. They may find they have more tow on their distaff than they know how to spin. Stand thou clear and give me space."

Both the foresters and the laborers had risen from their bench, and Dame Eliza and the travelling doctor had flung themselves between the two parties with soft words and soothing gestures, when the door of the "Pied Merlin" was flung violently open, and the attention of the company was drawn from their own quarrel to the new-comer who had burst so unceremoniously upon them.

VI

How Samkin Aylward Wagered his Feather-bed

He was a middle-sized man, of most massive and robust build, with an arching chest and extraordinary breadth of shoulder. His shaven face was as brown as a hazel-nut, tanned and dried by the weather, with harsh, well-marked features, which were not improved by a long white scar which stretched from the corner of his left nostril to the angle of the jaw. His eyes were bright and searching, with something of menace and of authority in their quick glitter, and his mouth was firm-set and hard, as befitted one who was wont to set his face against danger. A straight sword by his side and a painted long-bow jutting over his shoulder proclaimed his profession, while his scarred brigandine of chain-mail and his dinted steel cap showed that he was no holiday soldier, but one who was even now fresh from the wars. A white surcoat with the lion of St. George in red upon the centre covered his broad breast, while a sprig of new-plucked broom at the side of his head-gear gave a touch of gayety and grace to his grim, war-worn equipment.

"Ha!" he cried, blinking like an owl in the sudden glare. "Good even to you, comrades! Hola! a woman, by my soul!" and in an instant he had clipped Dame Eliza round the waist and was kissing her violently. His eye happening to wander upon the maid, however, he instantly abandoned the mistress and danced off after the other, who scurried in confusion up one of the ladders, and dropped the heavy trap-door upon her pursuer. He then turned back and saluted the landlady once more with the utmost relish and satisfaction.

"La petite is frightened," said he. "Ah, c'est l'amour, l'amour! Curse this trick of French, which will stick to my throat. I must wash it out with some good English ale. By my hilt! camarades, there is no drop of French blood in my body, and I am a true English bowman, Samkin Aylward by name; and I tell you, mes amis, that it warms my very heart-roots to set my feet on the dear old land once more. When I came off the galley at Hythe, this very day, I down on my bones, and I kissed the good brown earth, as I kiss thee now, ma belle, for it was eight long years since I had seen it. The very smell of it seemed life to me. But where are my six rascals? Hola, there! En avant!"

At the order, six men, dressed as common drudges, marched solemnly into the room, each bearing a huge bundle upon his head. They formed in military line, while the soldier stood in front of them with stern eyes, checking off their several packages.

"Number one—a French feather-bed with the two counter-panes of white sendall," said he.

"Here, worthy sir," answered the first of the bearers, laying a great package down in the corner.

"Number two—seven ells of red Turkey cloth and nine ells of cloth of gold. Put it down by the other. Good dame, I prythee give each of these men a bottrine of wine or a jack of ale. Three—a full piece of white Genoan velvet with twelve ells of purple silk. Thou rascal, there is dirt on the hem! Thou hast brushed it against some wall, coquin!"

"Not I, most worthy sir," cried the carrier, shrinking away from the fierce eyes of the bowman.

"I say yes, dog! By the three kings! I have seen a man gasp out his last breath for less. Had you gone through the pain and unease that I have done to earn these things you would be at more care. I swear by my ten finger-bones that there is not one of them that hath not cost its weight in French blood! Four—an incense-boat, a ewer of silver, a gold buckle and a cope worked in pearls. I found them, camarades, at the Church of St. Denis in the harrying of Narbonne, and I took them away with me lest they fall into the hands of the wicked. Five—a cloak of fur turned up with minever, a gold goblet with stand and cover, and a box of rose-colored sugar. See that you lay them together. Six—a box of monies, three pounds of Limousine gold-work, a pair of boots, silver tagged, and, lastly, a store of naping linen. So, the tally is complete! Here is a groat apiece, and you may go."

"Go whither, worthy sir?" asked one of the carriers.

"Whither? To the devil if ye will. What is it to me? Now, ma belle, to supper. A pair of cold capons, a mortress of brawn, or what you will, with a flask or two of the right Gascony. I have crowns in my pouch, my sweet, and I mean to spend them. Bring in wine while the food is dressing. Buvons my brave lads; you shall each empty a stoup with me."

Here was an offer which the company in an English inn at that or any other date are slow to refuse. The flagons were re-gathered and came back with the white foam dripping over their edges. Two of the woodmen and three of the laborers drank their portions off hurriedly and trooped off together, for their homes were distant and the hour late. The others, however, drew closer, leaving the place of honor to the right of the gleeman to the free-handed new-comer. He had thrown off his steel cap and his brigandine, and had placed them with his sword, his quiver and his painted long-bow, on the top of his varied heap of plunder in the corner. Now, with his thick and somewhat bowed legs stretched in front of the blaze, his green jerkin thrown open, and a great quart pot held in his corded fist, he looked the picture of comfort and of good-fellowship. His hard-set face had softened, and the thick crop of crisp brown curls which had been hidden by his helmet grew low upon his massive neck. He might have been forty years of age, though hard toil and harder pleasure had left their grim marks upon his features. Alleyne had ceased painting his pied merlin, and sat, brush in hand, staring with open eyes at a type of man so strange and so unlike any whom he had met. Men had been good or had been bad in his catalogue, but here was a man who was fierce one instant and gentle the next, with a curse on his lips and a smile in his eye. What was to be made of such a man as that?

It chanced that the soldier looked up and saw the questioning glance which the young clerk threw upon him. He raised his flagon and drank to him, with a merry flash of his white teeth.

"A toi, mon garcon," he cried. "Hast surely never seen a man-at-arms, that thou shouldst stare so?"

"I never have," said Alleyne frankly, "though I have oft heard talk of their deeds."

"By my hilt!" cried the other, "if you were to cross the narrow sea you would find them as thick as bees at a tee-hole. Couldst not shoot a bolt down any street of Bordeaux, I warrant, but you would pink archer, squire, or knight. There are more breastplates than gaberdines to be seen, I promise you."

"And where got you all these pretty things?" asked Hordle John, pointing at the heap in the corner.

"Where there is as much more waiting for any brave lad to pick it up. Where a good man can always earn a good wage, and where he need look upon no man as his paymaster, but just reach his hand out and help himself. Aye, it is a goodly and a proper life. And here I drink to mine old comrades, and the saints be with them! Arouse all together, mes enfants, under pain of my displeasure. To Sir Claude Latour and the White Company!"

"Sir Claude Latour and the White Company!" shouted the travellers, draining off their goblets.

"Well quaffed, mes braves! It is for me to fill your cups again, since you have drained them to my dear lads of the white jerkin. Hola! mon ange, bring wine and ale. How runs the old stave?—

We'll drink all together
To the gray goose feather
And the land where the gray goose flew."

He roared out the catch in a harsh, unmusical voice, and ended with a shout of laughter. "I trust that I am a better bowman than a minstrel," said he.

"Methinks I have some remembrance of the lilt," remarked the gleeman, running his fingers over the strings. "Hoping that it will give thee no offence, most holy sir"—with a vicious snap at Alleyne—"and with the kind permit of the company, I will even venture upon it."

Many a time in the after days Alleyne Edricson seemed to see that scene, for all that so many which were stranger and more stirring were soon to crowd upon him. The fat, red-faced gleeman, the listening group, the archer with upraised finger beating in time to the music, and the huge sprawling figure of Hordle John, all thrown into red light and black shadow by the flickering fire in the centre—memory was to come often lovingly back to it. At the time he was lost in admiration at the deft way in which the jongleur disguised the loss of his two missing strings, and the lusty, hearty fashion in which he trolled out his little ballad of the outland bowmen, which ran in some such fashion as this:

What of the bow?
The bow was made in England:
Of true wood, of yew wood,
The wood of English bows;
So men who are free
Love the old yew tree
And the land where the yew tree grows.

What of the cord?
The cord was made in England:
A rough cord, a tough cord,

A cord that bowmen love;
So we'll drain our jacks
To the English flax
And the land where the hemp was wove.

What of the shaft?
The shaft was cut in England:
A long shaft, a strong shaft,
Barbed and trim and true;
So we'll drink all together
To the gray goose feather
And the land where the gray goose flew.

What of the men?
The men were bred in England:
The bowman—the yeoman—
The lads of dale and fell
Here's to you—and to you;
To the hearts that are true
And the land where the true hearts dwell.

"Well sung, by my hilt!" shouted the archer in high delight. "Many a night have I heard that song, both in the old war-time and after in the days of the White Company, when Black Simon of Norwich would lead the stave, and four hundred of the best bowmen that ever drew string would come roaring in upon the chorus. I have seen old John Hawkwood, the same who has led half the Company into Italy, stand laughing in his beard as he heard it, until his plates rattled again. But to get the full smack of it ye must yourselves be English bowmen, and be far off upon an outland soil."

Whilst the song had been singing Dame Eliza and the maid had placed a board across two trestles, and had laid upon it the knife, the spoon, the salt, the tranchoir of bread, and finally the smoking dish which held the savory supper. The archer settled himself to it like one who had known what it was to find good food scarce; but his tongue still went as merrily as his teeth.

"It passes me," he cried, "how all you lusty fellows can bide scratching your backs at home when there are such doings over the seas. Look at me—what have I to do? It is but the eye to the cord, the cord to the shaft, and the shaft to the mark. There is the whole song of it. It is but what you do yourselves for pleasure upon a Sunday evening at the parish village butts."

"And the wage?" asked a laborer.

"You see what the wage brings," he answered. "I eat of the best, and I drink deep. I treat my friend, and I ask no friend to treat me. I clap a silk gown on my girl's back. Never a knight's lady shall be better betrimmed and betrinketed. How of all that, mon garcon? And how of the heap of trifles that you can see for yourselves in yonder corner? They are from the South French, every one, upon whom I have been making war. By my hilt! camarades, I think that I may let my plunder speak for itself."

"It seems indeed to be a goodly service," said the tooth-drawer.

"Tete bleu! yes, indeed. Then there is the chance of a ransom. Why, look you, in the affair at Brignais some four years back, when the companies slew James of Bourbon, and put his army to the sword, there was scarce a man of ours who had not count, baron, or knight. Peter Karsdale, who was but a common country lout newly brought over, with the English fleas still hopping under his doublet, laid his great hands upon the Sieur Amaury de Chatonville, who owns half Picardy, and had five thousand crowns out of him, with his horse and harness. 'Tis true that a French wench took it all off Peter as quick as the Frenchman paid it; but what then? By the twang of string! it would be a bad thing if money was not made to be spent; and how better than on woman—eh, ma belle?"

"It would indeed be a bad thing if we had not our brave archers to bring wealth and kindly customs into the country," quoth Dame Eliza, on whom the soldier's free and open ways had made a deep impression.

"A toi, ma cherie!" said he, with his hand over his heart. "Hola! there is la petite peeping from behind the door. A toi, aussi, ma petite! Mon Dieu! but the lass has a good color!"

"There is one thing, fair sir," said the Cambridge student in his piping voice, "which I would fain that you would make more clear. As I understand it, there was peace made at the town of Bretigny some six years back between our most gracious monarch and the King of the French. This being so, it seems most passing strange that you should talk so loudly of war and of companies when there is no quarrel between the French and us."

"Meaning that I lie," said the archer, laying down his knife.

"May heaven forfend!" cried the student hastily. "*Magna est veritas sed rara*, which means in the Latin tongue that archers are all honorable men. I come to you seeking knowledge, for it is my trade to learn."

"I fear that you are yet a 'prentice to that trade," quoth the soldier; "for there is no child over the water but could answer what you ask. Know then that though there may be peace between our own provinces and the French, yet within the marches of France there is always war, for the country is much divided against itself, and is furthermore harried by bands of flayers, skinners, Brabacons, tardvenus, and the rest of them. When every man's grip is on his neighbor's throat, and every five-sous-piece of a baron is marching with tuck of drum to fight whom he will, it would be a strange thing if five hundred brave English boys could not pick up a living. Now that Sir John Hawkwood hath gone with the East Anglian lads and the Nottingham woodmen into the service of the Marquis of Montferrat to fight against the Lord of Milan, there are but ten score of us left, yet I trust that I may be able to bring some back with me to fill the ranks of the White Company. By the tooth of Peter! it would be a bad thing if I could not muster many a Hamptonshire man who would be ready to strike in under the red flag of St. George, and the more so if Sir Nigel Loring, of Christchurch, should don hauberk once more and take the lead of us."

"Ah, you would indeed be in luck then," quoth a woodman; "for it is said that, setting aside the prince, and mayhap good old Sir John Chandos, there was not in the whole army a man of such tried courage."

"It is sooth, every word of it," the archer answered. "I have seen him with these two eyes in a stricken field, and never did man carry himself better. Mon Dieu! yes, ye would not credit it to look at him, or to hearken to his soft voice, but from the sailing from Orwell down to the foray to Paris, and that is clear twenty years, there was not a skirmish, onfall, sally, bushment, escalado or battle, but Sir Nigel was in the heart of it. I go now to Christchurch with a letter to him from Sir Claude Latour to ask him if he will take the place of Sir John Hawkwood; and there is the more chance that he will if I bring one or two likely men at my heels. What say you, woodman: wilt leave the bucks to loose a shaft at a nobler mark?"

The forester shook his head. "I have wife and child at Emery Down," quoth he; "I would not leave them for such a venture."

"You, then, young sir?" asked the archer.

"Nay, I am a man of peace," said Alleyne Edricson. "Besides, I have other work to do."

"Peste!" growled the soldier, striking his flagon on the board until the dishes danced again. "What, in the name of the devil, hath come over the folk? Why sit ye all moping by the fireside, like crows round a dead horse, when there is man's work to be done within a few short leagues of ye? Out upon you all, as a set of laggards and hang-backs! By my hilt I believe that the men of England are all in France already, and that what is left behind are in sooth the women dressed up in their paltocks and hosen."

"Archer," quoth Hordle John, "you have lied more than once and more than twice; for which, and also because I see much in you to dislike, I am sorely tempted to lay you upon your back."

"By my hilt! then, I have found a man at last!" shouted the bowman. "And, 'fore God, you are a better man than I take you for if you can lay me on my back, mon garcon. I have won the ram more times than there are toes to my feet, and for seven long years I have found no man in the Company who could make my jerkin dusty."

"We have had enough bobance and boasting," said Hordle John, rising and throwing off his doublet. "I will show you that there are better men left in England than ever went thieving to France."

"Pasques Dieu!" cried the archer, loosening his jerkin, and eyeing his foeman over with the keen glance of one who is a judge of manhood. "I have only once before seen such a body of a man. By your leave, my red-headed friend, I should be right sorry to exchange buffets with you; and I will allow that there is no man in the Company who would pull against you on a rope; so let that be a salve to your pride. On the other hand I should judge that you have led a life of ease for some months back, and that my muscle is harder than your own. I am ready to wager upon myself against you if you are not afeard."

"Afeard, thou lurden!" growled big John. "I never saw the face yet of the man that I was afeard of. Come out, and we shall see who is the better man."

"But the wager?"

"I have nought to wager. Come out for the love and the lust of the thing."

"Nought to wager!" cried the soldier. "Why, you have that which I covet above all things. It is that big body of thine that I am after. See, now, mon garcon. I have a French feather-bed there, which I have been at pains to keep these years back. I had it at the sacking of Issodun, and the King himself hath not such a bed. If you throw me, it is thine; but, if I throw you, then you are under a vow to take bow and bill and hie with me to France, there to serve in the White Company as long as we be enrolled."

"A fair wager!" cried all the travellers, moving back their benches and trestles, so as to give fair field for the wrestlers.

"Then you may bid farewell to your bed, soldier," said Hordle John.

"Nay; I shall keep the bed, and I shall have you to France in spite of your teeth, and you shall live to thank me for it. How shall it be, then, mon enfant? Collar and elbow, or close-lock, or catch how you can?"

"To the devil with your tricks," said John, opening and shutting his great red hands. "Stand forth, and let me clip thee."

"Shalt clip me as best you can then," quoth the archer, moving out into the open space, and keeping a most wary eye upon his opponent. He had thrown off his green jerkin, and his chest was covered only by a pink silk jupon, or undershirt, cut low in the neck and sleeveless. Hordle John was stripped from his waist upwards, and his huge body, with his great muscles swelling out like the gnarled roots of an oak, towered high above the soldier. The other, however, though near a foot shorter, was a man of great strength; and there was a gloss upon his white skin which was wanting in the heavier limbs of the renegade monk. He was quick on his feet, too, and skilled at the game; so that it was clear, from the poise of head and shine of eye, that he counted the chances to be in his favor. It would have been hard that night, through the whole length of England, to set up a finer pair in face of each other.

Big John stood waiting in the centre with a sullen, menacing eye, and his red hair in a bristle, while the archer paced lightly and swiftly to the right and the left with crooked knee and hands advanced. Then with a sudden dash, so swift and fierce that the eye could scarce follow it, he flew in upon his man and locked his leg round him. It was a grip that, between men of equal strength, would mean a fall; but Hordle John tore him off from him as he might a rat, and hurled him across the room, so that his head cracked up against the wooden wall.

"Ma foi!" cried the bowman, passing his fingers through his curls, "you were not far from the feather-bed then, mon gar. A little more and this good hostel would have a new window."

Nothing daunted, he approached his man once more, but this time with more caution than before. With a quick feint he threw the other off his guard, and then, bounding upon him, threw his legs round his waist and his arms round his bull-neck, in the hope of bearing him to the ground with the sudden shock. With a bellow of rage, Hordle John squeezed him limp in his huge arms; and then, picking him up, cast him down upon the floor with a force which might well have splintered a bone or two, had not the archer with the most perfect coolness clung to the other's forearms to break his fall. As it was, he dropped upon his feet and kept his balance, though it sent a jar through his frame which set every joint a-creaking. He bounded back from his perilous foeman; but the other, heated by the bout, rushed madly after him, and so gave the practised wrestler the very vantage for which he had planned. As big John flung himself upon him, the archer ducked under the great red hands that clutched for him, and, catching his man round the thighs, hurled him over his shoulder—helped as much by his own mad rush as by the trained strength of the heave. To Alleyne's eye, it was as if John had taken unto himself wings and flown. As he hurtled through the air, with giant limbs revolving, the lad's heart was in his mouth; for surely no man ever yet had such a fall and came scathless out of it. In truth, hardy as the man was, his neck had been assuredly broken had he not pitched head first on the very midriff of the drunken artist, who was slumbering so peacefully in the corner, all unaware of these stirring doings. The luckless limner, thus suddenly brought out from his dreams, sat up with a piercing yell, while Hordle John bounded back into the circle almost as rapidly as he had left it.

"One more fall, by all the saints!" he cried, throwing out his arms.

"Not I," quoth the archer, pulling on his clothes, "I have come well out of the business. I would sooner wrestle with the great bear of Navarre."

"It was a trick," cried John.

"Aye was it. By my ten finger-bones! it is a trick that will add a proper man to the ranks of the Company."

"Oh, for that," said the other, "I count it not a fly; for I had promised myself a good hour ago that I should go with thee, since the life seems to be a goodly and proper one. Yet I would fain have had the feather-bed."

"I doubt it not, mon ami," quoth the archer, going back to his tankard. "Here is to thee, lad, and may we be good comrades to each other! But, hola! what is it that ails our friend of the wrathful face?"

The unfortunate limner had been sitting up rubbing himself ruefully and staring about with a vacant gaze, which showed that he knew neither where he was nor what had occurred to him. Suddenly, however, a flash of intelligence had come over his sodden features, and he rose and staggered for the door. "'Ware the ale!" he said in a hoarse whisper, shaking a warning finger at the company. "Oh, holy Virgin, 'ware the ale!" and slapping his hands to his injury, he flitted off into the darkness, amid a shout of laughter, in which the vanquished joined as merrily as the victor. The remaining forester and the two laborers were also ready for the road, and the rest of the company turned to the blankets which Dame Eliza and the maid had laid out for them upon the floor. Alleyne, weary with the unwonted excitements of the day, was soon in a deep slumber broken only by fleeting visions of twittering legs, cursing beggars, black robbers, and the many strange folk whom he had met at the "Pied Merlin."

VII

How the Three Comrades Journeyed Through the Woodlands

At early dawn the country inn was all alive, for it was rare indeed that an hour of daylight would be wasted at a time when lighting was so scarce and dear. Indeed, early as it was when Dame Eliza began to stir, it seemed that others could be earlier still, for the door was ajar, and the learned student of Cambridge had taken himself off, with a mind which was too intent upon the high things of antiquity to stoop to consider the four-pence which he owed for bed and board. It was the shrill out-cry of the landlady when she found her loss, and the clucking of the hens, which had streamed in through the open door, that first broke in upon the slumbers of the tired wayfarers.

Once afoot, it was not long before the company began to disperse. A sleek mule with red trappings was brought round from some neighboring shed for the physician, and he ambled away with much dignity upon his road to Southampton. The tooth-drawer and the gleeman called for a cup of small ale apiece, and started off together for Ringwood fair, the old jongleur looking very yellow in the eye and swollen in the face after his overnight potations. The archer, however, who had drunk more than any man in the room, was as merry as a grig, and having kissed the matron and chased the maid up the ladder once more, he went out to the brook, and came back with the water dripping from his face and hair.

"Hola! my man of peace," he cried to Alleyne, "whither are you bent this morning?"

"To Minstead," quoth he. "My brother Simon Edricson is socman there, and I go to bide with him for a while. I prythee, let me have my score, good dame."

"Score, indeed!" cried she, standing with upraised hands in front of the panel on which Alleyne had worked the night before. "Say, rather what it is that I owe to thee, good youth. Aye, this is indeed a pied merlin, and with a leveret under its claws, as I am a living woman. By the rood of Waltham! but thy touch is deft and dainty."

"And see the red eye of it!" cried the maid.

"Aye, and the open beak."

"And the ruffled wing," added Hordle John.

"By my hilt!" cried the archer, "it is the very bird itself."

The young clerk flushed with pleasure at this chorus of praise, rude and indiscriminate indeed, and yet so much heartier and less grudging than any which he had ever heard from the critical brother Jerome, or the short-spoken Abbot. There was, it would seem, great kindness as well as great wickedness in this world, of which he had heard so little that was good. His hostess would hear nothing of his paying either for bed or for board, while the archer and Hordle John placed a hand upon either shoulder and led him off to the board, where some smoking fish, a dish of spinach, and a jug of milk were laid out for their breakfast.

"I should not be surprised to learn, mon camarade," said the soldier, as he heaped a slice of fish upon Alleyne's tranchoir of bread, "that you could read written things, since you are so ready with your brushes and pigments."

"It would be shame to the good brothers of Beaulieu if I could not," he answered, "seeing that I have been their clerk this ten years back."

The bowman looked at him with great respect. "Think of that!" said he. "And you with not a hair to your face, and a skin like a girl. I can shoot three hundred and fifty paces with my little popper there, and four hundred and twenty with the great war-bow; yet I can make nothing of this, nor read my own name if you were to set 'Sam Aylward' up against me. In the whole Company there was only one man who could read, and he fell down a well at the taking of Ventadour, which proves that the thing is not suited to a soldier, though most needful to a clerk."

"I can make some show at it," said big John; "though I was scarce long enough among the monks to catch the whole trick of it.

"Here, then, is something to try upon," quoth the archer, pulling a square of parchment from the inside of his tunic. It was tied securely with a broad band of purple silk, and firmly sealed at either end with a large red seal. John pored long and earnestly over the inscription upon the back, with his brows bent as one who bears up against great mental strain.

"Not having read much of late," he said, "I am loth to say too much about what this may be. Some might say one thing and some another, just as one bowman loves the yew, and a second will not shoot save with the ash. To me, by the length and the look of it, I should judge this to be a verse from one of the Psalms."

The bowman shook his head. "It is scarce likely," he said, "that Sir Claude Latour should send me all the way across seas with nought more weighty than a psalm-verse. You have clean overshot the butts this time, mon camarade. Give it to the little one. I will wager my feather-bed that he makes more sense of it."

"Why, it is written in the French tongue," said Alleyne, "and in a right clerkly hand. This is how it runs: 'A le moult puissant et moult honorable chevalier, Sir Nigel Loring de Christchurch, de son tres fidele ami Sir Claude Latour, capitaine de la Compagnie blanche, chatelain de Biscar, grand seigneur de Montchateau, vavaseur de le renomme Gaston, Comte de Foix, tenant les droits de la haute justice, de la milieu, et de la basse.' Which signifies in our speech: 'To the very powerful and very honorable knight, Sir Nigel Loring of Christchurch, from his very faithful friend Sir Claude Latour, captain of the White Company, chatelain of Biscar, grand lord of Montchateau and vassal to the renowned Gaston, Count of Foix, who holds the rights of the high justice, the middle and the low.'"

"Look at that now!" cried the bowman in triumph. "That is just what he would have said."

"I can see now that it is even so," said John, examining the parchment again. "Though I scarce understand this high, middle and low."

"By my hilt! you would understand it if you were Jacques Bonhomme. The low justice means that you may fleece him, and the middle that you may torture him, and the high that you may slay him. That is about the truth of it. But this is the letter which I am to take; and since the platter is clean it is time that we trussed up and were afoot. You come with me, mon gros Jean; and as to you, little one, where did you say that you journeyed?"

"To Minstead."

"Ah, yes. I know this forest country well, though I was born myself in the Hundred of Easebourne, in the Rape of Chichester, hard by the village of Midhurst. Yet I have not a word to say against the Hampton men, for there are no better comrades or truer archers in the whole Company than some who learned to loose the string in these very parts. We shall travel round with you to Minstead lad, seeing that it is little out of our way."

"I am ready," said Alleyne, right pleased at the thought of such company upon the road.

"So am not I. I must store my plunder at this inn, since the hostess is an honest woman. Hola! ma cherie, I wish to leave with you my gold-work, my velvet, my silk, my feather bed, my incense-boat, my ewer, my naping linen, and all the rest of it. I take only the money in a linen bag, and the box of rose colored sugar which is a gift from my captain to the Lady Loring. Wilt guard my treasure for me?"

"It shall be put in the safest loft, good archer. Come when you may, you shall find it ready for you."

"Now, there is a true friend!" cried the bowman, taking her hand. "There is a bonne amie! English land and English women, say I, and French wine and French plunder. I shall be back anon, mon ange. I am a lonely man, my sweeting, and I must settle some day when the wars are over and done. Mayhap you and I——Ah, mechante, mechante! There is la petite peeping from behind the door. Now, John, the sun is over the trees; you must be brisker than this when the bugleman blows 'Bows and Bills.'"

"I have been waiting this time back," said Hordle John gruffly.

"Then we must be off. Adieu, ma vie! The two livres shall settle the score and buy some ribbons against the next kermesse. Do not forget Sam Aylward, for his heart shall ever be thine alone—and thine, ma petite! So, marchons, and may St. Julian grant us as good quarters elsewhere!"

The sun had risen over Ashurst and Denny woods, and was shining brightly, though the eastern wind had a sharp flavor to it, and the leaves were flickering thickly from the trees. In the High Street of Lyndhurst the wayfarers had to pick their way, for the little town was crowded with the guardsmen, grooms, and yeomen prickers who were attached to the King's hunt. The King himself was staying at Castle Malwood, but several of his suite had been compelled to seek such quarters as they might find in the wooden or wattle-and-daub cottages of the village. Here and there a small escutcheon, peeping from a glassless window, marked the night's lodging of knight or baron. These coats-of-arms could be read, where a scroll would be meaningless, and the bowman, like most men of his age, was well versed in the common symbols of heraldry.

"There is the Saracen's head of Sir Bernard Brocas," quoth he. "I saw him last at the ruffle at Poictiers some ten years back, when he bore himself like a man. He is the master of the King's horse, and can sing a right jovial stave, though in that he cannot come nigh to Sir John Chandos, who is first at the board or in the saddle. Three martlets on a field azure, that must be one of the Luttrells. By the crescent upon it, it should be the second son of old Sir Hugh, who had a bolt through his ankle at the intaking of Romorantin, he having rushed into the fray ere his squire had time to clasp his solleret to his greave. There too is the hackle which is the old device of the De Brays. I have served under Sir Thomas de Bray, who was as jolly as a pie, and a lusty swordsman until he got too fat for his harness."

So the archer gossiped as the three wayfarers threaded their way among the stamping horses, the busy grooms, and the knots of pages and squires who disputed over the merits of their masters' horses and deer-hounds. As they passed the old church, which stood upon a mound at the left-hand side of the village street the door was flung open, and a stream of worshippers wound down the sloping path, coming from the morning mass, all chattering like a cloud of jays. Alleyne bent knee and doffed hat at the sight of the open door; but ere he had finished an ave his comrades were out of sight round the curve of the path, and he had to run to overtake them.

"What!" he said, "not one word of prayer before God's own open house? How can ye hope for His blessing upon the day?"

"My friend," said Hordle John, "I have prayed so much during the last two months, not only during the day, but at matins, lauds, and the like, when I could scarce keep my head upon my shoulders for nodding, that I feel that I have somewhat over-prayed myself."

"How can a man have too much religion?" cried Alleyne earnestly. "It is the one thing that availeth. A man is but a beast as he lives from day to day, eating and drinking, breathing and sleeping. It is only when he raises himself, and concerns himself with the immortal spirit within him, that he becomes in very truth a man. Bethink ye how sad a thing it would be that the blood of the Redeemer should be spilled to no purpose."

"Bless the lad, if he doth not blush like any girl, and yet preach like the whole College of Cardinals," cried the archer.

"In truth I blush that any one so weak and so unworthy as I should try to teach another that which he finds it so passing hard to follow himself."

"Prettily said, mon garcon. Touching that same slaying of the Redeemer, it was a bad business. A good padre in France read to us from a scroll the whole truth of the matter. The soldiers came upon him in the garden. In truth, these Apostles of His may have been holy men, but they were of no great account as men-at-arms. There was one, indeed, Sir Peter, who smote out like a true man; but, unless he is belied, he did but clip a varlet's ear, which was no very knightly deed. By these ten finger-bones! had I been there with Black Simon of Norwich, and but one score picked men of the Company, we had held them in play. Could we do no more, we had at least filled the false knight, Sir Judas, so full of English arrows that he would curse the day that ever he came on such an errand."

The young clerk smiled at his companion's earnestness. "Had He wished help," he said, "He could have summoned legions of archangels from heaven, so what need had He of your poor bow and arrow? Besides, bethink you of His own words—that those who live by the sword shall perish by the sword."

"And how could man die better?" asked the archer. "If I had my wish, it would be to fall so—not, mark you, in any mere skirmish of the Company, but in a stricken field, with the great lion banner waving over us and the red oriflamme in front, amid the shouting of my fellows and the twanging of the strings. But let it be sword, lance, or bolt that strikes me down: for I should think it shame to die from an iron ball from the fire-crake or bombard or any such unsoldierly weapon, which is only fitted to scare babes with its foolish noise and smoke."

"I have heard much even in the quiet cloisters of these new and dreadful engines," quoth Alleyne. "It is said, though I can scarce bring myself to believe it, that they will send a ball twice as far as a bowman can shoot his shaft, and with such force as to break through armor of proof."

"True enough, my lad. But while the armorer is thrusting in his devil's-dust, and dropping his ball, and lighting his flambeau, I can very easily loose six shafts, or eight maybe, so he hath no great vantage after all. Yet I will not deny that at the intaking of a town it is well to have good store of bombards. I am told that at Calais they made dints in the wall that a man might put his head into. But surely, comrades, some one who is grievously hurt hath passed along this road before us."

All along the woodland track there did indeed run a scattered straggling trail of blood-marks, sometimes in single drops, and in other places in broad, ruddy gouts, smudged over the dead leaves or crimsoning the white flint stones.

"It must be a stricken deer," said John.

"Nay, I am woodman enough to see that no deer hath passed this way this morning; and yet the blood is fresh. But hark to the sound!"

They stood listening all three with sidelong heads. Through the silence of the great forest there came a swishing, whistling sound, mingled with the most dolorous groans, and the voice of a man raised in a high quavering kind of song. The comrades hurried onwards eagerly, and topping the brow of a small rising they saw upon the other side the source from which these strange noises arose.

A tall man, much stooped in the shoulders, was walking slowly with bended head and clasped hands in the centre of the path. He was dressed from head to foot in a long white linen cloth, and a high white cap with a red cross printed upon it. His gown was turned back from his shoulders, and the flesh there was a sight to make a man wince, for it was all beaten to a pulp, and the blood was soaking into his gown and trickling down upon the ground. Behind him walked a smaller man with his hair touched with gray, who was clad in the same white garb. He intoned a long whining rhyme in the French tongue, and at the end of every line he raised a thick cord, all jagged with pellets of lead, and smote his companion across the shoulders until the blood spurted again. Even as the three wayfarers stared, however, there was a sudden change, for the smaller man, having finished his song, loosened his own gown and handed the scourge to the other, who took up the stave once more and lashed his companion with all the strength of his bare and sinewy arm. So, alternately beating and beaten, they made their dolorous way through the beautiful woods and under the amber arches of the fading beech-trees, where the calm strength and majesty of Nature might serve to rebuke the foolish energies and misspent strivings of mankind.

Such a spectacle was new to Hordle John or to Alleyne Edricson; but the archer treated it lightly, as a common matter enough.

"These are the Beating Friars, otherwise called the Flagellants," quoth he. "I marvel that ye should have come upon none of them before, for across the water they are as common as gallybaggers. I have heard that there are no English among them, but that they are from France, Italy and Bohemia. En avant, camarades! that we may have speech with them."

As they came up to them, Alleyne could hear the doleful dirge which the beater was chanting, bringing down his heavy whip at the end of each line, while the groans of the sufferer formed a sort of dismal chorus. It was in old French, and ran somewhat in this way:

Or avant, entre nous tous freres
Battons nos charognes bien fort
En remembrant la grant misere
De Dieu et sa piteuse mort

Qui fut pris en la gent amere
Et vendus et trais a tort
Et bastu sa chair, vierge et dere
Au nom de ce battons plus fort.

Then at the end of the verse the scourge changed hands and the chanting began anew.

"Truly, holy fathers," said the archer in French as they came abreast of them, "you have beaten enough for to-day. The road is all spotted like a shambles at Martinmas. Why should ye mishandle yourselves thus?"

"C'est pour vos peches—pour vos peches," they droned, looking at the travellers with sad lack-lustre eyes, and then bent to their bloody work once more without heed to the prayers and persuasions which were addressed to them. Finding all remonstrance useless, the three comrades hastened on their way, leaving these strange travellers to their dreary task.

"Mort Dieu!" cried the bowman, "there is a bucketful or more of my blood over in France, but it was all spilled in hot fight, and I should think twice before I drew it drop by drop as these friars are doing. By my hilt! our young one here is as white as a Picardy cheese. What is amiss then, mon cher?"

"It is nothing," Alleyne answered. "My life has been too quiet, I am not used to such sights."

"Ma foi!" the other cried, "I have never yet seen a man who was so stout of speech and yet so weak of heart."

"Not so, friend," quoth big John; "it is not weakness of heart for I know the lad well. His heart is as good as thine or mine but he hath more in his pate than ever you will carry under that tin pot of thine, and as a consequence he can see farther into things, so that they weigh upon him more."

"Surely to any man it is a sad sight," said Alleyne, "to see these holy men, who have done no sin themselves, suffering so for the sins of others. Saints are they, if in this age any may merit so high a name."

"I count them not a fly," cried Hordle John; "for who is the better for all their whipping and yowling? They are like other friars, I trow, when all is done. Let them leave their backs alone, and beat the pride out of their hearts."

"By the three kings! there is sooth in what you say," remarked the archer. "Besides, methinks if I were le bon Dieu, it would bring me little joy to see a poor devil cutting the flesh off his bones; and I should think that he had but a small opinion of me, that he should hope to please me by such provost-marshal work. No, by my hilt! I should look with a more loving eye upon a jolly archer who never harmed a fallen foe and never feared a hale one."

"Doubtless you mean no sin," said Alleyne. "If your words are wild, it is not for me to judge them. Can you not see that there are other foes in this world besides Frenchmen, and as much glory to be gained in conquering them? Would it not be a proud day for knight or squire if he could overthrow seven adversaries in the lists? Yet here are we in the lists of life, and there come the seven black champions against us Sir Pride, Sir Covetousness, Sir Lust, Sir Anger, Sir Gluttony, Sir Envy, and Sir Sloth. Let a man lay those seven low, and he shall have the prize of the day, from the hands of the fairest queen of beauty, even from the Virgin-Mother herself. It is for this that these men mortify their flesh, and to set us an example, who would pamper ourselves overmuch. I say again that they are God's own saints, and I bow my head to them."

"And so you shall, mon petit," replied the archer. "I have not heard a man speak better since old Dom Bertrand died, who was at one time chaplain to the White Company. He was a very valiant man, but at the battle of Brignais he was spitted through the body by a Hainault man-at-arms. For this we had an excommunication read against the man, when next we saw our holy father at Avignon; but as we had not his name, and knew nothing of him, save that he rode a dapple-gray roussin, I have feared sometimes that the blight may have settled upon the wrong man."

"Your Company has been, then, to bow knee before our holy father, the Pope Urban, the prop and centre of Christendom?" asked Alleyne, much interested. "Perchance you have yourself set eyes upon his august face?"

"Twice I saw him," said the archer. "He was a lean little rat of a man, with a scab on his chin. The first time we had five thousand crowns out of him, though he made much ado about it. The second time we asked ten thousand, but it was three days before we could come to terms, and I am of opinion myself that we might have done better by plundering the palace. His chamberlain and cardinals came forth, as I remember, to ask whether we would take seven thousand crowns with his blessing and a plenary absolution, or the ten thousand with his solemn ban by bell, book and candle. We were all of one mind that it was best to have the ten thousand with the curse; but in some way they prevailed upon

Sir John, so that we were blest and shriven against our will. Perchance it is as well, for the Company were in need of it about that time."

The pious Alleyne was deeply shocked by this reminiscence. Involuntarily he glanced up and around to see if there were any trace of those opportune levin-flashes and thunderbolts which, in the "Acta Sanctorum," were wont so often to cut short the loose talk of the scoffer. The autumn sun streamed down as brightly as ever, and the peaceful red path still wound in front of them through the rustling, yellow-tinted forest, Nature seemed to be too busy with her own concerns to heed the dignity of an outraged pontiff. Yet he felt a sense of weight and reproach within his breast, as though he had sinned himself in giving ear to such words. The teachings of twenty years cried out against such license. It was not until he had thrown himself down before one of the many wayside crosses, and had prayed from his heart both for the archer and for himself, that the dark cloud rolled back again from his spirit.

VIII

The Three Friends

His companions had passed on whilst he was at his orisons; but his young blood and the fresh morning air both invited him to a scamper. His staff in one hand and his scrip in the other, with springy step and floating locks, he raced along the forest path, as active and as graceful as a young deer. He had not far to go, however; for, on turning a corner, he came on a roadside cottage with a wooden fence-work around it, where stood big John and Aylward the bowman, staring at something within. As he came up with them, he saw that two little lads, the one about nine years of age and the other somewhat older, were standing on the plot in front of the cottage, each holding out a round stick in their left hands, with their arms stiff and straight from the shoulder, as silent and still as two small statues. They were pretty, blue-eyed, yellow-haired lads, well made and sturdy, with bronzed skins, which spoke of a woodland life.

"Here are young chips from an old bow stave!" cried the soldier in great delight. "This is the proper way to raise children. By my hilt! I could not have trained them better had I the ordering of it myself."

"What is it then?" asked Hordle John. "They stand very stiff, and I trust that they have not been struck so."

"Nay, they are training their left arms, that they may have a steady grasp of the bow. So my own father trained me, and six days a week I held out his walking-staff till my arm was heavy as lead. Hola, mes enfants! how long will you hold out?"

"Until the sun is over the great lime-tree, good master," the elder answered.

"What would ye be, then? Woodmen? Verderers?"

"Nay, soldiers," they cried both together.

"By the beard of my father! but ye are whelps of the true breed. Why so keen, then, to be soldiers?"

"That we may fight the Scots," they answered. "Daddy will send us to fight the Scots."

"And why the Scots, my pretty lads? We have seen French and Spanish galleys no further away than Southampton, but I doubt that it will be some time before the Scots find their way to these parts."

"Our business is with the Scots," quoth the elder; "for it was the Scots who cut off daddy's string fingers and his thumbs."

"Aye, lads, it was that," said a deep voice from behind Alleyne's shoulder. Looking round, the wayfarers saw a gaunt, big-boned man, with sunken cheeks and a sallow face, who had come up behind them. He held up his two hands as he spoke, and showed that the thumbs and two first fingers had been torn away from each of them.

"Ma foi, camarade!" cried Aylward. "Who hath served thee in so shameful a fashion?"

"It is easy to see, friend, that you were born far from the marches of Scotland," quoth the stranger, with a bitter smile. "North of Humber there is no man who would not know the handiwork of Devil Douglas, the black Lord James."

"And how fell you into his hands?" asked John.

"I am a man of the north country, from the town of Beverley and the wapentake of Holderness," he answered. "There was a day when, from Trent to Tweed, there was no better marksman than Robin Heathcot. Yet, as you see, he hath left me, as he hath left many another poor border archer, with no grip for bill or bow. Yet the king hath given me a living here in the southlands, and please God these two lads of mine will pay off a debt that hath been owing over long. What is the price of daddy's thumbs, boys?"

"Twenty Scottish lives," they answered together.

"And for the fingers?"

"Half a score."

"When they can bend my war-bow, and bring down a squirrel at a hundred paces, I send them to take service under Johnny Copeland, the Lord of the Marches and Governor of Carlisle. By my soul! I would give the rest of my fingers to see the Douglas within arrow-flight of them."

"May you live to see it," quoth the bowman. "And hark ye, mes enfants, take an old soldier's rede and lay your bodies to the bow, drawing from hip and thigh as much as from arm. Learn also, I pray you, to shoot with a dropping shaft; for though a bowman may at times be called upon to shoot straight and fast, yet it is more often that he has to do with a town-guard behind a wall, or an arbalestier with his mantlet raised when you cannot hope to do him scathe unless your shaft fall straight upon him from the clouds. I have not drawn string for two weeks, but I may be able to show ye how such shots should be made." He loosened his long-bow, slung his quiver round to the front, and then glanced keenly round for a fitting mark. There was a yellow and withered stump some way off, seen under the drooping branches of a lofty oak. The archer measured the distance with his eye; and then, drawing three shafts, he shot them off with such speed that the first had not reached the mark ere the last was on the string. Each arrow passed high over the oak; and, of the three, two stuck fair into the stump; while the third, caught in some wandering puff of wind, was driven a foot or two to one side.

"Good!" cried the north countryman. "Hearken to him lads! He is a master bowman. Your dad says amen to every word he says."

"By my hilt!" said Aylward, "if I am to preach on bowmanship, the whole long day would scarce give me time for my sermon. We have marksmen in the Company who will notch with a shaft every crevice and joint of a man-at-arm's harness, from the clasp of his bassinet to the hinge of his greave. But, with your favor, friend, I must gather my arrows again, for while a shaft costs a penny a poor man can scarce leave them sticking in wayside stumps. We must, then, on our road again, and I hope from my heart that you may train these two young goshawks here until they are ready for a cast even at such a quarry as you speak of."

Leaving the thumbless archer and his brood, the wayfarers struck through the scattered huts of Emery Down, and out on to the broad rolling heath covered deep in ferns and in heather, where droves of the half-wild black forest pigs were rooting about amongst the hillocks. The woods about this point fall away to the left and the right, while the road curves upwards and the wind sweeps keenly over the swelling uplands. The broad strips of bracken glowed red and yellow against the black peaty soil, and a queenly doe who grazed among them turned her white front and her great questioning eyes towards the wayfarers. Alleyne gazed in admiration at the supple beauty of the creature; but the archer's fingers played with his quiver, and his eyes glistened with the fell instinct which urges a man to slaughter.

"Tete Dieu!" he growled, "were this France, or even Guienne, we should have a fresh haunch for our none-meat. Law or no law, I have a mind to loose a bolt at her."

"I would break your stave across my knee first," cried John, laying his great hand upon the bow. "What! man, I am forest-born, and I know what comes of it. In our own township of Hordle two have lost their eyes and one his skin for this very thing. On my troth, I felt no great love when I first saw you, but since then I have conceived over much regard for you to wish to see the verderer's flayer at work upon you."

"It is my trade to risk my skin," growled the archer; but none the less he thrust his quiver over his hip again and turned his face for the west.

As they advanced, the path still tended upwards, running from heath into copses of holly and yew, and so back into heath again. It was joyful to hear the merry whistle of blackbirds as they darted from one clump of greenery to the other. Now and again a peaty amber colored stream rippled across their way, with ferny over-grown banks, where the blue kingfisher flitted busily from side to side, or the gray and pensive heron, swollen with trout and dignity, stood ankle-deep among the sedges. Chattering jays and loud wood-pigeons flapped thickly overhead, while ever and anon the measured tapping of Nature's carpenter, the great green woodpecker, sounded from each wayside grove. On either side, as the path mounted, the long sweep of country broadened and expanded, sloping down on the one side through yellow forest and brown moor to the distant smoke of Lymington and the blue misty channel which lay alongside the sky-line, while to the north the woods rolled away, grove topping grove, to where in the furthest distance the white spire of Salisbury stood out hard and clear against the cloudless sky. To Alleyne whose days had been spent in the low-lying coastland, the eager upland air and the wide free country-side gave a sense of life and of the joy of living which made his young blood tingle in his veins. Even the heavy John was not unmoved by the beauty of their road, while the bowman whistled lustily or sang snatches of French love songs in a voice which might have scared the most stout-hearted maiden that ever hearkened to serenade.

"I have a liking for that north countryman," he remarked presently. "He hath good power of hatred. Couldst see by his cheek and eye that he is as bitter as verjuice. I warm to a man who hath some gall in his liver."

"Ah me!" sighed Alleyne. "Would it not be better if he had some love in his heart?"

"I would not say nay to that. By my hilt! I shall never be said to be traitor to the little king. Let a man love the sex. Pasques Dieu! they are made to be loved, les petites, from whimple down to shoe-string! I am right glad, mon garcon, to see that the good monks have trained thee so wisely and so well."

"Nay, I meant not worldly love, but rather that his heart should soften towards those who have wronged him."

The archer shook his head. "A man should love those of his own breed," said he. "But it is not nature that an English-born man should love a Scot or a Frenchman. Ma foi! you have not seen a drove of

Nithsdale raiders on their Galloway nags, or you would not speak of loving them. I would as soon take Beelzebub himself to my arms. I fear, mon gar., that they have taught thee but badly at Beaulieu, for surely a bishop knows more of what is right and what is ill than an abbot can do, and I myself with these very eyes saw the Bishop of Lincoln hew into a Scottish hobeler with a battle-axe, which was a passing strange way of showing him that he loved him."

Alleyne scarce saw his way to argue in the face of so decided an opinion on the part of a high dignitary of the Church. "You have borne arms against the Scots, then?" he asked.

"Why, man, I first loosed string in battle when I was but a lad, younger by two years than you, at Neville's Cross, under the Lord Mowbray. Later, I served under the Warden of Berwick, that very John Copeland of whom our friend spake, the same who held the King of Scots to ransom. Ma foi! it is rough soldiering, and a good school for one who would learn to be hardy and war-wise."

"I have heard that the Scots are good men of war," said Hordle John.

"For axemen and for spearmen I have not seen their match," the archer answered. "They can travel, too, with bag of meal and gridiron slung to their sword-belt, so that it is ill to follow them. There are scant crops and few beeves in the borderland, where a man must reap his grain with sickle in one fist and brown bill in the other. On the other hand, they are the sorriest archers that I have ever seen, and cannot so much as aim with the arbalest, to say nought of the long-bow. Again, they are mostly poor folk, even the nobles among them, so that there are few who can buy as good a brigandine of chain-mail as that which I am wearing, and it is ill for them to stand up against our own knights, who carry the price of five Scotch farms upon their chest and shoulders. Man for man, with equal weapons, they are as worthy and valiant men as could be found in the whole of Christendom."

"And the French?" asked Alleyne, to whom the archer's light gossip had all the relish that the words of the man of action have for the recluse.

"The French are also very worthy men. We have had great good fortune in France, and it hath led to much bobance and camp-fire talk, but I have ever noticed that those who know the most have the least to say about it. I have seen Frenchmen fight both in open field, in the intaking and the defending of towns or castlewicks, in escalados, camisades, night forays, bushments, sallies, outfalls, and knightly spear-runnings. Their knights and squires, lad, are every whit as good as ours, and I could pick out a score of those who ride behind Du Guesclin who would hold the lists with sharpened lances against the best men in the army of England. On the other hand, their common folk are so crushed down with gabelle, and poll-tax, and every manner of cursed tallage, that the spirit has passed right out of them. It is a fool's plan to teach a man to be a cur in peace, and think that he will be a lion in war. Fleece them like sheep and sheep they will remain. If the nobles had not conquered the poor folk it is like enough that we should not have conquered the nobles."

"But they must be sorry folk to bow down to the rich in such a fashion," said big John. "I am but a poor commoner of England myself, and yet I know something of charters, liberties, franchises, usages, privileges, customs, and the like. If these be broken, then all men know that it is time to buy arrow-heads."

"Aye, but the men of the law are strong in France as well as the men of war. By my hilt! I hold that a man has more to fear there from the ink-pot of the one than from the iron of the other. There is ever some cursed sheepskin in their strong boxes to prove that the rich man should be richer and the poor man poorer. It would scarce pass in England, but they are quiet folk over the water."

"And what other nations have you seen in your travels, good sir?" asked Alleyne Edricson. His young mind hungered for plain facts of life, after the long course of speculation and of mysticism on which he had been trained.

"I have seen the low countryman in arms, and I have nought to say against him. Heavy and slow is he by nature, and is not to be brought into battle for the sake of a lady's eyelash or the twang of a minstrel's string, like the hotter blood of the south. But ma foi! lay hand on his wool-bales, or trifle with his velvet of Bruges, and out buzzes every stout burgher, like bees from the tee-hole, ready to lay on as though it were his one business in life. By our lady! they have shown the French at Courtrai and elsewhere that they are as deft in wielding steel as in welding it."

"And the men of Spain?"

"They too are very hardy soldiers, the more so as for many hundred years they have had to fight hard against the cursed followers of the black Mahound, who have pressed upon them from the south, and still, as I understand, hold the fairer half of the country. I had a turn with them upon the sea when they came over to Winchelsea and the good queen with her ladies sat upon the cliffs looking down at us, as if it had been joust or tourney. By my hilt! it was a sight that was worth the seeing, for all that was best in England was out on the water that day. We went forth in little ships and came back in great galleys—for of fifty tall ships of Spain, over two score flew the Cross of St. George ere the sun had set. But now, youngster, I have answered you freely, and I trow it is time that you answered me. Let things be plat and plain between us. I am a man who shoots straight at his mark. You saw the things I had with me at yonder hostel: name which you will, save only the box of rose-colored sugar which I take to the Lady Loring, and you shall have it if you will but come with me to France."

"Nay," said Alleyne, "I would gladly come with ye to France or where else ye will, just to list to your talk, and because ye are the only two friends that I have in the whole wide world outside of the cloisters; but, indeed, it may not be, for my duty is towards my brother, seeing that father and mother are dead, and he my elder. Besides, when ye talk of taking me to France, ye do not conceive how useless I should be to you, seeing that neither by training nor by nature am I fitted for the wars, and there seems to be nought but strife in those parts."

"That comes from my fool's talk," cried the archer; "for being a man of no learning myself, my tongue turns to blades and targets, even as my hand does. Know then that for every parchment in England there are twenty in France. For every statue, cut gem, shrine, carven screen, or what else might please the eye of a learned clerk, there are a good hundred to our one. At the spoiling of Carcasonne I have seen chambers stored with writing, though not one man in our Company could read them. Again, in Arles and Nimes, and other towns that I could name, there are the great arches and fortalices still standing which were built of old by giant men who came from the south. Can I not see by your brightened eye how you would love to look upon these things? Come then with me, and, by these ten finger-bones! there is not one of them which you shall not see."

"I should indeed love to look upon them," Alleyne answered; "but I have come from Beaulieu for a purpose, and I must be true to my service, even as thou art true to thine."

"Bethink you again, mon ami," quoth Aylward, "that you might do much good yonder, since there are three hundred men in the Company, and none who has ever a word of grace for them, and yet the Virgin knows that there was never a set of men who were in more need of it. Sickerly the one duty may balance the other. Your brother hath done without you this many a year, and, as I gather, he hath never walked as far as Beaulieu to see you during all that time, so he cannot be in any great need of you."

"Besides," said John, "the Socman of Minstead is a by-word through the forest, from Bramshaw Hill to Holmesley Walk. He is a drunken, brawling, perilous churl, as you may find to your cost."

"The more reason that I should strive to mend him," quoth Alleyne. "There is no need to urge me, friends, for my own wishes would draw me to France, and it would be a joy to me if I could go with you. But indeed and indeed it cannot be, so here I take my leave of you, for yonder square tower amongst the trees upon the right must surely be the church of Minstead, and I may reach it by this path through the woods."

"Well, God be with thee, lad!" cried the archer, pressing Alleyne to his heart. "I am quick to love, and quick to hate and 'fore God I am loth to part."

"Would it not be well," said John, "that we should wait here, and see what manner of greeting you have from your brother. You may prove to be as welcome as the king's purveyor to the village dame."

"Nay, nay," he answered; "ye must not bide for me, for where I go I stay."

"Yet it may be as well that you should know whither we go," said the archer. "We shall now journey south through the woods until we come out upon the Christchurch road, and so onwards, hoping to-night to reach the castle of Sir William Montacute, Earl of Salisbury, of which Sir Nigel Loring is constable. There we shall bide, and it is like enough that for a month or more you may find us there, ere we are ready for our viage back to France."

It was hard indeed for Alleyne to break away from these two new but hearty friends, and so strong was the combat between his conscience and his inclinations that he dared not look round, lest his resolution should slip away from him. It was not until he was deep among the tree trunks that he cast a glance backwards, when he found that he could still see them through the branches on the road above him. The archer was standing with folded arms, his bow jutting from over his shoulder, and the sun gleaming brightly upon his head-piece and the links of his chain-mail. Beside him stood his giant recruit, still clad in the home-spun and ill-fitting garments of the fuller of Lymington, with arms and legs shooting out of his scanty garb. Even as Alleyne watched them they turned upon their heels and plodded off together upon their way.

IX

How Strange Things Befell in Minstead Wood

The path which the young clerk had now to follow lay through a magnificent forest of the very heaviest timber, where the giant bowls of oak and of beech formed long aisles in every direction, shooting up their huge branches to build the majestic arches of Nature's own cathedral. Beneath lay a broad carpet of the softest and greenest moss, flecked over with fallen leaves, but yielding pleasantly to the foot of the traveller. The track which guided him was one so seldom used that in places it lost itself entirely among the grass, to reappear as a reddish rut between the distant tree trunks. It was very still here in the heart of the woodlands. The gentle rustle of the branches and the distant cooing of pigeons were the only sounds which broke in upon the silence, save that once Alleyne heard afar off a merry call upon a hunting bugle and the shrill yapping of the hounds.

It was not without some emotion that he looked upon the scene around him, for, in spite of his secluded life, he knew enough of the ancient greatness of his own family to be aware that the time had been when they had held undisputed and paramount sway over all that tract of country. His father could trace his pure Saxon lineage back to that Godfrey Malf who had held the manors of Bisterne and of Minstead at the time when the Norman first set mailed foot upon English soil. The afforestation of the district, however, and its conversion into a royal demesne had clipped off a large section of his estate, while other parts had been confiscated as a punishment for his supposed complicity in an abortive Saxon rising. The fate of the ancestor had been typical of that of his descendants. During three hundred years their domains had gradually contracted, sometimes through royal or feudal encroachment, and sometimes through such gifts to the Church as that with which Alleyne's father had opened the doors of Beaulieu Abbey to his younger son. The importance of the family had thus dwindled, but they still retained the old Saxon manor-house, with a couple of farms and a grove large enough to afford pannage to a hundred pigs—"sylva de centum porcis," as the old family parchments describe it. Above all, the owner of the soil could still hold his head high as the veritable Socman of Minstead—that is, as holding the land in free socage, with no feudal superior, and answerable to no man lower than the king. Knowing this, Alleyne felt some little glow of worldly pride as he looked for the first time upon the land with which so many generations of his ancestors had been associated. He pushed on the quicker, twirling his staff merrily, and looking out at every turn of the path for some sign of the old Saxon residence. He was suddenly arrested, however, by the appearance of a wild-looking fellow armed with a club, who sprang out from behind a tree and barred his passage. He was a rough, powerful peasant, with cap and tunic of untanned sheepskin, leather breeches, and galligaskins round legs and feet.

"Stand!" he shouted, raising his heavy cudgel to enforce the order. "Who are you who walk so freely through the wood? Whither would you go, and what is your errand?"

"Why should I answer your questions, my friend?" said Alleyne, standing on his guard.

"Because your tongue may save your pate. But where have I looked upon your face before?"

"No longer ago than last night at the 'Pied Merlin,'" the clerk answered, recognizing the escaped serf who had been so outspoken as to his wrongs.

"By the Virgin! yes. You were the little clerk who sat so mum in the corner, and then cried fy on the gleeman. What hast in the scrip?"

"Naught of any price."

"How can I tell that, clerk? Let me see."

"Not I."

"Fool! I could pull you limb from limb like a pullet. What would you have? Hast forgot that we are alone far from all men? How can your clerkship help you? Wouldst lose scrip and life too?"

"I will part with neither without fight."

"A fight, quotha? A fight betwixt spurred cock and new hatched chicken! Thy fighting days may soon be over."

"Hadst asked me in the name of charity I would have given freely," cried Alleyne. "As it stands, not one farthing shall you have with my free will, and when I see my brother, the Socman of Minstead, he will raise hue and cry from vill to vill, from hundred to hundred, until you are taken as a common robber and a scourge to the country."

The outlaw sank his club. "The Socman's brother!" he gasped. "Now, by the keys of Peter! I had rather that hand withered and tongue was palsied ere I had struck or miscalled you. If you are the Socman's brother you are one of the right side, I warrant, for all your clerkly dress."

"His brother I am," said Alleyne. "But if I were not, is that reason why you should molest me on the king's ground?"

"I give not the pip of an apple for king or for noble," cried the serf passionately. "Ill have I had from them, and ill I shall repay them. I am a good friend to my friends, and, by the Virgin! an evil foeman to my foes."

"And therefore the worst of foemen to thyself," said Alleyne. "But I pray you, since you seem to know him, to point out to me the shortest path to my brother's house."

The serf was about to reply, when the clear ringing call of a bugle burst from the wood close behind them, and Alleyne caught sight for an instant of the dun side and white breast of a lordly stag glancing swiftly betwixt the distant tree trunks. A minute later came the shaggy deer-hounds, a dozen or fourteen of them, running on a hot scent, with nose to earth and tail in air. As they streamed past the silent forest around broke suddenly into loud life, with galloping of hoofs, crackling of brushwood, and the short, sharp cries of the hunters. Close behind the pack rode a fourrier and a yeoman-pricker, whooping on the laggards and encouraging the leaders, in the shrill half-French jargon which was the language of venery and woodcraft. Alleyne was still gazing after them, listening to the loud "Hyke-a-Bayard! Hyke-a-Pomers! Hyke-a-Lebryt!" with which they called upon their favorite hounds, when a group of horsemen crashed out through the underwood at the very spot where the serf and he were standing.

The one who led was a man between fifty and sixty years of age, war-worn and weather-beaten, with a broad, thoughtful forehead and eyes which shone brightly from under his fierce and overhung brows. His beard, streaked thickly with gray, bristled forward from his chin, and spoke of a passionate nature, while the long, finely cut face and firm mouth marked the leader of men. His figure was erect and soldierly, and he rode his horse with the careless grace of a man whose life had been spent in the saddle. In common garb, his masterful face and flashing eye would have marked him as one who was born to rule; but now, with his silken tunic powdered with golden fleurs-de-lis, his velvet mantle lined with the royal minever, and the lions of England stamped in silver upon his harness, none could fail to recognize the noble Edward, most warlike and powerful of all the long line of fighting monarchs who had ruled the Anglo-Norman race. Alleyne doffed hat and bowed head at the sight of him, but the serf folded his hands and leaned them upon his cudgel, looking with little love at the knot of nobles and knights-in-waiting who rode behind the king.

"Ha!" cried Edward, reining up for an instant his powerful black steed. "Le cerf est passe? Non? Ici, Brocas; tu parles Anglais."

"The deer, clowns?" said a hard-visaged, swarthy-faced man, who rode at the king's elbow. "If ye have headed it back it is as much as your ears are worth."

"It passed by the blighted beech there," said Alleyne, pointing, "and the hounds were hard at its heels."

"It is well," cried Edward, still speaking in French: for, though he could understand English, he had never learned to express himself in so barbarous and unpolished a tongue. "By my faith, sirs," he continued, half turning in his saddle to address his escort, "unless my woodcraft is sadly at fault, it is a stag of six tines and the finest that we have roused this journey. A golden St. Hubert to the man who is the first to sound the mort." He shook his bridle as he spoke, and thundered away, his knights lying low upon their horses and galloping as hard as whip and spur would drive them, in the hope of winning the king's prize. Away they drove down the long green glade—bay horses, black and gray, riders clad in every shade of velvet, fur, or silk, with glint of brazen horn and flash of knife and spear. One only lingered, the black-browed Baron Brocas, who, making a gambade which brought him within arm-sweep of the serf, slashed him across the face with his riding-whip. "Doff, dog, doff," he hissed, "when a monarch deigns to lower his eyes to such as you!"—then spurred through the underwood and was gone, with a gleam of steel shoes and flutter of dead leaves.

The villein took the cruel blow without wince or cry, as one to whom stripes are a birthright and an inheritance. His eyes flashed, however, and he shook his bony hand with a fierce wild gesture after the retreating figure.

"Black hound of Gascony," he muttered, "evil the day that you and those like you set foot in free England! I know thy kennel of Rochecourt. The night will come when I may do to thee and thine what you and your class have wrought upon mine and me. May God smite me if I fail to smite thee, thou French robber, with thy wife and thy child and all that is under thy castle roof!"

"Forbear!" cried Alleyne. "Mix not God's name with these unhallowed threats! And yet it was a coward's blow, and one to stir the blood and loose the tongue of the most peaceful. Let me find some soothing simples and lay them on the weal to draw the sting."

"Nay, there is but one thing that can draw the sting, and that the future may bring to me. But, clerk, if you would see your brother you must on, for there is a meeting to-day, and his merry men will await him ere the shadows turn from west to east. I pray you not to hold him back, for it would be an evil thing if all the stout lads were there and the leader a-missing. I would come with you, but sooth to say I am stationed here and may not move. The path over yonder, betwixt the oak and the thorn, should bring you out into his nether field."

Alleyne lost no time in following the directions of the wild, masterless man, whom he left among the trees where he had found him. His heart was the heavier for the encounter, not only because all bitterness and wrath were abhorrent to his gentle nature, but also because it disturbed him to hear his brother spoken of as though he were a chief of outlaws or the leader of a party against the state. Indeed, of all the things which he had seen yet in the world to surprise him there was none more strange than the hate which class appeared to bear to class. The talk of laborer, woodman and villein in the inn had all pointed to the wide-spread mutiny, and now his brother's name was spoken as though he were the very centre of the universal discontent. In good truth, the commons throughout the length and breadth of the land were heart-weary of this fine game of chivalry which had been played so long at their expense. So long as knight and baron were a strength and a guard to the kingdom they might be endured, but now, when all men knew that the great battles in France had been won by English yeomen and Welsh stabbers, warlike fame, the only fame to which his class had ever aspired, appeared to have deserted the plate-clad horsemen. The sports of the lists had done much in days gone by to impress the minds of the people, but the plumed and unwieldy champion was no longer an object either of fear or of reverence to men whose fathers and brothers had shot into the press at Crecy or Poitiers, and seen the proudest chivalry in the world unable to make head against the weapons of disciplined peasants. Power had changed hands. The protector had become the protected, and the whole fabric of the feudal system was tottering to a fall. Hence the fierce mutterings of the lower classes and the constant discontent, breaking out into local tumult and outrage, and culminating some years later in the great rising of Tyler. What Alleyne saw and wondered at in Hampshire would have appealed equally to the traveller in any other English county from the Channel to the marches of Scotland.

He was following the track, his misgivings increasing with every step which took him nearer to that home which he had never seen, when of a sudden the trees began to thin and the sward to spread out onto a broad, green lawn, where five cows lay in the sunshine and droves of black swine wandered unchecked. A brown forest stream swirled down the centre of this clearing, with a rude bridge flung across it, and on the other side was a second field sloping up to a long, low-lying wooden house, with thatched roof and open squares for windows. Alleyne gazed across at it with flushed cheeks and sparkling eyes—for this, he knew, must be the home of his fathers. A wreath of blue smoke floated up through a hole in the thatch, and was the only sign of life in the place, save a great black hound which lay sleeping chained to the door-post. In the yellow shimmer of the autumn sunshine it lay as peacefully and as still as he had oft pictured it to himself in his dreams.

He was roused, however, from his pleasant reverie by the sound of voices, and two people emerged from the forest some little way to his right and moved across the field in the direction of the bridge. The one was a man with yellow flowing beard and very long hair of the same tint drooping over his shoulders; his dress of good Norwich cloth and his assured bearing marked him as a man of position, while the sombre hue of his clothes and the absence of all ornament contrasted with the flash and glitter which had marked the king's retinue. By his side walked a woman, tall and slight and dark, with lithe, graceful figure and clear-cut, composed features. Her jet-black hair was gathered back under a light pink coif, her head poised proudly upon her neck, and her step long and springy, like that of some wild, tireless woodland creature. She held her left hand in front of her, covered with a red velvet glove, and on the wrist a little brown falcon, very fluffy and bedraggled, which she smoothed and fondled as she walked. As she came out into the sunshine, Alleyne noticed that her light gown, slashed with pink, was all stained with earth and with moss upon one side from shoulder to hem. He stood in the shadow of an oak staring at her with parted lips, for this woman seemed to him to be the most beautiful and graceful creature that mind could conceive of. Such had he imagined the angels, and such he had tried to paint them in the Beaulieu missals; but here there was something human, were it only in the battered hawk and discolored dress, which sent a tingle and thrill through his nerves such as no dream of radiant and stainless spirit had ever yet been able to conjure up. Good, quiet, uncomplaining mother Nature, long slighted and miscalled, still bides her time and draws to her bosom the most errant of her children.

The two walked swiftly across the meadow to the narrow bridge, he in front and she a pace or two behind. There they paused, and stood for a few minutes face to face talking earnestly. Alleyne had read and had heard of love and of lovers. Such were these, doubtless—this golden-bearded man and the fair damsel with the cold, proud face. Why else should they wander together in the woods, or be so lost in talk by rustic streams? And yet as he watched, uncertain whether to advance from the cover or to choose some other path to the house, he soon came to doubt the truth of this first conjecture. The man stood, tall and square, blocking the entrance to the bridge, and throwing out his hands as he spoke in a wild eager fashion, while the deep tones of his stormy voice rose at times into accents of menace and of anger. She stood fearlessly in front of him, still stroking her bird; but twice she threw a swift questioning glance over her shoulder, as one who is in search of aid. So moved was the young clerk by these mute appeals, that he came forth from the trees and crossed the meadow, uncertain what to do, and yet loth to hold back from one who might need his aid. So intent were they upon each other that neither took note of his approach; until, when he was close upon them, the man threw his arm roughly round the damsel's waist and drew her towards him, she straining her lithe, supple figure away and striking fiercely at him, while the hooded hawk screamed with ruffled wings and pecked blindly in its mistress's defence. Bird and maid, however, had but little chance against their assailant who, laughing loudly, caught her wrist in one hand while he drew her towards him with the other.

"The best rose has ever the longest thorns," said he. "Quiet, little one, or you may do yourself a hurt. Must pay Saxon toll on Saxon land, my proud Maude, for all your airs and graces."

"You boor!" she hissed. "You base underbred clod! Is this your care and your hospitality? I would rather wed a branded serf from my father's fields. Leave go, I say——Ah! good youth, Heaven has sent you. Make him loose me! By the honor of your mother, I pray you to stand by me and to make this knave loose me."

"Stand by you I will, and that blithely," said Alleyne. "Surely, sir, you should take shame to hold the damsel against her will."

The man turned a face upon him which was lion-like in its strength and in its wrath. With his tangle of golden hair, his fierce blue eyes, and his large, well-marked features, he was the most comely man whom Alleyne had ever seen, and yet there was something so sinister and so fell in his expression that child or beast might well have shrunk from him. His brows were drawn, his cheek flushed, and there was a mad sparkle in his eyes which spoke of a wild, untamable nature.

"Young fool!" he cried, holding the woman still to his side, though every line of her shrinking figure spoke her abhorrence. "Do you keep your spoon in your own broth. I rede you to go on your way, lest worse befall you. This little wench has come with me and with me she shall bide."

"Liar!" cried the woman; and, stooping her head, she suddenly bit fiercely into the broad brown hand which held her. He whipped it back with an oath, while she tore herself free and slipped behind Alleyne, cowering up against him like the trembling leveret who sees the falcon poising for the swoop above him.

"Stand off my land!" the man said fiercely, heedless of the blood which trickled freely from his fingers. "What have you to do here? By your dress you should be one of those cursed clerks who overrun the land like vile rats, poking and prying into other men's concerns, too caitiff to fight and too lazy to work. By the rood! if I had my will upon ye, I should nail you upon the abbey doors, as they hang vermin before their holes. Art neither man nor woman, young shaveling. Get thee back to thy fellows ere I lay hands upon you: for your foot is on my land, and I may slay you as a common draw-latch."

"Is this your land, then?" gasped Alleyne.

"Would you dispute it, dog? Would you wish by trick or quibble to juggle me out of these last acres? Know, base-born knave, that you have dared this day to stand in the path of one whose race have been the advisers of kings and the leaders of hosts, ere ever this vile crew of Norman robbers came into the land, or such half-blood hounds as you were let loose to preach that the thief should have his booty and the honest man should sin if he strove to win back his own."

"You are the Socman of Minstead?"

"That am I; and the son of Edric the Socman, of the pure blood of Godfrey the thane, by the only daughter of the house of Aluric, whose forefathers held the white-horse banner at the fatal fight where our shield was broken and our sword shivered. I tell you, clerk, that my folk held this land from Bramshaw Wood to the Ringwood road; and, by the soul of my father! it will be a strange thing if I am to be bearded upon the little that is left of it. Begone, I say, and meddle not with my affair."

"If you leave me now," whispered the woman, "then shame forever upon your manhood."

"Surely, sir," said Alleyne, speaking in as persuasive and soothing a way as he could, "if your birth is gentle, there is the more reason that your manners should be gentle too. I am well persuaded that you did but jest with this lady, and that you will now permit her to leave your land either alone or with me as a guide, if she should need one, through the wood. As to birth, it does not become me to boast, and there is sooth in what you say as to the unworthiness of clerks, but it is none the less true that I am as well born as you."

"Dog!" cried the furious Socman, "there is no man in the south who can say as much."

"Yet can I," said Alleyne smiling; "for indeed I also am the son of Edric the Socman, of the pure blood of Godfrey the thane, by the only daughter of Aluric of Brockenhurst. Surely, dear brother," he continued, holding out his hand, "you have a warmer greeting than this for me. There are but two boughs left upon this old, old Saxon trunk."

His elder brother dashed his hand aside with an oath, while an expression of malignant hatred passed over his passion-drawn features. "You are the young cub of Beaulieu, then," said he. "I might have known it by the sleek face and the slavish manner too monk-ridden and craven in spirit to answer back a rough word. Thy father, shaveling, with all his faults, had a man's heart; and there were few who could look him in the eyes on the day of his anger. But you! Look there, rat, on yonder field where the cows graze, and on that other beyond, and on the orchard hard by the church. Do you know that all these were squeezed out of your dying father by greedy priests, to pay for your upbringing in the cloisters? I, the Socman, am shorn of my lands that you may snivel Latin and eat bread for which you never did hand's turn. You rob me first, and now you would come preaching and whining, in search mayhap of another field or two for your priestly friends. Knave! my dogs shall be set upon you; but, meanwhile, stand out of my path, and stop me at your peril!" As he spoke he rushed forward, and, throwing the lad to one side, caught the woman's wrist. Alleyne, however, as active as a young deer-hound, sprang to her aid and seized her by the other arm, raising his iron-shod staff as he did so.

"You may say what you will to me," he said between his clenched teeth—"it may be no better than I deserve; but, brother or no, I swear by my hopes of salvation that I will break your arm if you do not leave hold of the maid."

There was a ring in his voice and a flash in his eyes which promised that the blow would follow quick at the heels of the word. For a moment the blood of the long line of hot-headed thanes was too strong for the soft whisperings of the doctrine of meekness and mercy. He was conscious of a fierce wild thrill through his nerves and a throb of mad gladness at his heart, as his real human self burst for an instant the bonds of custom and of teaching which had held it so long. The socman sprang back, looking to left and to right for some stick or stone which might serve him for weapon; but finding none, he turned and ran at the top of his speed for the house, blowing the while upon a shrill whistle.

"Come!" gasped the woman. "Fly, friend, ere he come back."

"Nay, let him come!" cried Alleyne. "I shall not budge a foot for him or his dogs."

"Come, come!" she cried, tugging at his arm. "I know the man: he will kill you. Come, for the Virgin's sake, or for my sake, for I cannot go and leave you here."

"Come, then," said he; and they ran together to the cover of the woods. As they gained the edge of the brushwood, Alleyne, looking back, saw his brother come running out of the house again, with the sun gleaming upon his hair and his beard. He held something which flashed in his right hand, and he stooped at the threshold to unloose the black hound.

"This way!" the woman whispered, in a low eager voice. "Through the bushes to that forked ash. Do not heed me; I can run as fast as you, I trow. Now into the stream—right in, over ankles, to throw the dog off, though I think it is but a common cur, like its master." As she spoke, she sprang herself into the shallow stream and ran swiftly up the centre of it, with the brown water bubbling over her feet and her hand out-stretched toward the clinging branches of bramble or sapling. Alleyne followed close at her heels, with his mind in a whirl at this black welcome and sudden shifting of all his plans and hopes. Yet, grave as were his thoughts, they would still turn to wonder as he looked at the twinkling feet of his guide and saw her lithe figure bend this way and that, dipping under boughs, springing over stones, with a lightness and ease which made it no small task for him to keep up with her. At last, when he was almost out of breath, she suddenly threw herself down upon a mossy bank, between two holly-bushes, and looked ruefully at her own dripping feet and bedraggled skirt.

"Holy Mary!" said she, "what shall I do? Mother will keep me to my chamber for a month, and make me work at the tapestry of the nine bold knights. She promised as much last week, when I fell into Wilverley bog, and yet she knows that I cannot abide needle-work."

Alleyne, still standing in the stream, glanced down at the graceful pink-and-white figure, the curve of raven-black hair, and the proud, sensitive face which looked up frankly and confidingly at his own.

"We had best on," he said. "He may yet overtake us."

"Not so. We are well off his land now, nor can he tell in this great wood which way we have taken. But you—you had him at your mercy. Why did you not kill him?"

"Kill him! My brother!"

"And why not?"—with a quick gleam of her white teeth. "He would have killed you. I know him, and I read it in his eyes. Had I had your staff I would have tried—aye, and done it, too." She shook her clenched white hand as she spoke, and her lips tightened ominously.

"I am already sad in heart for what I have done," said he, sitting down on the bank, and sinking his face into his hands. "God help me!—all that is worst in me seemed to come uppermost. Another instant, and I had smitten him: the son of my own mother, the man whom I have longed to take to my heart. Alas! that I should still be so weak."

"Weak!" she exclaimed, raising her black eyebrows. "I do not think that even my father himself, who is a hard judge of manhood, would call you that. But it is, as you may think, sir, a very pleasant thing for me to hear that you are grieved at what you have done, and I can but rede that we should go back together, and you should make your peace with the Socman by handing back your prisoner. It is a sad thing that so small a thing as a woman should come between two who are of one blood."

Simple Alleyne opened his eyes at this little spurt of feminine bitterness. "Nay, lady," said he, "that were worst of all. What man would be so caitiff and thrall as to fail you at your need? I have turned my brother against me, and now, alas! I appear to have given you offence also with my clumsy tongue. But, indeed, lady, I am torn both ways, and can scarce grasp in my mind what it is that has befallen."

"Nor can I marvel at that," said she, with a little tinkling laugh. "You came in as the knight does in the jongleur's romances, between dragon and damsel, with small time for the asking of questions. Come," she went on, springing to her feet, and smoothing down her rumpled frock, "let us walk through the shaw together, and we may come upon

Bertrand with the horses. If poor Troubadour had not cast a shoe, we should not have had this trouble. Nay, I must have your arm: for, though I speak lightly, now that all is happily over I am as frightened as my brave Roland. See how his chest heaves, and his dear feathers all awry—the little knight who would not have his lady mishandled." So she prattled on to her hawk, while Alleyne walked by her side, stealing a glance from time to time at this queenly and wayward woman. In silence they wandered together over the velvet turf and on through the broad Minstead woods, where the old lichen-draped beeches threw their circles of black shadow upon the sunlit sward.

"You have no wish, then, to hear my story?" said she, at last.

"If it pleases you to tell it me," he answered.

"Oh!" she cried tossing her head, "if it is of so little interest to you, we had best let it bide."

"Nay," said he eagerly, "I would fain hear it."

"You have a right to know it, if you have lost a brother's favor through it. And yet——Ah well, you are, as I understand, a clerk, so I must think of you as one step further in orders, and make you my father-confessor. Know then that this man has been a suitor for my hand, less as I think for my own sweet sake than because he hath ambition and had it on his mind that he might improve his fortunes by dipping into my father's strong box—though the Virgin knows that he would have found little enough therein. My father, however, is a proud man, a gallant knight and tried soldier of the oldest blood, to whom this man's churlish birth and low descent——Oh, lackaday! I had forgot that he was of the same strain as yourself."

"Nay, trouble not for that," said Alleyne, "we are all from good mother Eve."

"Streams may spring from one source, and yet some be clear and some be foul," quoth she quickly. "But, to be brief over the matter, my father would have none of his wooing, nor in sooth would I. On that he swore a vow against us, and as he is known to be a perilous man, with many outlaws and others at his back, my father forbade that I should hawk or hunt in any part of the wood to the north of the Christchurch road. As it chanced, however, this morning my little Roland here was loosed at a strong-winged heron, and page Bertrand and I rode on, with no thoughts but for the sport, until we found ourselves in Minstead woods. Small harm then, but that my horse Troubadour trod with a tender foot upon a sharp stick, rearing and throwing me to the ground.

See to my gown, the third that I have befouled within the week. Woe worth me when Agatha the tire-woman sets eyes upon it!"

"And what then, lady?" asked Alleyne.

"Why, then away ran Troubadour, for belike I spurred him in falling, and Bertrand rode after him as hard as hoofs could bear him. When I rose there was the Socman himself by my side, with the news that I was on his land, but with so many courteous words besides, and such gallant bearing, that he prevailed upon me to come to his house for shelter, there to wait until the page return. By the grace of the Virgin and the help of my patron St. Magdalen, I stopped short ere I reached his door, though, as you saw, he strove to hale me up to it. And then—ah-h-h-h!"—she shivered and chattered like one in an ague-fit.

"What is it?" cried Alleyne, looking about in alarm.

"Nothing, friend, nothing! I was but thinking how I bit into his hand. Sooner would I bite living toad or poisoned snake. Oh, I shall loathe my lips forever! But you—how brave you were, and how quick! How meek for yourself, and how bold for a stranger! If I were a man, I should wish to do what you have done."

"It was a small thing," he answered, with a tingle of pleasure at these sweet words of praise. "But you—what will you do?"

"There is a great oak near here, and I think that Bertrand will bring the horses there, for it is an old hunting-tryst of ours. Then hey for home, and no more hawking to-day! A twelve-mile gallop will dry feet and skirt."

"But your father?"

"Not one word shall I tell him. You do not know him; but I can tell you he is not a man to disobey as I have disobeyed him. He would avenge me, it is true, but it is not to him that I shall look for vengeance. Some day, perchance, in joust or in tourney, knight may wish to wear my colors, and then I shall tell him that if he does indeed crave my favor there is wrong unredressed, and the wronger the Socman of Minstead. So my knight shall find a venture such as bold knights love, and my debt shall be paid, and my father none the wiser, and one rogue the less in the world. Say, is not that a brave plan?"

"Nay, lady, it is a thought which is unworthy of you. How can such as you speak of violence and of vengeance. Are none to be gentle and kind, none to be piteous and forgiving? Alas! it is a hard, cruel world, and I would that I had never left my abbey cell. To hear such words from your lips is as though I heard an angel of grace preaching the devil's own creed."

She started from him as a young colt who first feels the bit. "Gramercy for your rede, young sir!" she said, with a little curtsey. "As I understand your words, you are grieved that you ever met me, and look upon me as a preaching devil. Why, my father is a bitter man when he is wroth, but hath never called me such a name as that. It may be his right and duty, but certes it is none of thine. So it would be best, since you think so lowly of me, that you should take this path to the left while I keep on upon this one; for it is clear that I can be no fit companion for you." So saying, with downcast lids and a dignity which was somewhat marred by her bedraggled skirt, she swept off down the muddy track, leaving Alleyne standing staring ruefully after her. He waited in vain for some backward glance or sign of relenting, but she walked on with a rigid neck until her dress was only a white flutter among the leaves. Then, with a sunken head and a heavy heart, he plodded wearily down the other path, wroth with himself for the rude and uncouth tongue which had given offence where so little was intended.

He had gone some way, lost in doubt and in self-reproach, his mind all tremulous with a thousand new-found thoughts and fears and wonderments, when of a sudden there was a light rustle of the leaves behind him, and, glancing round, there was this graceful, swift-footed creature, treading in his very shadow, with her proud head bowed, even as his was—the picture of humility and repentance.

"I shall not vex you, nor even speak," she said; "but I would fain keep with you while we are in the wood."

"Nay, you cannot vex me," he answered, all warm again at the very sight of her. "It was my rough words which vexed you; but I have been thrown among men all my life, and indeed, with all the will, I scarce know how to temper my speech to a lady's ear."

"Then unsay it," cried she quickly; "say that I was right to wish to have vengeance on the Socman."

"Nay, I cannot do that," he answered gravely.

"Then who is ungentle and unkind now?" she cried in triumph. "How stern and cold you are for one so young! Art surely no mere clerk, but bishop or cardinal at the least. Shouldst have crozier for staff and mitre for cap. Well, well, for your sake I will forgive the Socman and take vengeance on none but on my own wilful self who must needs run into danger's path. So will that please you, sir?"

"There spoke your true self," said he; "and you will find more pleasure in such forgiveness than in any vengeance."

She shook her head, as if by no means assured of it, and then with a sudden little cry, which had more of surprise than of joy in it, "Here is Bertrand with the horses!"

Down the glade there came a little green-clad page with laughing eyes, and long curls floating behind him. He sat perched on a high bay horse, and held on to the bridle of a spirited black palfrey, the hides of both glistening from a long run.

"I have sought you everywhere, dear Lady Maude," said he in a piping voice, springing down from his horse and holding the stirrup. "Troubadour galloped as far as Holmhill ere I could catch him. I trust that you have had no hurt or scath?" He shot a questioning glance at Alleyne as he spoke.

"No, Bertrand," said she, "thanks to this courteous stranger. And now, sir," she continued, springing into her saddle, "it is not fit that I leave you without a word more. Clerk or no, you have acted this day as becomes a true knight. King Arthur and all his table could not have done more. It may be that, as some small return, my father or his kin may have power to advance your interest. He is not rich, but he is honored and hath great friends. Tell me what is your purpose, and see if he may not aid it."

"Alas! lady, I have now no purpose. I have but two friends in the world, and they have gone to Christchurch, where it is likely I shall join them."

"And where is Christchurch?"

"At the castle which is held by the brave knight, Sir Nigel Loring, constable to the Earl of Salisbury."

To his surprise she burst out a-laughing, and, spurring her palfrey, dashed off down the glade, with her page riding behind her. Not one word did she say, but as she vanished amid the trees she half turned in her saddle and waved a last greeting. Long time he stood, half hoping that she might again come back to him; but the thud of the hoofs had died away, and there was no sound in all the woods but the gentle rustle and dropping of the leaves. At last he turned away and made his way back to the high-road—another person from the light-hearted boy who had left it a short three hours before.

X

How Hordle John Found a Man whom he Might Follow

If he might not return to Beaulieu within the year, and if his brother's dogs were to be set upon him if he showed face upon Minstead land, then indeed he was adrift upon earth. North, south, east, and west—he might turn where he would, but all was equally chill and cheerless. The Abbot had rolled ten silver crowns in a lettuce-leaf and hid them away in the bottom of his scrip, but that would be a sorry support for twelve long months. In all the darkness there was but the one bright spot of the sturdy comrades whom he had left that morning; if he could find them again all would be well. The afternoon was not very advanced, for all that had befallen him. When a man is afoot at cock-crow much may be done in the day. If he walked fast he might yet overtake his friends ere they reached their destination. He pushed on therefore, now walking and now running. As he journeyed he bit into a crust which remained from his Beaulieu bread, and he washed it down by a draught from a woodland stream.

It was no easy or light thing to journey through this great forest, which was some twenty miles from east to west and a good sixteen from Bramshaw Woods in the north to Lymington in the south. Alleyne, however, had the good fortune to fall in with a woodman, axe upon shoulder, trudging along in the very direction that he wished to go. With his guidance he passed the fringe of Bolderwood Walk, famous for old ash and yew, through Mark Ash with its giant beech-trees, and on through the Knightwood groves, where the giant oak was already a great tree, but only one of many comely brothers. They plodded along together, the woodman and Alleyne, with little talk on either side, for their thoughts were as far asunder as the poles. The peasant's gossip had been of the hunt, of the bracken, of the gray-headed kites that had nested in Wood Fidley, and of the great catch of herring brought back by the boats of Pitt's Deep. The clerk's mind was on his brother, on his future—above all on this strange, fierce, melting, beautiful woman who had broken so suddenly into his life, and as suddenly passed out of it again. So *distrait* was he and so random his answers, that the woodman took to whistling, and soon branched off upon the track to Burley, leaving Alleyne upon the main Christchurch road.

Down this he pushed as fast as he might, hoping at every turn and rise to catch sight of his companions of the morning. From Vinney Ridge to Rhinefield Walk the woods grow thick and dense up to the very edges of the track, but beyond the country opens up into broad dun-colored moors, flecked with clumps of trees, and topping each other in long, low curves up to the dark lines of forest in the furthest distance. Clouds of insects danced and buzzed in the golden autumn light, and the air was full of the piping of the song-birds. Long, glinting dragonflies shot across the path, or hung tremulous with gauzy wings and gleaming bodies. Once a white-necked sea eagle soared screaming high over the traveller's head, and again a flock of brown bustards popped up from among the bracken, and blundered away in their clumsy fashion, half running, half flying, with strident cry and whirr of wings.

There were folk, too, to be met upon the road—beggars and couriers, chapmen and tinkers—cheery fellows for the most part, with a rough jest and homely greeting for each other and for Alleyne. Near Shotwood he came upon five seamen, on their way from Poole to Southampton—rude red-faced men, who shouted at him in a jargon which he could scarce understand, and held out to him a great pot from which they had been drinking—nor would they let him pass until he had dipped pannikin in and taken a mouthful, which set him coughing and choking, with the tears running down his cheeks. Further on he met a sturdy black-bearded man, mounted on a brown horse, with a rosary in his right hand and a long two-handed sword jangling against his stirrup-iron. By his black robe and the eight-pointed cross upon his sleeve, Alleyne recognized him as one of the Knights Hospitallers of St. John of Jerusalem, whose presbytery was at Baddesley. He held up two fingers as he passed, with a "*Benedic, fili mi!*" whereat Alleyne doffed hat and bent knee, looking with much reverence at one who had devoted his life to the overthrow of the infidel. Poor simple lad! he had not learned yet that what men are and what men profess to be are very wide asunder, and that the Knights of St. John, having come into large part of the riches of the ill-fated Templars, were very much too comfortable to think of exchanging their palace for a tent, or the cellars of England for the thirsty deserts of Syria. Yet ignorance may be more precious than wisdom, for Alleyne as he walked on braced himself to a higher life by the thought of this other's sacrifice, and strengthened himself by his example which he could scarce have done had he known that the Hospitaller's mind ran more upon malmsey than on Mamelukes, and on venison rather than victories.

As he pressed on the plain turned to woods once more in the region of Wilverley Walk, and a cloud swept up from the south with the sun shining through the chinks of it. A few great drops came pattering loudly down, and then in a moment the steady swish of a brisk shower, with the dripping and dropping of the leaves. Alleyne, glancing round for shelter, saw a thick and lofty holly-bush, so hollowed out beneath that no house could have been drier. Under this canopy of green two men were already squatted, who waved their hands to Alleyne that he should join them. As he approached he saw that they had five dried herrings laid out in front of them, with a great hunch of wheaten bread and a leathern flask full of milk, but instead of setting to at their food they appeared to have forgot all about it, and were disputing together with flushed faces and angry gestures. It was easy to see by their dress and manner that they were two of those wandering students who formed about this time so enormous a multitude in every country in Europe. The one was long and thin, with melancholy features, while the other was fat and sleek, with a loud voice and the air of a man who is not to be gainsaid.

"Come hither, good youth," he cried, "come hither! *Vultus ingenui puer*. Heed not the face of my good coz here. *Foenum habet in cornu*, as Don Horace has it; but I warrant him harmless for all that."

"Stint your bull's bellowing!" exclaimed the other. "If it come to Horace, I have a line in my mind: *Loquaces si sapiat*——How doth it run? The English o't being that a man of sense should ever avoid a great talker. That being so, if all were men of sense then thou wouldst be a lonesome man, coz."

"Alas! Dicon, I fear that your logic is as bad as your philosophy or your divinity—and God wot it would be hard to say a worse word than that for it. For, hark ye: granting, *propter argumentum*, that I am a talker, then the true reasoning runs that since all men of sense should avoid me, and thou hast not avoided me, but art at the present moment eating herrings with me under a holly-bush, ergo you are no man of sense, which is exactly what I have been dinning into your long ears ever since I first clapped eyes on your sunken chops."

"Tut, tut!" cried the other. "Your tongue goes like the clapper of a mill-wheel. Sit down here, friend, and partake of this herring. Understand first, however, that there are certain conditions attached to it."

"I had hoped," said Alleyne, falling into the humor of the twain, "that a tranchoir of bread and a draught of milk might be attached to it."

"Hark to him, hark to him!" cried the little fat man. "It is even thus, Dicon! Wit, lad, is a catching thing, like the itch or the sweating sickness. I exude it round me; it is an aura. I tell you, coz, that no man can come within seventeen feet of me without catching a spark. Look at your own case. A duller man never stepped, and yet within the week you have said three things which might pass, and one thing the day we left Fordingbridge which I should not have been ashamed of myself."

"Enough, rattle-pate, enough!" said the other. "The milk you shall have and the bread also, friend, together with the herring, but you must hold the scales between us."

"If he hold the herring he holds the scales, my sapient brother," cried the fat man. "But I pray you, good youth, to tell us whether you are a learned clerk, and, if so, whether you have studied at Oxenford or at Paris."

"I have some small stock of learning," Alleyne answered, picking at his herring, "but I have been at neither of these places. I was bred amongst the Cistercian monks at Beaulieu Abbey."

"Pooh, pooh!" they cried both together. "What sort of an upbringing is that?"

"*Non cuivis contingit adire Corinthum*," quoth Alleyne.

"Come, brother Stephen, he hath some tincture of letters," said the melancholy man more hopefully. "He may be the better judge, since he hath no call to side with either of us. Now, attention, friend, and let your ears work as well as your nether jaw. *Judex damnatur*—you know the old saw. Here am I upholding the good fame of the learned Duns Scotus against the foolish quibblings and poor silly reasonings of Willie Ockham."

"While I," quoth the other loudly, "do maintain the good sense and extraordinary wisdom of that most learned William against the crack-brained fantasies of the muddy Scotchman, who hath hid such little wit as he has under so vast a pile of words, that it is like one drop of Gascony in a firkin of ditch-water. Solomon his wisdom would not suffice to say what the rogue means."

"Certes, Stephen Hapgood, his wisdom doth not suffice," cried the other. "It is as though a mole cried out against the morning star, because he could not see it. But our dispute, friend, is concerning the nature of that subtle essence which we call thought. For I hold with the learned Scotus that thought is in very truth a thing, even as vapor or fumes, or many other substances which our gross bodily eyes are blind to. For, look you, that which produces a thing must be itself a thing, and if a man's thought may produce a written book, then must thought itself be a material thing, even as the book is. Have I expressed it? Do I make it plain?"

"Whereas I hold," shouted the other, "with my revered preceptor, *doctor, praeclarus et excellentissimus*, that all things are but thought; for when thought is gone I prythee where are the things then? Here are trees about us, and I see them because I think I see them, but if I have swooned, or sleep, or am in wine, then, my thought having gone forth from me, lo the trees go forth also. How now, coz, have I touched thee on the raw?"

Alleyne sat between them munching his bread, while the twain disputed across his knees, leaning forward with flushed faces and darting hands, in all the heat of argument. Never had he heard such jargon of scholastic philosophy, such fine-drawn distinctions, such cross-fire of major and minor, proposition, syllogism, attack and refutation. Question clattered upon answer like a sword on a buckler. The ancients, the fathers of the Church, the moderns, the Scriptures, the Arabians, were each sent hurtling against the other, while the rain still dripped and the dark holly-leaves glistened with the moisture. At last the fat man seemed to weary of it, for he set to work quietly upon his meal, while his opponent, as proud as the rooster who is left unchallenged upon the midden, crowed away in a last long burst of quotation and deduction. Suddenly, however, his eyes dropped upon his food, and he gave a howl of dismay.

"You double thief!" he cried, "you have eaten my herrings, and I without bite or sup since morning."

"That," quoth the other complacently, "was my final argument, my crowning effort, or *peroratio*, as the orators have it. For, coz, since all thoughts are things, you have but to think a pair of herrings, and then conjure up a pottle of milk wherewith to wash them down."

"A brave piece of reasoning," cried the other, "and I know of but one reply to it." On which, leaning forward, he caught his comrade a rousing smack across his rosy cheek. "Nay, take it not amiss," he said, "since all things are but thoughts, then that also is but a thought and may be disregarded."

This last argument, however, by no means commended itself to the pupil of Ockham, who plucked a great stick from the ground and signified his dissent by smiting the realist over the pate with it. By good fortune, the wood was so light and rotten that it went to a thousand splinters, but Alleyne thought it best to leave the twain to settle the matter at their leisure, the more so as the sun was shining brightly once more. Looking back down the pool-strewn road, he saw the two excited philosophers waving their hands and shouting at each other, but their babble soon became a mere drone in the distance, and a turn in the road hid them from his sight.

And now after passing Holmesley Walk and the Wooton Heath, the forest began to shred out into scattered belts of trees, with gleam of corn-field and stretch of pasture-land between. Here and there by the wayside stood little knots of wattle-and-daub huts with shock-haired laborers lounging by the doors and red-cheeked children sprawling in the roadway. Back among the groves he could see the high gable ends and thatched roofs of the franklins' houses, on whose fields these men found employment, or more often a thick dark column of smoke marked their position and hinted at the coarse plenty within. By these signs Alleyne knew that he was on the very fringe of the forest, and therefore no great way from Christchurch. The sun was lying low in the west and shooting its level rays across the long sweep of rich green country, glinting on the white-fleeced sheep and throwing long shadows from the red kine who waded knee-deep in the juicy clover. Right glad was the traveller to see the high tower of Christchurch Priory gleaming in the mellow evening light, and gladder still when, on rounding a corner, he came upon his comrades of the morning seated astraddle upon a fallen tree. They had a flat space before them, on which they alternately threw little square pieces of bone, and were so intent upon their occupation that they never raised eye as he approached them. He observed with astonishment, as he drew near, that the archer's bow was on John's back, the archer's sword by John's side, and the steel cap laid upon the tree-trunk between them.

"Mort de ma vie!" Aylward shouted, looking down at the dice. "Never had I such cursed luck. A murrain on the bones! I have not thrown a good main since I left Navarre. A one and a three! En avant, camarade!"

"Four and three," cried Hordle John, counting on his great fingers, "that makes seven. Ho, archer, I have thy cap! Now have at thee for thy jerkin!"

"Mon Dieu!" he growled, "I am like to reach Christchurch in my shirt." Then suddenly glancing up, "Hola, by the splendor of heaven, here is our cher petit! Now, by my ten finger bones! this is a rare sight to mine eyes." He sprang up and threw his arms round Alleyne's neck, while John, no less pleased, but more backward and Saxon in his habits, stood grinning and bobbing by the wayside, with his newly won steel cap stuck wrong side foremost upon his tangle of red hair.

"Hast come to stop?" cried the bowman, patting Alleyne all over in his delight. "Shall not get away from us again!"

"I wish no better," said he, with a pringling in the eyes at this hearty greeting.

"Well said, lad!" cried big John. "We three shall to the wars together, and the devil may fly away with the Abbot of Beaulieu! But your feet and hosen are all besmudged. Hast been in the water, or I am the more mistaken."

"I have in good sooth," Alleyne answered, and then as they journeyed on their way he told them the many things that had befallen him, his meeting with the villein, his sight of the king, his coming upon his brother, with all the tale of the black welcome and of the fair damsel. They strode on either side, each with an ear slanting towards him, but ere he had come to the end of his story the bowman had spun round upon his heel, and was hastening back the way they had come, breathing loudly through his nose.

"What then?" asked Alleyne, trotting after him and gripping at his jerkin.

"I am back for Minstead, lad."

"And why, in the name of sense?"

"To thrust a handful of steel into the Socman. What! hale a demoiselle against her will, and then loose dogs at his own brother! Let me go!"

"Nenny, nenny!" cried Alleyne, laughing. "There was no scath done. Come back, friend"—and so, by mingled pushing and entreaties, they got his head round for Christchurch once more. Yet he walked with his chin upon his shoulder, until, catching sight of a maiden by a wayside well, the smiles came back to his face and peace to his heart.

"But you," said Alleyne, "there have been changes with you also. Why should not the workman carry his tools? Where are bow and sword and cap—and why so warlike, John?"

"It is a game which friend Aylward hath been a-teaching of me."

"And I found him an over-apt pupil," grumbled the bowman. "He hath stripped me as though I had fallen into the hands of the tardvenus. But, by my hilt! you must render them back to me, camarade, lest you bring discredit upon my mission, and I will pay you for them at armorers' prices."

“Take them back, man, and never heed the pay,” said John. “I did but wish to learn the feel of them, since I am like to have such trinkets hung to my own girdle for some years to come.”

“Ma foi, he was born for a free companion!” cried Aylward, “He hath the very trick of speech and turn of thought. I take them back then, and indeed it gives me unease not to feel my yew-stave tapping against my leg bone. But see, mes garcons, on this side of the church rises the square and darkling tower of Earl Salisbury’s castle, and even from here I seem to see on yonder banner the red roebuck of the Montacutes.”

“Red upon white,” said Alleyne, shading his eyes; “but whether roebuck or no is more than I could vouch. How black is the great tower, and how bright the gleam of arms upon the wall! See below the flag, how it twinkles like a star!”

“Aye, it is the steel head-piece of the watchman,” remarked the archer. “But we must on, if we are to be there before the drawbridge rises at the vespers bugle; for it is likely that Sir Nigel, being so renowned a soldier, may keep hard discipline within the walls, and let no man enter after sundown.” So saying, he quickened his pace, and the three comrades were soon close to the straggling and broad-spread town which centered round the noble church and the frowning castle.

It chanced on that very evening that Sir Nigel Loring, having supped before sunset, as was his custom, and having himself seen that Pommers and Cadsand, his two war-horses, with the thirteen hacks, the five jennets, my lady’s three palfreys, and the great dapple-gray roussin, had all their needs supplied, had taken his dogs for an evening breather. Sixty or seventy of them, large and small, smooth and shaggy—deer-hound, boar-hound, blood-hound, wolf-hound, mastiff, alaun, talbot, lurcher, terrier, spaniel—snapping, yelling and whining, with score of lolling tongues and waving tails, came surging down the narrow lane which leads from the Twynham kennels to the bank of Avon. Two russet-clad varlets, with loud halloo and cracking whips, walked thigh-deep amid the swarm, guiding, controlling, and urging. Behind came Sir Nigel himself, with Lady Loring upon his arm, the pair walking slowly and sedately, as befitted both their age and their condition, while they watched with a smile in their eyes the scrambling crowd in front of them. They paused, however, at the bridge, and, leaning their elbows upon the stonework, they stood looking down at their own faces in the glassy stream, and at the swift flash of speckled trout against the tawny gravel.

Sir Nigel was a slight man of poor stature, with soft lisping voice and gentle ways. So short was he that his wife, who was no very tall woman, had the better of him by the breadth of three fingers. His sight having been injured in his early wars by a basketful of lime which had been emptied over him when he led the Earl of Derby's stormers up the breach at Bergerac, he had contracted something of a stoop, with a blinking, peering expression of face. His age was six and forty, but the constant practice of arms, together with a cleanly life, had preserved his activity and endurance unimpaired, so that from a distance he seemed to have the slight limbs and swift grace of a boy. His face, however, was tanned of a dull yellow tint, with a leathery, poreless look, which spoke of rough outdoor doings, and the little pointed beard which he wore, in deference to the prevailing fashion, was streaked and shot with gray. His features were small, delicate, and regular, with clear-cut, curving nose, and eyes which jutted forward from the lids. His dress was simple and yet spruce. A Flandrish hat of beevor, bearing in the band the token of Our Lady of Embrun, was drawn low upon the left side to hide that ear which had been partly shorn from his head by a Flemish man-at-arms in a camp broil before Tournay. His cote-hardie, or tunic, and trunk-hosen were of a purple plum color, with long weepers which hung from either sleeve to below his knees. His shoes were of red leather, daintily pointed at the toes, but not yet prolonged to the extravagant lengths which the succeeding reign was to bring into fashion. A gold-embroidered belt of knighthood encircled his loins, with his arms, five roses gules on a field argent, cunningly worked upon the clasp. So stood Sir Nigel Loring upon the bridge of Avon, and talked lightly with his lady.

And, certes, had the two visages alone been seen, and the stranger been asked which were the more likely to belong to the bold warrior whose name was loved by the roughest soldiery of Europe, he had assuredly selected the lady's. Her face was large and square and red, with fierce, thick brows, and the eyes of one who was accustomed to rule. Taller and broader than her husband, her flowing gown of sendall, and fur-lined tippet, could not conceal the gaunt and ungraceful outlines of her figure. It was the age of martial women. The deeds of black Agnes of Dunbar, of Lady Salisbury and of the Countess of Montfort, were still fresh in the public minds. With such examples before them the wives of the English captains had become as warlike as their mates, and ordered their castles in their absence with the prudence and discipline of veteran seneschals. Right easy were the Montacutes of their Castle of Twynham, and little had they to dread from roving galley or French squadron, while Lady Mary Loring had the ordering of it. Yet even in that age it was thought that, though a lady might have a soldier's heart, it was scarce as well that she should have a soldier's face. There were men who said that of all the stern passages and daring deeds by which Sir Nigel Loring had proved the true temper of his courage, not the least was his wooing and winning of so forbidding a dame.

"I tell you, my fair lord," she was saying, "that it is no fit training for a demoiselle: hawks and hounds, rotes and citoles singing a French rondel, or reading the Gestes de Doon de Mayence, as I found her yesternight, pretending sleep, the artful, with the corner of the scroll thrusting forth from under her pillow. Lent her by Father Christopher of the priory, forsooth—that is ever her answer. How shall all this help her when she has castle of her own to keep, with a hundred mouths all agape for beef and beer?"

"True, my sweet bird, true," answered the knight, picking a comfit from his gold drageoir. "The maid is like the young filly, which kicks heels and plunges for very lust of life. Give her time, dame, give her time."

"Well, I know that my father would have given me, not time, but a good hazel-stick across my shoulders. Ma foi! I know not what the world is coming to, when young maids may flout their elders. I wonder that you do not correct her, my fair lord."

"Nay, my heart's comfort, I never raised hand to woman yet, and it would be a passing strange thing if I began on my own flesh and blood. It was a woman's hand which cast this lime into mine eyes, and though I saw her stoop, and might well have stopped her ere she threw, I deemed it unworthy of my knighthood to hinder or balk one of her sex."

"The hussy!" cried Lady Loring clenching her broad right hand. "I would I had been at the side of her!"

"And so would I, since you would have been the nearer me my own. But I doubt not that you are right, and that Maude's wings need clipping, which I may leave in your hands when I am gone, for, in sooth, this peaceful life is not for me, and were it not for your gracious kindness and loving care I could not abide it a week. I hear that there is talk of warlike muster at Bordeaux once more, and by St. Paul! it would be a new thing if the lions of England and the red pile of Chandos were to be seen in the field, and the roses of Loring were not waving by their side."

"Now woe worth me but I feared it!" cried she, with the color all struck from her face. "I have noted your absent mind, your kindling eye, your trying and riveting of old harness. Consider my sweet lord, that you have already won much honor, that we have seen but little of each other, that you bear upon your body the scar of over twenty wounds received in I know not how many bloody encounters. Have you not done enough for honor and the public cause?"

"My lady, when our liege lord, the king, at three score years, and my Lord Chandos at three-score and ten, are blithe and ready to lay lance in rest for England's cause, it would ill be-seem me to prate of service done. It is sooth that I have received seven and twenty wounds. There is the more reason that I should be thankful that I am still long of breath and sound in limb. I have also seen some bickering and scuffling. Six great land battles I count, with four upon sea, and seven and fifty onfalls, skirmishes and bushments. I have held two and twenty towns, and I have been at the intaking of thirty-one. Surely then it would be bitter shame to me, and also to you, since my fame is yours, that I should now hold back if a man's work is to be done. Besides, bethink you how low is our purse, with bailiff and reeve ever croaking of empty farms and wasting lands. Were it not for this constableship which the Earl of Salisbury hath bestowed upon us we could scarce uphold the state which is fitting to our degree. Therefore, my sweeting, there is the more need that I should turn to where there is good pay to be earned and brave ransoms to be won."

"Ah, my dear lord," quoth she, with sad, weary eyes. "I thought that at last I had you to mine own self, even though your youth had been spent afar from my side. Yet my voice, as I know well, should speed you on to glory and renown, not hold you back when fame is to be won. Yet what can I say, for all men know that your valor needs the curb and not the spur. It goes to my heart that you should ride forth now a mere knight bachelor, when there is no noble in the land who hath so good a claim to the square pennon, save only that you have not the money to uphold it."

"And whose fault that, my sweet bird?" said he.

"No fault, my fair lord, but a virtue: for how many rich ransoms have you won, and yet have scattered the crowns among page and archer and varlet, until in a week you had not as much as would buy food and forage. It is a most knightly largesse, and yet withouten money how can man rise?"

"Dirt and dross!" cried he.

"What matter rise or fall, so that duty be done and honor gained. Banneret or bachelor, square pennon or forked, I would not give a denier for the difference, and the less since Sir John Chandos, chosen flower of English chivalry, is himself but a humble knight. But meanwhile fret not thyself, my heart's dove, for it is like that there may be no war waged, and we must await the news. But here are three strangers, and one, as I take it, a soldier fresh from service. It is likely that he may give us word of what is stirring over the water."

Lady Loring, glancing up, saw in the fading light three companions walking abreast down the road, all gray with dust, and stained with travel, yet chattering merrily between themselves. He in the midst was young and comely, with boyish open face and bright gray eyes, which glanced from right to left as though he found the world around him both new and pleasing. To his right walked a huge red-headed man, with broad smile and merry twinkle, whose clothes seemed to be bursting and splitting at every seam, as though he were some lusty chick who was breaking bravely from his shell. On the other side, with his knotted hand upon the young man's shoulder, came a stout and burly archer, brown and fierce eyed, with sword at belt and long yellow yew-stave peeping over his shoulder. Hard face, battered head piece, dinted brigandine, with faded red lion of St. George ramping on a discolored ground, all proclaimed as plainly as words that he was indeed from the land of war. He looked keenly at Sir Nigel as he approached, and then, plunging his hand under his breastplate, he stepped up to him with a rough, uncouth bow to the lady.

"Your pardon, fair sir," said he, "but I know you the moment I clap eyes on you, though in sooth I have seen you oftener in steel than in velvet. I have drawn string besides you at La Roche-d'Errien, Romorantin, Maupertuis, Nogent, Auray, and other places."

"Then, good archer, I am right glad to welcome you to Twynham Castle, and in the steward's room you will find provant for yourself and comrades. To me also your face is known, though mine eyes play such tricks with me that I can scarce be sure of my own squire. Rest awhile, and you shall come to the hall anon and tell us what is passing in France, for I have heard that it is likely that our pennons may flutter to the south of the great Spanish mountains ere another year be passed."

"There was talk of it in Bordeaux," answered the archer, "and I saw myself that the armorers and smiths were as busy as rats in a wheat-rick. But I bring you this letter from the valiant Gascon knight, Sir Claude Latour. And to you, Lady," he added after a pause, "I bring from him this box of red sugar of Narbonne, with every courteous and knightly greeting which a gallant cavalier may make to a fair and noble dame."

This little speech had cost the blunt bowman much pains and planning; but he might have spared his breath, for the lady was quite as much absorbed as her lord in the letter, which they held between them, a hand on either corner, spelling it out very slowly, with drawn brows and muttering lips. As they read it, Alleyne, who stood with Hordle John a few paces back from their comrade, saw the lady catch her breath, while the knight laughed softly to himself.

"You see, dear heart," said he, "that they will not leave the old dog in his kennel when the game is afoot. And what of this White Company, archer?"

"Ah, sir, you speak of dogs," cried Aylward; "but there are a pack of lusty hounds who are ready for any quarry, if they have but a good huntsman to halloo them on. Sir, we have been in the wars together, and I have seen many a brave following but never such a set of woodland boys as this. They do but want you at their head, and who will bar the way to them!"

"Pardieu!" said Sir Nigel, "if they are all like their messenger, they are indeed men of whom a leader may be proud. Your name, good archer?"

"Sam Aylward, sir, of the Hundred of Easebourne and the Rape of Chichester."

"And this giant behind you?"

"He is big John, of Hordle, a forest man, who hath now taken service in the Company."

"A proper figure of a man at-arms," said the little knight. "Why, man, you are no chicken, yet I warrant him the stronger man. See to that great stone from the coping which hath fallen upon the bridge. Four of my lazy varlets strove this day to carry it hence. I would that you two could put them to shame by budging it, though I fear that I overtask you, for it is of a grievous weight."

He pointed as he spoke to a huge rough-hewn block which lay by the roadside, deep sunken from its own weight in the reddish earth. The archer approached it, rolling back the sleeves of his jerkin, but with no very hopeful countenance, for indeed it was a mighty rock. John, however, put him aside with his left hand, and, stooping over the stone, he plucked it single-handed from its soft bed and swung it far into the stream. There it fell with mighty splash, one jagged end peaking out above the surface, while the waters bubbled and foamed with far-circling eddy.

"Good lack!" cried Sir Nigel, and "Good lack!" cried his lady, while John stood laughing and wiping the caked dirt from his fingers.

"I have felt his arms round my ribs," said the bowman, "and they crackle yet at the thought of it. This other comrade of mine is a right learned clerk, for all that he is so young, hight Alleyne, the son of Edric, brother to the Socman of Minstead."

"Young man," quoth Sir Nigel, sternly, "if you are of the same way of thought as your brother, you may not pass under portcullis of mine."

"Nay, fair sir," cried Aylward hastily, "I will be pledge for it that they have no thought in common; for this very day his brother hath set his dogs upon him, and driven him from his lands."

"And are you, too, of the White Company?" asked Sir Nigel. "Hast had small experience of war, if I may judge by your looks and bearing."

"I would fain to France with my friends here," Alleyne answered; "but I am a man of peace—a reader, exorcist, acolyte, and clerk."

"That need not hinder," quoth Sir Nigel.

"No, fair sir," cried the bowman joyously. "Why, I myself have served two terms with Arnold de Cervolles, he whom they called the archpriest. By my hilt! I have seen him ere now, with monk's gown trussed to his knees, over his sandals in blood in the fore-front of the battle. Yet, ere the last string had twanged, he would be down on his four bones among the stricken, and have them all houseled and shriven, as quick as shelling peas. Ma foi! there were those who wished that he would have less care for their souls and a little more for their bodies!"

"It is well to have a learned clerk in every troop," said Sir Nigel. "By St. Paul, there are men so caitiff that they think more of a scrivener's pen than of their lady's smile, and do their devoir in hopes that they may fill a line in a chronicle or make a tag to a jongleur's romance. I remember well that, at the siege of Retters, there was a little, sleek, fat clerk of the name of Chaucer, who was so apt at rondel, sirvente, or tonson, that no man dare give back a foot from the walls, lest he find it all set down in his rhymes and sung by every underling and varlet in the camp. But, my soul's bird, you hear me prate as though all were decided, when I have not yet taken counsel either with you or with my lady mother. Let us to the chamber, while these strangers find such fare as pantry and cellar may furnish."

"The night air strikes chill," said the lady, and turned down the road with her hand upon her lord's arm. The three comrades dropped behind and followed: Aylward much the lighter for having accomplished his mission, Alleyne full of wonderment at the humble bearing of so renowned a captain, and John loud with snorts and sneers, which spoke his disappointment and contempt.

"What ails the man?" asked Aylward in surprise.

"I have been cozened and bejaped," quoth he gruffly.

"By whom, Sir Samson the strong?"

"By thee, Sir Balaam the false prophet."

"By my hilt!" cried the archer, "though I be not Balaam, yet I hold converse with the very creature that spake to him. What is amiss, then, and how have I played you false?"

"Why, marry, did you not say, and Alleyne here will be my witness, that, if I would hie to the wars with you, you would place me under a leader who was second to none in all England for valor? Yet here you bring me to a shred of a man, peaky and ill-nourished, with eyes like a moulting owl, who must needs, forsooth, take counsel with his mother ere he buckle sword to girdle."

"Is that where the shoe galls?" cried the bowman, and laughed aloud. "I will ask you what you think of him three months hence, if we be all alive; for sure I am that— . . ."

Aylward's words were interrupted by an extraordinary hubbub which broke out that instant some little way down the street in the direction of the Priory. There was deep-mouthed shouting of men, frightened shrieks of women, howling and barking of curs, and over all a sullen, thunderous rumble, indescribably menacing and terrible. Round the corner of the narrow street there came rushing a brace of whining dogs with tails tucked under their legs, and after them a white-faced burgher, with outstretched hands and wide-spread fingers, his hair all abristle and his eyes glinting back from one shoulder to the other, as though some great terror were at his very heels. "Fly, my lady, fly!" he screeched, and whizzed past them like bolt from bow; while close behind came lumbering a huge black bear, with red tongue lolling from his mouth, and a broken chain jangling behind him. To right and left the folk flew for arch and doorway. Hordle John caught up the Lady Loring as though she had been a feather, and sprang with her into an open porch; while Aylward, with a whirl of French oaths, plucked at his quiver and tried to unsling his bow. Alleyne, all unnerved at so strange and unwonted a sight, shrunk up against the wall with his eyes fixed upon the frenzied creature, which came bounding along with ungainly speed, looking the larger in the uncertain light, its huge jaws agape, with blood and slaver trickling to the ground. Sir Nigel alone, unconscious to all appearance of the universal panic, walked with unfaltering step up the centre of the road, a silken handkerchief in one hand and his gold comfit-box in the other. It sent the blood cold through Alleyne's veins to see that as they came together—the man and the beast—the creature reared up, with eyes ablaze with fear and hate, and whirled its great paws above the knight to smite him to the earth. He, however, blinking with puckered eyes, reached up his kerchief, and flicked the beast twice across the snout with it. "Ah, saucy! saucy," quoth he, with gentle chiding; on which the bear, uncertain and puzzled, dropped its four legs to earth again, and, waddling back, was soon swathed in ropes by the bear-ward and a crowd of peasants who had been in close pursuit.

A scared man was the keeper; for, having chained the brute to a stake while he drank a stoup of ale at the inn, it had been baited by stray curs, until, in wrath and madness, it had plucked loose the chain, and smitten or bitten all who came in its path. Most scared of all was he to find that the creature had come nigh to harm the Lord and Lady of the castle, who had power to place him in the stretch-neck or to have the skin scourged from his shoulders. Yet, when he came with bowed head and humble entreaty for forgiveness, he was met with a handful of small silver from Sir Nigel, whose dame, however, was less charitably disposed, being much ruffled in her dignity by the manner in which she had been hustled from her lord's side.

As they passed through the castle gate, John plucked at Aylward's sleeve, and the two fell behind.

"I must crave your pardon, comrade," said he, bluntly. "I was a fool not to know that a little rooster may be the gamest. I believe that this man is indeed a leader whom we may follow."

XI

How a Young Shepherd Had a Perilous Flock

Black was the mouth of Twynham Castle, though a pair of torches burning at the further end of the gateway cast a red glare over the outer bailey, and sent a dim, ruddy flicker through the rough-hewn arch, rising and falling with fitful brightness. Over the door the travellers could discern the escutcheon of the Montacutes, a roebuck gules on a field argent, flanked on either side by smaller shields which bore the red roses of the veteran constable. As they passed over the drawbridge, Alleyne marked the gleam of arms in the embrasures to right and left, and they had scarce set foot upon the causeway ere a hoarse blare burst from a bugle, and, with screech of hinge and clank of chain, the ponderous bridge swung up into the air, drawn by unseen hands. At the same instant the huge portcullis came rattling down from above, and shut off the last fading light of day. Sir Nigel and his lady walked on in deep talk, while a fat under-steward took charge of the three comrades, and led them to the buttery, where beef, bread, and beer were kept ever in readiness for the wayfarer. After a hearty meal and a dip in the trough to wash the dust from them, they strolled forth into the bailey, where the bowman peered about through the darkness at wall and at keep, with the carping eyes of one who has seen something of sieges, and is not likely to be satisfied. To Alleyne and to John, however, it appeared to be as great and as stout a fortress as could be built by the hands of man.

Erected by Sir Balwin de Redvers in the old fighting days of the twelfth century, when men thought much of war and little of comfort, Castle Twynham had been designed as a stronghold pure and simple, unlike those later and more magnificent structures where warlike strength had been combined with the magnificence of a palace. From the time of the Edwards such buildings as Conway or Caernarvon castles, to say nothing of Royal Windsor, had shown that it was possible to secure luxury in peace as well as security in times of trouble. Sir Nigel's trust, however, still frowned above the smooth-flowing waters of the Avon, very much as the stern race of early Anglo-Normans had designed it. There were the broad outer and inner bailies, not paved, but sown with grass to nourish the sheep and cattle which might be driven in on sign of danger. All round were high and turreted walls, with at the corner a bare square-faced keep, gaunt and windowless, rearing up from a lofty mound, which made it almost inaccessible to an assailant. Against the bailey-walls were rows of frail wooden houses and leaning sheds, which gave shelter to the archers and men-at-arms who formed the garrison. The doors of these humble dwellings were mostly open, and against the yellow glare from within Alleyne could see the bearded fellows cleaning their harness, while their wives would come out for a gossip, with their needlework in their hands, and their long black shadows streaming across the yard. The air was full of the clack of their voices and the merry prattling of children, in strange contrast to the flash of arms and constant warlike challenge from the walls above.

"Methinks a company of school lads could hold this place against an army," quoth John.

"And so say I," said Alleyne.

"Nay, there you are wide of the clout," the bowman said gravely. "By my hilt! I have seen a stronger fortalice carried in a summer evening. I remember such a one in Picardy, with a name as long as a Gascon's pedigree. It was when I served under Sir Robert Knolles, before the days of the Company; and we came by good plunder at the sacking of it. I had myself a great silver bowl, with two goblets, and a plastron of Spanish steel. Pasques Dieu! there are some fine women over yonder! Mort de ma vie! see to that one in the doorway! I will go speak to her. But whom have we here?"

"Is there an archer here hight Sam Aylward?" asked a gaunt man-at-arms, clanking up to them across the courtyard.

"My name, friend," quoth the bowman.

"Then sure I have no need to tell thee mine," said the other.

"By the rood! if it is not Black Simon of Norwich!" cried Aylward. "A mon coeur, camarade, a mon coeur! Ah, but I am blithe to see thee!" The two fell upon each other and hugged like bears.

"And where from, old blood and bones?" asked the bowman.

"I am in service here. Tell me, comrade, is it sooth that we shall have another fling at these Frenchmen? It is so rumored in the guard-room, and that Sir Nigel will take the field once more."

"It is like enough, mon gar., as things go."

"Now may the Lord be praised!" cried the other. "This very night will I set apart a golden ouche to be offered on the shrine of my name-saint. I have pined for this, Aylward, as a young maid pines for her lover."

"Art so set on plunder then? Is the purse so light that there is not enough for a rouse? I have a bag at my belt, camarade, and you have but to put your fist into it for what you want. It was ever share and share between us."

"Nay, friend, it is not the Frenchman's gold, but the Frenchman's blood that I would have. I should not rest quiet in the grave, coz, if I had not another turn at them. For with us in France it has ever been fair and honest war—a shut fist for the man, but a bended knee for the woman. But how was it at Winchelsea when their galleys came down upon it some few years back? I had an old mother there, lad, who had come down thither from the Midlands to be the nearer her son. They found her afterwards by her own hearthstone, thrust through by a Frenchman's bill. My second sister, my brother's wife, and her two children, they were but ash-heaps in the smoking ruins of their house. I will not say that we have not wrought great scath upon France, but women and children have been safe from us. And so, old friend, my heart is hot within me, and I long to hear the old battle-cry again, and, by God's truth! if Sir Nigel unfurls his pennon, here is one who will be right glad to feel the saddle-flaps under his knees."

"We have seen good work together, old war-dog," quoth Aylward; "and, by my hilt! we may hope to see more ere we die. But we are more like to hawk at the Spanish woodcock than at the French heron, though certes it is rumored that Du Guesclin with all the best lances of France have taken service under the lions and towers of Castile. But, comrade, it is in my mind that there is some small matter of dispute still open between us."

"'Fore God, it is sooth!" cried the other; "I had forgot it. The provost-marshal and his men tore us apart when last we met."

"On which, friend, we vowed that we should settle the point when next we came together. Hast thy sword, I see, and the moon throws glimmer enough for such old night-birds as we. On guard, mon gar.! I have not heard clink of steel this month or more."

"Out from the shadow then," said the other, drawing his sword. "A vow is a vow, and not lightly to be broken."

"A vow to the saints," cried Alleyne, "is indeed not to be set aside; but this is a devil's vow, and, simple clerk as I am, I am yet the mouthpiece of the true church when I say that it were mortal sin to fight on such a quarrel. What! shall two grown men carry malice for years, and fly like snarling curs at each other's throats?"

"No malice, my young clerk, no malice," quoth Black Simon. "I have not a bitter drop in my heart for mine old comrade; but the quarrel, as he hath told you, is still open and unsettled. Fall on, Aylward!"

"Not whilst I can stand between you," cried Alleyne, springing before the bowman. "It is shame and sin to see two Christian Englishmen turn swords against each other like the frenzied bloodthirsty paynim."

"And, what is more," said Hordle John, suddenly appearing out of the buttery with the huge board upon which the pastry was rolled, "if either raise sword I shall flatten him like a Shrovetide pancake. By the black rood! I shall drive him into the earth, like a nail into a door, rather than see you do scath to each other."

"'Fore God, this is a strange way of preaching peace," cried Black Simon. "You may find the scath yourself, my lusty friend, if you raise your great cudgel to me. I had as lief have the castle drawbridge drop upon my pate."

"Tell me, Aylward," said Alleyne earnestly, with his hands outstretched to keep the pair asunder, "what is the cause of quarrel, that we may see whether honorable settlement may not be arrived at?"

The bowman looked down at his feet and then up at the moon. "Parbleu!" he cried, "the cause of quarrel? Why, mon petit, it was years ago in Limousin, and how can I bear in mind what was the cause of it? Simon there hath it at the end of his tongue."

"Not I, in troth," replied the other; "I have had other things to think of. There was some sort of bickering over dice, or wine, or was it a woman, coz?"

"Pasques Dieu! but you have nicked it," cried Aylward. "It was indeed about a woman; and the quarrel must go forward, for I am still of the same mind as before."

"What of the woman, then?" asked Simon. "May the murrain strike me if I can call to mind aught about her."

"It was La Blanche Rose, maid at the sign of the 'Trois Corbeaux' at Limoges. Bless her pretty heart! Why, mon gar., I loved her."

"So did a many," quoth Simon. "I call her to mind now. On the very day that we fought over the little hussy, she went off with Evan ap Price, a long-legged Welsh dagsman. They have a hostel of their own now, somewhere on the banks of the Garonne, where the landlord drinks so much of the liquor that there is little left for the customers."

"So ends our quarrel, then," said Aylward, sheathing his sword. "A Welsh dagsman, i' faith! C'etait mauvais gout, camarade, and the more so when she had a jolly archer and a lusty man-at-arms to choose from."

"True, old lad. And it is as well that we can compose our differences honorably, for Sir Nigel had been out at the first clash of steel; and he hath sworn that if there be quarrelling in the garrison he would smite the right hand from the broilers. You know him of old, and that he is like to be as good as his word."

"Mort-Dieu! yes. But there are ale, mead, and wine in the buttery, and the steward a merry rogue, who will not haggle over a quart or two. Buvons, mon gar., for it is not every day that two old friends come together."

The old soldiers and Hordle John strode off together in all good fellowship. Alleyne had turned to follow them, when he felt a touch upon his shoulder, and found a young page by his side.

"The Lord Loring commands," said the boy, "that you will follow me to the great chamber, and await him there."

"But my comrades?"

"His commands were for you alone."

Alleyne followed the messenger to the east end of the courtyard, where a broad flight of steps led up to the doorway of the main hall, the outer wall of which is washed by the waters of the Avon. As designed at first, no dwelling had been allotted to the lord of the castle and his family but the dark and dismal basement story of the keep. A more civilized or more effeminate generation, however, had refused to be pent up in such a cellar, and the hall with its neighboring chambers had been added for their accommodation. Up the broad steps Alleyne went, still following his boyish guide, until at the folding oak doors the latter paused, and ushered him into the main hall of the castle.

On entering the room the clerk looked round; but, seeing no one, he continued to stand, his cap in his hand, examining with the greatest interest a chamber which was so different to any to which he was accustomed. The days had gone by when a nobleman's hall was but a barn-like, rush-strewn enclosure, the common lounge and eating-room of every inmate of the castle. The Crusaders had brought back with them experiences of domestic luxuries, of Damascus carpets and rugs of Aleppo, which made them impatient of the hideous bareness and want of privacy which they found in their ancestral strongholds. Still stronger, however, had been the influence of the great French war; for, however well matched the nations might be in martial exercises, there could be no question but that our neighbors were infinitely superior to us in the arts of peace. A stream of returning knights, of wounded soldiers, and of unransomed French noblemen, had been for a quarter of a century continually pouring into England, every one of whom exerted an influence in the direction of greater domestic refinement, while shiploads of French furniture from Calais, Rouen, and other plundered towns, had supplied our own artisans with models on which to shape their work. Hence, in most English castles, and in Castle Twynham among the rest, chambers were to be found which would seem to be not wanting either in beauty or in comfort.

In the great stone fireplace a log fire was spurting and crackling, throwing out a ruddy glare which, with the four bracket-lamps which stood at each corner of the room, gave a bright and lightsome air to the whole apartment. Above was a wreath-work of blazonry, extending up to the carved and corniced oaken roof; while on either side stood the high canopied chairs placed for the master of the house and for his most honored guest. The walls were hung all round with most elaborate and brightly colored tapestry, representing the achievements of Sir Bevis of Hampton, and behind this convenient screen were stored the tables dormant and benches which would be needed for banquet or high festivity. The floor was of polished tiles, with a square of red and black diapered Flemish carpet in the centre; and many settees, cushions, folding chairs, and carved bancals littered all over it. At the further end was a long black buffet or dresser, thickly covered with gold cups, silver salvers, and other such valuables. All this Alleyne examined with curious eyes; but most interesting of all to him was a small ebony table at his very side, on which, by the side of a chess-board and the scattered chessmen, there lay an open manuscript written in a right clerkly hand, and set forth with brave flourishes and devices along the margins. In vain Alleyne bethought him of where he was, and of those laws of good breeding and decorum which should restrain him: those colored capitals and black even lines drew his hand down to them, as the loadstone draws the needle, until, almost before he knew it, he was standing with the romance of Garin de Montglane before his eyes, so absorbed in its contents as to be completely oblivious both of where he was and why he had come there.

He was brought back to himself, however, by a sudden little ripple of quick feminine laughter. Aghast, he dropped the manuscript among the chessmen and stared in bewilderment round the room. It was as empty and as still as ever. Again he stretched his hand out to the romance, and again came that roguish burst of merriment. He looked up at the ceiling, back at the closed door, and round at the stiff folds of motionless tapestry. Of a sudden, however, he caught a quick shimmer from the corner of a high-backed bancal in front of him, and, shifting a pace or two to the side, saw a white slender hand, which held a mirror of polished silver in such a way that the concealed observer could see without being seen. He stood irresolute, uncertain whether to advance or to take no notice; but, even as he hesitated, the mirror was whipped in, and a tall and stately young lady swept out from behind the oaken screen, with a dancing light of mischief in her eyes. Alleyne started with astonishment as he recognized the very maiden who had suffered from his brother's violence in the forest. She no longer wore her gay riding-dress, however, but was attired in a long sweeping robe of black velvet of Bruges, with delicate tracery of white lace at neck and at wrist, scarce to be seen against her ivory skin. Beautiful as she had seemed to him before, the lithe charm of her figure and the proud, free grace of her bearing were enhanced now by the rich simplicity of her attire.

"Ah, you start," said she, with the same sidelong look of mischief, "and I cannot marvel at it. Didst not look to see the distressed damosel again. Oh that I were a minstrel, that I might put it into rhyme, with the whole romance—the luckless maid, the wicked socman, and the virtuous clerk! So might our fame have gone down together for all time, and you be numbered with Sir Percival or Sir Galahad, or all the other rescuers of oppressed ladies."

"What I did," said Alleyne, "was too small a thing for thanks; and yet, if I may say it without offence, it was too grave and near a matter for mirth and raillery. I had counted on my brother's love, but God has willed that it should be otherwise. It is a joy to me to see you again, lady, and to know that you have reached home in safety, if this be indeed your home."

"Yes, in sooth, Castle Twynham is my home, and Sir Nigel Loring my father. I should have told you so this morning, but you said that you were coming thither, so I bethought me that I might hold it back as a surprise to you. Oh dear, but it was brave to see you!" she cried, bursting out a-laughing once more, and standing with her hand pressed to her side, and her half-closed eyes twinkling with amusement. "You drew back and came forward with your eyes upon my book there, like the mouse who sniffs the cheese and yet dreads the trap."

"I take shame," said Alleyne, "that I should have touched it."

"Nay, it warmed my very heart to see it. So glad was I, that I laughed for very pleasure. My fine preacher can himself be tempted then, thought I; he is not made of another clay to the rest of us."

"God help me! I am the weakest of the weak," groaned Alleyne. "I pray that I may have more strength."

"And to what end?" she asked sharply. "If you are, as I understand, to shut yourself forever in your cell within the four walls of an abbey, then of what use would it be were your prayer to be answered?"

"The use of my own salvation."

She turned from him with a pretty shrug and wave. "Is that all?" she said. "Then you are no better than Father Christopher and the rest of them. Your own, your own, ever your own! My father is the king's man, and when he rides into the press of fight he is not thinking ever of the saving of his own poor body; he recks little enough if he leave it on the field. Why then should you, who are soldiers of the Spirit, be ever moping or hiding in cell or in cave, with minds full of your own concerns, while the world, which you should be mending, is going on its way, and neither sees nor hears you? Were ye all as thoughtless of your own souls as the soldier is of his body, ye would be of more avail to the souls of others."

"There is sooth in what you say, lady," Alleyne answered; "and yet I scarce can see what you would have the clergy and the church to do."

"I would have them live as others and do men's work in the world, preaching by their lives rather than their words. I would have them come forth from their lonely places, mix with the borel folks, feel the pains and the pleasures, the cares and the rewards, the temptings and the stirrings of the common people. Let them toil and swinken, and labor, and plough the land, and take wives to themselves——"

"Alas! alas!" cried Alleyne aghast, "you have surely sucked this poison from the man Wicliffe, of whom I have heard such evil things."

"Nay, I know him not. I have learned it by looking from my own chamber window and marking these poor monks of the priory, their weary life, their profitless round. I have asked myself if the best which can be done with virtue is to shut it within high walls as though it were some savage creature. If the good will lock themselves up, and if the wicked will still wander free, then alas for the world!"

Alleyne looked at her in astonishment, for her cheek was flushed, her eyes gleaming, and her whole pose full of eloquence and conviction. Yet in an instant she had changed again to her old expression of merriment leavened with mischief.

"Wilt do what I ask?" said she.

"What is it, lady?"

"Oh, most ungallant clerk! A true knight would never have asked, but would have vowed upon the instant. 'Tis but to bear me out in what I say to my father."

"In what?"

"In saying, if he ask, that it was south of the Christchurch road that I met you. I shall be shut up with the tire-women else, and have a week of spindle and bodkin, when I would fain be galloping Troubadour up Wilverley Walk, or loosing little Roland at the Vinney Ridge herons."

"I shall not answer him if he ask."

"Not answer! But he will have an answer. Nay, but you must not fail me, or it will go ill with me."

"But, lady," cried poor Alleyne in great distress, "how can I say that it was to the south of the road when I know well that it was four miles to the north."

"You will not say it?"

"Surely you will not, too, when you know that it is not so?"

"Oh, I weary of your preaching!" she cried, and swept away with a toss of her beautiful head, leaving Alleyne as cast down and ashamed as though he had himself proposed some infamous thing. She was back again in an instant, however, in another of her varying moods.

"Look at that, my friend!" said she. "If you had been shut up in abbey or in cell this day you could not have taught a wayward maiden to abide by the truth. Is it not so? What avail is the shepherd if he leaves his sheep."

"A sorry shepherd!" said Alleyne humbly. "But here is your noble father."

"And you shall see how worthy a pupil I am. Father, I am much beholden to this young clerk, who was of service to me and helped me this very morning in Minstead Woods, four miles to the north of the Christchurch road, where I had no call to be, you having ordered it otherwise." All this she reeled off in a loud voice, and then glanced with sidelong, questioning eyes at Alleyne for his approval.

Sir Nigel, who had entered the room with a silvery-haired old lady upon his arm, stared aghast at this sudden outburst of candor.

"Maude, Maude!" said he, shaking his head, "it is more hard for me to gain obedience from you than from the ten score drunken archers who followed me to Guienne. Yet, hush! little one, for your fair lady-mother will be here anon, and there is no need that she should know it. We will keep you from the provost-marshal this journey. Away to your chamber, sweeting, and keep a blithe face, for she who confesses is shriven. And now, fair mother," he continued, when his daughter had gone, "sit you here by the fire, for your blood runs colder than it did. Alleyne Edricson, I would have a word with you, for I would fain that you should take service under me. And here in good time comes my lady, without whose counsel it is not my wont to decide aught of import; but, indeed, it was her own thought that you should come."

"For I have formed a good opinion of you, and can see that you are one who may be trusted," said the Lady Loring. "And in good sooth my dear lord hath need of such a one by his side, for he recks so little of himself that there should be one there to look to his needs and meet his wants. You have seen the cloisters; it were well that you should see the world too, ere you make choice for life between them."

"It was for that very reason that my father willed that I should come forth into the world at my twentieth year," said Alleyne.

"Then your father was a man of good counsel," said she, "and you cannot carry out his will better than by going on this path, where all that is noble and gallant in England will be your companions."

"You can ride?" asked Sir Nigel, looking at the youth with puckered eyes.

"Yes, I have ridden much at the abbey."

"Yet there is a difference betwixt a friar's hack and a warrior's destrier. You can sing and play?"

"On citole, flute and rebeck."

"Good! You can read blazonry?"

"Indifferent well."

"Then read this," quoth Sir Nigel, pointing upwards to one of the many quarterings which adorned the wall over the fireplace.

"Argent," Alleyne answered, "a fess azure charged with three lozenges dividing three mullets sable. Over all, on an escutcheon of the first, a jambe gules."

"A jambe gules erased," said Sir Nigel, shaking his head solemnly. "Yet it is not amiss for a monk-bred man. I trust that you are lowly and serviceable?"

"I have served all my life, my lord."

"Canst carve too?"

"I have carved two days a week for the brethren."

"A model truly! Wilt make a squire of squires. But tell me, I pray, canst curl hair?"

"No, my lord, but I could learn."

"It is of import," said he, "for I love to keep my hair well ordered, seeing that the weight of my helmet for thirty years hath in some degree frayed it upon the top." He pulled off his velvet cap of maintenance as he spoke, and displayed a pate which was as bald as an egg, and shone bravely in the firelight. "You see," said he, whisking round, and showing one little strip where a line of scattered hairs, like the last survivors in some fatal field, still barely held their own against the fate which had fallen upon their comrades; "these locks need some little oiling and curling, for I doubt not that if you look slantwise at my head, when the light is good, you will yourself perceive that there are places where the hair is sparse."

"It is for you also to bear the purse," said the lady; "for my sweet lord is of so free and gracious a temper that he would give it gayly to the first who asked alms of him. All these things, with some knowledge of venerie, and of the management of horse, hawk and hound, with the grace and hardihood and courtesy which are proper to your age, will make you a fit squire for Sir Nigel Loring."

"Alas! lady," Alleyne answered, "I know well the great honor that you have done me in deeming me worthy to wait upon so renowned a knight, yet I am so conscious of my own weakness that I scarce dare incur duties which I might be so ill-fitted to fulfil."

"Modesty and a humble mind," said she, "are the very first and rarest gifts in page or squire. Your words prove that you have these, and all the rest is but the work of use and time. But there is no call for haste. Rest upon it for the night, and let your orisons ask for guidance in the matter. We knew your father well, and would fain help his son, though we have small cause to love your brother the Socman, who is forever stirring up strife in the county."

"We can scarce hope," said Nigel, "to have all ready for our start before the feast of St. Luke, for there is much to be done in the time. You will have leisure, therefore, if it please you to take service under me, in which to learn your devoir. Bertrand, my daughter's page, is hot to go; but in sooth he is over young for such rough work as may be before us."

"And I have one favor to crave from you," added the lady of the castle, as Alleyne turned to leave their presence. "You have, as I understand, much learning which you have acquired at Beaulieu."

"Little enough, lady, compared with those who were my teachers."

"Yet enough for my purpose, I doubt not. For I would have you give an hour or two a day whilst you are with us in discoursing with my daughter, the Lady Maude; for she is somewhat backward, I fear, and hath no love for letters, save for these poor fond romances, which do but fill her empty head with dreams of enchanted maidens and of errant cavaliers. Father Christopher comes over after nones from the priory, but he is stricken with years and slow of speech, so that she gets small profit from his teaching. I would have you do what you can with her, and with Agatha my young tire-woman, and with Dorothy Pierpont."

And so Alleyne found himself not only chosen as squire to a knight but also as squire to three damosels, which was even further from the part which he had thought to play in the world. Yet he could but agree to do what he might, and so went forth from the castle hall with his face flushed and his head in a whirl at the thought of the strange and perilous paths which his feet were destined to tread.

XII

How Alleyne Learned More Than He Could Teach

And now there came a time of stir and bustle, of furbishing of arms and clang of hammer from all the southland counties. Fast spread the tidings from thorpe to thorpe and from castle to castle, that the old game was afoot once more, and the lions and lilies to be in the field with the early spring. Great news this for that fierce old country, whose trade for a generation had been war, her exports archers and her imports prisoners. For six years her sons had chafed under an unwonted peace. Now they flew to their arms as to their birthright. The old soldiers of Crecy, of Nogent, and of Poictiers were glad to think that they might hear the war-trumpet once more, and gladder still were the hot youth who had chafed for years under the martial tales of their sires. To pierce the great mountains of the south, to fight the tamers of the fiery Moors, to follow the greatest captain of the age, to find sunny cornfields and vineyards, when the marches of Picardy and Normandy were as rare and bleak as the Jedburgh forests—here was a golden prospect for a race of warriors. From sea to sea there was stringing of bows in the cottage and clang of steel in the castle.

Nor did it take long for every stronghold to pour forth its cavalry, and every hamlet its footmen. Through the late autumn and the early winter every road and country lane resounded with nakir and trumpet, with the neigh of the war-horse and the clatter of marching men. From the Wrekin in the Welsh marches to the Cotswolds in the west or Butser in the south, there was no hill-top from which the peasant might not have seen the bright shimmer of arms, the toss and flutter of plume and of pensil. From bye-path, from woodland clearing, or from winding moor-side track these little rivulets of steel united in the larger roads to form a broader stream, growing ever fuller and larger as it approached the nearest or most commodious seaport. And there all day, and day after day, there was bustle and crowding and labor, while the great ships loaded up, and one after the other spread their white pinions and darted off to the open sea, amid the clash of cymbals and rolling of drums and lusty shouts of those who went and of those who waited. From Orwell to the Dart there was no port which did not send forth its little fleet, gay with streamer and bunting, as for a joyous festival. Thus in the season of the waning days the might of England put forth on to the waters.

In the ancient and populous county of Hampshire there was no lack of leaders or of soldiers for a service which promised either honor or profit. In the north the Saracen's head of the Brocas and the scarlet fish of the De Roches were waving over a strong body of archers from Holt, Woolmer, and Harewood forests. De Borhunte was up in the east, and Sir John de Montague in the west. Sir Luke de Ponynges, Sir Thomas West, Sir Maurice de Bruin, Sir Arthur Lipscombe, Sir Walter Ramsey, and stout Sir Oliver Buttesthorn were all marching south with levies from Andover, Arlesford, Odiham and Winchester, while from Sussex came Sir John Clinton, Sir Thomas Cheyne, and Sir John Fallislee, with a troop of picked men-at-arms, making for their port at Southampton. Greatest of all the musters, however, was that of Twynham Castle, for the name and the fame of Sir Nigel Loring drew towards him the keenest and boldest spirits, all eager to serve under so valiant a leader. Archers from the New Forest and the Forest of Bere, billmen from the pleasant country which is watered by the Stour, the Avon, and the Itchen, young cavaliers from the ancient Hampshire houses, all were pushing for Christchurch to take service under the banner of the five scarlet roses.

And now, could Sir Nigel have shown the bachelles of land which the laws of rank required, he might well have cut his forked pennon into a square banner, and taken such a following into the field as would have supported the dignity of a banneret. But poverty was heavy upon him, his land was scant, his coffers empty, and the very castle which covered him the holding of another. Sore was his heart when he saw rare bowmen and war-hardened spearmen turned away from his gates, for the lack of the money which might equip and pay them. Yet the letter which Aylward had brought him gave him powers which he was not slow to use. In it Sir Claude Latour, the Gascon lieutenant of the White Company, assured him that there remained in his keeping enough to fit out a hundred archers and twenty men-at-arms, which, joined to the three hundred veteran companions already in France, would make a force which any leader might be proud to command. Carefully and sagaciously the veteran knight chose out his men from the swarm of volunteers. Many an anxious consultation he held with Black Simon, Sam Aylward, and other of his more experienced followers, as to who should come and who should stay. By All Saints' day, however ere the last leaves had fluttered to earth in the Wilverley and Holmesley glades, he had filled up his full numbers, and mustered under his banner as stout a following of Hampshire foresters as ever twanged their war-bows. Twenty men-at-arms, too, well mounted and equipped, formed the cavalry of the party, while young Peter Terlake of Fareham, and Walter Ford of Botley, the martial sons of martial sires, came at their own cost to wait upon Sir Nigel and to share with Alleyne Edricson the duties of his squireship.

Yet, even after the enrolment, there was much to be done ere the party could proceed upon its way. For armor, swords, and lances, there was no need to take much forethought, for they were to be had both better and cheaper in Bordeaux than in England. With the long-bow, however, it was different. Yew staves indeed might be got in Spain, but it was well to take enough and to spare with them. Then three spare cords should be carried for each bow, with a great store of arrow-heads, besides the brigandines of chain mail, the wadded steel caps, and the brassarts or arm-guards, which were the proper equipment of the archer. Above all, the women for miles round were hard at work cutting the white surcoats which were the badge of the Company, and adorning them with the red lion of St. George upon the centre of the breast. When all was completed and the muster called in the castle yard the oldest soldier of the French wars was fain to confess that he had never looked upon a better equipped or more warlike body of men, from the old knight with his silk jupon, sitting his great black war-horse in the front of them, to Hordle John, the giant recruit, who leaned carelessly upon a huge black bow-stave in the rear. Of the six score, fully half had seen service before, while a fair sprinkling were men who had followed the wars all their lives, and had a hand in those battles which had made the whole world ring with the fame and the wonder of the island infantry.

Six long weeks were taken in these preparations, and it was close on Martinmas ere all was ready for a start. Nigh two months had Alleyne Edricson been in Castle Twynham—months which were fated to turn the whole current of his life, to divert it from that dark and lonely bourne towards which it tended, and to guide it into freer and more sunlit channels. Already he had learned to bless his father for that wise provision which had made him seek to know the world ere he had ventured to renounce it.

For it was a different place from that which he had pictured—very different from that which he had heard described when the master of the novices held forth to his charges upon the ravening wolves who lurked for them beyond the peaceful folds of Beaulieu. There was cruelty in it, doubtless, and lust and sin and sorrow; but were there not virtues to atone, robust positive virtues which did not shrink from temptation, which held their own in all the rough blasts of the work-a-day world? How colorless by contrast appeared the sinlessness which came from inability to sin, the conquest which was attained by flying from the enemy! Monk-bred as he was, Alleyne had native shrewdness and a mind which was young enough to form new conclusions and to outgrow old ones. He could not fail to see that the men with whom he was thrown in contact, rough-tongued, fierce and quarrelsome as they were, were yet of deeper nature and of more service in the world than the ox-eyed brethren who rose and ate and slept from year's end to year's end in their own narrow, stagnant circle of existence. Abbot Berghersh was a good man, but how was he better than this kindly knight, who lived as simple a life, held as lofty and inflexible an ideal of duty, and did with all his fearless heart whatever came to his hand to do? In turning from the service of the one to that of the other, Alleyne could not feel that he was lowering his aims in life. True that his gentle and thoughtful nature recoiled from the grim work of war, yet in those days of martial orders and militant brotherhoods there was no gulf fixed betwixt the priest and the soldier. The man of God and the man of the sword might without scandal be united in the same individual. Why then should he, a mere clerk, have scruples when so fair a chance lay in his way of carrying out the spirit as well as the letter of his father's provision. Much struggle it cost him, anxious spirit-questionings and midnight prayings, with many a doubt and a misgiving; but the issue was that ere he had been three days in Castle Twynham he had taken service under Sir Nigel, and had accepted horse and harness, the same to be paid for out of his share of the profits of the expedition. Henceforth for seven hours a day he strove in the tilt-yard to qualify himself to be a worthy squire to so worthy a knight. Young, supple and active, with all the pent energies from years of pure and healthy living, it was not long before he could manage his horse and his weapon well enough to earn an approving nod from critical men-at-arms, or to hold his own against Terlake and Ford, his fellow-servitors.

But were there no other considerations which swayed him from the cloisters towards the world? So complex is the human spirit that it can itself scarce discern the deep springs which impel it to action. Yet to Alleyne had been opened now a side of life of which he had been as innocent as a child, but one which was of such deep import that it could not fail to influence him in choosing his path. A woman, in monkish precepts, had been the embodiment and concentration of what was dangerous and evil—a focus whence spread all that was to be dreaded and avoided. So defiling was their presence that a true Cistercian might not raise his eyes to their face or touch their finger-tips under ban of church and fear of deadly sin. Yet here, day after day for an hour after nones, and for an hour before vespers, he found himself in close communion with three maidens, all young, all fair, and all therefore doubly dangerous from the monkish standpoint. Yet he found that in their presence he was conscious of a quick sympathy, a pleasant ease, a ready response to all that was most gentle and best in himself, which filled his soul with a vague and new-found joy.

And yet the Lady Maude Loring was no easy pupil to handle. An older and more world-wise man might have been puzzled by her varying moods, her sudden prejudices, her quick resentment at all constraint and authority. Did a subject interest her, was there space in it for either romance or imagination, she would fly through it with her subtle, active mind, leaving her two fellow-students and even her teacher toiling behind her. On the other hand, were there dull patience needed with steady toil and strain of memory, no single fact could by any driving be fixed in her mind. Alleyne might talk to her of the stories of old gods and heroes, of gallant deeds and lofty aims, or he might hold forth upon moon and stars, and let his fancy wander over the hidden secrets of the universe, and he would have a rapt listener with flushed cheeks and eloquent eyes, who could repeat after him the very words which had fallen from his lips. But when it came to almagest and astrolabe, the counting of figures and reckoning of epicycles, away would go her thoughts to horse and hound, and a vacant eye and listless face would warn the teacher that he had lost his hold upon his scholar. Then he had but to bring out the old romance book from the priory, with befingered cover of sheepskin and gold letters upon a purple ground, to entice her wayward mind back to the paths of learning.

At times, too, when the wild fit was upon her, she would break into pertness and rebel openly against Alleyne's gentle firmness. Yet he would jog quietly on with his teachings, taking no heed to her mutiny, until suddenly she would be conquered by his patience, and break into self-revilings a hundred times stronger than her fault demanded. It chanced however that, on one of these mornings when the evil mood was upon her, Agatha the young tire-woman, thinking to please her mistress, began also to toss her head and make tart rejoinder to the teacher's questions. In an instant the Lady Maude had turned upon her two blazing eyes and a face which was blanched with anger.

"You would dare!" said she. "You would dare!" The frightened tire-woman tried to excuse herself. "But my fair lady," she stammered, "what have I done? I have said no more than I heard."

"You would dare!" repeated the lady in a choking voice. "You, a graceless baggage, a foolish lack-brain, with no thought above the hemming of shifts. And he so kindly and hendy and long-suffering! You would—ha, you may well flee the room!"

She had spoken with a rising voice, and a clasping and opening of her long white fingers, so that it was no marvel that ere the speech was over the skirts of Agatha were whisking round the door and the click of her sobs to be heard dying swiftly away down the corridor.

Alleyne stared open-eyed at this tigress who had sprung so suddenly to his rescue. "There is no need for such anger," he said mildly. "The maid's words have done me no scath. It is you yourself who have erred."

"I know it," she cried, "I am a most wicked woman. But it is bad enough that one should misuse you. Ma foi! I will see that there is not a second one."

"Nay, nay, no one has misused me," he answered. "But the fault lies in your hot and bitter words. You have called her a baggage and a lack-brain, and I know not what."

"And you are he who taught me to speak the truth," she cried. "Now I have spoken it, and yet I cannot please you. Lack-brain she is, and lack-brain I shall call her."

Such was a sample of the sudden janglings which marred the peace of that little class. As the weeks passed, however, they became fewer and less violent, as Alleyne's firm and constant nature gained sway and influence over the Lady Maude. And yet, sooth to say, there were times when he had to ask himself whether it was not the Lady Maude who was gaining sway and influence over him. If she were changing, so was he. In drawing her up from the world, he was day by day being himself dragged down towards it. In vain he strove and reasoned with himself as to the madness of letting his mind rest upon Sir Nigel's daughter. What was he—a younger son, a penniless clerk, a squire unable to pay for his own harness—that he should dare to raise his eyes to the fairest maid in Hampshire? So spake reason; but, in spite of all, her voice was ever in his ears and her image in his heart. Stronger than reason, stronger than cloister teachings, stronger than all that might hold him back, was that old, old tyrant who will brook no rival in the kingdom of youth.

And yet it was a surprise and a shock to himself to find how deeply she had entered into his life; how completely those vague ambitions and yearnings which had filled his spiritual nature centred themselves now upon this thing of earth. He had scarce dared to face the change which had come upon him, when a few sudden chance words showed it all up hard and clear, like a lightning flash in the darkness.

He had ridden over to Poole, one November day, with his fellow-squire, Peter Terlake, in quest of certain yew-staves from Wat Swathling, the Dorsetshire armorer. The day for their departure had almost come, and the two youths spurred it over the lonely downs at the top of their speed on their homeward course, for evening had fallen and there was much to be done. Peter was a hard, wiry, brown faced, country-bred lad who looked on the coming war as the schoolboy looks on his holidays. This day, however, he had been sombre and mute, with scarce a word a mile to bestow upon his comrade.

"Tell me Alleyne Edricson," he broke out, suddenly, as they clattered along the winding track which leads over the Bournemouth hills, "has it not seemed to you that of late the Lady Maude is paler and more silent than is her wont?"

"It may be so," the other answered shortly.

"And would rather sit distrait by her oriel than ride gayly to the chase as of old. Methinks, Alleyne, it is this learning which you have taught her that has taken all the life and sap from her. It is more than she can master, like a heavy spear to a light rider."

"Her lady-mother has so ordered it," said Alleyne.

"By our Lady! and withouten disrespect," quoth Terlake, "it is in my mind that her lady-mother is more fitted to lead a company to a storming than to have the upbringing of this tender and milk-white maid. Hark ye, lad Alleyne, to what I never told man or woman yet. I love the fair Lady Maude, and would give the last drop of my heart's blood to serve her." He spoke with a gasping voice, and his face flushed crimson in the moonlight.

Alleyne said nothing, but his heart seemed to turn to a lump of ice in his bosom.

"My father has broad acres," the other continued, "from Fareham Creek to the slope of the Portsdown Hill. There is filling of granges, hewing of wood, malting of grain, and herding of sheep as much as heart could wish, and I the only son. Sure am I that Sir Nigel would be blithe at such a match."

But how of the lady?" asked Alleyne, with dry lips.

"Ah, lad, there lies my trouble. It is a toss of the head and a droop of the eyes if I say one word of what is in my mind. 'Twere as easy to woo the snow-dame that we shaped last winter in our castle yard. I did but ask her yesternight for her green veil, that I might bear it as a token or lambrequin upon my helm; but she flashed out at me that she kept it for a better man, and then all in a breath asked pardon for that she had spoke so rudely. Yet she would not take back the words either, nor would she grant the veil. Has it seemed to thee, Alleyne, that she loves any one?"

"Nay, I cannot say," said Alleyne, with a wild throb of sudden hope in his heart.

"I have thought so, and yet I cannot name the man. Indeed, save myself, and Walter Ford, and you, who are half a clerk, and Father Christopher of the Priory, and Bertrand the page, who is there whom she sees?"

"I cannot tell," quoth Alleyne shortly; and the two squires rode on again, each intent upon his own thoughts.

Next day at morning lesson the teacher observed that his pupil was indeed looking pale and jaded, with listless eyes and a weary manner. He was heavy-hearted to note the grievous change in her.

"Your mistress, I fear, is ill, Agatha," he said to the tire-woman, when the Lady Maude had sought her chamber.

The maid looked aslant at him with laughing eyes. "It is not an illness that kills," quoth she.

"Pray God not!" he cried. "But tell me, Agatha, what it is that ails her?"

"Methinks that I could lay my hand upon another who is smitten with the same trouble," said she, with the same sidelong look. "Canst not give a name to it, and thou so skilled in leech-craft?"

"Nay, save that she seems aweary."

"Well, bethink you that it is but three days ere you will all be gone, and Castle Twynham be as dull as the Priory. Is there not enough there to cloud a lady's brow?"

"In sooth, yes," he answered; "I had forgot that she is about to lose her father."

"Her father!" cried the tire-woman, with a little trill of laughter. "Oh simple, simple!" And she was off down the passage like arrow from bow, while Alleyne stood gazing after her, betwixt hope and doubt, scarce daring to put faith in the meaning which seemed to underlie her words.

XIII

How the White Company Set Forth to the Wars

St. Luke's day had come and had gone, and it was in the season of Martinmas, when the oxen are driven in to the slaughter, that the White Company was ready for its journey. Loud shrieked the brazen bugles from keep and from gateway, and merry was the rattle of the war-drum, as the men gathered in the outer bailey, with torches to light them, for the morn had not yet broken. Alleyne, from the window of the armory, looked down upon the strange scene—the circles of yellow flickering light, the lines of stern and bearded faces, the quick shimmer of arms, and the lean heads of the horses. In front stood the bow-men, ten deep, with a fringe of under-officers, who paced hither and thither marshalling the ranks with curt precept or short rebuke. Behind were the little clump of steel-clad horsemen, their lances raised, with long pensils drooping down the oaken shafts. So silent and still were they, that they might have been metal-sheathed statues, were it not for the occasional quick, impatient stamp of their chargers, or the rattle of chamfron against neck-plates as they tossed and strained. A spear's length in front of them sat the spare and long-limbed figure of Black Simon, the Norwich fighting man, his fierce, deep-lined face framed in steel, and the silk guidon marked with the five scarlet roses slanting over his right shoulder. All round, in the edge of the circle of the light, stood the castle servants, the soldiers who were to form the garrison, and little knots of women, who sobbed in their aprons and called shrilly to their name-saints to watch over the Wat, or Will, or Peterkin who had turned his hand to the work of war.

The young squire was leaning forward, gazing at the stirring and martial scene, when he heard a short, quick gasp at his shoulder, and there was the Lady Maude, with her hand to her heart, leaning up against the wall, slender and fair, like a half-plucked lily. Her face was turned away from him, but he could see, by the sharp intake of her breath, that she was weeping bitterly.

"Alas! alas!" he cried, all unnerved at the sight, "why is it that you are so sad, lady?"

"It is the sight of these brave men," she answered; "and to think how many of them go and how few are like to find their way back. I have seen it before, when I was a little maid, in the year of the Prince's great battle. I remember then how they mustered in the bailey, even as they do now, and my lady-mother holding me in her arms at this very window that I might see the show."

"Please God, you will see them all back ere another year be out," said he.

She shook her head, looking round at him with flushed cheeks and eyes that sparkled in the lamp-light. "Oh, but I hate myself for being a woman!" she cried, with a stamp of her little foot. "What can I do that is good? Here I must bide, and talk and sew and spin, and spin and sew and talk. Ever the same dull round, with nothing at the end of it. And now you are going too, who could carry my thoughts out of these gray walls, and raise my mind above tapestry and distaffs. What can I do? I am of no more use or value than that broken bowstave."

"You are of such value to me," he cried, in a whirl of hot, passionate words, "that all else has become nought. You are my heart, my life, my one and only thought. Oh, Maude, I cannot live without you, I cannot leave you without a word of love. All is changed to me since I have known you. I am poor and lowly and all unworthy of you; but if great love may weigh down such defects, then mine may do it. Give me but one word of hope to take to the wars with me—but one. Ah, you shrink, you shudder! My wild words have frightened you."

Twice she opened her lips, and twice no sound came from them. At last she spoke in a hard and measured voice, as one who dare not trust herself to speak too freely.

"This is over sudden," she said; "it is not so long since the world was nothing to you. You have changed once; perchance you may change again."

"Cruel!" he cried, "who hath changed me?"

"And then your brother," she continued with a little laugh, disregarding his question. "Methinks this hath become a family custom amongst the Edricsons. Nay, I am sorry; I did not mean a jibe. But, indeed, Alleyne, this hath come suddenly upon me, and I scarce know what to say."

"Say some word of hope, however distant—some kind word that I may cherish in my heart."

"Nay, Alleyne, it were a cruel kindness, and you have been too good and true a friend to me that I should use you despitefully. There cannot be a closer link between us. It is madness to think of it. Were there no other reasons, it is enough that my father and your brother would both cry out against it."

"My brother, what has he to do with it? And your father——"

"Come, Alleyne, was it not you who would have me act fairly to all men, and, certes, to my father amongst them?"

"You say truly," he cried, "you say truly. But you do not reject me, Maude? You give me some ray of hope? I do not ask pledge or promise. Say only that I am not hateful to you—that on some happier day I may hear kinder words from you."

Her eyes softened upon him, and a kind answer was on her lips, when a hoarse shout, with the clatter of arms and stamping of steeds, rose up from the bailey below. At the sound her face set her eyes sparkled, and she stood with flushed cheek and head thrown back—a woman's body, with a soul of fire.

"My father hath gone down," she cried. "Your place is by his side. Nay, look not at me, Alleyne. It is no time for dallying. Win my father's love, and all may follow. It is when the brave soldier hath done his devoir that he hopes for his reward. Farewell, and may God be with you!" She held out her white, slim hand to him, but as he bent his lips over it she whisked away and was gone, leaving in his outstretched hand the very green veil for which poor Peter Terlake had craved in vain. Again the hoarse cheering burst out from below, and he heard the clang of the rising portcullis. Pressing the veil to his lips, he thrust it into the bosom of his tunic, and rushed as fast as feet could bear him to arm himself and join the muster.

The raw morning had broken ere the hot spiced ale had been served round and the last farewell spoken. A cold wind blew up from the sea and ragged clouds drifted swiftly across the sky.

The Christchurch townsfolk stood huddled about the Bridge of Avon, the women pulling tight their shawls and the men swathing themselves in their gaberdines, while down the winding path from the castle came the van of the little army, their feet clanging on the hard, frozen road. First came Black Simon with his banner, bestriding a lean and powerful dapple-gray charger, as hard and wiry and warwise as himself. After him, riding three abreast, were nine men-at-arms, all picked soldiers, who had followed the French wars before, and knew the marches of Picardy as they knew the downs of their native Hampshire. They were armed to the teeth with lance, sword, and mace, with square shields notched at the upper right-hand corner to serve as a spear-rest. For defence each man wore a coat of interlaced leathern thongs, strengthened at the shoulder, elbow, and upper arm with slips of steel. Greaves and knee-pieces were also of leather backed by steel, and their gauntlets and shoes were of iron plates, craftily jointed. So, with jingle of arms and clatter of hoofs, they rode across the Bridge of Avon, while the burghers shouted lustily for the flag of the five roses and its gallant guard.

Close at the heels of the horses came two-score archers bearded and burly, their round targets on their backs and their long yellow bows, the most deadly weapon that the wit of man had yet devised, thrusting forth from behind their shoulders. From each man's girdle hung sword or axe, according to his humor, and over the right hip there jutted out the leathern quiver with its bristle of goose, pigeon, and peacock feathers. Behind the bowmen strode two trumpeters blowing upon nakirs, and two drummers in parti-colored clothes. After them came twenty-seven sumpter horses carrying tent-poles, cloth, spare arms, spurs, wedges, cooking kettles, horse-shoes, bags of nails and the hundred other things which experience had shown to be needful in a harried and hostile country. A white mule with red trappings, led by a varlet, carried Sir Nigel's own napery and table comforts. Then came two-score more archers, ten more men-at-arms, and finally a rear guard of twenty bowmen, with big John towering in the front rank and the veteran Aylward marching by the side, his battered harness and faded surcoat in strange contrast with the snow-white jupons and shining brigandines of his companions. A quick cross-fire of greetings and questions and rough West Saxon jests flew from rank to rank, or were bandied about betwixt the marching archers and the gazing crowd.

"Hola, Gaffer Higginson!" cried Aylward, as he spied the portly figure of the village innkeeper. "No more of thy nut-brown, mon gar. We leave it behind us."

"By St. Paul, no!" cried the other. "You take it with you. Devil a drop have you left in the great kilderkin. It was time for you to go."

"If your cask is leer, I warrant your purse is full, gaffer," shouted Hordle John. "See that you lay in good store of the best for our home-coming."

"See that you keep your throat whole for the drinking of it archer," cried a voice, and the crowd laughed at the rough pleasantry.

"If you will warrant the beer, I will warrant the throat," said John composedly.

"Close up the ranks!" cried Aylward. "En avant, mes enfants! Ah, by my finger bones, there is my sweet Mary from the Priory Mill! Ma foi, but she is beautiful! Adieu, Mary ma cherie! Mon coeur est toujours a toi. Brace your belt, Watkins, man, and swing your shoulders as a free companion should. By my hilt! your jerkins will be as dirty as mine ere you clap eyes on Hengistbury Head again."

The Company had marched to the turn of the road ere Sir Nigel Loring rode out from the gateway, mounted on Pommers, his great black war-horse, whose ponderous footfall on the wooden drawbridge echoed loudly from the gloomy arch which spanned it. Sir Nigel was still in his velvet dress of peace, with flat velvet cap of maintenance, and curling ostrich feather clasped in a golden brooch. To his three squires riding behind him it looked as though he bore the bird's egg as well as its feather, for the back of his bald pate shone like a globe of ivory. He bore no arms save the long and heavy sword which hung at his saddle-bow; but Terlake carried in front of him the high wivern-crested bassinet, Ford the heavy ash spear with swallow-tail pennon, while Alleyne was entrusted with the emblazoned shield. The Lady Loring rode her palfrey at her lord's bridle-arm, for she would see him as far as the edge of the forest, and ever and anon she turned her hard-lined face up wistfully to him and ran a questioning eye over his apparel and appointments.

"I trust that there is nothing forgot," she said, beckoning to Alleyne to ride on her further side. "I trust him to you, Edricson. Hosen, shirts, cyclas, and under-jupons are in the brown basket on the left side of the mule. His wine he takes hot when the nights are cold, malvoisie or vernage, with as much spice as would cover the thumb-nail. See that he hath a change if he come back hot from the tilting. There is goose-grease in a box, if the old scars ache at the turn of the weather. Let his blankets be dry and——"

"Nay, my heart's life," the little knight interrupted, "trouble not now about such matters. Why so pale and wan, Edricson? Is it not enow to make a man's heart dance to see this noble Company, such valiant men-at-arms, such lusty archers? By St. Paul! I would be ill to please if I were not blithe to see the red roses flying at the head of so noble a following!"

"The purse I have already given you, Edricson," continued the lady. "There are in it twenty-three marks, one noble, three shillings and fourpence, which is a great treasure for one man to carry. And I pray you to bear in mind, Edricson, that he hath two pair of shoes, those of red leather for common use, and the others with golden toe-chains, which he may wear should he chance to drink wine with the Prince or with Chandos."

"My sweet bird," said Sir Nigel, "I am right loth to part from you, but we are now at the fringe of the forest, and it is not right that I should take the chatelaine too far from her trust."

"But oh, my dear lord," she cried with a trembling lip, "let me bide with you for one furlong further—or one and a half perhaps. You may spare me this out of the weary miles that you will journey along."

"Come, then, my heart's comfort," he answered. "But I must crave a gage from thee. It is my custom, dearling, and hath been since I have first known thee, to proclaim by herald in such camps, townships, or fortalices as I may chance to visit, that my lady-love, being beyond compare the fairest and sweetest in Christendom, I should deem it great honor and kindly condescension if any cavalier would run three courses against me with sharpened lances, should he chance to have a lady whose claim he was willing to advance. I pray you then my fair dove, that you will vouchsafe to me one of those doeskin gloves, that I may wear it as the badge of her whose servant I shall ever be."

"Alack and alas for the fairest and sweetest!" she cried. "Fair and sweet I would fain be for your dear sake, my lord, but old I am and ugly, and the knights would laugh should you lay lance in rest in such a cause."

"Edricson," quoth Sir Nigel, "you have young eyes, and mine are somewhat bedimmed. Should you chance to see a knight laugh, or smile, or even, look you, arch his brows, or purse his mouth, or in any way show surprise that I should uphold the Lady Mary, you will take particular note of his name, his coat-armor, and his lodging. Your glove, my life's desire!"

The Lady Mary Loring slipped her hand from her yellow leather gauntlet, and he, lifting it with dainty reverence, bound it to the front of his velvet cap.

"It is with mine other guardian angels," quoth he, pointing at the saints' medals which hung beside it. "And now, my dearest, you have come far enow. May the Virgin guard and prosper thee! One kiss!" He bent down from his saddle, and then, striking spurs into his horse's sides, he galloped at top speed after his men, with his three squires at his heels. Half a mile further, where the road topped a hill, they looked back, and the Lady Mary on her white palfrey was still where they had left her. A moment later they were on the downward slope, and she had vanished from their view.

XIV

How Sir Nigel Sought for a Wayside Venture

For a time Sir Nigel was very moody and downcast, with bent brows and eyes upon the pommel of his saddle. Edricson and Terlake rode behind him in little better case, while Ford, a careless and light-hearted youth, grinned at the melancholy of his companions, and flourished his lord's heavy spear, making a point to right and a point to left, as though he were a paladin contending against a host of assailants. Sir Nigel happened, however, to turn himself in his saddle—Ford instantly became as stiff and as rigid as though he had been struck with a palsy. The four rode alone, for the archers had passed a curve in the road, though Alleyne could still hear the heavy clump, clump of their marching, or catch a glimpse of the sparkle of steel through the tangle of leafless branches.

"Ride by my side, friends, I entreat of you," said the knight, reining in his steed that they might come abreast of him. "For, since it hath pleased you to follow me to the wars, it were well that you should know how you may best serve me. I doubt not, Terlake, that you will show yourself a worthy son of a valiant father; and you, Ford, of yours; and you, Edricson, that you are mindful of the old-time house from which all men know that you are sprung. And first I would have you bear very steadfastly in mind that our setting forth is by no means for the purpose of gaining spoil or exacting ransom, though it may well happen that such may come to us also. We go to France, and from thence I trust to Spain, in humble search of a field in which we may win advancement and perchance some small share of glory. For this purpose I would have you know that it is not my wont to let any occasion pass where it is in any way possible that honor may be gained. I would have you bear this in mind, and give great heed to it that you may bring me word of all cartels, challenges, wrongs, tyrannies, infamies, and wronging of damsels. Nor is any occasion too small to take note of, for I have known such trifles as the dropping of a gauntlet, or the flicking of a breadcrumb, when well and properly followed up, lead to a most noble spear-running. But, Edricson, do I not see a cavalier who rides down yonder road amongst the nether shaw? It would be well, perchance, that you should give him greeting from me. And, should he be of gentle blood it may be that he would care to exchange thrusts with me."

"Why, my lord," quoth Ford, standing in his stirrups and shading his eyes, "it is old Hob Davidson, the fat miller of Milton!"

"Ah, so it is, indeed," said Sir Nigel, puckering his cheeks; "but wayside ventures are not to be scorned, for I have seen no finer passages than are to be had from such chance meetings, when cavaliers are willing to advance themselves. I can well remember that two leagues from the town of Rheims I met a very valiant and courteous cavalier of France, with whom I had gentle and most honorable contention for upwards of an hour. It hath ever grieved me that I had not his name, for he smote upon me with a mace and went upon his way ere I was in condition to have much speech with him; but his arms were an allurion in chief above a fess azure. I was also on such an occasion thrust through the shoulder by Lyon de Montcourt, whom I met on the high road betwixt Libourne and Bordeaux. I met him but the once, but I have never seen a man for whom I bear a greater love and esteem. And so also with the squire Le Bourg Capillet, who would have been a very valiant captain had he lived."

"He is dead then?" asked Alleyne Edricson.

"Alas! it was my ill fate to slay him in a bickering which broke out in a field near the township of Tarbes. I cannot call to mind how the thing came about, for it was in the year of the Prince's ride through Languedoc, when there was much fine skirmishing to be had at barriers. By St. Paul! I do not think that any honorable cavalier could ask for better chance of advancement than might be had by spurring forth before the army and riding to the gateways of Narbonne, or Bergerac or Mont Giscar, where some courteous gentleman would ever be at wait to do what he might to meet your wish or ease you of your vow. Such a one at Ventadour ran three courses with me betwixt daybreak and sunrise, to the great exaltation of his lady."

"And did you slay him also, my lord?" asked Ford with reverence.

"I could never learn, for he was carried within the barrier, and as I had chanced to break the bone of my leg it was a great unease for me to ride or even to stand. Yet, by the goodness of heaven and the pious intercession of the valiant St. George, I was able to sit my charger in the ruffle of Poictiers, which was no very long time afterwards. But what have we here? A very fair and courtly maiden, or I mistake."

It was indeed a tall and buxom country lass, with a basket of spinach-leaves upon her head, and a great slab of bacon tucked under one arm. She bobbed a frightened curtsey as Sir Nigel swept his velvet hat from his head and reined up his great charger.

"God be with thee, fair maiden!" said he.

"God guard thee, my lord!" she answered, speaking in the broadest West Saxon speech, and balancing herself first on one foot and then on the other in her bashfulness.

"Fear not, my fair damsel," said Sir Nigel, "but tell me if perchance a poor and most unworthy knight can in any wise be of service to you. Should it chance that you have been used despitefully, it may be that I may obtain justice for you."

"Lawk no, kind sir," she answered, clutching her bacon the tighter, as though some design upon it might be hid under this knightly offer. "I be the milking wench o' fairmer Arnold, and he be as kind a maister as heart could wish."

"It is well," said he, and with a shake of the bridle rode on down the woodland path. "I would have you bear in mind," he continued to his squires, "that gentle courtesy is not, as is the base use of so many false knights, to be shown only to maidens of high degree, for there is no woman so humble that a true knight may not listen to her tale of wrong. But here comes a cavalier who is indeed in haste. Perchance it would be well that we should ask him whither he rides, for it may be that he is one who desires to advance himself in chivalry."

The bleak, hard, wind-swept road dipped down in front of them into a little valley, and then, writhing up the heathy slope upon the other side, lost itself among the gaunt pine-trees. Far away between the black lines of trunks the quick glitter of steel marked where the Company pursued its way. To the north stretched the tree country, but to the south, between two swelling downs, a glimpse might be caught of the cold gray shimmer of the sea, with the white fleck of a galley sail upon the distant sky-line. Just in front of the travellers a horseman was urging his steed up the slope, driving it on with whip and spur as one who rides for a set purpose. As he clattered up, Alleyne could see that the roan horse was gray with dust and flecked with foam, as though it had left many a mile behind it. The rider was a stern-faced man, hard of mouth and dry of eye, with a heavy sword clanking at his side, and a stiff white bundle swathed in linen balanced across the pommel of his saddle.

"The king's messenger," he bawled as he came up to them. "The messenger of the king. Clear the causeway for the king's own man."

"Not so loudly, friend," quoth the little knight, reining his horse half round to bar the path. "I have myself been the king's man for thirty years or more, but I have not been wont to halloo about it on a peaceful highway."

"I ride in his service," cried the other, "and I carry that which belongs to him. You bar my path at your peril."

"Yet I have known the king's enemies claim to ride in his same," said Sir Nigel. "The foul fiend may lurk beneath a garment of light. We must have some sign or warrant of your mission."

"Then must I hew a passage," cried the stranger, with his shoulder braced round and his hand upon his hilt. "I am not to be stopped on the king's service by every gadabout."

"Should you be a gentleman of quarterings and coat-armor," lisped Sir Nigel, "I shall be very blithe to go further into the matter with you. If not, I have three very worthy squires, any one of whom would take the thing upon himself, and debate it with you in a very honorable way."

The man scowled from one to the other, and his hand stole away from his sword.

"You ask me for a sign," he said. "Here is a sign for you, since you must have one." As he spoke he whirled the covering from the object in front of him and showed to their horror that it was a newly-severed human leg. "By God's tooth!" he continued, with a brutal laugh, "you ask me if I am a man of quarterings, and it is even so, for I am officer to the verderer's court at Lyndhurst. This thievish leg is to hang at Milton, and the other is already at Brockenhurst, as a sign to all men of what comes of being over-fond of venison pasty."

"Faugh!" cried Sir Nigel. "Pass on the other side of the road, fellow, and let us have the wind of you. We shall trot our horses, my friends, across this pleasant valley, for, by Our Lady! a breath of God's fresh air is right welcome after such a sight."

"We hoped to snare a falcon," said he presently, "but we netted a carrion-crow. Ma foi! but there are men whose hearts are tougher than a boar's hide. For me, I have played the old game of war since ever I had hair on my chin, and I have seen ten thousand brave men in one day with their faces to the sky, but I swear by Him who made me that I cannot abide the work of the butcher."

"And yet, my fair lord," said Edricson, "there has, from what I hear, been much of such devil's work in France."

"Too much, too much," he answered. "But I have ever observed that the foremost in the field are they who would scorn to mishandle a prisoner. By St. Paul! it is not they who carry the breach who are wont to sack the town, but the laggard knaves who come crowding in when a way has been cleared for them. But what is this among the trees?"

"It is a shrine of Our Lady," said Terlake, "and a blind beggar who lives by the alms of those who worship there."

"A shrine!" cried the knight. "Then let us put up an orison." Pulling off his cap, and clasping his hands, he chanted in a shrill voice: "Benedictus dominus Deus meus, qui docet manus meas ad proelium, et digitos meos ad bellum." A strange figure he seemed to his three squires, perched on his huge horse, with his eyes upturned and the wintry sun shimmering upon his bald head. "It is a noble prayer," he remarked, putting on his hat again, "and it was taught to me by the noble Chandos himself. But how fares it with you, father? Methinks that I should have ruth upon you, seeing that I am myself like one who looks through a horn window while his neighbors have the clear crystal. Yet, by St. Paul! there is a long stride between the man who hath a horn casement and him who is walled in on every hand."

"Alas! fair sir," cried the blind old man, "I have not seen the blessed blue of heaven this two-score years, since a levin flash burned the sight out of my head."

"You have been blind to much that is goodly and fair," quoth Sir Nigel, "but you have also been spared much that is sorry and foul. This very hour our eyes have been shocked with that which would have left you unmoved. But, by St. Paul! we must on, or our Company will think that they have lost their captain somewhat early in the venture. Throw the man my purse, Edricson, and let us go."

Alleyne, lingering behind, bethought him of the Lady Loring's counsel, and reduced the noble gift which the knight had so freely bestowed to a single penny, which the beggar with many mumbled blessings thrust away into his wallet. Then, spurring his steed, the young squire rode at the top of his speed after his companions, and overtook them just at the spot where the trees fringe off into the moor and the straggling hamlet of Hordle lies scattered on either side of the winding and deeply-rutted track. The Company was already well-nigh through the village; but, as the knight and his squires closed up upon them, they heard the clamor of a strident voice, followed by a roar of deep-chested laughter from the ranks of the archers. Another minute brought them up with the rear-guard, where every man marched with his beard on his shoulder and a face which was agrin with merriment. By the side of the column walked a huge red-headed bowman, with his hands thrown out in argument and expostulation, while close at his heels followed a little wrinkled woman who poured forth a shrill volley of abuse, varied by an occasional thwack from her stick, given with all the force of her body, though she might have been beating one of the forest trees for all the effect that she seemed likely to produce.

"I trust, Aylward," said Sir Nigel gravely, as he rode up, "that this doth not mean that any violence hath been offered to women. If such a thing happened, I tell you that the man shall hang, though he were the best archer that ever wore brassart."

"Nay, my fair lord," Aylward answered with a grin, "it is violence which is offered to a man. He comes from Hordle, and this is his mother who hath come forth to welcome him."

"You rammucky lurden," she was howling, with a blow between each catch of her breath, "you shammocking, yaping, over-long good-for-nought. I will teach thee! I will baste thee! Aye, by my faith!"

"Whist, mother," said John, looking back at her from the tail of his eye, "I go to France as an archer to give blows and to take them."

"To France, quotha?" cried the old dame. "Bide here with me, and I shall warrant you more blows than you are like to get in France. If blows be what you seek, you need not go further than Hordle."

"By my hilt! the good dame speaks truth," said Aylward. "It seems to be the very home of them."

"What have you to say, you clean-shaved galley-beggar?" cried the fiery dame, turning upon the archer. "Can I not speak with my own son but you must let your tongue clack? A soldier, quotha, and never a hair on his face. I have seen a better soldier with pap for food and swaddling clothes for harness."

"Stand to it, Aylward," cried the archers, amid a fresh burst of laughter.

"Do not thwart her, comrade," said big John. "She hath a proper spirit for her years and cannot abide to be thwarted. It is kindly and homely to me to hear her voice and to feel that she is behind me. But I must leave you now, mother, for the way is over-rough for your feet; but I will bring you back a silken gown, if there be one in France or Spain, and I will bring Jinny a silver penny; so good-bye to you, and God have you in His keeping!" Whipping up the little woman, he lifted her lightly to his lips, and then, taking his place in the ranks again, marched on with the laughing Company.

"That was ever his way," she cried, appealing to Sir Nigel, who reined up his horse and listened with the greatest courtesy. "He would jog on his own road for all that I could do to change him. First he must be a monk forsooth, and all because a wench was wise enough to turn her back on him. Then he joins a rascally crew and must needs trapse off to the wars, and me with no one to bait the fire if I be out, or tend the cow if I be home. Yet I have been a good mother to him. Three hazel switches a day have I broke across his shoulders, and he takes no more notice than you have seen him to-day."

"Doubt not that he will come back to you both safe and prosperous, my fair dame," quoth Sir Nigel. "Meanwhile it grieves me that as I have already given my purse to a beggar up the road I——"

"Nay, my lord," said Alleyne, "I still have some moneys remaining."

"Then I pray you to give them to this very worthy woman." He cantered on as he spoke, while Alleyne, having dispensed two more pence, left the old dame standing by the furthest cottage of Hordle, with her shrill voice raised in blessings instead of revilings.

There were two cross-roads before they reached the Lymington Ford, and at each of then Sir Nigel pulled up his horse, and waited with many a curvet and gambade, craning his neck this way and that to see if fortune would send him a venture. Crossroads had, as he explained, been rare places for knightly spear-runnings, and in his youth it was no uncommon thing for a cavalier to abide for weeks at such a point, holding gentle debate with all comers, to his own advancement and the great honor of his lady. The times were changed, however, and the forest tracks wound away from them deserted and silent, with no trample of war-horse or clang of armor which might herald the approach of an adversary—so that Sir Nigel rode on his way disconsolate. At the Lymington River they splashed through the ford, and lay in the meadows on the further side to eat the bread and salt meat which they carried upon the sumpter horses. Then, ere the sun was on the slope of the heavens, they had deftly trussed up again, and were swinging merrily upon their way, two hundred feet moving like two.

There is a third cross-road where the track from Boldre runs down to the old fishing village of Pitt's Deep. Down this, as they came abreast of it, there walked two men, the one a pace or two behind the other. The cavaliers could not but pull up their horses to look at them, for a stranger pair were never seen journeying together. The first was a misshapen, squalid man with cruel, cunning eyes and a shock of tangled red hair, bearing in his hands a small unpainted cross, which he held high so that all men might see it. He seemed to be in the last extremity of fright, with a face the color of clay and his limbs all ashake as one who hath an ague. Behind him, with his toe ever rasping upon the other's heels, there walked a very stern, black-bearded man with a hard eye and a set mouth. He bore over his shoulder a great knotted stick with three jagged nails stuck in the head of it, and from time to time he whirled it up in the air with a quivering arm, as though he could scarce hold back from dashing his companion's brains out. So in silence they walked under the spread of the branches on the grass-grown path from Boldre.

"By St. Paul!" quoth the knight, "but this is a passing strange sight, and perchance some very perilous and honorable venture may arise from it. I pray you, Edricson, to ride up to them and to ask them the cause of it."

There was no need, however, for him to move, for the twain came swiftly towards them until they were within a spear's length, when the man with the cross sat himself down sullenly upon a tussock of grass by the wayside, while the other stood beside him with his great cudgel still hanging over his head. So intent was he that he raised his eyes neither to knight nor squires, but kept them ever fixed with a savage glare upon his comrade.

"I pray you, friend," said Sir Nigel, "to tell us truthfully who you are, and why you follow this man with such bitter enmity?"

"So long as I am within the pale of the king's law," the stranger answered, "I cannot see why I should render account to every passing wayfarer."

"You are no very shrewd reasoner, fellow," quoth the knight; "for if it be within the law for you to threaten him with your club, then it is also lawful for me to threaten you with my sword."

The man with the cross was down in an instant on his knees upon the ground, with hands clasped above him and his face shining with hope. "For dear Christ's sake, my fair lord," he cried in a crackling voice, "I have at my belt a bag with a hundred rose nobles, and I will give it to you freely if you will but pass your sword through this man's body."

"How, you foul knave?" exclaimed Sir Nigel hotly. "Do you think that a cavalier's arm is to be bought like a packman's ware. By St. Paul! I have little doubt that this fellow hath some very good cause to hold you in hatred."

"Indeed, my fair sir, you speak sooth," quoth he with the club, while the other seated himself once more by the wayside. "For this man is Peter Peterson, a very noted rieve, draw-latch, and murtherer, who has wrought much evil for many years in the parts about Winchester. It was but the other day, upon the feasts of the blessed Simon and Jude, that he slew my younger brother William in Bere Forest—for which, by the black thorn of Glastonbury! I shall have his heart's blood, though I walk behind him to the further end of earth."

"But if this be indeed so," asked Sir Nigel, "why is it that you have come with him so far through the forest?"

"Because I am an honest Englishman, and will take no more than the law allows. For when the deed was done this foul and base wretch fled to sanctuary at St. Cross, and I, as you may think, after him with all the posse. The prior, however, hath so ordered that while he holds this cross no man may lay hand upon him without the ban of church, which heaven forfend from me or mine. Yet, if for an instant he lay the cross aside, or if he fail to journey to Pitt's Deep, where it is ordered that he shall take ship to outland parts, or if he take not the first ship, or if until the ship be ready he walk not every day into the sea as far as his loins, then he becomes outlaw, and I shall forthwith dash out his brains."

At this the man on the ground snarled up at him like a rat, while the other clenched his teeth, and shook his club, and looked down at him with murder in his eyes. Knight and squire gazed from rogue to avenger, but as it was a matter which none could mend they tarried no longer, but rode upon their way. Alleyne, looking back, saw that the murderer had drawn bread and cheese from his scrip, and was silently munching it, with the protecting cross still hugged to his breast, while the other, black and grim, stood in the sunlit road and threw his dark shadow athwart him.

XV

How the Yellow Cog Sailed Forth From Lepe

That night the Company slept at St. Leonard's, in the great monastic barns and spicarium—ground well known both to Alleyne and to John, for they were almost within sight of the Abbey of Beaulieu. A strange thrill it gave to the young squire to see the well-remembered white dress once more, and to hear the measured tolling of the deep vespers bell. At early dawn they passed across the broad, sluggish, reed-girt stream—men, horses, and baggage in the flat ferry barges—and so journeyed on through the fresh morning air past Exbury to Lepe. Topping the heathy down, they came of a sudden full in sight of the old sea-port—a cluster of houses, a trail of blue smoke, and a bristle of masts. To right and left the long blue curve of the Solent lapped in a fringe of foam upon the yellow beach. Some way out from the town a line of pessoners, creyers, and other small craft were rolling lazily on the gentle swell. Further out still lay a great merchant-ship, high ended, deep waisted, painted of a canary yellow, and towering above the fishing-boats like a swan among ducklings.

"By St. Paul!" said the knight, "our good merchant of Southampton hath not played us false, for methinks I can see our ship down yonder. He said that she would be of great size and of a yellow shade."

"By my hilt, yes!" muttered Aylward; "she is yellow as a kite's claw, and would carry as many men as there are pips in a pomegranate."

"It is as well," remarked Terlake; "for methinks, my fair lord, that we are not the only ones who are waiting a passage to Gascony. Mine eye catches at times a flash and sparkle among yonder houses which assuredly never came from shipman's jacket or the gaberdine of a burgher."

"I can also see it," said Alleyne, shading his eyes with his hand. "And I can see men-at-arms in yonder boats which ply betwixt the vessel and the shore. But methinks that we are very welcome here, for already they come forth to meet us."

A tumultuous crowd of fishermen, citizens, and women had indeed swarmed out from the northern gate, and approached them up the side of the moor, waving their hands and dancing with joy, as though a great fear had been rolled back from their minds. At their head rode a very large and solemn man with a long chin and a drooping lip. He wore a fur tippet round his neck and a heavy gold chain over it, with a medallion which dangled in front of him.

"Welcome, most puissant and noble lord," he cried, doffing his bonnet to Black Simon. "I have heard of your lordship's valiant deeds, and in sooth they might be expected from your lordship's face and bearing. Is there any small matter in which I may oblige you?"

"Since you ask me," said the man-at-arms, "I would take it kindly if you could spare a link or two of the chain which hangs round your neck."

"What, the corporation chain!" cried the other in horror. "The ancient chain of the township of Lepe! This is but a sorry jest, Sir Nigel."

"What the plague did you ask me for then?" said Simon. "But if it is Sir Nigel Loring with whom you would speak, that is he upon the black horse."

The Mayor of Lepe gazed with amazement on the mild face and slender frame of the famous warrior.

"Your pardon, my gracious lord," he cried. "You see in me the mayor and chief magistrate of the ancient and powerful town of Lepe. I bid you very heartily welcome, and the more so as you are come at a moment when we are sore put to it for means of defence."

"Ha!" cried Sir Nigel, pricking up his ears.

"Yes, my lord, for the town being very ancient and the walls as old as the town, it follows that they are very ancient too. But there is a certain villainous and bloodthirsty Norman pirate hight Tete-noire, who, with a Genoan called Tito Caracci, commonly known as Spade-beard, hath been a mighty scourge upon these coasts. Indeed, my lord, they are very cruel and black-hearted men, graceless and ruthless, and if they should come to the ancient and powerful town of Lepe then—"

"Then good-bye to the ancient and powerful town of Lepe," quoth Ford, whose lightness of tongue could at times rise above his awe of Sir Nigel.

The knight, however, was too much intent upon the matter in hand to give heed to the flippancy of his squire. "Have you then cause," he asked, "to think that these men are about to venture an attempt upon you?"

"They have come in two great galleys," answered the mayor, "with two bank of oars on either side, and great store of engines of war and of men-at-arms. At Weymouth and at Portland they have murdered and ravished. Yesterday morning they were at Cowes, and we saw the smoke from the burning crofts. To-day they lie at their ease near Freshwater, and we fear much lest they come upon us and do us a mischief."

"We cannot tarry," said Sir Nigel, riding towards the town, with the mayor upon his left side; "the Prince awaits us at Bordeaux, and we may not be behind the general muster. Yet I will promise you that on our way we shall find time to pass Freshwater and to prevail upon these rovers to leave you in peace."

"We are much beholden to you!" cried the mayor "But I cannot see, my lord, how, without a war-ship, you may venture against these men. With your archers, however, you might well hold the town and do them great scath if they attempt to land."

"There is a very proper cog out yonder," said Sir Nigel, "it would be a very strange thing if any ship were not a war-ship when it had such men as these upon her decks. Certes, we shall do as I say, and that no later than this very day."

"My lord," said a rough-haired, dark-faced man, who walked by the knight's other stirrup, with his head sloped to catch all that he was saying. "By your leave, I have no doubt that you are skilled in land fighting and the marshalling of lances, but, by my soul! you will find it another thing upon the sea. I am the master-shipman of this yellow cog, and my name is Goodwin Hawtayne. I have sailed since I was as high as this staff, and I have fought against these Normans and against the Genoese, as well as the Scotch, the Bretons, the Spanish, and the Moors. I tell you, sir, that my ship is over light and over frail for such work, and it will but end in our having our throats cut, or being sold as slaves to the Barbary heathen."

"I also have experienced one or two gentle and honorable ventures upon the sea," quoth Sir Nigel, "and I am right blithe to have so fair a task before us. I think, good master-shipman, that you and I may win great honor in this matter, and I can see very readily that you are a brave and stout man."

"I like it not," said the other sturdily. "In God's name, I like it not. And yet Goodwin Hawtayne is not the man to stand back when his fellows are for pressing forward. By my soul! be it sink or swim, I shall turn her beak into Freshwater Bay, and if good Master Witherton, of Southampton, like not my handling of his ship then he may find another master-shipman."

They were close by the old north gate of the little town, and Alleyne, half turning in his saddle, looked back at the motley crowd who followed. The bowmen and men-at-arms had broken their ranks and were intermingled with the fishermen and citizens, whose laughing faces and hearty gestures bespoke the weight of care from which this welcome arrival had relieved them. Here and there among the moving throng of dark jerkins and of white surcoats were scattered dashes of scarlet and blue, the whimples or shawls of the women. Aylward, with a fishing lass on either arm, was vowing constancy alternately to her on the right and her on the left, while big John towered in the rear with a little chubby maiden enthroned upon his great shoulder, her soft white arm curled round his shining headpiece. So the throng moved on, until at the very gate it was brought to a stand by a wondrously fat man, who came darting forth from the town with rage in every feature of his rubicund face.

"How now, Sir Mayor?" he roared, in a voice like a bull. "How now, Sir Mayor? How of the clams and the scallops?"

"By Our Lady! my sweet Sir Oliver," cried the mayor. "I have had so much to think of, with these wicked villains so close upon us, that it had quite gone out of my head."

"Words, words!" shouted the other furiously. "Am I to be put off with words? I say to you again, how of the clams and scallops?"

"My fair sir, you flatter me," cried the mayor. "I am a peaceful trader, and I am not wont to be so shouted at upon so small a matter."

"Small!" shrieked the other. "Small! Clams and scallops! Ask me to your table to partake of the dainty of the town, and when I come a barren welcome and a bare board! Where is my spear-bearer?"

"Nay, Sir Oliver, Sir Oliver!" cried Sir Nigel, laughing.

"Let your anger be appeased, since instead of this dish you come upon an old friend and comrade."

"By St. Martin of Tours!" shouted the fat knight, his wrath all changed in an instant to joy, "if it is not my dear little game rooster of the Garonne. Ah, my sweet coz, I am right glad to see you. What days we have seen together!"

"Aye, by my faith," cried Sir Nigel, with sparkling eyes, "we have seen some valiant men, and we have shown our pennons in some noble skirmishes. By St. Paul! we have had great joys in France."

"And sorrows also," quoth the other. "I have some sad memories of the land. Can you recall that which befell us at Libourne?"

"Nay, I cannot call to mind that we ever so much as drew sword at the place."

"Man, man," cried Sir Oliver, "your mind still runs on nought but blades and bassinets. Hast no space in thy frame for the softer joys. Ah, even now I can scarce speak of it unmoved. So noble a pie, such tender pigeons, and sugar in the gravy instead of salt! You were by my side that day, as were Sir Claude Latour and the Lord of Pommers."

"I remember it," said Sir Nigel, laughing, "and how you harried the cook down the street, and spoke of setting fire to the inn. By St. Paul! most worthy mayor, my old friend is a perilous man, and I rede you that you compose your difference with him on such terms as you may."

"The clams and scallops shall be ready within the hour," the mayor answered. "I had asked Sir Oliver Buttesthorn to do my humble board the honor to partake at it of the dainty upon which we take some little pride, but in sooth this alarm of pirates hath cast such a shadow on my wits that I am like one distrait. But I trust, Sir Nigel, that you will also partake of none-meat with me?"

"I have overmuch to do," Sir Nigel answered, "for we must be aboard, horse and man, as early as we may. How many do you muster, Sir Oliver?"

"Three and forty. The forty are drunk, and the three are but indifferent sober. I have them all safe upon the ship."

"They had best find their wits again, for I shall have work for every man of them ere the sun set. It is my intention, if it seems good to you, to try a venture against these Norman and Genoese rovers."

"They carry caviare and certain very noble spices from the Levant aboard of ships from Genoa," quoth Sir Oliver. "We may come to great profit through the business. I pray you, master-shipman, that when you go on board you pour a helmetful of sea-water over any of my rogues whom you may see there."

Leaving the lusty knight and the Mayor of Lepe, Sir Nigel led the Company straight down to the water's edge, where long lines of flat lighters swiftly bore them to their vessel. Horse after horse was slung by main force up from the barges, and after kicking and plunging in empty air was dropped into the deep waist of the yellow cog, where rows of stalls stood ready for their safe keeping. Englishmen in those days were skilled and prompt in such matters, for it was so not long before that Edward had embarked as many as fifty thousand men in the port of Orwell, with their horses and their baggage, all in the space of four-and-twenty hours. So urgent was Sir Nigel on the shore, and so prompt was Goodwin Hawtayne on the cog, that Sir Oliver Buttesthorn had scarce swallowed his last scallop ere the peal of the trumpet and clang of nakir announced that all was ready and the anchor drawn. In the last boat which left the shore the two commanders sat together in the sheets, a strange contrast to one another, while under the feet of the rowers was a litter of huge stones which Sir Nigel had ordered to be carried to the cog. These once aboard, the ship set her broad mainsail, purple in color, and with a golden St. Christopher bearing Christ upon his shoulder in the centre of it. The breeze blew, the sail bellied, over heeled the portly vessel, and away she plunged through the smooth blue rollers, amid the clang of the minstrels on her poop and the shouting of the black crowd who fringed the yellow beach. To the left lay the green Island of Wight, with its long, low, curving hills peeping over each other's shoulders to the sky-line; to the right the wooded Hampshire coast as far as eye could reach; above a steel-blue heaven, with a wintry sun shimmering down upon them, and enough of frost to set the breath a-smoking.

"By St. Paul!" said Sir Nigel gayly, as he stood upon the poop and looked on either side of him, "it is a land which is very well worth fighting for, and it were pity to go to France for what may be had at home. Did you not spy a crooked man upon the beach?"

"Nay, I spied nothing," grumbled Sir Oliver, "for I was hurried down with a clam stuck in my gizzard and an untasted goblet of Cyprus on the board behind me."

"I saw him, my fair lord," said Terlake, "an old man with one shoulder higher than the other."

"'Tis a sign of good fortune," quoth Sir Nigel. "Our path was also crossed by a woman and by a priest, so all should be well with us. What say you, Edricson?"

"I cannot tell, my fair lord. The Romans of old were a very wise people, yet, certes, they placed their faith in such matters. So, too, did the Greeks, and divers other ancient peoples who were famed for their learning. Yet of the moderns there are many who scoff at all omens."

"There can be no manner of doubt about it," said Sir Oliver Buttesthorn. "I can well remember that in Navarre one day it thundered on the left out of a cloudless sky. We knew that ill would come of it, nor had we long to wait. Only thirteen days after, a haunch of prime venison was carried from my very tent door by the wolves, and on the same day two flasks of old vernage turned sour and muddy."

"You may bring my harness from below," said Sir Nigel to his squires, "and also, I pray you, bring up Sir Oliver's and we shall don it here. Ye may then see to your own gear; for this day you will, I hope, make a very honorable entrance into the field of chivalry, and prove yourselves to be very worthy and valiant squires. And now, Sir Oliver, as to our dispositions: would it please you that I should order them or will you?"

"You, my cockerel, you. By Our Lady! I am no chicken, but I cannot claim to know as much of war as the squire of Sir Walter Manny. Settle the matter to your own liking."

"You shall fly your pennon upon the fore part, then, and I upon the poop. For foreguard I shall give you your own forty men, with two-score archers. Two-score men, with my own men-at-arms and squires, will serve as a poop-guard. Ten archers, with thirty shipmen, under the master, may hold the waist while ten lie aloft with stones and arbalests. How like you that?"

"Good, by my faith, good! But here comes my harness, and I must to work, for I cannot slip into it as I was wont when first I set my face to the wars."

Meanwhile there had been bustle and preparation in all parts of the great vessel. The archers stood in groups about the decks, new-stringing their bows, and testing that they were firm at the nocks. Among them moved Aylward and other of the older soldiers, with a few whispered words of precept here and of warning there.

"Stand to it, my hearts of gold," said the old bowman as he passed from knot to knot. "By my hilt! we are in luck this journey. Bear in mind the old saying of the Company."

"What is that, Aylward?" cried several, leaning on their bows and laughing at him.

"'Tis the master-bowyer's rede: 'Every bow well bent. Every shaft well sent. Every stave well nocked. Every string well locked.' There, with that jingle in his head, a bracer on his left hand, a shooting glove on his right, and a farthing's-worth of wax in his girdle, what more doth a bowman need?"

"It would not be amiss," said Hordle John, "if under his girdle he had four farthings'-worth of wine."

"Work first, wine afterwards, mon camarade. But it is time that we took our order, for methinks that between the Needle rocks and the Alum cliffs yonder I can catch a glimpse of the topmasts of the galleys. Hewett, Cook, Johnson, Cunningham, your men are of the poop-guard. Thornbury, Walters, Hackett, Baddlesmere, you are with Sir Oliver on the forecastle. Simon, you bide with your lord's banner; but ten men must go forward."

Quietly and promptly the men took their places, lying flat upon their faces on the deck, for such was Sir Nigel's order. Near the prow was planted Sir Oliver's spear, with his arms—a boar's head gules upon a field of gold. Close by the stern stood Black Simon with the pennon of the house of Loring. In the waist gathered the Southampton mariners, hairy and burly men, with their jerkins thrown off, their waists braced tight, swords, mallets, and pole-axes in their hands. Their leader, Goodwin Hawtayne, stood upon the poop and talked with Sir Nigel, casting his eye up sometimes at the swelling sail, and then glancing back at the two seamen who held the tiller.

"Pass the word," said Sir Nigel, "that no man shall stand to arms or draw his bow-string until my trumpeter shall sound. It would be well that we should seem to be a merchant-ship from Southampton and appear to flee from them."

"We shall see them anon," said the master-shipman. "Ha, said I not so? There they lie, the water-snakes, in Freshwater Bay; and mark the reek of smoke from yonder point, where they have been at their devil's work. See how their shallops pull from the land! They have seen us and called their men aboard. Now they draw upon the anchor. See them like ants upon the forecastle! They stoop and heave like handy ship men. But, my fair lord, these are no niefs. I doubt but we have taken in hand more than we can do. Each of these ships is a galeasse, and of the largest and swiftest make."

"I would I had your eyes," said Sir Nigel, blinking at the pirate galleys. "They seem very gallant ships, and I trust that we shall have much pleasance from our meeting with them. It would be well to pass the word that we should neither give nor take quarter this day. Have you perchance a priest or friar aboard this ship, Master Hawtayne?"

"No, my fair lord."

"Well, well, it is no great matter for my Company, for they were all houseled and shriven ere we left Twynham Castle; and Father Christopher of the Priory gave me his word that they were as fit to march to heaven as to Gascony. But my mind misdoubts me as to these Winchester men who have come with Sir Oliver, for they appear to be a very ungodly crew. Pass the word that the men kneel, and that the under-officers repeat to them the pater, the ave, and the credo."

With a clank of arms, the rough archers and seamen took to their knees, with bent heads and crossed hands, listening to the hoarse mutter from the file-leaders. It was strange to mark the hush; so that the lapping of the water, the straining of the sail, and the creaking of the timbers grew louder of a sudden upon the ear. Many of the bowmen had drawn amulets and relics from their bosoms, while he who possessed some more than usually sanctified treasure passed it down the line of his comrades, that all might kiss and reap the virtue.

The yellow cog had now shot out from the narrow waters of the Solent, and was plunging and rolling on the long heave of the open channel. The wind blew freshly from the east, with a very keen edge to it; and the great sail bellied roundly out, laying the vessel over until the water hissed beneath her lee bulwarks. Broad and ungainly, she floundered from wave to wave, dipping her round bows deeply into the blue rollers, and sending the white flakes of foam in a spatter over her decks. On her larboard quarter lay the two dark galleys, which had already hoisted sail, and were shooting out from Freshwater Bay in swift pursuit, their double line of oars giving them a vantage which could not fail to bring them up with any vessel which trusted to sails alone. High and bluff the English cog; long, black and swift the pirate galleys, like two fierce lean wolves which have seen a lordly and unsuspecting stag walk past their forest lair.

"Shall we turn, my fair lord, or shall we carry on?" asked the master-shipman, looking behind him with anxious eyes.

"Nay, we must carry on and play the part of the helpless merchant."

"But your pennons? They will see that we have two knights with us."

"Yet it would not be to a knight's honor or good name to lower his pennon. Let them be, and they will think that we are a wine-ship for Gascony, or that we bear the wool-bales of some mercer of the Staple. Ma foi, but they are very swift! They swoop upon us like two goshawks on a heron. Is there not some symbol or device upon their sails?"

"That on the right," said Edricson, "appears to have the head of an Ethiop upon it."

"'Tis the badge of Tete-noire, the Norman," cried a seaman-mariner. "I have seen it before, when he harried us at Winchelsea. He is a wondrous large and strong man, with no ruth for man, woman, or beast. They say that he hath the strength of six; and, certes, he hath the crimes of six upon his soul. See, now, to the poor souls who swing at either end of his yard-arm!"

At each end of the yard there did indeed hang the dark figure of a man, jolting and lurching with hideous jerkings of its limbs at every plunge and swoop of the galley.

"By St. Paul!" said Sir Nigel, "and by the help of St. George and Our Lady, it will be a very strange thing if our black-headed friend does not himself swing thence ere he be many hours older. But what is that upon the other galley?"

"It is the red cross of Genoa. This Spade-beard is a very noted captain, and it is his boast that there are no seamen and no archers in the world who can compare with those who serve the Doge Boccanegra."

"That we shall prove," said Goodwin Hawtayne; "but it would be well, ere they close with us, to raise up the mantlets and pavises as a screen against their bolts." He shouted a hoarse order, and his seamen worked swiftly and silently, heightening the bulwarks and strengthening them. The three ship's anchors were at Sir Nigel's command carried into the waist, and tied to the mast, with twenty feet of cable between, each under the care of four seamen. Eight others were stationed with leather water-bags to quench any fire-arrows which might come aboard, while others were sent up the mast, to lie along the yard and drop stones or shoot arrows as the occasion served.

"Let them be supplied with all that is heavy and weighty in the ship," said Sir Nigel.

"Then we must send them up Sir Oliver Buttesthorn," quoth Ford.

The knight looked at him with a face which struck the smile from his lips. "No squire of mine," he said, "shall ever make jest of a belted knight. And yet," he added, his eyes softening, "I know that it is but a boy's mirth, with no sting in it. Yet I should ill do my part towards your father if I did not teach you to curb your tongue-play."

"They will lay us aboard on either quarter, my lord," cried the master. "See how they stretch out from each other! The Norman hath a mangonel or a trabuch upon the forecastle. See, they bend to the levers! They are about to loose it."

"Aylward," cried the knight, "pick your three trustiest archers, and see if you cannot do something to hinder their aim. Methinks they are within long arrow flight."

"Seventeen score paces," said the archer, running his eye backwards and forwards. "By my ten finger-bones! it would be a strange thing if we could not notch a mark at that distance. Here, Watkin of Sowley, Arnold, Long Williams, let us show the rogues that they have English bowmen to deal with."

The three archers named stood at the further end of the poop, balancing themselves with feet widely spread and bows drawn, until the heads of the cloth-yard arrows were level with the centre of the stave. "You are the surer, Watkin," said Aylward, standing by them with shaft upon string. "Do you take the rogue with the red coif. You two bring down the man with the head-piece, and I will hold myself ready if you miss. Ma foi! they are about to loose her. Shoot, mes garcons, or you will be too late."

The throng of pirates had cleared away from the great wooden catapult, leaving two of their number to discharge it. One in a scarlet cap bent over it, steadying the jagged rock which was balanced on the spoon-shaped end of the long wooden lever. The other held the loop of the rope which would release the catch and send the unwieldy missile hurtling through the air. So for an instant they stood, showing hard and clear against the white sail behind them. The next, redcap had fallen across the stone with an arrow between his ribs; and the other, struck in the leg and in the throat, was writhing and spluttering upon the ground. As he toppled backwards he had loosed the spring, and the huge beam of wood, swinging round with tremendous force, cast the corpse of his comrade so close to the English ship that its mangled and distorted limbs grazed their very stern. As to the stone, it glanced off obliquely and fell midway between the vessels. A roar of cheering and of laughter broke from the rough archers and seamen at the sight, answered by a yell of rage from their pursuers.

"Lie low, mes enfants," cried Aylward, motioning with his left hand. "They will learn wisdom. They are bringing forward shield and mantlet. We shall have some pebbles about our ears ere long."

XVI

How the Yellow Cog Fought the Two Rover Galleys

The three vessels had been sweeping swiftly westwards, the cog still well to the front, although the galleys were slowly drawing in upon either quarter. To the left was a hard skyline unbroken by a sail. The island already lay like a cloud behind them, while right in front was St. Alban's Head, with Portland looming mistily in the farthest distance. Alleyne stood by the tiller, looking backwards, the fresh wind full in his teeth, the crisp winter air tingling on his face and blowing his yellow curls from under his bassinet. His cheeks were flushed and his eyes shining, for the blood of a hundred fighting Saxon ancestors was beginning to stir in his veins.

"What was that?" he asked, as a hissing, sharp-drawn voice seemed to whisper in his ear. The steersman smiled, and pointed with his foot to where a short heavy cross-bow quarrel stuck quivering in the boards. At the same instant the man stumbled forward upon his knees, and lay lifeless upon the deck, a blood-stained feather jutting out from his back. As Alleyne stooped to raise him, the air seemed to be alive with the sharp zip-zip of the bolts, and he could hear them pattering on the deck like apples at a tree-shaking.

"Raise two more mantlets by the poop-lanthorn," said Sir Nigel quietly.

"And another man to the tiller," cried the master-shipman.

"Keep them in play, Aylward, with ten of your men," the knight continued. "And let ten of Sir Oliver's bowmen do as much for the Genoese. I have no mind as yet to show them how much they have to fear from us."

Ten picked shots under Aylward stood in line across the broad deck, and it was a lesson to the young squires who had seen nothing of war to note how orderly and how cool were these old soldiers, how quick the command, and how prompt the carrying out, ten moving like one. Their comrades crouched beneath the bulwarks, with many a rough jest and many a scrap of criticism or advice. "Higher, Wat, higher!" "Put thy body into it, Will!" "Forget not the wind, Hal!" So ran the muttered chorus, while high above it rose the sharp twanging of the strings, the hiss of the shafts, and the short "Draw your arrow! Nick your arrow! Shoot wholly together!" from the master-bowman.

And now both mangonels were at work from the galleys, but so covered and protected that, save at the moment of discharge, no glimpse could be caught of them. A huge brown rock from the Genoese sang over their heads, and plunged sullenly into the slope of a wave. Another from the Norman whizzed into the waist, broke the back of a horse, and crashed its way through the side of the vessel. Two others, flying together, tore a great gap in the St. Christopher upon the sail, and brushed three of Sir Oliver's men-at-arms from the forecastle. The master-shipman looked at the knight with a troubled face.

"They keep their distance from us," said he. "Our archery is over-good, and they will not close. What defence can we make against the stones?"

"I think I may trick them," the knight answered cheerfully, and passed his order to the archers. Instantly five of them threw up their hands and fell prostrate upon the deck. One had already been slain by a bolt, so that there were but four upon their feet.

"That should give them heart," said Sir Nigel, eyeing the galleys, which crept along on either side, with a slow, measured swing of their great oars, the water swirling and foaming under their sharp stems.

"They still hold aloof," cried Hawtayne.

"Then down with two more," shouted their leader. "That will do. Ma foi! but they come to our lure like chicks to the fowler. To your arms, men! The pennon behind me, and the squires round the pennon. Stand fast with the anchors in the waist, and be ready for a cast. Now blow out the trumpets, and may God's benison be with the honest men!"

As he spoke a roar of voices and a roll of drums came from either galley, and the water was lashed into spray by the hurried beat of a hundred oars. Down they swooped, one on the right, one on the left, the sides and shrouds black with men and bristling with weapons. In heavy clusters they hung upon the forecastle all ready for a spring—faces white, faces brown, faces yellow, and faces black, fair Norsemen, swarthy Italians, fierce rovers from the Levant, and fiery Moors from the Barbary States, of all hues and countries, and marked solely by the common stamp of a wild-beast ferocity. Rasping up on either side, with oars trailing to save them from snapping, they poured in a living torrent with horrid yell and shrill whoop upon the defenceless merchantman.

But wilder yet was the cry, and shriller still the scream, when there rose up from the shadow of those silent bulwarks the long lines of the English bowmen, and the arrows whizzed in a deadly sleet among the unprepared masses upon the pirate decks. From the higher sides of the cog the bowmen could shoot straight down, at a range which was so short as to enable a cloth-yard shaft to pierce through mail-coats or to transfix a shield, though it were an inch thick of toughened wood. One moment Alleyne saw the galley's poop crowded with rushing figures, waving arms, exultant faces; the next it was a blood-smeared shambles, with bodies piled three deep upon each other, the living cowering behind the dead to shelter themselves from that sudden storm-blast of death. On either side the seamen whom Sir Nigel had chosen for the purpose had cast their anchors over the side of the galleys, so that the three vessels, locked in an iron grip, lurched heavily forward upon the swell.

And now set in a fell and fierce fight, one of a thousand of which no chronicler has spoken and no poet sung. Through all the centuries and over all those southern waters nameless men have fought in nameless places, their sole monuments a protected coast and an unravaged country-side.

Fore and aft the archers had cleared the galleys' decks, but from either side the rovers had poured down into the waist, where the seamen and bowmen were pushed back and so mingled with their foes that it was impossible for their comrades above to draw string to help them. It was a wild chaos where axe and sword rose and fell, while Englishman, Norman, and Italian staggered and reeled on a deck which was cumbered with bodies and slippery with blood. The clang of blows, the cries of the stricken, the short, deep shout of the islanders, and the fierce whoops of the rovers, rose together in a deafening tumult, while the breath of the panting men went up in the wintry air like the smoke from a furnace. The giant Tete-noire, towering above his fellows and clad from head to foot in plate of proof, led on his boarders, waving a huge mace in the air, with which he struck to the deck every man who approached him. On the other side, Spade-beard, a dwarf in height, but of great breadth of shoulder and length of arm, had cut a road almost to the mast, with three-score Genoese men-at-arms close at his heels. Between these two formidable assailants the seamen were being slowly wedged more closely together, until they stood back to back under the mast with the rovers raging upon every side of them.

But help was close at hand. Sir Oliver Buttesthorn with his men-at-arms had swarmed down from the forecastle, while Sir Nigel, with his three squires, Black Simon, Aylward, Hordle John, and a score more, threw themselves from the poop and hurled themselves into the thickest of the fight. Alleyne, as in duty bound, kept his eyes fixed ever on his lord and pressed forward close at his heels. Often had he heard of Sir Nigel's prowess and skill with all knightly weapons, but all the tales that had reached his ears fell far short of the real quickness and coolness of the man. It was as if the devil was in him, for he sprang here and sprang there, now thrusting and now cutting, catching blows on his shield, turning them with his blade, stooping under the swing of an axe, springing over the sweep of a sword, so swift and so erratic that the man who braced himself for a blow at him might find him six paces off ere he could bring it down. Three pirates had fallen before him, and he had wounded Spade-beard in the neck, when the Norman giant sprang at him from the side with a slashing blow from his deadly mace. Sir Nigel stooped to avoid it, and at the same instant turned a thrust from the Genoese swordsman, but, his foot slipping in a pool of blood, he fell heavily to the ground. Alleyne sprang in front of the Norman, but his sword was shattered and he himself beaten to the ground by a second blow from the ponderous weapon. Ere the pirate chief could repeat it, however, John's iron grip fell upon his wrist, and he found that for once he was in the hands of a stronger man than himself.

Fiercely he strove to disengage his weapon, but Hordle John bent his arm slowly back until, with a sharp crack, like a breaking stave, it turned limp in his grasp, and the mace dropped from the nerveless fingers. In vain he tried to pluck it up with the other hand. Back and back still his foeman bent him, until, with a roar of pain and of fury, the giant clanged his full length upon the boards, while the glimmer of a knife before the bars of his helmet warned him that short would be his shrift if he moved.

Cowed and disheartened by the loss of their leader, the Normans had given back and were now streaming over the bulwarks on to their own galley, dropping a dozen at a time on to her deck. But the anchor still held them in its crooked claw, and Sir Oliver with fifty men was hard upon their heels. Now, too, the archers had room to draw their bows once more, and great stones from the yard of the cog came thundering and crashing among the flying rovers. Here and there they rushed with wild screams and curses, diving under the sail, crouching behind booms, huddling into corners like rabbits when the ferrets are upon them, as helpless and as hopeless. They were stern days, and if the honest soldier, too poor for a ransom, had no prospect of mercy upon the battle-field, what ruth was there for sea robbers, the enemies of humankind, taken in the very deed, with proofs of their crimes still swinging upon their yard-arm.

But the fight had taken a new and a strange turn upon the other side. Spade-beard and his men had given slowly back, hard pressed by Sir Nigel, Aylward, Black Simon, and the poop-guard. Foot by foot the Italian had retreated, his armor running blood at every joint, his shield split, his crest shorn, his voice fallen away to a mere gasping and croaking. Yet he faced his foemen with dauntless courage, dashing in, springing back, sure-footed, steady-handed, with a point which seemed to menace three at once. Beaten back on to the deck of his own vessel, and closely followed by a dozen Englishmen, he disengaged himself from them, ran swiftly down the deck, sprang back into the cog once more, cut the rope which held the anchor, and was back in an instant among his crossbow-men. At the same time the Genoese sailors thrust with their oars against the side of the cog, and a rapidly widening rift appeared between the two vessels.

"By St. George!" cried Ford, "we are cut off from Sir Nigel."

"He is lost," gasped Terlake. "Come, let us spring for it." The two youths jumped with all their strength to reach the departing galley. Ford's feet reached the edge of the bulwarks, and his hand clutching a rope he swung himself on board. Terlake fell short, crashed in among the oars, and bounded off into the sea. Alleyne, staggering to the side, was about to hurl himself after him, but Hordle John dragged him back by the girdle.

"You can scarce stand, lad, far less jump," said he. "See how the blood rips from your bassinet."

"My place is by the flag," cried Alleyne, vainly struggling to break from the other's hold.

"Bide here, man. You would need wings ere you could reach Sir Nigel's side."

The vessels were indeed so far apart now that the Genoese could use the full sweep of their oars, and draw away rapidly from the cog.

"My God, but it is a noble fight!" shouted big John, clapping his hands. "They have cleared the poop, and they spring into the waist. Well struck, my lord! Well struck, Aylward! See to Black Simon, how he storms among the shipmen! But this Spade-beard is a gallant warrior. He rallies his men upon the forecastle. He hath slain an archer. Ha! my lord is upon him. Look to it, Alleyne! See to the whirl and glitter of it!"

"By heaven, Sir Nigel is down!" cried the squire.

"Up!" roared John. "It was but a feint. He bears him back. He drives him to the side. Ah, by Our Lady, his sword is through him! They cry for mercy. Down goes the red cross, and up springs Simon with the scarlet roses!"

The death of the Genoese leader did indeed bring the resistance to an end. Amid a thunder of cheering from cog and from galleys the forked pennon fluttered upon the forecastle, and the galley, sweeping round, came slowly back, as the slaves who rowed it learned the wishes of their new masters.

The two knights had come aboard the cog, and the grapplings having been thrown off, the three vessels now moved abreast. Through all the storm and rush of the fight Alleyne had been aware of the voice of Goodwin Hawtayne, the master-shipman, with his constant "Hale the bowline! Veer the sheet!" and strange it was to him to see how swiftly the blood-stained sailors turned from the strife to the ropes and back. Now the cog's head was turned Francewards, and the shipman walked the deck, a peaceful master-mariner once more.

"There is sad scath done to the cog, Sir Nigel," said he. "Here is a hole in the side two ells across, the sail split through the centre, and the wood as bare as a friar's poll. In good sooth, I know not what I shall say to Master Witherton when I see the Itchen once more."

"By St. Paul! it would be a very sorry thing if we suffered you to be the worse of this day's work," said Sir Nigel. "You shall take these galleys back with you, and Master Witherton may sell them. Then from the moneys he shall take as much as may make good the damage, and the rest he shall keep until our home-coming, when every man shall have his share. An image of silver fifteen inches high I have vowed to the Virgin, to be placed in her chapel within the Priory, for that she was pleased to allow me to come upon this Spade-beard, who seemed to me from what I have seen of him to be a very sprightly and valiant gentleman. But how fares it with you, Edricson?"

"It is nothing, my fair lord," said Alleyne, who had now loosened his bassinet, which was cracked across by the Norman's blow. Even as he spoke, however, his head swirled round, and he fell to the deck with the blood gushing from his nose and mouth.

"He will come to anon," said the knight, stooping over him and passing his fingers through his hair. "I have lost one very valiant and gentle squire this day. I can ill afford to lose another. How many men have fallen?"

"I have pricked off the tally," said Aylward, who had come aboard with his lord. "There are seven of the Winchester men, eleven seamen, your squire, young Master Terlake, and nine archers."

"And of the others?"

"They are all dead—save only the Norman knight who stands behind you. What would you that we should do with him?"

"He must hang on his own yard," said Sir Nigel. "It was my vow and must be done."

The pirate leader had stood by the bulwarks, a cord round his arms, and two stout archers on either side. At Sir Nigel's words he started violently, and his swarthy features blanched to a livid gray.

"How, Sir Knight?" he cried in broken English. "Que dites vous? To hang, le mort du chien! To hang!"

"It is my vow," said Sir Nigel shortly. "From what I hear, you thought little enough of hanging others."

"Peasants, base roturiers," cried the other. "It is their fitting death. Mais Le Seigneur d'Andelys, avec le sang des rois dans ses veins! C'est incroyable!"

Sir Nigel turned upon his heel, while two seamen cast a noose over the pirate's neck. At the touch of the cord he snapped the bonds which bound him, dashed one of the archers to the deck, and seizing the other round the waist sprang with him into the sea.

"By my hilt, he is gone!" cried Aylward, rushing to the side. "They have sunk together like a stone."

"I am right glad of it," answered Sir Nigel; "for though it was against my vow to loose him, I deem that he has carried himself like a very gentle and debonnaire cavalier."

XVII

How the Yellow Cog Crossed the Bar of Gironde

For two days the yellow cog ran swiftly before a northeasterly wind, and on the dawn of the third the high land of Ushant lay like a mist upon the shimmering sky-line. There came a plump of rain towards mid-day and the breeze died down, but it freshened again before nightfall, and Goodwin Hawtayne veered his sheet and held head for the south. Next morning they had passed Belle Isle, and ran through the midst of a fleet of transports returning from Guienne. Sir Nigel Loring and Sir Oliver Buttesthorn at once hung their shields over the side, and displayed their pennons as was the custom, noting with the keenest interest the answering symbols which told the names of the cavaliers who had been constrained by ill health or wounds to leave the prince at so critical a time.

That evening a great dun-colored cloud banked up in the west, and an anxious man was Goodwin Hawtayne, for a third part of his crew had been slain, and half the remainder were aboard the galleys, so that, with an injured ship, he was little fit to meet such a storm as sweeps over those waters. All night it blew in short fitful puffs, heeling the great cog over until the water curled over her lee bulwarks. As the wind still freshened the yard was lowered half way down the mast in the morning. Alleyne, wretchedly ill and weak, with his head still ringing from the blow which he had received, crawled up upon deck. Water-swept and aslant, it was preferable to the noisome, rat-haunted dungeons which served as cabins. There, clinging to the stout halliards of the sheet, he gazed with amazement at the long lines of black waves, each with its curling ridge of foam, racing in endless succession from out the inexhaustible west. A huge sombre cloud, flecked with livid blotches, stretched over the whole seaward sky-line, with long ragged streamers whirled out in front of it. Far behind them the two galleys labored heavily, now sinking between the rollers until their yards were level with the waves, and again shooting up with a reeling, scooping motion until every spar and rope stood out hard against the sky. On the left the low-lying land stretched in a dim haze, rising here and there into a darker blur which marked the higher capes and headlands. The land of France! Alleyne's eyes shone as he gazed upon it. The land of France!—the very words sounded as the call of a bugle in the ears of the youth of England. The land where their fathers had bled, the home of chivalry and of knightly deeds, the country of gallant men, of courtly women, of princely buildings, of the wise, the polished and the sainted. There it lay, so still and gray beneath the drifting wrack—the home of things noble and of things shameful—the theatre where a new name might be made or an old one marred. From his bosom to his lips came the crumpled veil, and he breathed a vow that if valor and goodwill could raise him to his lady's side, then death alone should hold him back from her. His thoughts were still in the woods of Minstead and the old armory of Twynham Castle, when the hoarse voice of the master-shipman brought them back once more to the Bay of Biscay.

"By my troth, young sir," he said, "you are as long in the face as the devil at a christening, and I cannot marvel at it, for I have sailed these waters since I was as high as this whinyard, and yet I never saw more sure promise of an evil night."

"Nay, I had other things upon my mind," the squire answered.

"And so has every man," cried Hawtayne in an injured voice. "Let the shipman see to it. It is the master-shipman's affair. Put it all upon good Master Hawtayne! Never had I so much care since first I blew trumpet and showed cartel at the west gate of Southampton."

"What is amiss then?" asked Alleyne, for the man's words were as gusty as the weather.

"Amiss, quotha? Here am I with but half my mariners, and a hole in the ship where that twenty-devil stone struck us big enough to fit the fat widow of Northam through. It is well enough on this tack, but I would have you tell me what I am to do on the other. We are like to have salt water upon us until we be found pickled like the herrings in an Easterling's barrels."

"What says Sir Nigel to it?"

"He is below pricking out the coat-armor of his mother's uncle. 'Pester me not with such small matters!' was all that I could get from him. Then there is Sir Oliver. 'Fry them in oil with a dressing of Gascony,' quoth he, and then swore at me because I had not been the cook. 'Walawa,' thought I, 'mad master, sober man'—so away forward to the archers. Harrow and alas! but they were worse than the others."

"Would they not help you then?"

"Nay, they sat tway and tway at a board, him that they call Aylward and the great red-headed man who snapped the Norman's arm-bone, and the black man from Norwich, and a score of others, rattling their dice in an archer's gauntlet for want of a box. 'The ship can scarce last much longer, my masters,' quoth I. 'That is your business, old swine's-head,' cried the black galliard. 'Le diable t'emporte,' says Aylward. 'A five, a four and the main,' shouted the big man, with a voice like the flap of a sail. Hark to them now, young sir, and say if I speak not sooth."

As he spoke, there sounded high above the shriek of the gale and the straining of the timbers a gust of oaths with a roar of deep-chested mirth from the gamblers in the forecastle.

"Can I be of avail?" asked Alleyne. "Say the word and the thing is done, if two hands may do it."

"Nay, nay, your head I can see is still totty, and i' faith little head would you have, had your bassinet not stood your friend. All that may be done is already carried out, for we have stuffed the gape with sails and corded it without and within. Yet when we bale our bowline and veer the sheet our lives will hang upon the breach remaining blocked. See how yonder headland looms upon us through the mist! We must tack within three arrow flights, or we may find a rock through our timbers. Now, St. Christopher be praised! here is Sir Nigel, with whom I may confer."

"I prythee that you will pardon me," said the knight, clutching his way along the bulwark. "I would not show lack of courtesy toward a worthy man, but I was deep in a matter of some weight, concerning which, Alleyne, I should be glad of your rede. It touches the question of dimidiation or impalement in the coat of mine uncle, Sir John Leighton of Shropshire, who took unto wife the widow of Sir Henry Oglander of Nunwell. The case has been much debated by pursuivants and kings-of-arms. But how is it with you, master shipman?"

"Ill enough, my fair lord. The cog must go about anon, and I know not how we may keep the water out of her."

"Go call Sir Oliver!" said Sir Nigel, and presently the portly knight made his way all astraddle down the slippery deck.

"By my soul, master-shipman, this passes all patience!" he cried wrathfully. "If this ship of yours must needs dance and skip like a clown at a kermesse, then I pray you that you will put me into one of these galeasses. I had but sat down to a flask of malvoisie and a mortress of brawn, as is my use about this hour, when there comes a cherking, and

I find my wine over my legs and the flask in my lap, and then as I stoop to clip it there comes another cursed cherk, and there is a mortress of brawn stuck fast to the nape of my neck. At this moment I have two pages coursing after it from side to side, like hounds behind a leveret. Never did living pig gambol more lightly. But you have sent for me, Sir Nigel?"

"I would fain have your rede, Sir Oliver, for Master Hawtayne hath fears that when we veer there may come danger from the hole in our side."

"Then do not veer," quoth Sir Oliver hastily. "And now, fair sir, I must hasten back to see how my rogues have fared with the brawn."

"Nay, but this will scarce suffice," cried the shipman. "If we do not veer we will be upon the rocks within the hour."

"Then veer," said Sir Oliver. "There is my rede; and now, Sir Nigel, I must crave——"

At this instant, however, a startled shout rang out from two seamen upon the forecastle. "Rocks!" they yelled, stabbing into the air with their forefingers. "Rocks beneath our very bows!" Through the belly of a great black wave, not one hundred paces to the front of them, there thrust forth a huge jagged mass of brown stone, which spouted spray as though it were some crouching monster, while a dull menacing boom and roar filled the air.

"Yare! yare!" screamed Goodwin Hawtayne, flinging himself upon the long pole which served as a tiller. "Cut the halliard! Haul her over! Lay her two courses to the wind!"

Over swung the great boom, and the cog trembled and quivered within five spear-lengths of the breakers.

"She can scarce draw clear," cried Hawtayne, with his eyes from the sail to the seething line of foam. "May the holy Julian stand by us and the thrice-sainted Christopher!"

"If there be such peril, Sir Oliver," quoth Sir Nigel, "it would be very knightly and fitting that we should show our pennons. I pray you, Edricson, that you will command my guidon-bearer to put forward my banner."

"And sound the trumpets!" cried Sir Oliver. "In manus tuas, Domine! I am in the keeping of James of Compostella, to whose shrine I shall make pilgrimage, and in whose honor I vow that I will eat a carp each year upon his feast-day. Mon Dieu, but the waves roar! How is it with us now, master-shipman?"

"We draw! We draw!" cried Hawtayne, with his eyes still fixed upon the foam which hissed under the very bulge of the side. "Ah, Holy Mother, be with us now!"

As he spoke the cog rasped along the edge of the reef, and a long white curling sheet of wood was planed off from her side from waist to poop by a jutting horn of the rock. At the same instant she lay suddenly over, the sail drew full, and she plunged seawards amid the shoutings of the seamen and the archers.

"The Virgin be praised!" cried the shipman, wiping his brow. "For this shall bell swing and candle burn when I see Southampton Water once more. Cheerily, my hearts! Pull yarely on the bowline!"

"By my soul! I would rather have a dry death," quoth Sir Oliver. "Though, Mort Dieu! I have eaten so many fish that it were but justice that the fish should eat me. Now I must back to the cabin, for I have matters there which crave my attention."

"Nay, Sir Oliver, you had best bide with us, and still show your ensign," Sir Nigel answered; "for, if I understand the matter aright, we have but turned from one danger to the other."

"Good Master Hawtayne," cried the boatswain, rushing aft, "the water comes in upon us apace. The waves have driven in the sail wherewith we strove to stop the hole." As he spoke the seamen came swarming on to the poop and the forecastle to avoid the torrent which poured through the huge leak into the waist. High above the roar of the wind and the clash of the sea rose the shrill half-human cries of the horses, as they found the water rising rapidly around them.

"Stop it from without!" cried Hawtayne, seizing the end of the wet sail with which the gap had been plugged. "Speedily, my hearts, or we are gone!" Swiftly they rove ropes to the corners, and then, rushing forward to the bows, they lowered them under the keel, and drew them tight in such a way that the sail should cover the outer face of the gap. The force of the rush of water was checked by this obstacle, but it still squirted plentifully from every side of it. At the sides the horses were above the belly, and in the centre a man from the poop could scarce touch the deck with a seven-foot spear. The cog lay lower in the water and the waves splashed freely over the weather bulwark.

"I fear that we can scarce bide upon this tack," cried Hawtayne; "and yet the other will drive us on the rocks."

"Might we not haul down sail and wait for better times?" suggested Sir Nigel.

"Nay, we should drift upon the rocks. Thirty years have I been on the sea, and never yet in greater straits. Yet we are in the hands of the Saints."

"Of whom," cried Sir Oliver, "I look more particularly to St. James of Compostella, who hath already befriended us this day, and on whose feast I hereby vow that I shall eat a second carp, if he will but interpose a second time."

The wrack had thickened to seaward, and the coast was but a blurred line. Two vague shadows in the offing showed where the galeasses rolled and tossed upon the great Atlantic rollers. Hawtayne looked wistfully in their direction.

"If they would but lie closer we might find safety, even should the cog founder. You will bear me out with good Master Witherton of Southampton that I have done all that a shipman might. It would be well that you should doff camail and greaves, Sir Nigel, for, by the black rood! it is like enough that we shall have to swim for it."

"Nay," said the little knight, "it would be scarce fitting that a cavalier should throw off his harness for the fear of every puff of wind and puddle of water. I would rather that my Company should gather round me here on the poop, where we might abide together whatever God may be pleased to send. But, certes, Master Hawtayne, for all that my sight is none of the best, it is not the first time that I have seen that headland upon the left."

The seaman shaded his eyes with his hand, and gazed earnestly through the haze and spray. Suddenly he threw up his arms and shouted aloud in his joy.

"'Tis the point of La Tremblade!" he cried. "I had not thought that we were as far as Oleron. The Gironde lies before us, and once over the bar, and under shelter of the Tour de Cordouan, all will be well with us. Veer again, my hearts, and bring her to try with the main course!"

The sail swung round once more, and the cog, battered and torn and well-nigh water-logged, staggered in for this haven of refuge. A bluff cape to the north and a long spit to the south marked the mouth of the noble river, with a low-lying island of silted sand in the centre, all shrouded and curtained by the spume of the breakers. A line of broken water traced the dangerous bar, which in clear day and balmy weather has cracked the back of many a tall ship.

"There is a channel," said Hawtayne, "which was shown to me by the Prince's own pilot. Mark yonder tree upon the bank, and see the tower which rises behind it. If these two be held in a line, even as we hold them now, it may be done, though our ship draws two good ells more than when she put forth."

"God speed you, Master Hawtayne!" cried Sir Oliver. "Twice have we come scathless out of peril, and now for the third time I commend me to the blessed James of Compostella, to whom I vow——"

"Nay, nay, old friend," whispered Sir Nigel. "You are like to bring a judgment upon us with these vows, which no living man could accomplish. Have I not already heard you vow to eat two carp in one day, and now you would venture upon a third?"

"I pray you that you will order the Company to lie down," cried Hawtayne, who had taken the tiller and was gazing ahead with a fixed eye. "In three minutes we shall either be lost or in safety."

Archers and seamen lay flat upon the deck, waiting in stolid silence for whatever fate might come. Hawtayne bent his weight upon the tiller, and crouched to see under the bellying sail. Sir Oliver and Sir Nigel stood erect with hands crossed in front of the poop. Down swooped the great cog into the narrow channel which was the portal to safety. On either bow roared the shallow bar. Right ahead one small lane of black swirling water marked the pilot's course. But true was the eye and firm the hand which guided. A dull scraping came from beneath, the vessel quivered and shook, at the waist, at the quarter, and behind sounded that grim roaring of the waters, and with a plunge the yellow cog was over the bar and speeding swiftly up the broad and tranquil estuary of the Gironde.

XVIII

How Sir Nigel Loring Put a Patch Upon His Eye

It was on the morning of Friday, the eight-and-twentieth day of November, two days before the feast of St. Andrew, that the cog and her two prisoners, after a weary tacking up the Gironde and the Garonne, dropped anchor at last in front of the noble city of Bordeaux. With wonder and admiration, Alleyne, leaning over the bulwarks, gazed at the forest of masts, the swarm of boats darting hither and thither on the bosom of the broad curving stream, and the gray crescent-shaped city which stretched with many a tower and minaret along the western shore. Never had he in his quiet life seen so great a town, nor was there in the whole of England, save London alone, one which might match it in size or in wealth. Here came the merchandise of all the fair countries which are watered by the Garonne and the Dordogne—the cloths of the south, the skins of Guienne, the wines of the Medoc—to be borne away to Hull, Exeter, Dartmouth, Bristol or Chester, in exchange for the wools and woolfels of England. Here too dwelt those famous smelters and welders who had made the Bordeaux steel the most trusty upon earth, and could give a temper to lance or to sword which might mean dear life to its owner. Alleyne could see the smoke of their forges reeking up in the clear morning air. The storm had died down now to a gentle breeze, which wafted to his ears the long-drawn stirring bugle-calls which sounded from the ancient ramparts.

"Hola, mon petit!" said Aylward, coming up to where he stood. "Thou art a squire now, and like enough to win the golden spurs, while I am still the master-bowman, and master-bowman I shall bide. I dare scarce wag my tongue so freely with you as when we tramped together past Wilverley Chase, else I might be your guide now, for indeed I know every house in Bordeaux as a friar knows the beads on his rosary."

"Nay, Aylward," said Alleyne, laying his hand upon the sleeve of his companion's frayed jerkin, "you cannot think me so thrall as to throw aside an old friend because I have had some small share of good fortune. I take it unkind that you should have thought such evil of me."

"Nay, mon gar. 'Twas but a flight shot to see if the wind blew steady, though I were a rogue to doubt it."

"Why, had I not met you, Aylward, at the Lynhurst inn, who can say where I had now been! Certes, I had not gone to Twynham Castle, nor become squire to Sir Nigel, nor met——" He paused abruptly and flushed to his hair, but the bowman was too busy with his own thoughts to notice his young companion's embarrassment.

"It was a good hostel, that of the 'Pied Merlin,'" he remarked. "By my ten finger bones! when I hang bow on nail and change my brigandine for a tunic, I might do worse than take over the dame and her business."

"I thought," said Alleyne, "that you were betrothed to some one at Christchurch."

"To three," Aylward answered moodily, "to three. I fear I may not go back to Christchurch. I might chance to see hotter service in Hampshire than I have ever done in Gascony. But mark you now yonder lofty turret in the centre, which stands back from the river and hath a broad banner upon the summit. See the rising sun flashes full upon it and sparkles on the golden lions. 'Tis the royal banner of England, crossed by the prince's label. There he dwells in the Abbey of St. Andrew, where he hath kept his court these years back. Beside it is the minster of the same saint, who hath the town under his very special care."

"And how of yon gray turret on the left?"

"'Tis the fane of St. Michael, as that upon the right is of St. Remi. There, too, above the poop of yonder nief, you see the towers of Saint Croix and of Pey Berland. Mark also the mighty ramparts which are pierced by the three water-gates, and sixteen others to the landward side."

"And how is it, good Aylward, that there comes so much music from the town? I seem to hear a hundred trumpets, all calling in chorus."

"It would be strange else, seeing that all the great lords of England and of Gascony are within the walls, and each would have his trumpeter blow as loud as his neighbor, lest it might be thought that his dignity had been abated. Ma foi! they make as much louster as a Scotch army, where every man fills himself with girdle-cakes, and sits up all night to blow upon the toodle-pipe. See all along the banks how the pages water the horses, and there beyond the town how they gallop them over the plain! For every horse you see a belted knight hath herbergage in the town, for, as I learn, the men-at-arms and archers have already gone forward to Dax."

"I trust, Aylward," said Sir Nigel, coming upon deck, "that the men are ready for the land. Go tell them that the boats will be for them within the hour."

The archer raised his hand in salute, and hastened forward. In the meantime Sir Oliver had followed his brother knight, and the two paced the poop together, Sir Nigel in his plum-colored velvet suit with flat cap of the same, adorned in front with the Lady Loring's glove and girt round with a curling ostrich feather. The lusty knight, on the other hand, was clad in the very latest mode, with cote-hardie, doublet, pourpoint, court-pie, and paltock of olive-green, picked out with pink and jagged at the edges. A red chaperon or cap, with long hanging cornette, sat daintily on the back of his black-curled head, while his gold-hued shoes were twisted up *a la poulaine*, as though the toes were shooting forth a tendril which might hope in time to entwine itself around his massive leg.

"Once more, Sir Oliver," said Sir Nigel, looking shorewards with sparkling eyes, "do we find ourselves at the gate of honor, the door which hath so often led us to all that is knightly and worthy. There flies the prince's banner, and it would be well that we haste ashore and pay our obeisance to him. The boats already swarm from the bank."

"There is a goodly hostel near the west gate, which is famed for the stewing of spiced pullets," remarked Sir Oliver. "We might take the edge of our hunger off ere we seek the prince, for though his tables are gay with damask and silver he is no trencherman himself, and hath no sympathy for those who are his betters."

"His betters!"

"His betters before the tranchoir, lad. Sniff not treason where none is meant. I have seen him smile in his quiet way because I had looked for the fourth time towards the carving squire. And indeed to watch him dallying with a little gobbet of bread, or sipping his cup of thrice-watered wine, is enough to make a man feel shame at his own hunger. Yet war and glory, my good friend, though well enough in their way, will not serve to tighten such a belt as clasps my waist."

"How read you that coat which hangs over yonder galley, Alleyne?" asked Sir Nigel.

"Argent, a bend vert between cotises dancette gules."

"It is a northern coat. I have seen it in the train of the Percies. From the shields, there is not one of these vessels which hath not knight or baron aboard. I would mine eyes were better. How read you this upon the left?"

"Argent and azure, a barry wavy of six."

"Ha, it is the sign of the Wiltshire Stourtons! And there beyond I see the red and silver of the Worsleys of Apuldercombe, who like myself are of Hampshire lineage. Close behind us is the moline cross of the gallant William Molyneux, and beside it the bloody chevrons of the Norfork Woodhouses, with the amulets of the Musgraves of Westmoreland. By St. Paul! it would be a very strange thing if so noble a company were to gather without some notable deed of arms arising from it. And here is our boat, Sir Oliver, so it seems best to me that we should go to the abbey with our squires, leaving Master Hawtayne to have his own way in the unloading."

The horses both of knights and squires were speedily lowered into a broad lighter, and reached the shore almost as soon as their masters. Sir Nigel bent his knee devoutly as he put foot on land, and taking a small black patch from his bosom he bound it tightly over his left eye.

"May the blessed George and the memory of my sweet lady-love raise high my heart!" quoth he. "And as a token I vow that I will not take this patch from my eye until I have seen something of this country of Spain, and done such a small deed as it lies in me to do. And this I swear upon the cross of my sword and upon the glove of my lady."

"In truth, you take me back twenty years, Nigel," quoth Sir Oliver, as they mounted and rode slowly through the water-gate. "After Cadsand, I deem that the French thought that we were an army of the blind, for there was scarce a man who had not closed an eye for the greater love and honor of his lady. Yet it goes hard with you that you should darken one side, when with both open you can scarce tell a horse from a mule. In truth, friend, I think that you step over the line of reason in this matter."

"Sir Oliver Buttesthorn," said the little knight shortly, "I would have you to understand that, blind as I am, I can yet see the path of honor very clearly, and that that is the road upon which I do not crave another man's guidance."

"By my soul," said Sir Oliver, "you are as tart as verjuice this morning! If you are bent upon a quarrel with me I must leave you to your humor and drop into the 'Tete d'Or' here, for I marked a varlet pass the door who bare a smoking dish, which had, methought, a most excellent smell."

"Nenny, nenny," cried his comrade, laying his hand upon his knee; "we have known each other over long to fall out, Oliver, like two raw pages at their first epreuves. You must come with me first to the prince, and then back to the hostel; though sure I am that it would grieve his heart that any gentle cavalier should turn from his board to a common tavern. But is not that my Lord Delewar who waves to us? Ha! my fair lord, God and Our Lady be with you! And there is Sir Robert Cheney. Good-morrow, Robert! I am right glad to see you."

The two knights walked their horses abreast, while Alleyne and Ford, with John Norbury, who was squire to Sir Oliver, kept some paces behind them, a spear's-length in front of Black Simon and of the Winchester guidon-bearer. Norbury, a lean, silent man, had been to those parts before, and sat his horse with a rigid neck; but the two young squires gazed eagerly to right or left, and plucked each other's sleeves to call attention to the many strange things on every side of them.

"See to the brave stalls!" cried Alleyne. "See to the noble armor set forth, and the costly taffeta—and oh, Ford, see to where the scrivener sits with the pigments and the ink-horns, and the rolls of sheepskin as white as the Beaulieu napery! Saw man ever the like before?"

"Nay, man, there are finer stalls in Cheapside," answered Ford, whose father had taken him to London on occasion of one of the Smithfield joustings. "I have seen a silversmith's booth there which would serve to buy either side of this street. But mark these houses, Alleyne, how they thrust forth upon the top. And see to the coats-of-arms at every window, and banner or pensil on the roof."

"And the churches!" cried Alleyne. "The Priory at Christchurch was a noble pile, but it was cold and bare, methinks, by one of these, with their frettings, and their carvings, and their traceries, as though some great ivy-plant of stone had curled and wantoned over the walls."

"And hark to the speech of the folk!" said Ford. "Was ever such a hissing and clacking? I wonder that they have not wit to learn English now that they have come under the English crown. By Richard of Hampole! there are fair faces amongst them. See the wench with the brown whimple! Out on you, Alleyne, that you would rather gaze upon dead stone than on living flesh!"

It was little wonder that the richness and ornament, not only of church and of stall, but of every private house as well, should have impressed itself upon the young squires. The town was now at the height of its fortunes. Besides its trade and its armorers, other causes had combined to pour wealth into it. War, which had wrought evil upon so many fair cities around, had brought nought but good to this one. As her French sisters decayed she increased, for here, from north, and from east, and from south, came the plunder to be sold and the ransom money to be spent. Through all her sixteen landward gates there had set for many years a double tide of empty-handed soldiers hurrying Francewards, and of enriched and laden bands who brought their spoils home. The prince's court, too, with its swarm of noble barons and wealthy knights, many of whom, in imitation of their master, had brought their ladies and their children from England, all helped to swell the coffers of the burghers. Now, with this fresh influx of noblemen and cavaliers, food and lodging were scarce to be had, and the prince was hurrying forward his forces to Dax in Gascony to relieve the overcrowding of his capital.

In front of the minster and abbey of St. Andrew's was a large square crowded with priests, soldiers, women, friars, and burghers, who made it their common centre for sight-seeing and gossip. Amid the knot of noisy and gesticulating townsfolk, many small parties of mounted knights and squires threaded their way towards the prince's quarters, where the huge iron-clamped doors were thrown back to show that he held audience within. Two-score archers stood about the gateway, and beat back from time to time with their bow-staves the inquisitive and chattering crowd who swarmed round the portal. Two knights in full armor, with lances raised and closed visors, sat their horses on either side, while in the centre, with two pages to tend upon him, there stood a noble-faced man in flowing purple gown, who pricked off upon a sheet of parchment the style and title of each applicant, marshalling them in their due order, and giving to each the place and facility which his rank demanded. His long white beard and searching eyes imparted to him an air of masterful dignity, which was increased by his tabardlike vesture and the heraldic barret cap with triple plume which bespoke his office.

"It is Sir William de Pakington, the prince's own herald and scrivener," whispered Sir Nigel, as they pulled up amid the line of knights who waited admission. "Ill fares it with the man who would venture to deceive him. He hath by rote the name of every knight of France or of England; and all the tree of his family, with his kinships, coat-armor, marriages, augmentations, abatements, and I know not what beside. We may leave our horses here with the varlets, and push forward with our squires."

Following Sir Nigel's counsel, they pressed on upon foot until they were close to the prince's secretary, who was in high debate with a young and foppish knight, who was bent upon making his way past him.

"Mackworth!" said the king-at-arms. "It is in my mind, young sir, that you have not been presented before."

"Nay, it is but a day since I set foot in Bordeaux, but I feared lest the prince should think it strange that I had not waited upon him."

"The prince hath other things to think upon," quoth Sir William de Pakington; "but if you be a Mackworth you must be a Mackworth of Normanton, and indeed I see now that your coat is sable and ermine."

"I am a Mackworth of Normanton," the other answered, with some uneasiness of manner.

"Then you must be Sir Stephen Mackworth, for I learn that when old Sir Guy died he came in for the arms and the name, the war-cry and the profit."

"Sir Stephen is my elder brother, and I am Arthur, the second son," said the youth.

"In sooth and in sooth!" cried the king-at-arms with scornful eyes. "And pray, sir second son, where is the cadency mark which should mark your rank. Dare you to wear your brother's coat without the crescent which should stamp you as his cadet. Away to your lodgings, and come not nigh the prince until the armorer hath placed the true charge upon your shield." As the youth withdrew in confusion, Sir William's keen eye singled out the five red roses from amid the overlapping shields and cloud of pennons which faced him.

"Ha!" he cried, "there are charges here which are above counterfeit. The roses of Loring and the boar's head of Buttesthorn may stand back in peace, but by my faith! they are not to be held back in war. Welcome, Sir Oliver, Sir Nigel! Chandos will be glad to his very heart-roots when he sees you. This way, my fair sirs. Your squires are doubtless worthy the fame of their masters. Down this passage, Sir Oliver! Edricson! Ha! one of the old strain of Hampshire Edricsons, I doubt not. And Ford, they are of a south Saxon stock, and of good repute. There are Norburys in Cheshire and in Wiltshire, and also, as I have heard, upon the borders. So, my fair sirs, and I shall see that you are shortly admitted."

He had finished his professional commentary by flinging open a folding door, and ushering the party into a broad hall, which was filled with a great number of people who were waiting, like themselves, for an audience. The room was very spacious, lighted on one side by three arched and mullioned windows, while opposite was a huge fireplace in which a pile of faggots was blazing merrily. Many of the company had crowded round the flames, for the weather was bitterly cold; but the two knights seated themselves upon a bancal, with their squires standing behind them. Looking down the room, Alleyne marked that both floor and ceiling were of the richest oak, the latter spanned by twelve arching beams, which were adorned at either end by the lilies and the lions of the royal arms. On the further side was a small door, on each side of which stood men-at-arms. From time to time an elderly man in black with rounded shoulders and a long white wand in his hand came softly forth from this inner room, and beckoned to one or other of the company, who doffed cap and followed him.

The two knights were deep in talk, when Alleyne became aware of a remarkable individual who was walking round the room in their direction. As he passed each knot of cavaliers every head turned to look after him, and it was evident, from the bows and respectful salutations on all sides, that the interest which he excited was not due merely to his strange personal appearance. He was tall and straight as a lance, though of a great age, for his hair, which curled from under his velvet cap of maintenance, was as white as the new-fallen snow. Yet, from the swing of his stride and the spring of his step, it was clear that he had not yet lost the fire and activity of his youth. His fierce hawk-like face was clean shaven like that of a priest, save for a long thin wisp of white moustache which drooped down half way to his shoulder. That he had been handsome might be easily judged from his high aquiline nose and clear-cut chin; but his features had been so distorted by the seams and scars of old wounds, and by the loss of one eye which had been torn from the socket, that there was little left to remind one of the dashing young knight who had been fifty years ago the fairest as well as the boldest of the English chivalry. Yet what knight was there in that hall of St. Andrew's who would not have gladly laid down youth, beauty, and all that he possessed to win the fame of this man? For who could be named with Chandos, the stainless knight, the wise councillor, the valiant warrior, the hero of Crecy, of Winchelsea, of Poictiers, of Auray, and of as many other battles as there were years to his life?

"Ha, my little heart of gold!" he cried, darting forward suddenly and throwing his arms round Sir Nigel. "I heard that you were here and have been seeking you."

"My fair and dear lord," said the knight, returning the warrior's embrace, "I have indeed come back to you, for where else shall I go that I may learn to be a gentle and a hardy knight?"

"By my troth!" said Chandos with a smile, "it is very fitting that we should be companions, Nigel, for since you have tied up one of your eyes, and I have had the mischance to lose one of mine, we have but a pair between us. Ah, Sir Oliver! you were on the blind side of me and I saw you not. A wise woman hath made prophecy that this blind side will one day be the death of me. We shall go in to the prince anon; but in truth he hath much upon his hands, for what with Pedro, and the King of Majorca, and the King of Navarre, who is no two days of the same mind, and the Gascon barons who are all chaffering for terms like so many hucksters, he hath an uneasy part to play. But how left you the Lady Loring?"

"She was well, my fair lord, and sent her service and greetings to you."

"I am ever her knight and slave. And your journey, I trust that it was pleasant?"

"As heart could wish. We had sight of two rover galleys, and even came to have some slight bickering with them."

"Ever in luck's way, Nigel!" quoth Sir John. "We must hear the tale anon. But I deem it best that ye should leave your squires and come with me, for, howsoe'er pressed the prince may be, I am very sure that he would be loth to keep two old comrades-in-arms upon the further side of the door. Follow close behind me, and I will forestall old Sir William, though I can scarce promise to roll forth your style and rank as is his wont." So saying, he led the way to the inner chamber, the two companions treading close at his heels, and nodding to right and left as they caught sight of familiar faces among the crowd.

XIX

How There Was Stir at the Abbey of St. Andrew's

The prince's reception-room, although of no great size, was fitted up with all the state and luxury which the fame and power of its owner demanded. A high dais at the further end was roofed in by a broad canopy of scarlet velvet spangled with silver fleurs-de-lis, and supported at either corner by silver rods. This was approached by four steps carpeted with the same material, while all round were scattered rich cushions, oriental mats and costly rugs of fur. The choicest tapestries which the looms of Arras could furnish draped the walls, whereon the battles of Judas Maccabaeus were set forth, with the Jewish warriors in plate of proof, with crest and lance and banderole, as the naive artists of the day were wont to depict them. A few rich settles and bancals, choicely carved and decorated with glazed leather hangings of the sort termed *or basane*, completed the furniture of the apartment, save that at one side of the dais there stood a lofty perch, upon which a cast of three solemn Prussian gerfalcons sat, hooded and jesseled, as silent and motionless as the royal fowler who stood beside them.

In the centre of the dais were two very high chairs with dorserets, which arched forwards over the heads of the occupants, the whole covered with light-blue silk thickly powdered with golden stars. On that to the right sat a very tall and well formed man with red hair, a livid face, and a cold blue eye, which had in it something peculiarly sinister and menacing. He lounged back in a careless position, and yawned repeatedly as though heartily weary of the proceedings, stooping from time to time to fondle a shaggy Spanish greyhound which lay stretched at his feet. On the other throne there was perched bolt upright, with prim demeanor, as though he felt himself to be upon his good behavior, a little, round, pippin faced person, who smiled and bobbed to every one whose eye he chanced to meet. Between and a little in front of them on a humble charette or stool, sat a slim, dark young man, whose quiet attire and modest manner would scarce proclaim him to be the most noted prince in Europe. A jupon of dark blue cloth, tagged with buckles and pendants of gold, seemed but a sombre and plain attire amidst the wealth of silk and ermine and gilt tissue of fustian with which he was surrounded. He sat with his two hands clasped round his knee, his head slightly bent, and an expression of impatience and of trouble upon his clear, well-chiselled features. Behind the thrones there stood two men in purple gowns, with ascetic, clean-shaven faces, and half a dozen other high dignitaries and office-holders of Aquitaine. Below on either side of the steps were forty or fifty barons, knights, and courtiers, ranged in a triple row to the right and the left, with a clear passage in the centre.

"There sits the prince," whispered Sir John Chandos, as they entered. "He on the right is Pedro, whom we are about to put upon the Spanish throne. The other is Don James, whom we purpose with the aid of God to help to his throne in Majorca. Now follow me, and take it not to heart if he be a little short in his speech, for indeed his mind is full of many very weighty concerns."

The prince, however, had already observed their entrance, and, springing to his feet, he had advanced with a winning smile and the light of welcome in his eyes.

"We do not need your good offices as herald here, Sir John," said he in a low but clear voice; "these valiant knights are very well known to me. Welcome to Aquitaine, Sir Nigel Loring and Sir Oliver Buttesthorn. Nay, keep your knee for my sweet father at Windsor. I would have your hands, my friends. We are like to give you some work to do ere you see the downs of Hampshire once more. Know you aught of Spain, Sir Oliver?"

"Nought, my sire, save that I have heard men say that there is a dish named an olla which is prepared there, though I have never been clear in my mind as to whether it was but a ragout such as is to be found in the south, or whether there is some seasoning such as fennel or garlic which is peculiar to Spain."

"Your doubts, Sir Oliver, shall soon be resolved," answered the prince, laughing heartily, as did many of the barons who surrounded them. "His majesty here will doubtless order that you have this dish hotly seasoned when we are all safely in Castile."

"I will have a hotly seasoned dish for some folk I know of," answered Don Pedro with a cold smile.

"But my friend Sir Oliver can fight right hardily without either bite or sup," remarked the prince. "Did I not see him at Poictiers, when for two days we had not more than a crust of bread and a cup of foul water, yet carrying himself most valiantly. With my own eyes I saw him in the rout sweep the head from a knight of Picardy with one blow of his sword."

"The rogue got between me and the nearest French victual wain," muttered Sir Oliver, amid a fresh titter from those who were near enough to catch his words.

"How many have you in your train?" asked the prince, assuming a graver mien.

"I have forty men-at-arms, sire," said Sir Oliver.

"And I have one hundred archers and a score of lancers, but there are two hundred men who wait for me on this side of the water upon the borders of Navarre."

"And who are they, Sir Nigel?"

"They are a free company, sire, and they are called the White Company."

To the astonishment of the knight, his words provoked a burst of merriment from the barons round, in which the two kings and the prince were fain to join. Sir Nigel blinked mildly from one to the other, until at last perceiving a stout black-bearded knight at his elbow, whose laugh rang somewhat louder than the others, he touched him lightly upon the sleeve.

"Perchance, my fair sir," he whispered, "there is some small vow of which I may relieve you. Might we not have some honorable debate upon the matter. Your gentle courtesy may perhaps grant me an exchange of thrusts."

"Nay, nay, Sir Nigel," cried the prince, "fasten not the offence upon Sir Robert Briquet, for we are one and all bogged in the same mire. Truth to say, our ears have just been vexed by the doings of the same company, and I have even now made vow to hang the man who held the rank of captain over it. I little thought to find him among the bravest of my own chosen chieftains. But the vow is now nought, for, as you have never seen your company, it would be a fool's act to blame you for their doings."

"My liege," said Sir Nigel, "it is a very small matter that I should be hanged, albeit the manner of death is somewhat more ignoble than I had hoped for. On the other hand, it would be a very grievous thing that you, the Prince of England and the flower of knighthood, should make a vow, whether in ignorance or no, and fail to bring it to fulfilment."

"Vex not your mind on that," the prince answered, smiling. "We have had a citizen from Montauban here this very day, who told us such a tale of sack and murder and pillage that it moved our blood; but our wrath was turned upon the man who was in authority over them."

"My dear and honored master," cried Nigel, in great anxiety, "I fear me much that in your gentleness of heart you are straining this vow which you have taken. If there be so much as a shadow of a doubt as to the form of it, it were a thousand times best——"

"Peace! peace!" cried the prince impatiently. "I am very well able to look to my own vows and their performance. We hope to see you both in the banquet-hall anon. Meanwhile you will attend upon us with our train." He bowed, and Chandos, plucking Sir Oliver by the sleeve, led them both away to the back of the press of courtiers.

"Why, little coz," he whispered, "you are very eager to have your neck in a noose. By my soul! had you asked as much from our new ally Don Pedro, he had not baulked you. Between friends, there is overmuch of the hangman in him, and too little of the prince. But indeed this White Company is a rough band, and may take some handling ere you find yourself safe in your captaincy."

"I doubt not, with the help of St. Paul, that I shall bring them to some order," Sir Nigel answered. "But there are many faces here which are new to me, though others have been before me since first I waited upon my dear master, Sir Walter. I pray you to tell me, Sir John, who are these priests upon the dais?"

"The one is the Archbishop of Bordeaux, Nigel, and the other the Bishop of Agen."

"And the dark knight with gray-streaked beard? By my troth, he seems to be a man of much wisdom and valor."

"He is Sir William Felton, who, with my unworthy self, is the chief counsellor of the prince, he being high steward and I the seneschal of Aquitaine."

"And the knights upon the right, beside Don Pedro?"

"They are cavaliers of Spain who have followed him in his exile. The one at his elbow is Fernando de Castro, who is as brave and true a man as heart could wish. In front to the right are the Gascon lords. You may well tell them by their clouded brows, for there hath been some ill-will of late betwixt the prince and them. The tall and burly man is the Captal de Buch, whom I doubt not that you know, for a braver knight never laid lance in rest. That heavy-faced cavalier who plucks his skirts and whispers in his ear is Lord Oliver de Clisson, known also as the butcher. He it is who stirs up strife, and forever blows the dying embers into flame. The man with the mole upon his cheek is the Lord Pommers, and his two brothers stand behind him, with the Lord Lesparre, Lord de Rosem, Lord de Mucident, Sir Perducas d'Albret, the Souldich de la Trane, and others. Further back are knights from Quercy, Limousin, Saintonge, Poitou, and Aquitaine, with the valiant Sir Guiscard d'Angle. That is he in the rose-colored doublet with the ermine."

"And the knights upon this side?"

"They are all Englishmen, some of the household and others who like yourself, are captains of companies. There is Lord Neville, Sir Stephen Cossington, and Sir Matthew Gourney, with Sir Walter Huet, Sir Thomas Banaster, and Sir Thomas Felton, who is the brother of the high steward. Mark well the man with the high nose and flaxen beard who hath placed his hand upon the shoulder of the dark hard-faced cavalier in the rust-stained jupon."

"Aye, by St. Paul!" observed Sir Nigel, "they both bear the print of their armor upon their cotes-hardies. Methinks they are men who breathe freer in a camp than a court."

"There are many of us who do that, Nigel," said Chandos, "and the head of the court is, I dare warrant, among them. But of these two men the one is Sir Hugh Calverley, and the other is Sir Robert Knolles."

Sir Nigel and Sir Oliver craned their necks to have the clearer view of these famous warriors, the one a chosen leader of free companies, the other a man who by his fierce valor and energy had raised himself from the lowest ranks until he was second only to Chandos himself in the esteem of the army.

"He hath no light hand in war, hath Sir Robert," said Chandos. "If he passes through a country you may tell it for some years to come. I have heard that in the north it is still the use to call a house which hath but the two gable ends left, without walls or roof, a Knolles' mitre."

"I have often heard of him," said Nigel, "and I have hoped to be so far honored as to run a course with him. But hark, Sir John, what is amiss with the prince?"

Whilst Chandos had been conversing with the two knights a continuous stream of suitors had been ushered in, adventurers seeking to sell their swords and merchants clamoring over some grievance, a ship detained for the carriage of troops, or a tun of sweet wine which had the bottom knocked out by a troop of thirsty archers. A few words from the prince disposed of each case, and, if the applicant liked not the judgment, a quick glance from the prince's dark eyes sent him to the door with the grievance all gone out of him. The younger ruler had sat listlessly upon his stool with the two puppet monarchs enthroned behind him, but of a sudden a dark shadow passed over his face, and he sprang to his feet in one of those gusts of passion which were the single blot upon his noble and generous character.

"How now, Don Martin de la Carra?" he cried. "How now, sirrah? What message do you bring to us from our brother of Navarre?"

The new-comer to whom this abrupt query had been addressed was a tall and exceedingly handsome cavalier who had just been ushered into the apartment. His swarthy cheek and raven black hair spoke of the fiery south, and he wore his long black cloak swathed across his chest and over his shoulders in a graceful sweeping fashion, which was neither English nor French. With stately steps and many profound bows, he advanced to the foot of the dais before replying to the prince's question.

"My powerful and illustrious master," he began, "Charles, King of Navarre, Earl of Evreux, Count of Champagne, who also writeth himself Overlord of Bearn, hereby sends his love and greetings to his dear cousin Edward, the Prince of Wales, Governor of Aquitaine, Grand Commander of——"

"Tush! tush! Don Martin!" interrupted the prince, who had been beating the ground with his foot impatiently during this stately preamble. "We already know our cousin's titles and style, and, certes, we know our own. To the point, man, and at once. Are the passes open to us, or does your master go back from his word pledged to me at Libourne no later than last Michaelmas?"

"It would ill become my gracious master, sire, to go back from promise given. He does but ask some delay and certain conditions and hostages——"

"Conditions! Hostages! Is he speaking to the Prince of England, or is it to the bourgeois provost of some half-captured town! Conditions, quotha? He may find much to mend in his own condition ere long. The passes are, then, closed to us?"

"Nay, sire——"

"They are open, then?"

"Nay, sire, if you would but——"

"Enough, enough, Don Martin," cried the prince. "It is a sorry sight to see so true a knight pleading in so false a cause. We know the doings of our cousin Charles. We know that while with the right hand he takes our fifty thousand crowns for the holding of the passes open, he hath his left outstretched to Henry of Trastamare, or to the King of France, all ready to take as many more for the keeping them closed. I know our good Charles, and, by my blessed name-saint the Confessor, he shall learn that I know him. He sets his kingdom up to the best bidder, like some scullion farrier selling a glandered horse. He is——"

"My lord," cried Don Martin, "I cannot stand there to hear such words of my master. Did they come from other lips, I should know better how to answer them."

Don Pedro frowned and curled his lip, but the prince smiled and nodded his approbation.

"Your bearing and your words, Don Martin, are such I should have looked for in you," he remarked. "You will tell the king, your master, that he hath been paid his price and that if he holds to his promise he hath my word for it that no scath shall come to his people, nor to their houses or gear. If, however, we have not his leave, I shall come close at the heels of this message without his leave, and bearing a key with me which shall open all that he may close." He stooped and whispered to Sir Robert Knolles and Sir Huge Calverley, who smiled as men well pleased, and hastened from the room.

"Our cousin Charles has had experience of our friendship," the prince continued, "and now, by the Saints! he shall feel a touch of our displeasure. I send now a message to our cousin Charles which his whole kingdom may read. Let him take heed lest worse befall him. Where is my Lord Chandos? Ha, Sir John, I commend this worthy knight to your care. You will see that he hath refection, and such a purse of gold as may defray his charges, for indeed it is great honor to any court to have within it so noble and gentle a cavalier. How say you, sire?" he asked, turning to the Spanish refugee, while the herald of Navarre was conducted from the chamber by the old warrior.

"It is not our custom in Spain to reward pertness in a messenger," Don Pedro answered, patting the head of his greyhound. "Yet we have all heard the lengths to which your royal generosity runs."

"In sooth, yes," cried the King of Majorca.

"Who should know it better than we?" said Don Pedro bitterly, "since we have had to fly to you in our trouble as to the natural protector of all who are weak."

"Nay, nay, as brothers to a brother," cried the prince, with sparkling eyes. "We doubt not, with the help of God, to see you very soon restored to those thrones from which you have been so traitorously thrust."

"When that happy day comes," said Pedro, "then Spain shall be to you as Aquitaine, and, be your project what it may, you may ever count on every troop and every ship over which flies the banner of Castile."

"And," added the other, "upon every aid which the wealth and power of Majorca can bestow."

"Touching the hundred thousand crowns in which I stand your debtor," continued Pedro carelessly, "it can no doubt——"

"Not a word, sire, not a word!" cried the prince. "It is not now when you are in grief that I would vex your mind with such base and sordid matters. I have said once and forever that I am yours with every bow-string of my army and every florin in my coffers."

"Ah! here is indeed a mirror of chivalry," said Don Pedro. "I think, Sir Fernando, since the prince's bounty is stretched so far, that we may make further use of his gracious goodness to the extent of fifty thousand crowns. Good Sir William Felton, here, will doubtless settle the matter with you."

The stout old English counsellor looked somewhat blank at this prompt acceptance of his master's bounty.

"If it please you, sire," he said, "the public funds are at their lowest, seeing that I have paid twelve thousand men of the companies, and the new taxes—the hearth-tax and the wine-tax—not yet come in. If you could wait until the promised help from England comes——"

"Nay, nay, my sweet cousin," cried Don Pedro. "Had we known that your own coffers were so low, or that this sorry sum could have weighed one way or the other, we had been loth indeed——"

"Enough, sire, enough!" said the prince, flushing with vexation. "If the public funds be, indeed, so backward, Sir William, there is still, I trust, my own private credit, which hath never been drawn upon for my own uses, but is now ready in the cause of a friend in adversity. Go, raise this money upon our own jewels, if nought else may serve, and see that it be paid over to Don Fernando."

"In security I offer——" cried Don Pedro.

"Tush! tush!" said the prince. "I am not a Lombard, sire. Your kingly pledge is my security, without bond or seal. But I have tidings for you, my lords and lieges, that our brother of Lancaster is on his way for our capital with four hundred lances and as many archers to aid us in our venture. When he hath come, and when our fair consort is recovered in her health, which I trust by the grace of God may be ere many weeks be past, we shall then join the army at Dax, and set our banners to the breeze once more."

A buzz of joy at the prospect of immediate action rose up from the group of warriors. The prince smiled at the martial ardor which shone upon every face around him.

"It will hearten you to know," he continued, "that I have sure advices that this Henry is a very valiant leader, and that he has it in his power to make such a stand against us as promises to give us much honor and pleasure. Of his own people he hath brought together, as I learn, some fifty thousand, with twelve thousand of the French free companies, who are, as you know very valiant and expert men-at-arms. It is certain also, that the brave and worthy Bertrand de Guesclin hath ridden into France to the Duke of Anjou, and purposes to take back with him great levies from Picardy and Brittany. We hold Bertrand in high esteem, for he has oft before been at great pains to furnish us with an honorable encounter. What think you of it, my worthy Captal? He took you at Cocherel, and, by my soul! you will have the chance now to pay that score."

The Gascon warrior winced a little at the allusion, nor were his countrymen around him better pleased, for on the only occasion when they had encountered the arms of France without English aid they had met with a heavy defeat.

"There are some who say, sire," said the burly De Clisson, "that the score is already overpaid, for that without Gascon help Bertrand had not been taken at Auray, nor had King John been overborne at Poictiers."

"By heaven! but this is too much," cried an English nobleman. "Methinks that Gascony is too small a cock to crow so lustily."

"The smaller cock, my Lord Audley, may have the longer spur," remarked the Captal de Buch.

"May have its comb clipped if it make over-much noise," broke in an Englishman.

"By our Lady of Rocamadour!" cried the Lord of Mucident, "this is more than I can abide. Sir John Charnell, you shall answer to me for those words!"

"Freely, my lord, and when you will," returned the Englishman carelessly.

"My Lord de Clisson," cried Lord Audley, "you look somewhat fixedly in my direction. By God's soul! I should be right glad to go further into the matter with you."

"And you, my Lord of Pommers," said Sir Nigel, pushing his way to the front, "it is in my mind that we might break a lance in gentle and honorable debate over the question."

For a moment a dozen challenges flashed backwards and forwards at this sudden bursting of the cloud which had lowered so long between the knights of the two nations. Furious and gesticulating the Gascons, white and cold and sneering the English, while the prince with a half smile glanced from one party to the other, like a man who loved to dwell upon a fiery scene, and yet dreaded least the mischief go so far that he might find it beyond his control.

"Friends, friends!" he cried at last, "this quarrel must go no further. The man shall answer to me, be he Gascon or English, who carries it beyond this room. I have overmuch need for your swords that you should turn them upon each other. Sir John Charnell, Lord Audley, you do not doubt the courage of our friends of Gascony?"

"Not I, sire," Lord Audley answered. "I have seen them fight too often not to know that they are very hardy and valiant gentlemen."

"And so say I," quoth the other Englishman; "but, certes, there is no fear of our forgetting it while they have a tongue in their heads."

"Nay, Sir John," said the prince reprovingly, "all peoples have their own use and customs. There are some who might call us cold and dull and silent. But you hear, my lords of Gascony, that these gentlemen had no thought to throw a slur upon your honor or your valor, so let all anger fade from your mind. Clisson, Captal, De Pommers, I have your word?"

"We are your subjects, sire," said the Gascon barons, though with no very good grace. "Your words are our law."

"Then shall we bury all cause of unkindness in a flagon of Malvoisie," said the prince, cheerily. "Ho, there! the doors of the banquet-hall! I have been over long from my sweet spouse but I shall be back with you anon. Let the sewers serve and the minstrels play, while we drain a cup to the brave days that are before us in the south!" He turned away, accompanied by the two monarchs, while the rest of the company, with many a compressed lip and menacing eye, filed slowly through the side-door to the great chamber in which the royal tables were set forth.

XX

How Alleyne Won His Place in an Honorable Guild

Whilst the prince's council was sitting, Alleyne and Ford had remained in the outer hall, where they were soon surrounded by a noisy group of young Englishmen of their own rank, all eager to hear the latest news from England.

"How is it with the old man at Windsor?" asked one.

"And how with the good Queen Philippa?"

"And how with Dame Alice Perrers?" cried a third.

"The devil take your tongue, Wat!" shouted a tall young man, seizing the last speaker by the collar and giving him an admonitory shake. "The prince would take your head off for those words."

"By God's coif! Wat would miss it but little," said another. "It is as empty as a beggar's wallet."

"As empty as an English squire, coz," cried the first speaker. "What a devil has become of the maitre-des-tables and his sewers? They have not put forth the trestles yet."

"Mon Dieu! if a man could eat himself into knighthood, Humphrey, you had been a banneret at the least," observed another, amid a burst of laughter.

"And if you could drink yourself in, old leather-head, you had been first baron of the realm," cried the aggrieved Humphrey. "But how of England, my lads of Loring?"

"I take it," said Ford, "that it is much as it was when you were there last, save that perchance there is a little less noise there."

"And why less noise, young Solomon?"

"Ah, that is for your wit to discover."

"Pardieu! here is a paladin come over, with the Hampshire mud still sticking to his shoes. He means that the noise is less for our being out of the country."

"They are very quick in these parts," said Ford, turning to Alleyne.

"How are we to take this, sir?" asked the ruffling squire.

"You may take it as it comes," said Ford carelessly.

"Here is pertness!" cried the other.

"Sir, I honor your truthfulness," said Ford.

"Stint it, Humphrey," said the tall squire, with a burst of laughter. "You will have little credit from this gentleman, I perceive. Tongues are sharp in Hampshire, sir."

"And swords?"

"Hum! we may prove that. In two days' time is the vepres du tournoi, when we may see if your lance is as quick as your wit."

"All very well, Roger Harcomb," cried a burly, bull-necked young man, whose square shoulders and massive limbs told of exceptional personal strength. "You pass too lightly over the matter. We are not to be so easily overcrowed. The Lord Loring hath given his proofs; but we know nothing of his squires, save that one of them hath a railing tongue. And how of you, young sir?" bringing his heavy hand down on Alleyne's shoulder.

"And what of me, young sir?"

"Ma foi! this is my lady's page come over. Your cheek will be browner and your hand harder ere you see your mother again."

"If my hand is not hard, it is ready."

"Ready? Ready for what? For the hem of my lady's train?"

"Ready to chastise insolence, sir," cried Alleyne with flashing eyes.

"Sweet little coz!" answered the burly squire. "Such a dainty color! Such a mellow voice! Eyes of a bashful maid, and hair like a three years' babe! Voila!" He passed his thick fingers roughly through the youth's crisp golden curls.

"You seek to force a quarrel, sir," said the young man, white with anger.

"And what then?"

"Why, you do it like a country boor, and not like a gentle squire. Hast been ill bred and as ill taught. I serve a master who could show you how such things should be done."

"And how would he do it, O pink of squires?"

"He would neither be loud nor would he be unmannerly, but rather more gentle than is his wont. He would say, 'Sir, I should take it as an honor to do some small deed of arms against you, not for mine own glory or advancement, but rather for the fame of my lady and for the upholding of chivalry.' Then he would draw his glove, thus, and throw it on the ground; or, if he had cause to think that he had to deal with a churl, he might throw it in his face—as I do now!"

A buzz of excitement went up from the knot of squires as Alleyne, his gentle nature turned by this causeless attack into fiery resolution, dashed his glove with all his strength into the sneering face of his antagonist. From all parts of the hall squires and pages came running, until a dense, swaying crowd surrounded the disputants.

"Your life for this!" said the bully, with a face which was distorted with rage.

"If you can take it," returned Alleyne.

"Good lad!" whispered Ford. "Stick to it close as wax."

"I shall see justice," cried Norbury, Sir Oliver's silent attendant.

"You brought it upon yourself, John Tranter," said the tall squire, who had been addressed as Roger Harcomb. "You must ever plague the new-comers. But it were shame if this went further. The lad hath shown a proper spirit."

"But a blow! a blow!" cried several of the older squires. "There must be a finish to this."

"Nay; Tranter first laid hand upon his head," said Harcomb. "How say you, Tranter? The matter may rest where it stands?"

"My name is known in these parts," said Tranter, proudly, "I can let pass what might leave a stain upon another. Let him pick up his glove and say that he has done amiss."

"I would see him in the claws of the devil first," whispered Ford.

"You hear, young sir?" said the peacemaker. "Our friend will overlook the matter if you do but say that you have acted in heat and haste."

"I cannot say that," answered Alleyne.

"It is our custom, young sir, when new squires come amongst us from England, to test them in some such way. Bethink you that if a man have a destrier or a new lance he will ever try it in time of peace, lest in days of need it may fail him. How much more then is it proper to test those who are our comrades in arms."

"I would draw out if it may honorably be done," murmured Norbury in Alleyne's ear. "The man is a noted swordsman and far above your strength."

Edricson came, however, of that sturdy Saxon blood which is very slowly heated, but once up not easily to be cooled. The hint of danger which Norbury threw out was the one thing needed to harden his resolution.

"I came here at the back of my master," he said, "and I looked on every man here as an Englishman and a friend. This gentleman hath shown me a rough welcome, and if I have answered him in the same spirit he has but himself to thank. I will pick the glove up; but, certes,

I shall abide what I have done unless he first crave my pardon for what he hath said and done."

Tranter shrugged his shoulders. "You have done what you could to save him, Harcomb," said he. "We had best settle at once."

"So say I," cried Alleyne.

"The council will not break up until the banquet," remarked a gray-haired squire. "You have a clear two hours."

"And the place?"

"The tilting-yard is empty at this hour."

"Nay; it must not be within the grounds of the court, or it may go hard with all concerned if it come to the ears of the prince."

"But there is a quiet spot near the river," said one youth. "We have but to pass through the abbey grounds, along the armory wall, past the church of St. Remi, and so down the Rue des Apotres."

"En avant, then!" cried Tranter shortly, and the whole assembly flocked out into the open air, save only those whom the special orders of their masters held to their posts. These unfortunates crowded to the small casements, and craned their necks after the throng as far as they could catch a glimpse of them.

Close to the banks of the Garonne there lay a little tract of green sward, with the high wall of a prior's garden upon one side and an orchard with a thick bristle of leafless apple-trees upon the other. The river ran deep and swift up to the steep bank; but there were few boats upon it, and the ships were moored far out in the centre of the stream. Here the two combatants drew their swords and threw off their doublets, for neither had any defensive armor. The duello with its stately etiquette had not yet come into vogue, but rough and sudden encounters were as common as they must ever be when hot-headed youth goes abroad with a weapon strapped to its waist. In such combats, as well as in the more formal sports of the tilting-yard, Tranter had won a name for strength and dexterity which had caused Norbury to utter his well-meant warning. On the other hand, Alleyne had used his weapons in constant exercise and practice on every day for many months, and being by nature quick of eye and prompt of hand, he might pass now as no mean swordsman. A strangely opposed pair they appeared as they approached each other: Tranter dark and stout and stiff, with hairy chest and corded arms, Alleyne a model of comeliness and grace, with his golden hair and his skin as fair as a woman's. An unequal fight it seemed to most; but there were a few, and they the most experienced, who saw something in the youth's steady gray eye and wary step which left the issue open to doubt.

"Hold, sirs, hold!" cried Norbury, ere a blow had been struck. "This gentleman hath a two-handed sword, a good foot longer than that of our friend."

"Take mine, Alleyne," said Ford.

"Nay, friends," he answered, "I understand the weight and balance of mine own. To work, sir, for our lord may need us at the abbey!"

Tranter's great sword was indeed a mighty vantage in his favor. He stood with his feet close together, his knees bent outwards, ready for a dash inwards or a spring out. The weapon he held straight up in front of him with blade erect, so that he might either bring it down with a swinging blow, or by a turn of the heavy blade he might guard his own head and body. A further protection lay in the broad and powerful guard which crossed the hilt, and which was furnished with a deep and narrow notch, in which an expert swordsman might catch his foeman's blade, and by a quick turn of his wrist might snap it across. Alleyne, on the other hand, must trust for his defence to his quick eye and active foot—for his sword, though keen as a whetstone could make it, was of a light and graceful build with a narrow, sloping pommel and a tapering steel.

Tranter well knew his advantage and lost no time in putting it to use. As his opponent walked towards him he suddenly bounded forward and sent in a whistling cut which would have severed the other in twain had he not sprung lightly back from it. So close was it that the point ripped a gash in the jutting edge of his linen cyclas. Quick as a panther, Alleyne sprang in with a thrust, but Tranter, who was as active as he was strong, had already recovered himself and turned it aside with a movement of his heavy blade. Again he whizzed in a blow which made the spectators hold their breath, and again Alleyne very quickly and swiftly slipped from under it, and sent back two lightning thrusts which the other could scarce parry. So close were they to each other that Alleyne had no time to spring back from the next cut, which beat down his sword and grazed his forehead, sending the blood streaming into his eyes and down his cheeks. He sprang out beyond sword sweep, and the pair stood breathing heavily, while the crowd of young squires buzzed their applause.

"Bravely struck on both sides!" cried Roger Harcomb. "You have both won honor from this meeting, and it would be sin and shame to let it go further."

"You have done enough, Edricson," said Norbury.

"You have carried yourself well," cried several of the older squires.

"For my part, I have no wish to slay this young man," said Tranter, wiping his heated brow.

"Does this gentleman crave my pardon for having used me despitefully?" asked Alleyne.

"Nay, not I."

"Then stand on your guard, sir!" With a clatter and dash the two blades met once more, Alleyne pressing in so as to keep within the full sweep of the heavy blade, while Tranter as continually sprang back to have space for one of his fatal cuts. A three-parts-parried blow drew blood from Alleyne's left shoulder, but at the same moment he wounded Tranter slightly upon the thigh. Next instant, however, his blade had slipped into the fatal notch, there was a sharp cracking sound with a tinkling upon the ground, and he found a splintered piece of steel fifteen inches long was all that remained to him of his weapon.

"Your life is in my hands!" cried Tranter, with a bitter smile.

"Nay, nay, he makes submission!" broke in several squires.

"Another sword!" cried Ford.

"Nay, sir," said Harcomb, "that is not the custom."

"Throw down your hilt, Edricson," cried Norbury.

"Never!" said Alleyne. "Do you crave my pardon, sir?"

"You are mad to ask it."

"Then on guard again!" cried the young squire, and sprang in with a fire and a fury which more than made up for the shortness of his weapon. It had not escaped him that his opponent was breathing in short, hoarse gasps, like a man who is dizzy with fatigue. Now was the time for the purer living and the more agile limb to show their value. Back and back gave Tranter, ever seeking time for a last cut. On and on came Alleyne, his jagged point now at his foeman's face, now at his throat, now at his chest, still stabbing and thrusting to pass the line of steel which covered him. Yet his experienced foeman knew well that such efforts could not be long sustained. Let him relax for one instant, and his death-blow had come. Relax he must! Flesh and blood could not stand the strain. Already the thrusts were less fierce, the foot less ready, although there was no abatement of the spirit in the steady gray eyes. Tranter, cunning and wary from years of fighting, knew that his chance had come. He brushed aside the frail weapon which was opposed to him, whirled up his great blade, sprang back to get the fairer sweep—and vanished into the waters of the Garonne.

So intent had the squires, both combatants and spectators, been on the matter in hand, that all thought of the steep bank and swift still stream had gone from their minds. It was not until Tranter, giving back before the other's fiery rush, was upon the very brink, that a general cry warned him of his danger. That last spring, which he hoped would have brought the fight to a bloody end, carried him clear of the edge, and he found himself in an instant eight feet deep in the ice-cold stream. Once and twice his gasping face and clutching fingers broke up through the still green water, sweeping outwards in the swirl of the current. In vain were sword-sheaths, apple-branches and belts linked together thrown out to him by his companions. Alleyne had dropped his shattered sword and was standing, trembling in every limb, with his rage all changed in an instant to pity. For the third time the drowning man came to the surface, his hands full of green slimy water-plants, his eyes turned in despair to the shore. Their glance fell upon Alleyne, and he could not withstand the mute appeal which he read in them. In an instant he, too, was in the Garonne, striking out with powerful strokes for his late foeman.

Yet the current was swift and strong, and, good swimmer as he was, it was no easy task which Alleyne had set himself. To clutch at Tranter and to seize him by the hair was the work of a few seconds, but to hold his head above water and to make their way out of the current was another matter. For a hundred strokes he did not seem to gain an inch. Then at last, amid a shout of joy and praise from the bank, they slowly drew clear into more stagnant water, at the instant that a rope, made of a dozen sword-belts linked together by the buckles, was thrown by Ford into their very hands. Three pulls from eager arms, and the two combatants, dripping and pale, were dragged up the bank, and lay panting upon the grass.

John Tranter was the first to come to himself, for although he had been longer in the water, he had done nothing during that fierce battle with the current. He staggered to his feet and looked down upon his rescuer, who had raised himself upon his elbow, and was smiling faintly at the buzz of congratulation and of praise which broke from the squires around him.

"I am much beholden to you, sir," said Tranter, though in no very friendly voice. "Certes, I should have been in the river now but for you, for I was born in Warwickshire, which is but a dry county, and there are few who swim in those parts."

"I ask no thanks," Alleyne answered shortly. "Give me your hand to rise, Ford."

"The river has been my enemy," said Tranter, "but it hath been a good friend to you, for it has saved your life this day."

"That is as it may be," returned Alleyne.

"But all is now well over," quoth Harcomb, "and no scath come of it, which is more than I had at one time hoped for. Our young friend here hath very fairly and honestly earned his right to be craftsman of the Honorable Guild of the Squires of Bordeaux. Here is your doublet, Tranter."

"Alas for my poor sword which lies at the bottom of the Garonne!" said the squire.

"Here is your pourpoint, Edricson," cried Norbury. "Throw it over your shoulders, that you may have at least one dry garment."

"And now away back to the abbey!" said several.

"One moment, sirs," cried Alleyne, who was leaning on Ford's shoulder, with the broken sword, which he had picked up, still clutched in his right hand. "My ears may be somewhat dulled by the water, and perchance what has been said has escaped me, but I have not yet heard this gentleman crave pardon for the insults which he put upon me in the hall."

"What! do you still pursue the quarrel?" asked Tranter.

"And why not, sir? I am slow to take up such things, but once afoot I shall follow it while I have life or breath."

"Ma foi! you have not too much of either, for you are as white as marble," said Harcomb bluntly. "Take my rede, sir, and let it drop, for you have come very well out from it."

"Nay," said Alleyne, "this quarrel is none of my making; but, now that I am here, I swear to you that I shall never leave this spot until I have that which I have come for: so ask my pardon, sir, or choose another glaive and to it again."

The young squire was deadly white from his exertions, both on the land and in the water. Soaking and stained, with a smear of blood on his white shoulder and another on his brow, there was still in his whole pose and set of face the trace of an inflexible resolution. His opponent's duller and more material mind quailed before the fire and intensity of a higher spiritual nature.

"I had not thought that you had taken it so amiss," said he awkwardly. "It was but such a jest as we play upon each other, and, if you must have it so, I am sorry for it."

"Then I am sorry too," quoth Alleyne warmly, "and here is my hand upon it."

"And the none-meat horn has blown three times," quoth Harcomb, as they all streamed in chattering groups from the ground. "I know not what the prince's maitre-de-cuisine will say or think. By my troth! master Ford, your friend here is in need of a cup of wine, for he hath drunk deeply of Garonne water. I had not thought from his fair face that he had stood to this matter so shrewdly."

"Faith," said Ford, "this air of Bordeaux hath turned our turtle-dove into a game-cock. A milder or more courteous youth never came out of Hampshire."

"His master also, as I understand, is a very mild and courteous gentleman," remarked Harcomb; "yet I do not think that they are either of them men with whom it is very safe to trifle."

XXI

How Agostino Pisano Risked His Head

Even the squires' table at the Abbey of St. Andrew's at Bordeaux was on a very sumptuous scale while the prince held his court there. Here first, after the meagre fare of Beaulieu and the stinted board of the Lady Loring, Alleyne learned the lengths to which luxury and refinement might be pushed. Roasted peacocks, with the feathers all carefully replaced, so that the bird lay upon the dish even as it had strutted in life, boars' heads with the tusks gilded and the mouth lined with silver foil, jellies in the shape of the Twelve Apostles, and a great pasty which formed an exact model of the king's new castle at Windsor—these were a few of the strange dishes which faced him. An archer had brought him a change of clothes from the cog, and he had already, with the elasticity of youth, shaken off the troubles and fatigues of the morning. A page from the inner banqueting-hall had come with word that their master intended to drink wine at the lodgings of the Lord Chandos that night, and that he desired his squires to sleep at the hotel of the "Half Moon" on the Rue des Apotres. Thither then they both set out in the twilight after the long course of juggling tricks and glee-singing with which the principal meal was concluded.

A thin rain was falling as the two youths, with their cloaks over their heads, made their way on foot through the streets of the old town, leaving their horses in the royal stables. An occasional oil lamp at the corner of a street, or in the portico of some wealthy burgher, threw a faint glimmer over the shining cobblestones, and the varied motley crowd who, in spite of the weather, ebbed and flowed along every highway. In those scattered circles of dim radiance might be seen the whole busy panorama of life in a wealthy and martial city. Here passed the round-faced burgher, swollen with prosperity, his sweeping dark-clothed gaberdine, flat velvet cap, broad leather belt and dangling pouch all speaking of comfort and of wealth. Behind him his serving wench, her blue whimple over her head, and one hand thrust forth to bear the lanthorn which threw a golden bar of light along her master's path. Behind them a group of swaggering, half-drunken Yorkshire dalesmen, speaking a dialect which their own southland countrymen could scarce comprehend, their jerkins marked with the pelican, which showed that they had come over in the train of the north-country Stapletons. The burgher glanced back at their fierce faces and quickened his step, while the girl pulled her whimple closer round her, for there was a meaning in their wild eyes, as they stared at the purse and the maiden, which men of all tongues could understand. Then came archers of the guard, shrill-voiced women of the camp, English pages with their fair skins and blue wondering eyes, dark-robed friars, lounging men-at-arms, swarthy loud-tongued Gascon serving-men, seamen from the river, rude peasants of the Medoc, and becloaked and befeathered squires of the court, all jostling and pushing in an ever-changing, many-colored stream, while English, French, Welsh, Basque, and the varied dialects of Gascony and Guienne filled the air with their babel. From time to time the throng would be burst asunder and a lady's horse-litter would trot past towards the abbey, or there would come a knot of torch-bearing archers walking in front of Gascon baron or English knight, as he sought his lodgings after the palace revels. Clatter of hoofs, clinking of weapons, shouts from the drunken brawlers, and high laughter of women, they all rose up, like the mist from a marsh, out of the crowded streets of the dim-lit city.

One couple out of the moving throng especially engaged the attention of the two young squires, the more so as they were going in their own direction and immediately in front of them. They consisted of a man and a girl, the former very tall with rounded shoulders, a limp of one foot, and a large flat object covered with dark cloth under his arm. His companion was young and straight, with a quick, elastic step and graceful bearing, though so swathed in a black mantle that little could be seen of her face save a flash of dark eyes and a curve of raven hair. The tall man leaned heavily upon her to take the weight off his tender foot, while he held his burden betwixt himself and the wall, cuddling it jealously to his side, and thrusting forward his young companion to act as a buttress whenever the pressure of the crowd threatened to bear him away. The evident anxiety of the man, the appearance of his attendant, and the joint care with which they defended their concealed possession, excited the interest of the two young Englishmen who walked within hand-touch of them.

"Courage, child!" they heard the tall man exclaim in strange hybrid French. "If we can win another sixty paces we are safe."

"Hold it safe, father," the other answered, in the same soft, mincing dialect. "We have no cause for fear."

"Verily, they are heathens and barbarians," cried the man; "mad, howling, drunken barbarians! Forty more paces, Tita mia, and I swear to the holy Eloi, patron of all learned craftsmen, that I will never set foot over my door again until the whole swarm are safely hived in their camp of Dax, or wherever else they curse with their presence. Twenty more paces, my treasure! Ah, my God! how they push and brawl! Get in their way, Tita mia! Put your little elbow bravely out! Set your shoulders squarely against them, girl! Why should you give way to these mad islanders? Ah, cospetto! we are ruined and destroyed!"

The crowd had thickened in front, so that the lame man and the girl had come to a stand. Several half-drunken English archers, attracted, as the squires had been, by their singular appearance, were facing towards them, and peering at them through the dim light.

"By the three kings!" cried one, "here is an old dotard shrew to have so goodly a crutch! Use the leg that God hath given you, man, and do not bear so heavily upon the wench."

"Twenty devils fly away with him!" shouted another. "What, how, man! are brave archers to go maidless while an old man uses one as a walking-staff?"

"Come with me, my honey-bird!" cried a third, plucking at the girl's mantle.

"Nay, with me, my heart's desire!" said the first. "By St. George! our life is short, and we should be merry while we may. May I never see Chester Bridge again, if she is not a right winsome lass!"

"What hath the old toad under his arm?" cried one of the others. "He hugs it to him as the devil hugged the pardoner."

"Let us see, old bag of bones; let us see what it is that you have under your arm!" They crowded in upon him, while he, ignorant of their language, could but clutch the girl with one hand and the parcel with the other, looking wildly about in search of help.

"Nay, lads, nay!" cried Ford, pushing back the nearest archer. "This is but scurvy conduct. Keep your hands off, or it will be the worse for you."

"Keep your tongue still, or it will be the worse for you," shouted the most drunken of the archers. "Who are you to spoil sport?"

"A raw squire, new landed," said another. "By St. Thomas of Kent! we are at the beck of our master, but we are not to be ordered by every babe whose mother hath sent him as far as Aquitaine."

"Oh, gentlemen," cried the girl in broken French, "for dear Christ's sake stand by us, and do not let these terrible men do us an injury."

"Have no fears, lady," Alleyne answered. "We shall see that all is well with you. Take your hand from the girl's wrist, you north-country rogue!"

"Hold to her, Wat!" said a great black-bearded man-at-arms, whose steel breast-plate glimmered in the dusk. "Keep your hands from your bodkins, you two, for that was my trade before you were born, and, by God's soul! I will drive a handful of steel through you if you move a finger."

"Thank God!" said Alleyne suddenly, as he spied in the lamp-light a shock of blazing red hair which fringed a steel cap high above the heads of the crowd. "Here is John, and Aylward, too! Help us, comrades, for there is wrong being done to this maid and to the old man."

"Hola, mon petit," said the old bowman, pushing his way through the crowd, with the huge forester at his heels. "What is all this, then? By the twang of string! I think that you will have some work upon your hands if you are to right all the wrongs that you may see upon this side of the water. It is not to be thought that a troop of bowmen, with the wine buzzing in their ears, will be as soft-spoken as so many young clerks in an orchard. When you have been a year with the Company you will think less of such matters. But what is amiss here? The provost-marshal with his archers is coming this way, and some of you may find yourselves in the stretch-neck, if you take not heed."

"Why, it is old Sam Aylward of the White Company!" shouted the man-at-arms. "Why, Samkin, what hath come upon thee? I can call to mind the day when you were as roaring a blade as ever called himself a free companion. By my soul! from Limoges to Navarre, who was there who would kiss a wench or cut a throat as readily as bowman Aylward of Hawkwood's company?"

"Like enough, Peter," said Aylward, "and, by my hilt! I may not have changed so much. But it was ever a fair loose and a clear mark with me. The wench must be willing, or the man must be standing up against me, else, by these ten finger bones! either were safe enough for me."

A glance at Aylward's resolute face, and at the huge shoulders of Hordle John, had convinced the archers that there was little to be got by violence. The girl and the old man began to shuffle on in the crowd without their tormentors venturing to stop them. Ford and Alleyne followed slowly behind them, but Aylward caught the latter by the shoulder.

"By my hilt! camarade," said he, "I hear that you have done great things at the Abbey to-day, but I pray you to have a care, for it was I who brought you into the Company, and it would be a black day for me if aught were to befall you."

"Nay, Aylward, I will have a care."

"Thrust not forward into danger too much, mon petit. In a little time your wrist will be stronger and your cut more shrewd. There will be some of us at the 'Rose de Guienne' to-night, which is two doors from the hotel of the 'Half Moon,' so if you would drain a cup with a few simple archers you will be right welcome."

Alleyne promised to be there if his duties would allow, and then, slipping through the crowd, he rejoined Ford, who was standing in talk with the two strangers, who had now reached their own doorstep.

"Brave young signor," cried the tall man, throwing his arms round Alleyne, "how can we thank you enough for taking our parts against those horrible drunken barbarians. What should we have done without you? My Tita would have been dragged away, and my head would have been shivered into a thousand fragments."

"Nay, I scarce think that they would have mishandled you so," said Alleyne in surprise.

"Ho, ho!" cried he with a high crowing laugh, "it is not the head upon my shoulders that I think of. Cospetto! no. It is the head under my arm which you have preserved."

"Perhaps the signori would deign to come under our roof, father," said the maiden. "If we bide here, who knows that some fresh tumult may not break out."

"Well said, Tita! Well said, my girl! I pray you, sirs, to honor my unworthy roof so far. A light, Giacomo! There are five steps up. Now two more. So! Here we are at last in safety. Corpo di Bacco! I would not have given ten maravedi for my head when those children of the devil were pushing us against the wall. Tita mia, you have been a brave girl, and it was better that you should be pulled and pushed than that my head should be broken."

"Yes indeed, father," said she earnestly.

"But those English! Ach! Take a Goth, a Hun, and a Vandal, mix them together and add a Barbary rover; then take this creature and make him drunk—and you have an Englishman. My God! were ever such people upon earth! What place is free from them? I hear that they swarm in Italy even as they swarm here. Everywhere you will find them, except in heaven."

"Dear father," cried Tita, still supporting the angry old man, as he limped up the curved oaken stair. "You must not forget that these good signori who have preserved us are also English."

"Ah, yes. My pardon, sirs! Come into my rooms here. There are some who might find some pleasure in these paintings, but I learn the art of war is the only art which is held in honor in your island."

The low-roofed, oak-panelled room into which he conducted them was brilliantly lit by four scented oil lamps. Against the walls, upon the table, on the floor, and in every part of the chamber were great sheets of glass painted in the most brilliant colors. Ford and Edricson gazed around them in amazement, for never had they seen such magnificent works of art.

"You like them then," the lame artist cried, in answer to the look of pleasure and of surprise in their faces. "There are then some of you who have a taste for such trifling."

"I could not have believed it," exclaimed Alleyne. "What color! What outlines! See to this martyrdom of the holy Stephen, Ford. Could you not yourself pick up one of these stones which lie to the hand of the wicked murtherers?"

"And see this stag, Alleyne, with the cross betwixt its horns. By my faith! I have never seen a better one at the Forest of Bere."

"And the green of this grass—how bright and clear! Why all the painting that I have seen is but child's play beside this. This worthy gentleman must be one of those great painters of whom I have oft heard brother Bartholomew speak in the old days at Beaulieu."

The dark mobile face of the artist shone with pleasure at the unaffected delight of the two young Englishmen. His daughter had thrown off her mantle and disclosed a face of the finest and most delicate Italian beauty, which soon drew Ford's eyes from the pictures in front of him. Alleyne, however, continued with little cries of admiration and of wonderment to turn from the walls to the table and yet again to the walls.

"What think you of this, young sir?" asked the painter, tearing off the cloth which concealed the flat object which he had borne beneath his arm. It was a leaf-shaped sheet of glass bearing upon it a face with a halo round it, so delicately outlined, and of so perfect a tint, that it might have been indeed a human face which gazed with sad and thoughtful eyes upon the young squire. He clapped his hands, with that thrill of joy which true art will ever give to a true artist.

"It is great!" he cried. "It is wonderful! But I marvel, sir, that you should have risked a work of such beauty and value by bearing it at night through so unruly a crowd."

"I have indeed been rash," said the artist. "Some wine, Tita, from the Florence flask! Had it not been for you, I tremble to think of what might have come of it. See to the skin tint: it is not to be replaced, for paint as you will, it is not once in a hundred times that it is not either burned too brown in the furnace or else the color will not hold, and you get but a sickly white. There you can see the very veins and the throb of the blood. Yes, diavolo! if it had broken, my heart would have broken too. It is for the choir window in the church of St. Remi, and we had gone, my little helper and I, to see if it was indeed of the size for the stonework. Night had fallen ere we finished, and what could we do save carry it home as best we might? But you, young sir, you speak as if you too knew something of the art."

"So little that I scarce dare speak of it in your presence," Alleyne answered. "I have been cloister-bred, and it was no very great matter to handle the brush better than my brother novices."

"There are pigments, brush, and paper," said the old artist. "I do not give you glass, for that is another matter, and takes much skill in the mixing of colors. Now I pray you to show me a touch of your art. I thank you, Tita! The Venetian glasses, cara mia, and fill them to the brim. A seat, signor!"

While Ford, in his English-French, was conversing with Tita in her Italian-French, the old man was carefully examining his precious head to see that no scratch had been left upon its surface. When he glanced up again, Alleyne had, with a few bold strokes of the brush, tinted in a woman's face and neck upon the white sheet in front of him.

"Diavolo!" exclaimed the old artist, standing with his head on one side, "you have power; yes, cospetto! you have power, it is the face of an angel!"

"It is the face of the Lady Maude Loring!" cried Ford, even more astonished.

"Why, on my faith, it is not unlike her!" said Alleyne, in some confusion.

"Ah! a portrait! So much the better. Young man, I am Agostino Pisano, the son of Andrea Pisano, and I say again that you have power. Further, I say, that, if you will stay with me, I will teach you all the secrets of the glass-stainers' mystery: the pigments and their thickening, which will fuse into the glass and which will not, the furnace and the glazing—every trick and method you shall know."

"I would be right glad to study under such a master," said Alleyne; "but I am sworn to follow my lord whilst this war lasts."

"War! war!" cried the old Italian. "Ever this talk of war. And the men that you hold to be great—what are they? Have I not heard their names? Soldiers, butchers, destroyers! Ah, per Bacco! we have men in Italy who are in very truth great. You pull down, you despoil; but they build up, they restore. Ah, if you could but see my own dear Pisa, the Duomo, the cloisters of Campo Santo, the high Campanile, with the mellow throb of her bells upon the warm Italian air! Those are the works of great men. And I have seen them with my own eyes, these very eyes which look upon you. I have seen Andrea Orcagna, Taddeo Gaddi, Giottino, Stefano, Simone Memmi—men whose very colors I am not worthy to mix. And I have seen the aged Giotto, and he in turn was pupil to Cimabue, before whom there was no art in Italy, for the Greeks were brought to paint the chapel of the Gondi at Florence. Ah, signori, there are the real great men whose names will be held in honor when your soldiers are shown to have been the enemies of humankind."

"Faith, sir," said Ford, "there is something to say for the soldiers also, for, unless they be defended, how are all these gentlemen whom you have mentioned to preserve the pictures which they have painted?"

"And all these!" said Alleyne. "Have you indeed done them all?—and where are they to go?"

"Yes, signor, they are all from my hand. Some are, as you see, upon one sheet, and some are in many pieces which may fasten together. There are some who do but paint upon the glass, and then, by placing another sheet of glass upon the top and fastening it, they keep the air from their painting. Yet I hold that the true art of my craft lies as much in the furnace as in the brush. See this rose window, which is from the model of the Church of the Holy Trinity at Vendome, and this other of the 'Finding of the Grail,' which is for the apse of the Abbey church. Time was when none but my countrymen could do these things; but there is Clement of Chartres and others in France who are very worthy workmen. But, ah! there is that ever shrieking brazen tongue which will not let us forget for one short hour that it is the arm of the savage, and not the hand of the master, which rules over the world."

A stern, clear bugle call had sounded close at hand to summon some following together for the night.

"It is a sign to us as well," said Ford. "I would fain stay here forever amid all these beautiful things—" staring hard at the blushing Tita as he spoke— "but we must be back at our lord's hostel ere he reach it."

Amid renewed thanks and with promises to come again, the two squires bade their leave of the old Italian glass-stainer and his daughter. The streets were clearer now, and the rain had stopped, so they made their way quickly from the Rue du Roi, in which their new friends dwelt, to the Rue des Apotres, where the hostel of the "Half Moon" was situated.

XXII

How the Bowmen Held Wassail at the "Rose De Guienne"

"Mon Dieu! Alleyne, saw you ever so lovely a face?" cried Ford as they hurried along together. "So pure, so peaceful, and so beautiful!"

"In sooth, yes. And the hue of the skin the most perfect that ever I saw. Marked you also how the hair curled round the brow? It was wonder fine."

"Those eyes, too!" cried Ford. "How clear and how tender—simple, and yet so full of thought!"

"If there was a weakness it was in the chin," said Alleyne.

"Nay. I saw none."

"It was well curved, it is true."

"Most daintily so."

"And yet——"

"What then, Alleyne? Wouldst find flaw in the sun?"

"Well, bethink you, Ford, would not more power and expression have been put into the face by a long and noble beard?"

"Holy Virgin!" cried Ford, "the man is mad. A beard on the face of little Tita!"

"Tita! Who spoke of Tita?"

"Who spoke of aught else?"

"It was the picture of St. Remi, man, of which I have been discoursing."

"You are indeed," cried Ford, laughing, "a Goth, Hun, and Vandal, with all the other hard names which the old man called us. How could you think so much of a smear of pigments, when there was such a picture painted by the good God himself in the very room with you? But who is this?"

"If it please you, sirs," said an archer, running across to them, "Aylward and others would be right glad to see you. They are within here. He bade me say to you that the Lord Loring will not need your service to-night, as he sleeps with the Lord Chandos."

"By my faith!" said Ford, "we do not need a guide to lead us to their presence." As he spoke there came a roar of singing from the tavern upon the right, with shouts of laughter and stamping of feet. Passing under a low door, and down a stone-flagged passage, they found themselves in a long narrow hall lit up by a pair of blazing torches, one at either end. Trusses of straw had been thrown down along the walls, and reclining on them were some twenty or thirty archers, all of the Company, their steel caps and jacks thrown off, their tunics open and their great limbs sprawling upon the clay floor. At every man's elbow stood his leathern blackjack of beer, while at the further end a hogshead with its end knocked in promised an abundant supply for the future. Behind the hogshead, on a half circle of kegs, boxes, and rude settles, sat Aylward, John, Black Simon and three or four other leading men of the archers, together with Goodwin Hawtayne, the master-shipman, who had left his yellow cog in the river to have a last rouse with his friends of the Company. Ford and Alleyne took their seats between Aylward and Black Simon, without their entrance checking in any degree the hubbub which was going on.

"Ale, mes camarades?" cried the bowman, "or shall it be wine? Nay, but ye must have the one or the other. Here, Jacques, thou limb of the devil, bring a bottrine of the oldest vernage, and see that you do not shake it. Hast heard the news?"

"Nay," cried both the squires.

"That we are to have a brave tourney."

"A tourney?"

"Aye, lads. For the Captal du Buch hath sworn that he will find five knights from this side of the water who will ride over any five Englishmen who ever threw leg over saddle; and Chandos hath taken up the challenge, and the prince hath promised a golden vase for the man who carries himself best, and all the court is in a buzz over it."

"Why should the knights have all the sport?" growled Hordle John. "Could they not set up five archers for the honor of Aquitaine and of Gascony?"

"Or five men-at-arms," said Black Simon.

"But who are the English knights?" asked Hawtayne.

"There are three hundred and forty-one in the town," said Aylward, "and I hear that three hundred and forty cartels and defiances have already been sent in, the only one missing being Sir John Ravensholme, who is in his bed with the sweating sickness, and cannot set foot to ground."

"I have heard of it from one of the archers of the guard," cried a bowman from among the straw; "I hear that the prince wished to break a lance, but that Chandos would not hear of it, for the game is likely to be a rough one."

"Then there is Chandos."

"Nay, the prince would not permit it. He is to be marshal of the lists, with Sir William Felton and the Duc d'Armagnac. The English will be the Lord Audley, Sir Thomas Percy, Sir Thomas Wake, Sir William Beauchamp, and our own very good lord and leader."

"Hurrah for him, and God be with him!" cried several. "It is honor to draw string in his service."

"So you may well say," said Aylward. "By my ten finger-bones! if you march behind the pennon of the five roses you are like to see all that a good bowman would wish to see. Ha! yes, mes garcons, you laugh, but, by my hilt! you may not laugh when you find yourselves where he will take you, for you can never tell what strange vow he may not have sworn to. I see that he has a patch over his eye, even as he had at Poictiers. There will come bloodshed of that patch, or I am the more mistaken."

"How chanced it at Poictiers, good Master Aylward?" asked one of the young archers, leaning upon his elbows, with his eyes fixed respectfully upon the old bowman's rugged face.

"Aye, Aylward, tell us of it," cried Hordle John.

"Here is to old Samkin Aylward!" shouted several at the further end of the room, waving their blackjacks in the air.

"Ask him!" said Aylward modestly, nodding towards Black Simon. "He saw more than I did. And yet, by the holy nails! there was not very much that I did not see either."

"Ah, yes," said Simon, shaking his head, "it was a great day. I never hope to see such another. There were some fine archers who drew their last shaft that day. We shall never see better men, Aylward."

"By my hilt! no. There was little Robby Withstaff, and Andrew Salblaster, and Wat Alspaye, who broke the neck of the German. Mon Dieu! what men they were! Take them how you would, at long butts or short, hoyles, rounds, or rovers, better bowmen never twirled a shaft over their thumb-nails."

"But the fight, Aylward, the fight!" cried several impatiently.

"Let me fill my jack first, boys, for it is a thirsty tale. It was at the first fall of the leaf that the prince set forth, and he passed through Auvergne, and Berry, and Anjou, and Touraine. In Auvergne the maids are kind, but the wines are sour. In Berry it is the women that are sour, but the wines are rich. Anjou, however, is a very good land for bowmen, for wine and women are all that heart could wish. In Touraine I got nothing save a broken pate, but at Vierzon I had a great good fortune, for I had a golden pyx from the minster, for which I afterwards got nine Genoan janes from the goldsmith in the Rue Mont Olive. From thence we went to Bourges, where I had a tunic of flame-colored silk and a very fine pair of shoes with tassels of silk and drops of silver."

"From a stall, Aylward?" asked one of the young archers.

"Nay, from a man's feet, lad. I had reason to think that he might not need them again, seeing that a thirty-inch shaft had feathered in his back."

"And what then, Aylward?"

"On we went, coz, some six thousand of us, until we came to Issodun, and there again a very great thing befell."

"A battle, Aylward?"

"Nay, nay; a greater thing than that. There is little to be gained out of a battle, unless one have the fortune to win a ransom. At Issodun I and three Welshmen came upon a house which all others had passed, and we had the profit of it to ourselves. For myself, I had a fine feather-bed—a thing which you will not see in a long day's journey in England. You have seen it, Alleyne, and you, John. You will bear me out that it is a noble bed. We put it on a sutler's mule, and bore it after the army. It was on my mind that I would lay it by until I came to start house of mine own, and I have it now in a very safe place near Lyndhurst."

"And what then, master-bowman?" asked Hawtayne. "By St. Christopher! it is indeed a fair and goodly life which you have chosen, for you gather up the spoil as a Warsash man gathers lobsters, without grace or favor from any man."

"You are right, master-shipman," said another of the older archers. "It is an old bowyer's rede that the second feather of a fenny goose is better than the pinion of a tame one. Draw on old lad, for I have come between you and the clout."

"On we went then," said Aylward, after a long pull at his blackjack. "There were some six thousand of us, with the prince and his knights, and the feather-bed upon a sutler's mule in the centre. We made great havoc in Touraine, until we came into Romorantin, where I chanced upon a gold chain and two bracelets of jasper, which were stolen from me the same day by a black-eyed wench from the Ardennes. Mon Dieu! there are some folk who have no fear of Domesday in them, and no sign of grace in their souls, for ever clutching and clawing at another man's chattels."

"But the battle, Aylward, the battle!" cried several, amid a burst of laughter.

"I come to it, my young war-pups. Well, then, the King of France had followed us with fifty thousand men, and he made great haste to catch us, but when he had us he scarce knew what to do with us, for we were so drawn up among hedges and vineyards that they could not come nigh us, save by one lane. On both sides were archers, men-at-arms and knights behind, and in the centre the baggage, with my feather-bed upon a sutler's mule. Three hundred chosen knights came straight for it, and, indeed, they were very brave men, but such a drift of arrows met them that few came back. Then came the Germans, and they also fought very bravely, so that one or two broke through the archers and came as far as the feather-bed, but all to no purpose. Then out rides our own little hothead with the patch over his eye, and my Lord Audley with his four Cheshire squires, and a few others of like kidney, and after them went the prince and Chandos, and then the whole throng of us, with axe and sword, for we had shot away our arrows. Ma foi! it was a foolish thing, for we came forth from the hedges, and there was naught to guard the baggage had they ridden round behind us. But all went well with us, and the king was taken, and little Robby Withstaff and I fell in with a wain with twelve firkins of wine for the king's own table, and, by my hilt! if you ask me what happened after that, I cannot answer you, nor can little Robby Withstaff either."

"And next day?"

"By my faith! we did not tarry long, but we hied back to Bordeaux, where we came in safety with the King of France and also the feather-bed. I sold my spoil, mes garcons, for as many gold-pieces as I could hold in my hufken, and for seven days I lit twelve wax candles upon the altar of St. Andrew; for if you forget the blessed when things are well with you, they are very likely to forget you when you have need of them. I have a score of one hundred and nineteen pounds of wax against the holy Andrew, and, as he was a very just man, I doubt not that I shall have full weigh and measure when I have most need of it."

"Tell me, master Aylward," cried a young fresh-faced archer at the further end of the room, "what was this great battle about?"

"Why, you jack-fool, what would it be about save who should wear the crown of France?"

"I thought that mayhap it might be as to who should have this feather-bed of thine."

"If I come down to you, Silas, I may lay my belt across your shoulders," Aylward answered, amid a general shout of laughter. "But it is time young chickens went to roost when they dare cackle against their elders. It is late, Simon."

"Nay, let us have another song."

"Here is Arnold of Sowley will troll as good a stave as any man in the Company."

"Nay, we have one here who is second to none," said Hawtayne, laying his hand upon big John's shoulder. "I have heard him on the cog with a voice like the wave upon the shore. I pray you, friend, to give us 'The Bells of Milton,' or, if you will, 'The Franklin's Maid.'"

Hordle John drew the back of his hand across his mouth, fixed his eyes upon the corner of the ceiling, and bellowed forth, in a voice which made the torches flicker, the southland ballad for which he had been asked:

The franklin he hath gone to roam,
The franklin's maid she bides at home,
But she is cold and coy and staid,
And who may win the franklin's maid?

There came a knight of high renown
In bassinet and ciclatoun;
On bended knee full long he prayed,
He might not win the franklin's maid.

There came a squire so debonair
His dress was rich, his words were fair,
He sweetly sang, he deftly played:
He could not win the franklin's maid.

There came a mercer wonder-fine
With velvet cap and gaberdine;
For all his ships, for all his trade
He could not buy the franklin's maid.

There came an archer bold and true,
With bracer guard and stave of yew;
His purse was light, his jerkin frayed;
Haro, alas! the franklin's maid!

Oh, some have laughed and some have cried
And some have scoured the country-side!
But off they ride through wood and glade,
The bowman and the franklin's maid.

A roar of delight from his audience, with stamping of feet and beating of blackjacks against the ground, showed how thoroughly the song was to their taste, while John modestly retired into a quart pot, which he drained in four giant gulps. "I sang that ditty in Hordle ale-house ere I ever thought to be an archer myself," quoth he.

"Fill up your stoups!" cried Black Simon, thrusting his own goblet into the open hogshead in front of him. "Here is a last cup to the White Company, and every brave boy who walks behind the roses of Loring!"

"To the wood, the flax, and the gander's wing!" said an old gray-headed archer on the right.

"To a gentle loose, and the King of Spain for a mark at fourteen score!" cried another.

"To a bloody war!" shouted a fourth. "Many to go and few to come!"

"With the most gold to the best steel!" added a fifth.

"And a last cup to the maids of our heart!" cried Aylward. "A steady hand and a true eye, boys; so let two quarts be a bowman's portion." With shout and jest and snatch of song they streamed from the room, and all was peaceful once more in the "Rose de Guienne."

XXIII

How England Held the Lists at Bordeaux

So used were the good burghers of Bordeaux to martial display and knightly sport, that an ordinary joust or tournament was an everyday matter with them. The fame and brilliancy of the prince's court had drawn the knights-errant and pursuivants-of-arms from every part of Europe. In the long lists by the Garonne on the landward side of the northern gate there had been many a strange combat, when the Teutonic knight, fresh from the conquest of the Prussian heathen, ran a course against the knight of Calatrava, hardened by continual struggle against the Moors, or cavaliers from Portugal broke a lance with Scandinavian warriors from the further shore of the great Northern Ocean. Here fluttered many an outland pennon, bearing symbol and blazonry from the banks of the Danube, the wilds of Lithuania and the mountain strongholds of Hungary; for chivalry was of no clime and of no race, nor was any land so wild that the fame and name of the prince had not sounded through it from border to border.

Great, however, was the excitement through town and district when it was learned that on the third Wednesday in Advent there would be held a passage-at-arms in which five knights of England would hold the lists against all comers. The great concourse of noblemen and famous soldiers, the national character of the contest, and the fact that this was a last trial of arms before what promised to be an arduous and bloody war, all united to make the event one of the most notable and brilliant that Bordeaux had ever seen. On the eve of the contest the peasants flocked in from the whole district of the Medoc, and the fields beyond the walls were whitened with the tents of those who could find no warmer lodging. From the distant camp of Dax, too, and from Blaye, Bourge, Libourne, St. Emilion, Castillon, St. Macaire, Cardillac, Ryons, and all the cluster of flourishing towns which look upon Bordeaux as their mother, there thronged an unceasing stream of horsemen and of footmen, all converging upon the great city. By the morning of the day on which the courses were to be run, not less than eighty people had assembled round the lists and along the low grassy ridge which looks down upon the scene of the encounter.

It was, as may well be imagined, no easy matter among so many noted cavaliers to choose out five on either side who should have precedence over their fellows. A score of secondary combats had nearly arisen from the rivalries and bad blood created by the selection, and it was only the influence of the prince and the efforts of the older barons which kept the peace among so many eager and fiery soldiers. Not till the day before the courses were the shields finally hung out for the inspection of the ladies and the heralds, so that all men might know the names of the champions and have the opportunity to prefer any charge against them, should there be stain upon them which should disqualify them from taking part in so noble and honorable a ceremony.

Sir Hugh Calverley and Sir Robert Knolles had not yet returned from their raid into the marches of the Navarre, so that the English party were deprived of two of their most famous lances. Yet there remained so many good names that Chandos and Felton, to whom the selection had been referred, had many an earnest consultation, in which every feat of arms and failure or success of each candidate was weighed and balanced against the rival claims of his companions. Lord Audley of Cheshire, the hero of Poictiers, and Loring of Hampshire, who was held to be the second lance in the army, were easily fixed upon. Then, of the younger men, Sir Thomas Percy of Northumberland, Sir Thomas Wake of Yorkshire, and Sir William Beauchamp of Gloucestershire, were finally selected to uphold the honor of England. On the other side were the veteran Captal de Buch and the brawny Olivier de Clisson, with the free companion Sir Perducas d'Albret, the valiant Lord of Mucident, and Sigismond von Altenstadt, of the Teutonic Order. The older soldiers among the English shook their heads as they looked upon the escutcheons of these famous warriors, for they were all men who had spent their lives upon the saddle, and bravery and strength can avail little against experience and wisdom of war.

"By my faith! Sir John," said the prince as he rode through the winding streets on his way to the list, "I should have been glad to have splintered a lance to-day. You have seen me hold a spear since I had strength to lift one, and should know best whether I do not merit a place among this honorable company."

"There is no better seat and no truer lance, sire," said Chandos; "but, if I may say so without fear of offence, it were not fitting that you should join in this debate."

"And why, Sir John?"

"Because, sire, it is not for you to take part with Gascons against English, or with English against Gascons, seeing that you are lord of both. We are not too well loved by the Gascons now, and it is but the golden link of your princely coronet which holds us together. If that be snapped I know not what would follow."

"Snapped, Sir John!" cried the prince, with an angry sparkle in his dark eyes. "What manner of talk is this? You speak as though the allegiance of our people were a thing which might be thrown off or on like a falcon's jessel."

"With a sorry hack one uses whip and spur, sire," said Chandos; "but with a horse of blood and spirit a good cavalier is gentle and soothing, coaxing rather than forcing. These folk are strange people, and you must hold their love, even as you have it now, for you will get from their kindness what all the pennons in your army could not wring from them."

"You are over-grave to-day, John," the prince answered. "We may keep such questions for our council-chamber. But how now, my brothers of Spain, and of Majorca, what think you of this challenge?"

"I look to see some handsome joisting," said Don Pedro, who rode with the King of Majorca upon the right of the prince, while Chandos was on the left. "By St. James of Compostella! but these burghers would bear some taxing. See to the broadcloth and velvet that the rogues bear upon their backs! By my troth! if they were my subjects they would be glad enough to wear falding and leather ere I had done with them. But mayhap it is best to let the wool grow long ere you clip it."

"It is our pride," the prince answered coldly, "that we rule over freemen and not slaves."

"Every man to his own humor," said Pedro carelessly. "Carajo! there is a sweet face at yonder window! Don Fernando, I pray you to mark the house, and to have the maid brought to us at the abbey."

"Nay, brother, nay!" cried the prince impatiently. "I have had occasion to tell you more than once that things are not ordered in this way in Aquitaine."

"A thousand pardons, dear friend," the Spaniard answered quickly, for a flush of anger had sprung to the dark cheek of the English prince. "You make my exile so like a home that I forget at times that I am not in very truth back in Castile. Every land hath indeed its ways and manners; but I promise you, Edward, that when you are my guest in Toledo or Madrid you shall not yearn in vain for any commoner's daughter on whom you may deign to cast your eye."

"Your talk, sire," said the prince still more coldly, "is not such as I love to hear from your lips. I have no taste for such amours as you speak of, and I have sworn that my name shall be coupled with that of no woman save my ever dear wife."

"Ever the mirror of true chivalry!" exclaimed Pedro, while James of Majorca, frightened at the stern countenance of their all-powerful protector, plucked hard at the mantle of his brother exile.

"Have a care, cousin," he whispered; "for the sake of the Virgin have a care, for you have angered him."

"Pshaw! fear not," the other answered in the same low tone. "If I miss one stoop I will strike him on the next. Mark me else. Fair cousin," he continued, turning to the prince, "these be rare men-at-arms and lusty bowmen. It would be hard indeed to match them."

"They have journeyed far, sire, but they have never yet found their match."

"Nor ever will, I doubt not. I feel myself to be back upon my throne when I look at them. But tell me, dear coz, what shall we do next, when we have driven this bastard Henry from the kingdom which he hath filched?"

"We shall then compel the King of Aragon to place our good friend and brother James of Majorca upon the throne."

"Noble and generous prince!" cried the little monarch.

"That done," said King Pedro, glancing out of the corners of his eyes at the young conqueror, "we shall unite the forces of England, of Aquitaine, of Spain and of Majorca. It would be shame to us if we did not do some great deed with such forces ready to our hand."

"You say truly, brother," cried the prince, his eyes kindling at the thought. "Methinks that we could not do anything more pleasing to Our Lady than to drive the heathen Moors out of the country."

"I am with you, Edward, as true as hilt to blade. But, by St. James! we shall not let these Moors make mock at us from over the sea. We must take ship and thrust them from Africa."

"By heaven, yes!" cried the prince. "And it is the dream of my heart that our English pennons shall wave upon the Mount of Olives, and the lions and lilies float over the holy city."

"And why not, dear coz? Your bowmen have cleared a path to Paris, and why not to Jerusalem? Once there, your arms might rest."

"Nay, there is more to be done," cried the prince, carried away by the ambitious dream. "There is still the city of Constantine to be taken, and war to be waged against the Soldan of Damascus. And beyond him again there is tribute to be levied from the Cham of Tartary and from the kingdom of Cathay. Ha! John, what say you? Can we not go as far eastward as Richard of the Lion Heart?"

"Old John will bide at home, sire," said the rugged soldier. "By my soul! as long as I am seneschal of Aquitaine I will find enough to do in guarding the marches which you have entrusted to me. It would be a blithe day for the King of France when he heard that the seas lay between him and us."

"By my soul! John," said the prince, "I have never known you turn laggard before."

"The babbling hound, sire, is not always the first at the mort," the old knight answered.

"Nay, my true-heart! I have tried you too often not to know. But, by my soul! I have not seen so dense a throng since the day that we brought King John down Cheapside."

It was indeed an enormous crowd which covered the whole vast plain from the line of vineyards to the river bank. From the northern gate the prince and his companions looked down at a dark sea of heads, brightened here and there by the colored hoods of the women, or by the sparkling head-pieces of archers and men-at-arms. In the centre of this vast assemblage the lists seemed but a narrow strip of green marked out with banners and streamers, while a gleam of white with a flutter of pennons at either end showed where the marquees were pitched which served as the dressing-rooms of the combatants. A path had been staked off from the city gate to the stands which had been erected for the court and the nobility. Down this, amid the shouts of the enormous multitude, the prince cantered with his two attendant kings, his high officers of state, and his long train of lords and ladies, courtiers, counsellors, and soldiers, with toss of plume and flash of jewel, sheen of silk and glint of gold—as rich and gallant a show as heart could wish. The head of the cavalcade had reached the lists ere the rear had come clear of the city gate, for the fairest and the bravest had assembled from all the broad lands which are watered by the Dordogne and the Garonne. Here rode dark-browed cavaliers from the sunny south, fiery soldiers from Gascony, graceful courtiers of Limousin or Saintonge, and gallant young Englishmen from beyond the seas. Here too were the beautiful brunettes of the Gironde, with eyes which out-flashed their jewels, while beside them rode their blonde sisters of England, clear cut and aquiline, swathed in swans'-down and in ermine, for the air was biting though the sun was bright. Slowly the long and glittering train wound into the lists, until every horse had been tethered by the varlets in waiting, and every lord and lady seated in the long stands which stretched, rich in tapestry and velvet and blazoned arms, on either side of the centre of the arena.

The holders of the lists occupied the end which was nearest to the city gate. There, in front of their respective pavilions, flew the martlets of Audley, the roses of Loring, the scarlet bars of Wake, the lion of the Percies and the silver wings of the Beauchamps, each supported by a squire clad in hanging green stuff to represent so many Tritons, and bearing a huge conch-shell in their left hands. Behind the tents the great war-horses, armed at all points, champed and reared, while their masters sat at the doors of their pavilions, with their helmets upon their knees, chatting as to the order of the day's doings. The English archers and men-at-arms had mustered at that end of the lists, but the vast majority of the spectators were in favor of the attacking party, for the English had declined in popularity ever since the bitter dispute as to the disposal of the royal captive after the battle of Poictiers. Hence the applause was by no means general when the herald-at-arms proclaimed, after a flourish of trumpets, the names and styles of the knights who were prepared, for the honor of their country and for the love of their ladies, to hold the field against all who might do them the favor to run a course with them. On the other hand, a deafening burst of cheering greeted the rival herald, who, advancing from the other end of the lists, rolled forth the well-known titles of the five famous warriors who had accepted the defiance.

"Faith, John," said the prince, "it sounds as though you were right. Ha! my grace D'Armagnac, it seems that our friends on this side will not grieve if our English champions lose the day."

"It may be so, sire," the Gascon nobleman answered. "I have little doubt that in Smithfield or at Windsor an English crowd would favor their own countrymen."

"By my faith! that's easily seen," said the prince, laughing, "for a few score English archers at yonder end are bellowing as though they would out-shout the mighty multitude. I fear that they will have little to shout over this tourney, for my gold vase has small prospect of crossing the water. What are the conditions, John?"

"They are to tilt singly not less than three courses, sire, and the victory to rest with that party which shall have won the greater number of courses, each pair continuing till one or other have the vantage. He who carries himself best of the victors hath the prize, and he who is judged best of the other party hath a jewelled clasp. Shall I order that the nakirs sound, sire?"

The prince nodded, and the trumpets rang out, while the champions rode forth one after the other, each meeting his opponent in the centre of the lists. Sir William Beauchamp went down before the practiced lance of the Captal de Buch. Sir Thomas Percy won the vantage over the Lord of Mucident, and the Lord Audley struck Sir Perducas d'Albret from the saddle. The burly De Clisson, however, restored the hopes of the attackers by beating to the ground Sir Thomas Wake of Yorkshire. So far, there was little to choose betwixt challengers and challenged.

"By Saint James of Santiago!" cried Don Pedro, with a tinge of color upon his pale cheeks, "win who will, this has been a most notable contest."

"Who comes next for England, John?" asked the prince in a voice which quivered with excitement.

"Sir Nigel Loring of Hampshire, sire."

"Ha! he is a man of good courage, and skilled in the use of all weapons."

"He is indeed, sire. But his eyes, like my own, are the worse for wars. Yet he can tilt or play his part at hand-strokes as merrily as ever. It was he, sire, who won the golden crown which Queen Philippa, your royal mother, gave to be jousted for by all the knights of England after the harrying of Calais. I have heard that at Twynham Castle there is a buffet which groans beneath the weight of his prizes."

"I pray that my vase may join them," said the prince. "But here is the cavalier of Germany, and by my soul! he looks like a man of great valor and hardiness. Let them run their full three courses, for the issue is over-great to hang upon one."

As the prince spoke, amid a loud flourish of trumpets and the shouting of the Gascon party, the last of the assailants rode gallantly into the lists. He was a man of great size, clad in black armor without blazonry or ornament of any kind, for all worldly display was forbidden by the rules of the military brotherhood to which he belonged. No plume or nobloy fluttered from his plain tilting salade, and even his lance was devoid of the customary banderole. A white mantle fluttered behind him, upon the left side of which was marked the broad black cross picked out with silver which was the well-known badge of the

Teutonic Order. Mounted upon a horse as large, as black, and as forbidding as himself, he cantered slowly forward, with none of those prancings and gambades with which a cavalier was accustomed to show his command over his charger. Gravely and sternly he inclined his head to the prince, and took his place at the further end of the arena.

He had scarce done so before Sir Nigel rode out from the holders' enclosure, and galloping at full speed down the lists, drew his charger up before the prince's stand with a jerk which threw it back upon its haunches. With white armor, blazoned shield, and plume of ostrich-feathers from his helmet, he carried himself in so jaunty and joyous a fashion, with tossing pennon and curveting charger, that a shout of applause ran the full circle of the arena. With the air of a man who hastes to a joyous festival, he waved his lance in salute, and reining the pawing horse round without permitting its fore-feet to touch the ground, he hastened back to his station.

A great hush fell over the huge multitude as the two last champions faced each other. A double issue seemed to rest upon their contest, for their personal fame was at stake as well as their party's honor. Both were famous warriors, but as their exploits had been performed in widely sundered countries, they had never before been able to cross lances. A course between such men would have been enough in itself to cause the keenest interest, apart from its being the crisis which would decide who should be the victors of the day. For a moment they waited—the German sombre and collected, Sir Nigel quivering in every fibre with eagerness and fiery resolution. Then, amid a long-drawn breath from the spectators, the glove fell from the marshal's hand, and the two steel-clad horsemen met like a thunderclap in front of the royal stand. The German, though he reeled for an instant before the thrust of the Englishman, struck his opponent so fairly upon the vizor that the laces burst, the plumed helmet flew to pieces, and Sir Nigel galloped on down the lists with his bald head shimmering in the sunshine. A thousand waving scarves and tossing caps announced that the first bout had fallen to the popular party.

The Hampshire knight was not a man to be disheartened by a reverse. He spurred back to the pavilion, and was out in a few instants with another helmet. The second course was so equal that the keenest judges could not discern any vantage. Each struck fire from the other's shield, and each endured the jarring shock as though welded to the horse beneath him. In the final bout, however, Sir Nigel struck his opponent with so true an aim that the point of the lance caught between the bars of his vizor and tore the front of his helmet out, while the German, aiming somewhat low, and half stunned by the shock, had the misfortune to strike his adversary upon the thigh, a breach of the rules of the tilting-yard, by which he not only sacrificed his chances of success, but would also have forfeited his horse and his armor, had the English knight chosen to claim them. A roar of applause from the English soldiers, with an ominous silence from the vast crowd who pressed round the barriers, announced that the balance of victory lay with the holders. Already the ten champions had assembled in front of the prince to receive his award, when a harsh bugle call from the further end of the lists drew all eyes to a new and unexpected arrival.

XXIV

How a Champion Came Forth From the East

The Bordeaux lists were, as has already been explained, situated upon the plain near the river upon those great occasions when the tilting-ground in front of the Abbey of St. Andrew's was deemed to be too small to contain the crowd. On the eastern side of this plain the country-side sloped upwards, thick with vines in summer, but now ridged with the brown bare enclosures. Over the gently rising plain curved the white road which leads inland, usually flecked with travellers, but now with scarce a living form upon it, so completely had the lists drained all the district of its inhabitants. Strange it was to see such a vast concourse of people, and then to look upon that broad, white, empty highway which wound away, bleak and deserted, until it narrowed itself to a bare streak against the distant uplands.

Shortly after the contest had begun, any one looking from the lists along this road might have remarked, far away in the extreme distance, two brilliant and sparkling points which glittered and twinkled in the bright shimmer of the winter sun. Within an hour these had become clearer and nearer, until they might be seen to come from the reflection from the head-pieces of two horsemen who were riding at the top of their speed in the direction of Bordeaux. Another half-hour had brought them so close that every point of their bearing and equipment could be discerned. The first was a knight in full armor, mounted upon a brown horse with a white blaze upon breast and forehead. He was a short man of great breadth of shoulder, with vizor closed, and no blazonry upon his simple white surcoat or plain black shield. The other, who was evidently his squire and attendant, was unarmed save for the helmet upon his head, but bore in his right hand a very long and heavy oaken spear which belonged to his master. In his left hand the squire held not only the reins of his own horse but those of a great black war-horse, fully harnessed, which trotted along at his side. Thus the three horses and their two riders rode swiftly to the lists, and it was the blare of the trumpet sounded by the squire as his lord rode into the arena which had broken in upon the prize-giving and drawn away the attention and interest of the spectators.

"Ha, John!" cried the prince, craning his neck, "who is this cavalier, and what is it that he desires?"

"On my word, sire," replied Chandos, with the utmost surprise upon his face, "it is my opinion that he is a Frenchman."

"A Frenchman!" repeated Don Pedro. "And how can you tell that, my Lord Chandos, when he has neither coat-armor, crest, or blazonry?"

"By his armor, sire, which is rounder at elbow and at shoulder than any of Bordeaux or of England. Italian he might be were his bassinet more sloped, but I will swear that those plates were welded betwixt this and Rhine. Here comes his squire, however, and we shall hear what strange fortune hath brought him over the marches."

As he spoke the attendant cantered up the grassy enclosure, and pulling up his steed in front of the royal stand, blew a second fanfare upon his bugle. He was a raw-boned, swarthy-cheeked man, with black bristling beard and a swaggering bearing.

Having sounded his call, he thrust the bugle into his belt, and, pushing his way betwixt the groups of English and of Gascon knights, he reined up within a spear's length of the royal party.

"I come," he shouted in a hoarse, thick voice, with a strong Breton accent, "as squire and herald from my master, who is a very valiant pursuivant-of-arms, and a liegeman to the great and powerful monarch, Charles, king of the French. My master has heard that there is jousting here, and prospect of honorable advancement, so he has come to ask that some English cavalier will vouchsafe for the love of his lady to run a course with sharpened lances with him, or to meet him with sword, mace, battle-axe, or dagger. He bade me say, however, that he would fight only with a true Englishman, and not with any mongrel who is neither English nor French, but speaks with the tongue of the one, and fights under the banner of the other."

"Sir!" cried De Clisson, with a voice of thunder, while his countrymen clapped their hands to their swords. The squire, however, took no notice of their angry faces, but continued with his master's message.

"He is now ready, sire," he said, "albeit his destrier has travelled many miles this day, and fast, for we were in fear lest we come too late for the jousting."

"Ye have indeed come too late," said the prince, "seeing that the prize is about to be awarded; yet I doubt not that one of these gentlemen will run a course for the sake of honor with this cavalier of France."

"And as to the prize, sire," quoth Sir Nigel, "I am sure that I speak for all when I say this French knight hath our leave to bear it away with him if he can fairly win it."

"Bear word of this to your master," said the prince, "and ask him which of these five Englishmen he would desire to meet. But stay; your master bears no coat-armor, and we have not yet heard his name."

"My master, sire, is under vow to the Virgin neither to reveal his name nor to open his vizor until he is back upon French ground once more."

"Yet what assurance have we," said the prince, "that this is not some varlet masquerading in his master's harness, or some caitiff knight, the very touch of whose lance might bring infamy upon an honorable gentleman?"

"It is not so, sire," cried the squire earnestly. "There is no man upon earth who would demean himself by breaking a lance with my master."

"You speak out boldly, squire," the prince answered; "but unless I have some further assurance of your master's noble birth and gentle name I cannot match the choicest lances of my court against him."

"You refuse, sire?"

"I do refuse."

"Then, sire, I was bidden to ask you from my master whether you would consent if Sir John Chandos, upon hearing my master's name, should assure you that he was indeed a man with whom you might yourself cross swords without indignity."

"I ask no better," said the prince.

"Then I must ask, Lord Chandos, that you will step forth. I have your pledge that the name shall remain ever a secret, and that you will neither say nor write one word which might betray it. The name is——" He stooped down from his horse and whispered something into the old knight's ear which made him start with surprise, and stare with much curiosity at the distant Knight, who was sitting his charger at the further end of the arena.

"Is this indeed sooth?" he exclaimed.

"It is, my lord, and I swear it by St. Ives of Brittany."

"I might have known it," said Chandos, twisting his moustache, and still looking thoughtfully at the cavalier.

"What then, Sir John?" asked the prince.

"Sire, this is a knight whom it is indeed great honor to meet, and I would that your grace would grant me leave to send my squire for my harness, for I would dearly love to run a course with him."

"Nay, nay, Sir John, you have gained as much honor as one man can bear, and it were hard if you could not rest now. But I pray you, squire, to tell your master that he is very welcome to our court, and that wines and spices will be served him, if he would refresh himself before jousting."

"My master will not drink," said the squire.

"Let him then name the gentleman with whom he would break a spear."

"He would contend with these five knights, each to choose such weapons as suit him best."

"I perceive," said the prince, "that your master is a man of great heart and high of enterprise. But the sun already is low in the west, and there will scarce be light for these courses. I pray you, gentlemen, to take your places, that we may see whether this stranger's deeds are as bold as his words."

The unknown knight had sat like a statue of steel, looking neither to the right nor to the left during these preliminaries. He had changed from the horse upon which he had ridden, and bestrode the black charger which his squire had led beside him. His immense breadth, his stern composed appearance, and the mode in which he handled his shield and his lance, were enough in themselves to convince the thousands of critical spectators that he was a dangerous opponent. Aylward, who stood in the front row of the archers with Simon, big John, and others of the Company, had been criticising the proceedings from the commencement with the ease and freedom of a man who had spent his life under arms and had learned in a hard school to know at a glance the points of a horse and his rider. He stared now at the stranger with a wrinkled brow and the air of a man who is striving to stir his memory.

"By my hilt! I have seen the thick body of him before to-day. Yet I cannot call to mind where it could have been. At Nogent belike, or was it at Auray? Mark me, lads, this man will prove to be one of the best lances of France, and there are no better in the world."

"It is but child's play, this poking game," said John. "I would fain try my hand at it, for, by the black rood! I think that it might be amended."

"What then would you do, John?" asked several.

"There are many things which might be done," said the forester thoughtfully. "Methinks that I would begin by breaking my spear."

"So they all strive to do."

"Nay, but not upon another man's shield. I would break it over my own knee."

"And what the better for that, old beef and bones?" asked Black Simon.

"So I would turn what is but a lady's bodkin of a weapon into a very handsome club."

"And then, John?"

"Then I would take the other's spear into my arm or my leg, or where it pleased him best to put it, and I would dash out his brains with my club."

"By my ten finger-bones! old John," said Aylward, "I would give my feather-bed to see you at a spear-running. This is a most courtly and gentle sport which you have devised."

"So it seems to me," said John seriously. "Or, again, one might seize the other round the middle, pluck him off his horse and bear him to the pavilion, there to hold him to ransom."

"Good!" cried Simon, amid a roar of laughter from all the archers round. "By Thomas of Kent! we shall make a camp-marshal of thee, and thou shalt draw up rules for our jousting. But, John, who is it that you would uphold in this knightly and pleasing fashion?"

"What mean you?"

"Why, John, so strong and strange a tilter must fight for the brightness of his lady's eyes or the curve of her eyelash, even as Sir Nigel does for the Lady Loring."

"I know not about that," said the big archer, scratching his head in perplexity. "Since Mary hath played me false, I can scarce fight for her."

"Yet any woman will serve."

"There is my mother then," said John. "She was at much pains at my upbringing, and, by my soul! I will uphold the curve of her eyelashes, for it tickleth my very heart-root to think of her. But who is here?"

"It is Sir William Beauchamp. He is a valiant man, but I fear that he is scarce firm enough upon the saddle to bear the thrust of such a tilter as this stranger promises to be."

Aylward's words were speedily justified, for even as he spoke the two knights met in the centre of the lists. Beauchamp struck his opponent a shrewd blow upon the helmet, but was met with so frightful a thrust that he whirled out of his saddle and rolled over and over upon the ground. Sir Thomas Percy met with little better success, for his shield was split, his vambrace torn and he himself wounded slightly in the side. Lord Audley and the unknown knight struck each other fairly upon the helmet; but, while the stranger sat as firm and rigid as ever upon his charger, the Englishman was bent back to his horse's cropper by the weight of the blow, and had galloped half-way down the lists ere he could recover himself. Sir Thomas Wake was beaten to the ground with a battle-axe—that being the weapon which he had selected—and had to be carried to his pavilion. These rapid successes, gained one after the other over four celebrated warriors, worked the crowd up to a pitch of wonder and admiration. Thunders of applause from the English soldiers, as well as from the citizens and peasants, showed how far the love of brave and knightly deeds could rise above the rivalries of race.

"By my soul! John," cried the prince, with his cheek flushed and his eyes shining, "this is a man of good courage and great hardiness. I could not have thought that there was any single arm upon earth which could have overthrown these four champions."

"He is indeed, as I have said, sire, a knight from whom much honor is to be gained. But the lower edge of the sun is wet, and it will be beneath the sea ere long."

"Here is Sir Nigel Loring, on foot and with his sword," said the prince. "I have heard that he is a fine swordsman."

"The finest in your army, sire," Chandos answered. "Yet I doubt not that he will need all his skill this day."

As he spoke, the two combatants advanced from either end in full armor with their two-handed swords sloping over their shoulders. The stranger walked heavily and with a measured stride, while the English knight advanced as briskly as though there was no iron shell to weigh down the freedom of his limbs. At four paces distance they stopped, eyed each other for a moment, and then in an instant fell to work with a clatter and clang as though two sturdy smiths were busy upon their anvils. Up and down went the long, shining blades, round and round they circled in curves of glimmering light, crossing, meeting, disengaging, with flash of sparks at every parry. Here and there bounded Sir Nigel, his head erect, his jaunty plume fluttering in the air, while his dark opponent sent in crashing blow upon blow, following fiercely up with cut and with thrust, but never once getting past the practised blade of the skilled swordsman. The crowd roared with delight as Sir Nigel would stoop his head to avoid a blow, or by some slight movement of his body allow some terrible thrust to glance harmlessly past him. Suddenly, however, his time came. The Frenchman, whirling up his sword, showed for an instant a chink betwixt his shoulder piece and the rerebrace which guarded his upper arm. In dashed Sir Nigel, and out again so swiftly that the eye could not follow the quick play of his blade, but a trickle of blood from the stranger's shoulder, and a rapidly widening red smudge upon his white surcoat, showed where the thrust had taken effect. The wound was, however, but a slight one, and the Frenchman was about to renew his onset, when, at a sign from the prince, Chandos threw down his baton, and the marshals of the lists struck up the weapons and brought the contest to an end.

"It were time to check it," said the prince, smiling, "for Sir Nigel is too good a man for me to lose, and, by the five holy wounds! if one of those cuts came home I should have fears for our champion. What think you, Pedro?"

"I think, Edward, that the little man was very well able to take care of himself. For my part, I should wish to see so well matched a pair fight on while a drop of blood remained in their veins."

"We must have speech with him. Such a man must not go from my court without rest or sup. Bring him hither, Chandos, and, certes, if the Lord Loring hath resigned his claim upon this goblet, it is right and proper that this cavalier should carry it to France with him as a sign of the prowess that he has shown this day."

As he spoke, the knight-errant, who had remounted his warhorse, galloped forward to the royal stand, with a silken kerchief bound round his wounded arm. The setting sun cast a ruddy glare upon his burnished arms, and sent his long black shadow streaming behind him up the level clearing. Pulling up his steed, he slightly inclined his head, and sat in the stern and composed fashion with which he had borne himself throughout, heedless of the applauding shouts and the flutter of kerchiefs from the long lines of brave men and of fair women who were looking down upon him.

"Sir knight," said the prince, "we have all marvelled this day at this great skill and valor with which God has been pleased to endow you. I would fain that you should tarry at our court, for a time at least, until your hurt is healed and your horses rested."

"My hurt is nothing, sire, nor are my horses weary," returned the stranger in a deep, stern voice.

"Will you not at least hie back to Bordeaux with us, that you may drain a cup of muscadine and sup at our table?"

"I will neither drink your wine nor sit at your table," returned the other. "I bear no love for you or for your race, and there is nought that I wish at your hands until the day when I see the last sail which bears you back to your island vanishing away against the western sky."

"These are bitter words, sir knight," said Prince Edward, with an angry frown.

"And they come from a bitter heart," answered the unknown knight. "How long is it since there has been peace in my hapless country? Where are the steadings, and orchards, and vineyards, which made France fair? Where are the cities which made her great? From Providence to Burgundy we are beset by every prowling hireling in Christendom, who rend and tear the country which you have left too weak to guard her own marches. Is it not a by-word that a man may ride all day in that unhappy land without seeing thatch upon roof or hearing the crow of cock? Does not one fair kingdom content you, that you should strive so for this other one which has no love for you? Pardieu! a true Frenchman's words may well be bitter, for bitter is his lot and bitter his thoughts as he rides through his thrice unhappy country."

"Sir knight," said the prince, "you speak like a brave man, and our cousin of France is happy in having a cavalier who is so fit to uphold his cause either with tongue or with sword. But if you think such evil of us, how comes it that you have trusted yourselves to us without warranty or safe-conduct?"

"Because I knew that you would be here, sire. Had the man who sits upon your right been ruler of this land, I had indeed thought twice before I looked to him for aught that was knightly or generous." With a soldierly salute, he wheeled round his horse, and, galloping down the lists, disappeared amid the dense crowd of footmen and of horsemen who were streaming away from the scene of the tournament.

"The insolent villain!" cried Pedro, glaring furiously after him. "I have seen a man's tongue torn from his jaws for less. Would it not be well even now, Edward, to send horsemen to hale him back? Bethink you that it may be one of the royal house of France, or at least some knight whose loss would be a heavy blow to his master. Sir William Felton, you are well mounted, gallop after the caitiff, I pray you."

"Do so, Sir William," said the prince, "and give him this purse of a hundred nobles as a sign of the respect which I bear for him; for, by St. George! he has served his master this day even as I would wish liegeman of mine to serve me." So saying, the prince turned his back upon the King of Spain, and springing upon his horse, rode slowly homewards to the Abbey of Saint Andrew's.

XXV

How Sir Nigel Wrote to Twynham Castle

On the morning after the jousting, when Alleyne Edricson went, as was his custom, into his master's chamber to wait upon him in his dressing and to curl his hair, he found him already up and very busily at work. He sat at a table by the window, a deer-hound on one side of him and a lurcher on the other, his feet tucked away under the trestle on which he sat, and his tongue in his cheek, with the air of a man who is much perplexed. A sheet of vellum lay upon the board in front of him, and he held a pen in his hand, with which he had been scribbling in a rude schoolboy hand. So many were the blots, however, and so numerous the scratches and erasures, that he had at last given it up in despair, and sat with his single uncovered eye cocked upwards at the ceiling, as one who waits upon inspiration.

"By Saint Paul!" he cried, as Alleyne entered, "you are the man who will stand by me in this matter. I have been in sore need of you, Alleyne."

"God be with you, my fair lord!" the squire answered. "I trust that you have taken no hurt from all that you have gone through yesterday."

"Nay; I feel the fresher for it, Alleyne. It has eased my joints, which were somewhat stiff from these years of peace. I trust, Alleyne, that thou didst very carefully note and mark the bearing and carriage of this knight of France; for it is time, now when you are young, that you should see all that is best, and mould your own actions in accordance. This was a man from whom much honor might be gained, and I have seldom met any one for whom I have conceived so much love and esteem. Could I but learn his name, I should send you to him with my cartel, that we might have further occasion to watch his goodly feats of arms."

"It is said, my fair lord, that none know his name save only the Lord Chandos, and that he is under vow not to speak it. So ran the gossip at the squires' table."

"Be he who he might, he was a very hardy gentleman. But I have a task here, Alleyne, which is harder to me than aught that was set before me yesterday."

"Can I help you, my lord?"

"That indeed you can. I have been writing my greetings to my sweet wife; for I hear that a messenger goes from the prince to Southampton within the week, and he would gladly take a packet for me. I pray you, Alleyne, to cast your eyes upon what I have written, and see it they are such words as my lady will understand. My fingers, as you can see, are more used to iron and leather than to the drawing of strokes and turning of letters. What then? Is there aught amiss, that you should stare so?"

"It is this first word, my lord. In what tongue were you pleased to write?"

"In English; for my lady talks it more than she doth French.

"Yet this is no English word, my sweet lord. Here are four t's and never a letter betwixt them."

"By St. Paul! it seemed strange to my eye when I wrote it," said Sir Nigel. "They bristle up together like a clump of lances. We must break their ranks and set them farther apart. The word is 'that.' Now I will read it to you, Alleyne, and you shall write it out fair; for we leave Bordeaux this day, and it would be great joy to me to think that the Lady Loring had word from me."

Alleyne sat down as ordered, with a pen in his hand and a fresh sheet of parchment before him, while Sir Nigel slowly spelled out his letter, running his forefinger on from word to word.

"That my heart is with thee, my dear sweeting, is what thine own heart will assure thee of. All is well with us here, save that Pepin hath the mange on his back, and Pommers hath scarce yet got clear of his stiffness from being four days on ship-board, and the more so because the sea was very high, and we were like to founder on account of a hole in her side, which was made by a stone cast at us by certain sea-rovers, who may the saints have in their keeping, for they have gone from amongst us, as has young Terlake, and two-score mariners and archers, who would be the more welcome here as there is like to be a very fine war, with much honor and all hopes of advancement, for which I go to gather my Company together, who are now at Montaubon, where they pillage and destroy; yet I hope that, by God's help, I may be able to show that I am their master, even as, my sweet lady, I am thy servant."

"How of that, Alleyne?" continued Sir Nigel, blinking at his squire, with an expression of some pride upon his face. "Have I not told her all that hath befallen us?"

"You have said much, my fair lord; and yet, if I may say so, it is somewhat crowded together, so that my Lady Loring can, mayhap, scarce follow it. Were it in shorter periods——"

"Nay, it boots me not how you marshal them, as long as they are all there at the muster. Let my lady have the words, and she will place them in such order as pleases her best. But I would have you add what it would please her to know."

"That will I," said Alleyne, blithely, and bent to the task.

"My fair lady and mistress," he wrote, "God hath had us in His keeping, and my lord is well and in good cheer. He hath won much honor at the jousting before the prince, when he alone was able to make it good against a very valiant man from France. Touching the moneys, there is enough and to spare until we reach Montaubon. Herewith, my fair lady, I send my humble regards, entreating you that you will give the same to your daughter, the Lady Maude. May the holy saints have you both in their keeping is ever the prayer of thy servant,

ALLEYNE EDRICSON.

"That is very fairly set forth," said Sir Nigel, nodding his bald head as each sentence was read to him. "And for thyself, Alleyne, if there be any dear friend to whom you would fain give greeting, I can send it for thee within this packet."

"There is none," said Alleyne, sadly.

"Have you no kinsfolk, then?"

"None, save my brother."

"Ha! I had forgotten that there was ill blood betwixt you. But are there none in all England who love thee?"

"None that I dare say so."

"And none whom you love?"

"Nay, I will not say that," said Alleyne.

Sir Nigel shook his head and laughed softly to himself, "I see how it is with you," he said. "Have I not noted your frequent sighs and vacant eye? Is she fair?"

"She is indeed," cried Alleyne from his heart, all tingling at this sudden turn of the talk.

"And good?"

"As an angel."

"And yet she loves you not?"

"Nay, I cannot say that she loves another."

"Then you have hopes?"

"I could not live else."

"Then must you strive to be worthy of her love. Be brave and pure, fearless to the strong and humble to the weak; and so, whether this love prosper or no, you will have fitted yourself to be honored by a maiden's love, which is, in sooth, the highest guerdon which a true knight can hope for."

"Indeed, my lord, I do so strive," said Alleyne; "but she is so sweet, so dainty, and of so noble a spirit, that I fear me that I shall never be worthy of her."

"By thinking so you become worthy. Is she then of noble birth?"

"She is, my lord," faltered Alleyne.

"Of a knightly house?"

"Yes."

"Have a care, Alleyne, have a care!" said Sir Nigel, kindly. "The higher the steed the greater the fall. Hawk not at that which may be beyond thy flight."

"My lord, I know little of the ways and usages of the world," cried Alleyne, "but I would fain ask your rede upon the matter. You have known my father and my kin: is not my family one of good standing and repute?"

"Beyond all question."

"And yet you warn me that I must not place my love too high."

"Were Minstead yours, Alleyne, then, by St. Paul! I cannot think that any family in the land would not be proud to take you among them, seeing that you come of so old a strain. But while the Socman lives—— Ha, by my soul! if this is not Sir Oliver's step I am the more mistaken."

As he spoke, a heavy footfall was heard without, and the portly knight flung open the door and strode into the room.

"Why, my little coz," said he, "I have come across to tell you that I live above the barber's in the Rue de la Tour, and that there is a venison pasty in the oven and two flasks of the right vintage on the table. By St. James! a blind man might find the place, for one has but to get in the wind from it, and follow the savory smell. Put on your cloak, then, and come, for Sir Walter Hewett and Sir Robert Briquet, with one or two others, are awaiting us."

"Nay, Oliver, I cannot be with you, for I must to Montaubon this day."

"To Montaubon? But I have heard that your Company is to come with my forty Winchester rascals to Dax."

"If you will take charge of them, Oliver. For I will go to Montaubon with none save my two squires and two archers. Then, when I have found the rest of my Company I shall lead them to Dax. We set forth this morning."

"Then I must back to my pasty," said Sir Oliver. "You will find us at Dax, I doubt not, unless the prince throw me into prison, for he is very wroth against me."

"And why, Oliver?"

"Pardieu! because I have sent my cartel, gauntlet, and defiance to Sir John Chandos and to Sir William Felton."

"To Chandos? In God's name, Oliver, why have you done this?"

"Because he and the other have used me despitefully."

"And how?"

"Because they have passed me over in choosing those who should joust for England. Yourself and Audley I could pass, coz, for you are mature men; but who are Wake, and Percy, and Beauchamp? By my soul! I was prodding for my food into a camp-kettle when they were howling for their pap. Is a man of my weight and substance to be thrown aside for the first three half-grown lads who have learned the trick of the tilt-yard? But hark ye, coz, I think of sending my cartel also to the prince."

"Oliver! Oliver! You are mad!"

"Not I, i' faith! I care not a denier whether he be prince or no. By Saint James! I see that your squire's eyes are starting from his head like a trussed crab. Well, friend, we are all three men of Hampshire, and not lightly to be jeered at."

"Has he jeered at you than?"

"Pardieu! yes, 'Old Sir Oliver's heart is still stout,' said one of his court. 'Else had it been out of keeping with the rest of him,' quoth the prince. 'And his arm is strong,' said another. 'So is the backbone of his horse,' quoth the prince. This very day I will send him my cartel and defiance."

"Nay, nay, my dear Oliver," said Sir Nigel, laying his hand upon his angry friend's arm. "There is naught in this, for it was but saying that you were a strong and robust man, who had need of a good destrier. And as to Chandos and Felton, bethink you that if when you yourself were young the older lances had ever been preferred, how would you then have had the chance to earn the good name and fame which you now bear? You do not ride as light as you did, Oliver, and I ride lighter by the weight of my hair, but it would be an ill thing if in the evening of our lives we showed that our hearts were less true and loyal than of old. If such a knight as Sir Oliver Buttesthorn may turn against his own prince for the sake of a light word, then where are we to look for steadfast faith and constancy?"

"Ah! my dear little coz, it is easy to sit in the sunshine and preach to the man in the shadow. Yet you could ever win me over to your side with that soft voice of yours. Let us think no more of it then. But, holy Mother! I had forgot the pasty, and it will be as scorched as Judas Iscariot! Come, Nigel, lest the foul fiend get the better of me again."

"For one hour, then; for we march at mid-day. Tell Aylward, Alleyne, that he is to come with me to Montaubon, and to choose one archer for his comrade. The rest will to Dax when the prince starts, which will be before the feast of the Epiphany. Have Pommers ready at mid-day with my sycamore lance, and place my harness on the sumpter mule."

With these brief directions, the two old soldiers strode off together, while Alleyne hastened to get all in order for their journey.

XXVI

How the Three Comrades Gained a Mighty Treasure

It was a bright, crisp winter's day when the little party set off from Bordeaux on their journey to Montaubon, where the missing half of their Company had last been heard of. Sir Nigel and Ford had ridden on in advance, the knight upon his hackney, while his great war-horse trotted beside his squire. Two hours later Alleyne Edricson followed; for he had the tavern reckoning to settle, and many other duties which fell to him as squire of the body. With him came Aylward and Hordle John, armed as of old, but mounted for their journey upon a pair of clumsy Landes horses, heavy-headed and shambling, but of great endurance, and capable of jogging along all day, even when between the knees of the huge archer, who turned the scale at two hundred and seventy pounds. They took with them the sumpter mules, which carried in panniers the wardrobe and table furniture of Sir Nigel; for the knight, though neither fop nor epicure, was very dainty in small matters, and loved, however bare the board or hard the life, that his napery should still be white and his spoon of silver.

There had been frost during the night, and the white hard road rang loud under their horses' irons as they spurred through the east gate of the town, along the same broad highway which the unknown French champion had traversed on the day of the jousts. The three rode abreast, Alleyne Edricson with his eyes cast down and his mind distrait, for his thoughts were busy with the conversation which he had had with Sir Nigel in the morning. Had he done well to say so much, or had he not done better to have said more? What would the knight have said had he confessed to his love for the Lady Maude? Would he cast him off in disgrace, or might he chide him as having abused the shelter of his roof? It had been ready upon his tongue to tell him all when Sir Oliver had broken in upon them. Perchance Sir Nigel, with his love of all the dying usages of chivalry, might have contrived some strange ordeal or feat of arms by which his love should be put to the test. Alleyne smiled as he wondered what fantastic and wondrous deed would be exacted from him. Whatever it was, he was ready for it, whether it were to hold the lists in the court of the King of Tartary, to carry a cartel to the Sultan of Baghdad, or to serve a term against the wild heathen of Prussia. Sir Nigel had said that his birth was high enough for any lady, if his fortune could but be amended. Often had Alleyne curled his lip at the beggarly craving for land or for gold which blinded man to the higher and more lasting issues of life. Now it seemed as though it were only by this same land and gold that he might hope to reach his heart's desire. But then, again, the Socman of Minstead was no friend to the Constable of Twynham Castle. It might happen that, should he amass riches by some happy fortune of war, this feud might hold the two families aloof. Even if Maude loved him, he knew her too well to think that she would wed him without the blessing of her father. Dark and murky was it all, but hope mounts high in youth, and it ever fluttered over all the turmoil of his thoughts like a white plume amid the shock of horsemen.

If Alleyne Edricson had enough to ponder over as he rode through the bare plains of Guienne, his two companions were more busy with the present and less thoughtful of the future. Aylward rode for half a mile with his chin upon his shoulder, looking back at a white kerchief which fluttered out of the gable window of a high house which peeped over the corner of the battlements. When at last a dip of the road hid it from his view, he cocked his steel cap, shrugged his broad shoulders, and rode on with laughter in his eyes, and his weather-beaten face all ashine with pleasant memories. John also rode in silence, but his eyes wandered slowly from one side of the road to the other, and he stared and pondered and nodded his head like a traveller who makes his notes and saves them up for the re-telling.

"By the rood!" he broke out suddenly, slapping his thigh with his great red hand, "I knew that there was something a-missing, but I could not bring to my mind what it was."

"What was it then?" asked Alleyne, coming with a start out of his reverie.

"Why, it is the hedgerows," roared John, with a shout of laughter. "The country is all scraped as clear as a friar's poll. But indeed I cannot think much of the folk in these parts. Why do they not get to work and dig up these long rows of black and crooked stumps which I see on every hand? A franklin of Hampshire would think shame to have such litter upon his soil."

"Thou foolish old John!" quoth Aylward. "You should know better, since I have heard that the monks of Beaulieu could squeeze a good cup of wine from their own grapes. Know then that if these rows were dug up the wealth of the country would be gone, and mayhap there would be dry throats and gaping mouths in England, for in three months' time these black roots will blossom and shoot and burgeon, and from them will come many a good ship-load of Medoc and Gascony which will cross the narrow seas. But see the church in the hollow, and the folk who cluster in the churchyard! By my hilt! it is a burial, and there is a passing bell!" He pulled off his steel cap as he spoke and crossed himself, with a muttered prayer for the repose of the dead.

"There too," remarked Alleyne, as they rode on again, "that which seems to the eye to be dead is still full of the sap of life, even as the vines were. Thus God hath written Himself and His laws very broadly on all that is around us, if our poor dull eyes and duller souls could but read what He hath set before us."

"Ha! mon petit," cried the bowman, "you take me back to the days when you were new fledged, as sweet a little chick as ever pecked his way out of a monkish egg. I had feared that in gaining our debonair young man-at-arms we had lost our soft-spoken clerk. In truth, I have noted much change in you since we came from Twynham Castle."

"Surely it would be strange else, seeing that I have lived in a world so new to me. Yet I trust that there are many things in which I have not changed. If I have turned to serve an earthly master, and to carry arms for an earthly king, it would be an ill thing if I were to lose all thought of the great high King and Master of all, whose humble and unworthy servant I was ere ever I left Beaulieu. You, John, are also from the cloisters, but I trow that you do not feel that you have deserted the old service in taking on the new."

"I am a slow-witted man," said John, "and, in sooth, when I try to think about such matters it casts a gloom upon me. Yet I do not look upon myself as a worse man in an archer's jerkin than I was in a white cowl, if that be what you mean."

"You have but changed from one white company to the other," quoth Aylward. "But, by these ten finger-bones! it is a passing strange thing to me to think that it was but in the last fall of the leaf that we walked from Lyndhurst together, he so gentle and maidenly, and you, John, like a great red-limbed overgrown moon-calf; and now here you are as sprack a squire and as lusty an archer as ever passed down the highway from Bordeaux, while I am still the same old Samkin Aylward, with never a change, save that I have a few more sins on my soul and a few less crowns in my pouch. But I have never yet heard, John, what the reason was why you should come out of Beaulieu."

"There were seven reasons," said John thoughtfully. "The first of them was that they threw me out."

"Ma foi! camarade, to the devil with the other six! That is enough for me and for thee also. I can see that they are very wise and discreet folk at Beaulieu. Ah! mon ange, what have you in the pipkin?"

"It is milk, worthy sir," answered the peasant-maid, who stood by the door of a cottage with a jug in her hand. "Would it please you, gentles, that I should bring you out three horns of it?"

"Nay, ma petite, but here is a two-sous piece for thy kindly tongue and for the sight of thy pretty face. Ma foi! but she has a bonne mine. I have a mind to bide and speak with her."

"Nay, nay, Aylward," cried Alleyne. "Sir Nigel will await us, and he in haste."

"True, true, camarade! Adieu, ma cherie! mon coeur est toujours a toi. Her mother is a well-grown woman also. See where she digs by the wayside. Ma foi! the riper fruit is ever the sweeter. Bon jour, ma belle dame! God have you in his keeping! Said Sir Nigel where he would await us?"

"At Marmande or Aiguillon. He said that we could not pass him, seeing that there is but the one road."

"Aye, and it is a road that I know as I know the Midhurst parish butts," quoth the bowman. "Thirty times have I journeyed it, forward and backward, and, by the twang of string! I am wont to come back this way more laden than I went. I have carried all that I had into France in a wallet, and it hath taken four sumpter-mules to carry it back again. God's benison on the man who first turned his hand to the making of war! But there, down in the dingle, is the church of Cardillac, and you may see the inn where three poplars grow beyond the village. Let us on, for a stoup of wine would hearten us upon our way."

The highway had lain through the swelling vineyard country, which stretched away to the north and east in gentle curves, with many a peeping spire and feudal tower, and cluster of village houses, all clear cut and hard in the bright wintry air. To their right stretched the blue Garonne, running swiftly seawards, with boats and barges dotted over its broad bosom. On the other side lay a strip of vineyard, and beyond it the desolate and sandy region of the Landes, all tangled with faded gorse and heath and broom, stretching away in unbroken gloom to the blue hills which lay low upon the furthest sky-line. Behind them might still be seen the broad estuary of the Gironde, with the high towers of Saint Andre and Saint Remi shooting up from the plain. In front, amid radiating lines of poplars, lay the riverside townlet of Cardillac—gray walls, white houses, and a feather of blue smoke.

"This is the 'Mouton d'Or,'" said Aylward, as they pulled up their horses at a whitewashed straggling hostel. "What ho there!" he continued, beating upon the door with the hilt of his sword. "Tapster, ostler, varlet, hark hither, and a wannion on your lazy limbs! Ha! Michel, as red in the nose as ever! Three jacks of the wine of the country, Michel—for the air bites shrewdly. I pray you, Alleyne, to take note of this door, for I have a tale concerning it."

"Tell me, friend," said Alleyne to the portly red-faced inn-keeper, "has a knight and a squire passed this way within the hour?"

"Nay, sir, it would be two hours back. Was he a small man, weak in the eyes, with a want of hair, and speaks very quiet when he is most to be feared?"

"The same," the squire answered. "But I marvel how you should know how he speaks when he is in wrath, for he is very gentle-minded with those who are beneath him."

"Praise to the saints! it was not I who angered him," said the fat Michel.

"Who, then?"

"It was young Sieur de Crespigny of Saintonge, who chanced to be here, and made game of the Englishman, seeing that he was but a small man and hath a face which is full of peace. But indeed this good knight was a very quiet and patient man, for he saw that the Sieur de Crespigny was still young and spoke from an empty head, so he sat his horse and quaffed his wine, even as you are doing now, all heedless of the clacking tongue."

"And what then, Michel?"

"Well, messieurs, it chanced that the Sieur de Crespigny, having said this and that, for the laughter of the varlets, cried out at last about the glove that the knight wore in his coif, asking if it was the custom in England for a man to wear a great archer's glove in his cap. Pardieu! I have never seen a man get off his horse as quick as did that stranger Englishman. Ere the words were past the other's lips he was beside him, his face nigh touching, and his breath hot upon his cheeks. 'I think, young sir,' quoth he softly, looking into the other's eyes, 'that now that

I am nearer you will very clearly see that the glove is not an archer's glove.' 'Perchance not,' said the Sieur de Crespigny with a twitching lip. 'Nor is it large, but very small,' quoth the Englishman. 'Less large than I had thought,' said the other, looking down, for the knight's gaze was heavy upon his eyelids. 'And in every way such a glove as might be worn by the fairest and sweetest lady in England,' quoth the Englishman. 'It may be so,' said the Sieur de Crespigny, turning his face from him. 'I am myself weak in the eyes, and have often taken one thing for another,' quoth the knight, as he sprang back into his saddle and rode off, leaving the Sieur de Crespigny biting his nails before the door. Ha! by the five wounds, many men of war have drunk my wine, but never one was more to my fancy than this little Englishman."

"By my hilt! he is our master, Michel," quoth Aylward, "and such men as we do not serve under a laggart. But here are four deniers, Michel, and God be with you! En avant, camarades! for we have a long road before us."

At a brisk trot the three friends left Cardillac and its wine-house behind them, riding without a halt past St. Macaire, and on by ferry over the river Dorpt. At the further side the road winds through La Reolle, Bazaille, and Marmande, with the sunlit river still gleaming upon the right, and the bare poplars bristling up upon either side. John and Alleyne rode silent on either side, but every inn, farm-steading, or castle brought back to Aylward some remembrance of love, foray, or plunder, with which to beguile the way.

"There is the smoke from Bazas, on the further side of Garonne," quoth he. "There were three sisters yonder, the daughters of a farrier, and, by these ten finger-bones! a man might ride for a long June day and never set eyes upon such maidens. There was Marie, tall and grave, and Blanche petite and gay, and the dark Agnes, with eyes that went through you like a waxed arrow. I lingered there as long as four days, and was betrothed to them all; for it seemed shame to set one above her sisters, and might make ill blood in the family. Yet, for all my care, things were not merry in the house, and I thought it well to come away. There, too, is the mill of Le Souris. Old Pierre Le Caron, who owned it, was a right good comrade, and had ever a seat and a crust for a weary archer. He was a man who wrought hard at all that he turned his hand to; but he heated himself in grinding bones to mix with his flour, and so through over-diligence he brought a fever upon himself and died."

"Tell me, Aylward," said Alleyne, "what was amiss with the door of yonder inn that you should ask me to observe it."

"Pardieu! yes, I had well-nigh forgot. What saw you on yonder door?"

"I saw a square hole, through which doubtless the host may peep when he is not too sure of those who knock."

"And saw you naught else?"

"I marked that beneath this hole there was a deep cut in the door, as though a great nail had been driven in."

"And naught else?"

"No."

"Had you looked more closely you might have seen that there was a stain upon the wood. The first time that I ever heard my comrade Black Simon laugh was in front of that door. I heard him once again when he slew a French squire with his teeth, he being unarmed and the Frenchman having a dagger."

"And why did Simon laugh in front of the inn-door!" asked John.

"Simon is a hard and perilous man when he hath the bitter drop in him; and, by my hilt! he was born for war, for there is little sweetness or rest in him. This inn, the 'Mouton d'Or,' was kept in the old days by one Francois Gourval, who had a hard fist and a harder heart. It was said that many and many an archer coming from the wars had been served with wine with simples in it, until he slept, and had then been stripped of all by this Gourval. Then on the morrow, if he made complaint, this wicked Gourval would throw him out upon the road or beat him, for he was a very lusty man, and had many stout varlets in his service. This chanced to come to Simon's ears when we were at Bordeaux together, and he would have it that we should ride to Cardillac with a good hempen cord, and give this Gourval such a scourging as he merited. Forth we rode then, but when we came to the 'Mouton d'Or,' Gourval had had word of our coming and its purpose, so that the door was barred, nor was there any way into the house. 'Let us in, good Master Gourval!' cried Simon, and 'Let us in, good Master Gourval!' cried I, but no word could we get through the hole in the door, save that he would draw an arrow upon us unless we went on our way. 'Well, Master Gourval,' quoth Simon at last, 'this is but a sorry welcome, seeing that we have ridden so far just to shake you by the hand.' 'Canst shake me by the hand without coming in,' said Gourval. 'And how that?' asked Simon. 'By passing in your hand through the hole,' said he. 'Nay, my hand is wounded,' quoth Simon, 'and of such a size that I cannot pass it in.' 'That need not hinder,' said Gourval, who was hot to be rid of us, 'pass in your left hand.' 'But I have something for thee, Gourval,' said

Simon. 'What then?' he asked. 'There was an English archer who slept here last week of the name of Hugh of Nutbourne.' 'We have had many rogues here,' said Gourval. 'His conscience hath been heavy within him because he owes you a debt of fourteen deniers, having drunk wine for which he hath never paid. For the easing of his soul, he asked me to pay the money to you as I passed.' Now this Gourval was very greedy for money, so he thrust forth his hand for the fourteen deniers, but Simon had his dagger ready and he pinned his hand to the door. 'I have paid the Englishman's debt, Gourval!' quoth he, and so rode away, laughing so that he could scarce sit his horse, leaving mine host still nailed to his door. Such is the story of the hole which you have marked, and of the smudge upon the wood. I have heard that from that time English archers have been better treated in the auberge of Cardillac. But what have we here by the wayside?"

"It appears to be a very holy man," said Alleyne.

"And, by the rood! he hath some strange wares," cried John. "What are these bits of stone, and of wood, and rusted nails, which are set out in front of him?"

The man whom they had remarked sat with his back against a cherry-tree, and his legs shooting out in front of him, like one who is greatly at his ease. Across his thighs was a wooden board, and scattered over it all manner of slips of wood and knobs of brick and stone, each laid separate from the other, as a huckster places his wares. He was dressed in a long gray gown, and wore a broad hat of the same color, much weather-stained, with three scallop-shells dangling from the brim. As they approached, the travellers observed that he was advanced in years, and that his eyes were upturned and yellow.

"Dear knights and gentlemen," he cried in a high crackling voice, "worthy Christian cavaliers, will ye ride past and leave an aged pilgrim to die of hunger? The sight hast been burned from mine eyes by the sands of the Holy Land, and I have had neither crust of bread nor cup of wine these two days past."

"By my hilt! father," said Aylward, looking keenly at him, "it is a marvel to me that thy girdle should have so goodly a span and clip thee so closely, if you have in sooth had so little to place within it."

"Kind stranger," answered the pilgrim, "you have unwittingly spoken words which are very grievous to me to listen to. Yet I should be loth to blame you, for I doubt not that what you said was not meant to sadden me, nor to bring my sore affliction back to my mind. It ill becomes me to prate too much of what I have endured for the faith, and yet, since you have observed it, I must tell you that this thickness and roundness of the waist is caused by a dropsy brought on by over-haste in journeying from the house of Pilate to the Mount of Olives."

"There, Aylward," said Alleyne, with a reddened cheek, "let that curb your blunt tongue. How could you bring a fresh pang to this holy man, who hath endured so much and hath journeyed as far as Christ's own blessed tomb?"

"May the foul fiend strike me dumb!" cried the bowman in hot repentance; but both the palmer and Alleyne threw up their hands to stop him.

"I forgive thee from my heart, dear brother," piped the blind man. "But, oh, these wild words of thine are worse to mine ears than aught which you could say of me."

"Not another word shall I speak," said Aylward; "but here is a franc for thee and I crave thy blessing."

"And here is another," said Alleyne.

"And another," cried Hordle John.

But the blind palmer would have none of their alms. "Foolish, foolish pride!" he cried, beating upon his chest with his large brown hand. "Foolish, foolish pride! How long then will it be ere I can scourge it forth? Am I then never to conquer it? Oh, strong, strong are the ties of flesh, and hard it is to subdue the spirit! I come, friends, of a noble house, and I cannot bring myself to touch this money, even though it be to save me from the grave."

"Alas! father," said Alleyne, "how then can we be of help to thee?"

"I had sat down here to die," quoth the palmer; "but for many years I have carried in my wallet these precious things which you see set forth now before me. It were sin, thought I, that my secret should perish with me. I shall therefore sell these things to the first worthy passers-by, and from them I shall have money enough to take me to the shrine of Our Lady at Rocamadour, where I hope to lay these old bones."

"What are these treasures, then, father?" asked Hordle John. "I can but see an old rusty nail, with bits of stone and slips of wood."

"My friend," answered the palmer, "not all the money that is in this country could pay a just price for these wares of mine. This nail," he continued, pulling off his hat and turning up his sightless orbs, "is one of those wherewith man's salvation was secured. I had it, together with this piece of the true rood, from the five-and-twentieth descendant of

Joseph of Arimathea, who still lives in Jerusalem alive and well, though latterly much afflicted by boils. Aye, you may well cross yourselves, and I beg that you will not breathe upon it or touch it with your fingers."

"And the wood and stone, holy father?" asked Alleyne, with bated breath, as he stared awe-struck at his precious relics.

"This cantle of wood is from the true cross, this other from Noah his ark, and the third is from the door-post of the temple of the wise King Solomon. This stone was thrown at the sainted Stephen, and the other two are from the Tower of Babel. Here, too, is part of Aaron's rod, and a lock of hair from Elisha the prophet."

"But, father," quoth Alleyne, "the holy Elisha was bald, which brought down upon him the revilements of the wicked children."

"It is very true that he had not much hair," said the palmer quickly, "and it is this which makes this relic so exceeding precious. Take now your choice of these, my worthy gentlemen, and pay such a price as your consciences will suffer you to offer; for I am not a chapman nor a huckster, and I would never part with them, did I not know that I am very near to my reward."

"Aylward," said Alleyne excitedly, "this is such a chance as few folk have twice in one life. The nail I must have, and I will give it to the abbey of Beaulieu, so that all the folk in England may go thither to wonder and to pray."

"And I will have the stone from the temple," cried Hordle John. "What would not my old mother give to have it hung over her bed?"

"And I will have Aaron's rod," quoth Aylward. "I have but five florins in the world, and here are four of them."

"Here are three more," said John.

"And here are five more," added Alleyne. "Holy father, I hand you twelve florins, which is all that we can give, though we well know how poor a pay it is for the wondrous things which you sell us."

"Down, pride, down!" cried the pilgrim, still beating upon his chest. "Can I not bend myself then to take this sorry sum which is offered me for that which has cost me the labors of a life. Give me the dross! Here are the precious relics, and, oh, I pray you that you will handle them softly and with reverence, else had I rather left my unworthy bones here by the wayside."

With doffed caps and eager hands, the comrades took their new and precious possessions, and pressed onwards upon their journey, leaving the aged palmer still seated under the cherry-tree. They rode in silence, each with his treasure in his hand, glancing at it from time to time, and scarce able to believe that chance had made them sole owners of relics of such holiness and worth that every abbey and church in Christendom would have bid eagerly for their possession. So they journeyed, full of this good fortune, until opposite the town of Le Mas, where John's horse cast a shoe, and they were glad to find a wayside smith who might set the matter to rights. To him Aylward narrated the good hap which had befallen them; but the smith, when his eyes lit upon the relics, leaned up against his anvil and laughed, with his hand to his side, until the tears hopped down his sooty cheeks.

"Why, masters," quoth he, "this man is a coquillart, or seller of false relics, and was here in the smithy not two hours ago. This nail that he hath sold you was taken from my nail-box, and as to the wood and the stones, you will see a heap of both outside from which he hath filled his scrip."

"Nay, nay," cried Alleyne, "this was a holy man who had journeyed to Jerusalem, and acquired a dropsy by running from the house of Pilate to the Mount of Olives."

"I know not about that," said the smith; "but I know that a man with a gray palmer's hat and gown was here no very long time ago, and that he sat on yonder stump and ate a cold pullet and drank a flask of wine. Then he begged from me one of my nails, and filling his scrip with stones, he went upon his way. Look at these nails, and see if they are not the same as that which he has sold you."

"Now may God save us!" cried Alleyne, all aghast. "Is there no end then to the wickedness of humankind? He so humble, so aged, so loth to take our money—and yet a villain and a cheat. Whom can we trust or believe in?"

"I will after him," said Aylward, flinging himself into the saddle. "Come, Alleyne, we may catch him ere John's horse be shod."

Away they galloped together, and ere long they saw the old gray palmer walking slowly along in front of them. He turned, however, at the sound of their hoofs, and it was clear that his blindness was a cheat like all the rest of him, for he ran swiftly through a field and so into a wood, where none could follow him. They hurled their relics after him, and so rode back to the blacksmith's the poorer both in pocket and in faith.

XXVII

How Roger Club-foot Was Passed Into Paradise

It was evening before the three comrades came into Aiguillon. There they found Sir Nigel Loring and Ford safely lodged at the sign of the "Baton Rouge," where they supped on good fare and slept between lavender-scented sheets. It chanced, however, that a knight of Poitou, Sir Gaston d'Estelle, was staying there on his way back from Lithuania, where he had served a term with the Teutonic knights under the land-master of the presbytery of Marienberg. He and Sir Nigel sat late in high converse as to bushments, outfalls, and the intaking of cities, with many tales of warlike men and valiant deeds. Then their talk turned to minstrelsy, and the stranger knight drew forth a cittern, upon which he played the minne-lieder of the north, singing the while in a high cracked voice of Hildebrand and Brunhild and Siegfried, and all the strength and beauty of the land of Almain. To this Sir Nigel answered with the romances of Sir Eglamour, and of Sir Isumbras, and so through the long winter night they sat by the crackling wood-fire answering each other's songs until the crowing cocks joined in their concert. Yet, with scarce an hour of rest, Sir Nigel was as blithe and bright as ever as they set forth after breakfast upon their way.

"This Sir Gaston is a very worthy man," said he to his squires as they rode from the "Baton Rouge." "He hath a very strong desire to advance himself, and would have entered upon some small knightly debate with me, had he not chanced to have his arm-bone broken by the kick of a horse. I have conceived a great love for him, and I have promised him that when his bone is mended I will exchange thrusts with him. But we must keep to this road upon the left."

"Nay, my fair lord," quoth Aylward. "The road to Montaubon is over the river, and so through Quercy and the Agenois."

"True, my good Aylward; but I have learned from this worthy knight, who hath come over the French marches, that there is a company of Englishmen who are burning and plundering in the country round Villefranche. I have little doubt, from what he says, that they are those whom we seek."

"By my hilt! it is like enough," said Aylward. "By all accounts they had been so long at Montaubon, that there would be little there worth the taking. Then as they have already been in the south, they would come north to the country of the Aveyron."

"We shall follow the Lot until we come to Cahors, and then cross the marches into Villefranche," said Sir Nigel. "By St. Paul! as we are but a small band, it is very likely that we may have some very honorable and pleasing adventure, for I hear that there is little peace upon the French border."

All morning they rode down a broad and winding road, barred with the shadows of poplars. Sir Nigel rode in front with his squires, while the two archers followed behind with the sumpter mule between them. They had left Aiguillon and the Garonne far to the south, and rode now by the tranquil Lot, which curves blue and placid through a gently rolling country. Alleyne could not but mark that, whereas in Guienne there had been many townlets and few castles, there were now many castles and few houses. On either hand gray walls and square grim keeps peeped out at every few miles from amid the forests while the few villages which they passed were all ringed round with rude walls, which spoke of the constant fear and sudden foray of a wild frontier land. Twice during the morning there came bands of horsemen swooping down upon them from the black gateways of wayside strongholds, with short, stern questions as to whence they came and what their errand. Bands of armed men clanked along the highway, and the few lines of laden mules which carried the merchandise of the trader were guarded by armed varlets, or by archers hired for the service.

"The peace of Bretigny hath not made much change in these parts," quoth Sir Nigel, "for the country is overrun with free companions and masterless men. Yonder towers, between the wood and the hill, mark the town of Cahors, and beyond it is the land of France. But here is a man by the wayside, and as he hath two horses and a squire I make little doubt that he is a knight. I pray you, Alleyne, to give him greeting from me, and to ask him for his titles and coat-armor. It may be that I can relieve him of some vow, or perchance he hath a lady whom he would wish to advance."

"Nay, my fair lord," said Alleyne, "these are not horses and a squire, but mules and a varlet. The man is a mercer, for he hath a great bundle beside him."

"Now, God's blessing on your honest English voice!" cried the stranger, pricking up his ears at the sound of Alleyne's words. "Never have I heard music that was so sweet to mine ear. Come, Watkin lad, throw the bales over Laura's back! My heart was nigh broke, for it seemed that I had left all that was English behind me, and that I would never set eyes upon Norwich market square again." He was a tall, lusty, middle-aged man with a ruddy face, a brown forked beard shot with gray, and a broad Flanders hat set at the back of his head. His servant, as tall as himself, but gaunt and raw-boned, had swung the bales on the back of one mule, while the merchant mounted upon the other and rode to join the party. It was easy to see, as he approached, from the quality of his dress and the richness of his trappings, that he was a man of some wealth and position.

"Sir knight," said he, "my name is David Micheldene, and I am a burgher and alderman of the good town of Norwich, where I live five doors from the church of Our Lady, as all men know on the banks of Yare. I have here my bales of cloth which I carry to Cahors—woe worth the day that ever I started on such an errand! I crave your gracious protection upon the way for me, my servant, and my mercery; for I have already had many perilous passages, and have now learned that Roger Club-foot, the robber-knight of Quercy, is out upon the road in front of me. I hereby agree to give you one rose-noble if you bring me safe to the inn of the 'Angel' in Cahors, the same to be repaid to me or my heirs if any harm come to me or my goods."

"By Saint Paul!" answered Sir Nigel, "I should be a sorry knight if I ask pay for standing by a countryman in a strange land. You may ride with me and welcome, Master Micheldene, and your varlet may follow with my archers."

"God's benison upon thy bounty!" cried the stranger. "Should you come to Norwich you may have cause to remember that you have been of service to Alderman Micheldene. It is not very far to Cahors, for surely I see the cathedral towers against the sky-line; but I have heard much of this Roger Clubfoot, and the more I hear the less do I wish to look upon his face. Oh, but I am sick and weary of it all, and I would give half that I am worth to see my good dame sitting in peace beside me, and to hear the bells of Norwich town."

"Your words are strange to me," quoth Sir Nigel, "for you have the appearance of a stout man, and I see that you wear a sword by your side."

"Yet it is not my trade," answered the merchant. "I doubt not that if I set you down in my shop at Norwich you might scarce tell fustian from falding, and know little difference between the velvet of Genoa and the three-piled cloth of Bruges. There you might well turn to me for help. But here on a lone roadside, with thick woods and robber-knights, I turn to you, for it is the business to which you have been reared."

"There is sooth in what you say, Master Micheldene," said Sir Nigel, "and I trust that we may come upon this Roger Clubfoot, for I have heard that he is a very stout and skilful soldier, and a man from whom much honor is to be gained."

"He is a bloody robber," said the trader, curtly, "and I wish I saw him kicking at the end of a halter."

"It is such men as he," Sir Nigel remarked, "who give the true knight honorable deeds to do, whereby he may advance himself."

"It is such men as he," retorted Micheldene, "who are like rats in a wheat-rick or moths in a woolfels, a harm and a hindrance to all peaceful and honest men."

"Yet, if the dangers of the road weigh so heavily upon you, master alderman, it is a great marvel to me that you should venture so far from home."

"And sometimes, sir knight, it is a marvel to myself. But I am a man who may grutch and grumble, but when I have set my face to do a thing I will not turn my back upon it until it be done. There is one, Francois Villet, at Cahors, who will send me wine-casks for my cloth-bales, so to Cahors I will go, though all the robber-knights of Christendom were to line the roads like yonder poplars."

"Stoutly spoken, master alderman! But how have you fared hitherto?"

"As a lamb fares in a land of wolves. Five times we have had to beg and pray ere we could pass. Twice I have paid toll to the wardens of the road. Three times we have had to draw, and once at La Reolle we stood over our wool-bales, Watkin and I, and we laid about us for as long as a man might chant a litany, slaying one rogue and wounding two others. By God's coif! we are men of peace, but we are free English burghers, not to be mishandled either in our country or abroad. Neither lord, baron, knight, or commoner shall have as much as a strike of flax of mine whilst I have strength to wag this sword."

"And a passing strange sword it is," quoth Sir Nigel. "What make you, Alleyne, of these black lines which are drawn across the sheath?"

"I cannot tell what they are, my fair lord."

"Nor can I," said Ford.

The merchant chuckled to himself. "It was a thought of mine own," said he; "for the sword was made by Thomas Wilson, the armorer, who is betrothed to my second daughter Margery. Know then that the sheath is one cloth-yard, in length, marked off according to feet and inches to serve me as a measuring wand. It is also of the exact weight of two pounds, so that I may use it in the balance."

"By Saint Paul!" quoth Sir Nigel, "it is very clear to me that the sword is like thyself, good alderman, apt either for war or for peace. But I doubt not that even in England you have had much to suffer from the hands of robbers and outlaws."

"It was only last Lammastide, sir knight, that I was left for dead near Reading as I journeyed to Winchester fair. Yet I had the rogues up at the court of pie-powder, and they will harm no more peaceful traders."

"You travel much then!"

"To Winchester, Linn mart, Bristol fair, Stourbridge, and Bartholomew's in London Town. The rest of the year you may ever find me five doors from the church of Our Lady, where I would from my heart that I was at this moment, for there is no air like Norwich air, and no water like the Yare, nor can all the wines of France compare with the beer of old Sam Yelverton who keeps the 'Dun Cow.' But, out and alack, here is an evil fruit which hangs upon this chestnut-tree!"

As he spoke they had ridden round a curve of the road and come upon a great tree which shot one strong brown branch across their path. From the centre of this branch there hung a man, with his head at a horrid slant to his body and his toes just touching the ground. He was naked save for a linen under shirt and pair of woollen drawers. Beside him on a green bank there sat a small man with a solemn face, and a great bundle of papers of all colors thrusting forth from the scrip which lay beside him. He was very richly dressed, with furred robes, a scarlet hood, and wide hanging sleeves lined with flame-colored silk. A great gold chain hung round his neck, and rings glittered from every finger of his hands. On his lap he had a little pile of gold and of silver, which he was dropping, coin by coin, into a plump pouch which hung from his girdle.

"May the saints be with you, good travellers!" he shouted, as the party rode up. "May the four Evangelists watch over you! May the twelve Apostles bear you up! May the blessed army of martyrs direct your feet and lead you to eternal bliss!"

"Gramercy for these good wishes!" said Sir Nigel. "But I perceive, master alderman, that this man who hangs here is, by mark of foot, the very robber-knight of whom we have spoken. But there is a cartel pinned upon his breast, and I pray you, Alleyne, to read it to me."

The dead robber swung slowly to and fro in the wintry wind, a fixed smile upon his swarthy face, and his bulging eyes still glaring down the highway of which he had so long been the terror; on a sheet of parchment upon his breast was printed in rude characters;

ROGER PIED-BOT.

Par l'ordre du Senechal de
Castelnau, et de l'Echevin de
Cahors, servantes fideles du
tres vaillant et tres puissant
Edouard, Prince de Galles et
d'Aquitaine.
Ne touchez pas,
Ne coutez pas,
Ne depechez pas.

"He took a sorry time in dying," said the man who sat beside him. "He could stretch one toe to the ground and bear himself up, so that I thought he would never have done. Now at last, however, he is safely in paradise, and so I may jog on upon my earthly way." He mounted, as he spoke, a white mule which had been grazing by the wayside, all gay with fustian of gold and silver bells, and rode onward with Sir Nigel's party.

"How know you then that he is in paradise?" asked Sir Nigel. "All things are possible to God, but, certes, without a miracle, I should scarce expect to find the soul of Roger Clubfoot amongst the just."

"I know that he is there because I have just passed him in there," answered the stranger, rubbing his bejewelled hands together in placid satisfaction. "It is my holy mission to be a sompnour or pardoner. I am the unworthy servant and delegate of him who holds the keys. A contrite heart and ten nobles to holy mother Church may stave off perdition; but he hath a pardon of the first degree, with a twenty-five livre benison, so that I doubt if he will so much as feel a twinge of purgatory. I came up even as the seneschal's archers were tying him up, and I gave him my fore-word that I would bide with him until he had passed. There were two leaden crowns among the silver, but I would not for that stand in the way of his salvation."

"By Saint Paul!" said Sir Nigel, "if you have indeed this power to open and to shut the gates of hope, then indeed you stand high above mankind. But if you do but claim to have it, and yet have it not, then it seems to me, master clerk, that you may yourself find the gate barred when you shall ask admittance."

"Small of faith! Small of faith!" cried the sompnour. "Ah, Sir Didymus yet walks upon earth! And yet no words of doubt can bring anger to mine heart, or a bitter word to my lip, for am I not a poor unworthy worker in the cause of gentleness and peace? Of all these pardons which I bear every one is stamped and signed by our holy father, the prop and centre of Christendom."

"Which of them?" asked Sir Nigel.

"Ha, ha!" cried the pardoner, shaking a jewelled forefinger. "Thou wouldst be deep in the secrets of mother Church? Know then that I have both in my scrip. Those who hold with Urban shall have Urban's pardon, while I have Clement's for the Clementist—or he who is in doubt may have both, so that come what may he shall be secure. I pray you that you will buy one, for war is bloody work, and the end is sudden with little time for thought or shrift. Or you, sir, for you seem to me to be a man who would do ill to trust to your own merits." This to the alderman of Norwich, who had listened to him with a frowning brow and a sneering lip.

"When I sell my cloth," quoth he, "he who buys may weigh and feel and handle. These goods which you sell are not to be seen, nor is there any proof that you hold them. Certes, if mortal man might control God's mercy, it would be one of a lofty and God-like life, and not one who is decked out with rings and chains and silks, like a pleasure-wench at a kermesse.

"Thou wicked and shameless man!" cried the clerk. "Dost thou dare to raise thy voice against the unworthy servant of mother Church?"

"Unworthy enough!" quoth David Micheldene. "I would have you to know, clerk, that I am a free English burgher, and that I dare say my mind to our father the Pope himself, let alone such a lacquey's lacquey as you!"

"Base-born and foul-mouthed knave!" cried the sompnour. "You prate of holy things, to which your hog's mind can never rise. Keep silence, lest I call a curse upon you!"

"Silence yourself!" roared the other. "Foul bird! we found thee by the gallows like a carrion-crow. A fine life thou hast of it with thy silks and thy baubles, cozening the last few shillings from the pouches of dying men. A fig for thy curse! Bide here, if you will take my rede, for we will make England too hot for such as you, when Master Wicliff has the ordering of it. Thou vile thief! it is you, and such as you, who bring an evil name upon the many churchmen who lead a pure and a holy life. Thou outside the door of heaven! Art more like to be inside the door of hell."

At this crowning insult the sompnour, with a face ashen with rage, raised up a quivering hand and began pouring Latin imprecations upon the angry alderman. The latter, however, was not a man to be quelled by words, for he caught up his ell-measure sword-sheath and belabored the cursing clerk with it. The latter, unable to escape from the shower of blows, set spurs to his mule and rode for his life, with his enemy thundering behind him. At sight of his master's sudden departure, the varlet Watkin set off after him, with the pack-mule beside him, so that the four clattered away down the road together, until they swept round a curve and their babble was but a drone in the distance. Sir Nigel and Alleyne gazed in astonishment at one another, while Ford burst out a-laughing.

"Pardieu!" said the knight, "this David Micheldene must be one of those Lollards about whom Father Christopher of the priory had so much to say. Yet he seemed to be no bad man from what I have seen of him."

"I have heard that Wicliff hath many followers in Norwich," answered Alleyne.

"By St. Paul! I have no great love for them," quoth Sir Nigel. "I am a man who am slow to change; and, if you take away from me the faith that I have been taught, it would be long ere I could learn one to set in its place. It is but a chip here and a chip there, yet it may bring the tree down in time. Yet, on the other hand, I cannot but think it shame that a man should turn God's mercy on and off, as a cellarman doth wine with a spigot."

"Nor is it," said Alleyne, "part of the teachings of that mother Church of which he had so much to say. There was sooth in what the alderman said of it."

"Then, by St. Paul! they may settle it betwixt them," quoth Sir Nigel. "For me, I serve God, the king and my lady; and so long as I can keep the path of honor I am well content. My creed shall ever be that of Chandos:

"Fais ce que dois—adviegne que peut,
C'est commande au chevalier."

XXVIII

How the Comrades Came Over the Marches of France

After passing Cahors, the party branched away from the main road, and leaving the river to the north of them, followed a smaller track which wound over a vast and desolate plain. This path led them amid marshes and woods, until it brought them out into a glade with a broad stream swirling swiftly down the centre of it. Through this the horses splashed their way, and on the farther shore Sir Nigel announced to them that they were now within the borders of the land of France. For some miles they still followed the same lonely track, which led them through a dense wood, and then widening out, curved down to an open rolling country, such as they had traversed between Aiguillon and Cahors.

If it were grim and desolate upon the English border, however, what can describe the hideous barrenness of this ten times harried tract of France? The whole face of the country was scarred and disfigured, mottled over with the black blotches of burned farm-steadings, and the gray, gaunt gable-ends of what had been chateaux. Broken fences, crumbling walls, vineyards littered with stones, the shattered arches of bridges—look where you might, the signs of ruin and rapine met the eye. Here and there only, on the farthest sky-line, the gnarled turrets of a castle, or the graceful pinnacles of church or of monastery showed where the forces of the sword or of the spirit had preserved some small islet of security in this universal flood of misery. Moodily and in silence the little party rode along the narrow and irregular track, their hearts weighed down by this far-stretching land of despair. It was indeed a stricken and a blighted country, and a man might have ridden from Auvergne in the north to the marches of Foix, nor ever seen a smiling village or a thriving homestead.

From time to time as they advanced they saw strange lean figures scraping and scratching amid the weeds and thistles, who, on sight of the band of horsemen, threw up their arms and dived in among the brushwood, as shy and as swift as wild animals. More than once, however, they came on families by the wayside, who were too weak from hunger and disease to fly, so that they could but sit like hares on a tussock, with panting chests and terror in their eyes. So gaunt were these poor folk, so worn and spent—with bent and knotted frames, and sullen, hopeless, mutinous faces—that it made the young Englishman heart-sick to look upon them. Indeed, it seemed as though all hope and light had gone so far from them that it was not to be brought back; for when Sir Nigel threw down a handful of silver among them there came no softening of their lined faces, but they clutched greedily at the coins, peering questioningly at him, and champing with their animal jaws. Here and there amid the brushwood the travellers saw the rude bundle of sticks which served them as a home—more like a fowl's nest than the dwelling-place of man. Yet why should they build and strive, when the first adventurer who passed would set torch to their thatch, and when their own feudal lord would wring from them with blows and curses the last fruits of their toil? They sat at the lowest depth of human misery, and hugged a bitter comfort to their souls as they realized that they could go no lower. Yet they had still the human gift of speech, and would take council among themselves in their brushwood hovels, glaring with bleared eyes and pointing with thin fingers at the great widespread chateaux which ate like a cancer into the life of the country-side. When such men, who are beyond hope and fear, begin in their dim minds to see the source of their woes, it may be an evil time for those who have wronged them. The weak man becomes strong when he has nothing, for then only can he feel the wild, mad thrill of despair. High and strong the chateaux, lowly and weak the brushwood hut; but God help the seigneur and his lady when the men of the brushwood set their hands to the work of revenge!

Through such country did the party ride for eight or it might be nine miles, until the sun began to slope down in the west and their shadows to stream down the road in front of them. Wary and careful they must be, with watchful eyes to the right and the left, for this was no man's land, and their only passports were those which hung from their belts. Frenchmen and Englishmen, Gascon and Provencal, Brabanter, Tardvenu, Scorcher, Flayer, and Free Companion, wandered and struggled over the whole of this accursed district. So bare and cheerless was the outlook, and so few and poor the dwellings, that Sir Nigel began to have fears as to whether he might find food and quarters for his little troop. It was a relief to him, therefore, when their narrow track opened out upon a larger road, and they saw some little way down it a square white house with a great bunch of holly hung out at the end of a stick from one of the upper windows.

"By St. Paul!" said he, "I am right glad; for I had feared that we might have neither provant nor herbergage. Ride on, Alleyne, and tell this inn-keeper that an English knight with his party will lodge with him this night."

Alleyne set spurs to his horse and reached the inn door a long bow-shot before his companions. Neither varlet nor ostler could be seen, so he pushed open the door and called loudly for the landlord. Three times he shouted, but, receiving no reply, he opened an inner door and advanced into the chief guest-room of the hostel.

A very cheerful wood-fire was sputtering and cracking in an open grate at the further end of the apartment. At one side of this fire, in a high-backed oak chair, sat a lady, her face turned towards the door. The firelight played over her features, and Alleyne thought that he had never seen such queenly power, such dignity and strength, upon a woman's face. She might have been five-and-thirty years of age, with aquiline nose, firm yet sensitive mouth, dark curving brows, and deep-set eyes which shone and sparkled with a shifting brilliancy. Beautiful as she was, it was not her beauty which impressed itself upon the beholder; it was her strength, her power, the sense of wisdom which hung over the broad white brow, the decision which lay in the square jaw and delicately moulded chin. A chaplet of pearls sparkled amid her black hair, with a gauze of silver network flowing back from it over her shoulders; a black mantle was swathed round her, and she leaned back in her chair as one who is fresh from a journey.

In the opposite corner there sat a very burly and broad-shouldered man, clad in a black jerkin trimmed with sable, with a black velvet cap with curling white feather cocked upon the side of his head. A flask of red wine stood at his elbow, and he seemed to be very much at his ease, for his feet were stuck up on a stool, and between his thighs he held a dish full of nuts. These he cracked between his strong white teeth and chewed in a leisurely way, casting the shells into the blaze. As Alleyne gazed in at him he turned his face half round and cocked an eye at him over his shoulder. It seemed to the young Englishman that he had never seen so hideous a face, for the eyes were of the lightest green, the nose was broken and driven inwards, while the whole countenance was seared and puckered with wounds. The voice, too, when he spoke, was as deep and as fierce as the growl of a beast of prey.

"Young man," said he, "I know not who you may be, and I am not much inclined to bestir myself, but if it were not that I am bent upon taking my ease, I swear, by the sword of Joshua! that I would lay my dog-whip across your shoulders for daring to fill the air with these discordant bellowings."

Taken aback at this ungentle speech, and scarce knowing how to answer it fitly in the presence of the lady, Alleyne stood with his hand upon the handle of the door, while Sir Nigel and his companions dismounted. At the sound of these fresh voices, and of the tongue in which they spoke, the stranger crashed his dish of nuts down upon the floor, and began himself to call for the landlord until the whole house re-echoed with his roarings. With an ashen face the white-aproned host came running at his call, his hands shaking and his very hair bristling with apprehension. "For the sake of God, sirs," he whispered as he passed, "speak him fair and do not rouse him! For the love of the Virgin, be mild with him!"

"Who is this, then?" asked Sir Nigel.

Alleyne was about to explain, when a fresh roar from the stranger interrupted him.

"Thou villain inn-keeper," he shouted, "did I not ask you when I brought my lady here whether your inn was clean?"

"You did, sire."

"Did I not very particularly ask you whether there were any vermin in it?"

"You did, sire."

"And you answered me?"

"That there were not, sire."

"And yet ere I have been here an hour I find Englishmen crawling about within it. Where are we to be free from this pestilent race? Can a Frenchman upon French land not sit down in a French auberge without having his ears pained by the clack of their hideous talk? Send them packing, inn-keeper, or it may be the worse for them and for you."

"I will, sire, I will!" cried the frightened host, and bustled from the room, while the soft, soothing voice of the woman was heard remonstrating with her furious companion.

"Indeed, gentlemen, you had best go," said mine host. "It is but six miles to Villefranche, where there are very good quarters at the sign of the 'Lion Rouge.'"

"Nay," answered Sir Nigel, "I cannot go until I have seen more of this person, for he appears to be a man from whom much is to be hoped. What is his name and title?"

"It is not for my lips to name it unless by his desire. But I beg and pray you, gentlemen, that you will go from my house, for I know not what may come of it if his rage should gain the mastery of him."

"By Saint Paul!" lisped Sir Nigel, "this is certainly a man whom it is worth journeying far to know. Go tell him that a humble knight of England would make his further honorable acquaintance, not from any presumption, pride, or ill-will, but for the advancement of chivalry and the glory of our ladies. Give him greeting from Sir Nigel Loring, and say that the glove which I bear in my cap belongs to the most peerless and lovely of her sex, whom I am now ready to uphold against any lady whose claim he might be desirous of advancing."

The landlord was hesitating whether to carry this message or no, when the door of the inner room was flung open, and the stranger bounded out like a panther from its den, his hair bristling and his deformed face convulsed with anger.

"Still here!" he snarled. "Dogs of England, must ye be lashed hence? Tiphaine, my sword!" He turned to seize his weapon, but as he did so his gaze fell upon the blazonry of sir Nigel's shield, and he stood staring, while the fire in his strange green eyes softened into a sly and humorous twinkle.

"Mort Dieu!" cried he, "it is my little swordsman of Bordeaux. I should remember that coat-armor, seeing that it is but three days since I looked upon it in the lists by Garonne. Ah! Sir Nigel, Sir Nigel! you owe me a return for this," and he touched his right arm, which was girt round just under the shoulder with a silken kerchief.

But the surprise of the stranger at the sight of Sir Nigel was as nothing compared with the astonishment and the delight which shone upon the face of the knight of Hampshire as he looked upon the strange face of the Frenchman. Twice he opened his mouth and twice he peered again, as though to assure himself that his eyes had not played him a trick.

"Bertrand!" he gasped at last. "Bertrand du Guesclin!"

"By Saint Ives!" shouted the French soldier, with a hoarse roar of laughter, "it is well that I should ride with my vizor down, for he that has once seen my face does not need to be told my name. It is indeed I, Sir Nigel, and here is my hand! I give you my word that there are but three Englishmen in this world whom I would touch save with the sharp edge of the sword: the prince is one, Chandos the second, and you the third; for I have heard much that is good of you."

"I am growing aged, and am somewhat spent in the wars," quoth Sir Nigel; "but I can lay by my sword now with an easy mind, for I can say that I have crossed swords with him who hath the bravest heart and the strongest arm of all this great kingdom of France. I have longed for it, I have dreamed of it, and now I can scarce bring my mind to understand that this great honor hath indeed been mine."

"By the Virgin of Rennes! you have given me cause to be very certain of it," said Du Guesclin, with a gleam of his broad white teeth.

"And perhaps, most honored sir, it would please you to continue the debate. Perhaps you would condescend to go farther into the matter. God He knows that I am unworthy of such honor, yet I can show my four-and-sixty quarterings, and I have been present at some bickerings and scufflings during these twenty years."

"Your fame is very well known to me, and I shall ask my lady to enter your name upon my tablets," said Sir Bertrand. "There are many who wish to advance themselves, and who bide their turn, for I refuse no man who comes on such an errand. At present it may not be, for mine arm is stiff from this small touch, and I would fain do you full honor when we cross swords again. Come in with me, and let your squires come also, that my sweet spouse, the Lady Tiphaine, may say that she hath seen so famed and gentle a knight."

Into the chamber they went in all peace and concord, where the Lady Tiphaine sat like queen on throne for each in turn to be presented to her. Sooth to say, the stout heart of Sir Nigel, which cared little for the wrath of her lion-like spouse, was somewhat shaken by the calm, cold face of this stately dame, for twenty years of camp-life had left him more at ease in the lists than in a lady's boudoir. He bethought him, too, as he looked at her set lips and deep-set questioning eyes, that he had heard strange tales of this same Lady Tiphaine du Guesclin. Was it not she who was said to lay hands upon the sick and raise them from their couches when the leeches had spent their last nostrums? Had she not forecast the future, and were there not times when in the loneliness of her chamber she was heard to hold converse with some being upon whom mortal eye never rested—some dark familiar who passed where doors were barred and windows high? Sir Nigel sunk his eye and marked a cross on the side of his leg as he greeted this dangerous dame, and yet ere five minutes had passed he was hers, and not he only but his two young squires as well. The mind had gone out of them, and they could but look at this woman and listen to the words which fell from her lips—words which thrilled through their nerves and stirred their souls like the battle-call of a bugle.

Often in peaceful after-days was Alleyne to think of that scene of the wayside inn of Auvergne. The shadows of evening had fallen, and the corners of the long, low, wood-panelled room were draped in darkness. The sputtering wood fire threw out a circle of red flickering light which played over the little group of wayfarers, and showed up every line and shadow upon their faces. Sir Nigel sat with elbows upon knees, and chin upon hands, his patch still covering one eye, but his other shining like a star, while the ruddy light gleamed upon his smooth white head. Ford was seated at his left, his lips parted, his eyes staring, and a fleck of deep color on either cheek, his limbs all rigid as one who fears to move. On the other side the famous French captain leaned back in his chair, a litter of nut-shells upon his lap, his huge head half buried in a cushion, while his eyes wandered with an amused gleam from his dame to the staring, enraptured Englishmen. Then, last of all, that pale clear-cut face, that sweet clear voice, with its high thrilling talk of the deathlessness of glory, of the worthlessness of life, of the pain of ignoble joys, and of the joy which lies in all pains which lead to a noble end. Still, as the shadows deepened, she spoke of valor and virtue, of loyalty, honor, and fame, and still they sat drinking in her words while the fire burned down and the red ash turned to gray.

"By the sainted Ives!" cried Du Guesclin at last, "it is time that we spoke of what we are to do this night, for I cannot think that in this wayside auberge there are fit quarters for an honorable company."

Sir Nigel gave a long sigh as he came back from the dreams of chivalry and hardihood into which this strange woman's words had wafted him. "I care not where I sleep," said he; "but these are indeed somewhat rude lodgings for this fair lady."

"What contents my lord contents me," quoth she. "I perceive, Sir Nigel, that you are under vow," she added, glancing at his covered eye.

"It is my purpose to attempt some small deed," he answered.

"And the glove—is it your lady's?"

"It is indeed my sweet wife's."

"Who is doubtless proud of you."

"Say rather I of her," quoth he quickly. "God He knows that I am not worthy to be her humble servant. It is easy, lady, for a man to ride forth in the light of day, and do his devoir when all men have eyes for him. But in a woman's heart there is a strength and truth which asks no praise, and can but be known to him whose treasure it is."

The Lady Tiphaine smiled across at her husband. "You have often told me, Bertrand, that there were very gentle knights amongst the English," quoth she.

"Aye, aye," said he moodily. "But to horse, Sir Nigel, you and yours and we shall seek the chateau of Sir Tristram de Rochefort, which is two miles on this side of Villefranche. He is Seneschal of Auvergne, and mine old war companion."

"Certes, he would have a welcome for you," quoth Sir Nigel; "but indeed he might look askance at one who comes without permit over the marches."

"By the Virgin! when he learns that you have come to draw away these rascals he will be very blithe to look upon your face. Inn-keeper, here are ten gold pieces. What is over and above your reckoning you may take off from your charges to the next needy knight who comes this way. Come then, for it grows late and the horses are stamping in the roadway."

The Lady Tiphaine and her spouse sprang upon their steeds without setting feet to stirrup, and away they jingled down the white moonlit highway, with Sir Nigel at the lady's bridle-arm, and Ford a spear's length behind them. Alleyne had lingered for an instant in the passage, and as he did so there came a wild outcry from a chamber upon the left, and out there ran Aylward and John, laughing together like two schoolboys who are bent upon a prank. At sight of Alleyne they slunk past him with somewhat of a shame-faced air, and springing upon their horses galloped after their party. The hubbub within the chamber did not cease, however, but rather increased, with yells of: "A moi, mes amis! A moi, camarades! A moi, l'honorable champion de l'Eveque de Montaubon! A la recousse de l'eglise sainte!" So shrill was the outcry that both the inn-keeper and Alleyne, with every varlet within hearing, rushed wildly to the scene of the uproar.

It was indeed a singular scene which met their eyes. The room was a long and lofty one, stone floored and bare, with a fire at the further end upon which a great pot was boiling. A deal table ran down the centre, with a wooden wine-pitcher upon it and two horn cups. Some way from it was a smaller table with a single beaker and a broken wine-bottle. From the heavy wooden rafters which formed the roof there hung rows of hooks which held up sides of bacon, joints of smoked beef, and strings of onions for winter use. In the very centre of all these, upon the largest hook of all, there hung a fat little red-faced man with enormous whiskers, kicking madly in the air and clawing at rafters, hams, and all else that was within hand-grasp. The huge steel hook had been passed through the collar of his leather jerkin, and there he hung like a fish on a line, writhing, twisting, and screaming, but utterly unable to free himself from his extraordinary position. It was not until Alleyne and the landlord had mounted on the table that they were able to lift him down, when he sank gasping with rage into a seat, and rolled his eyes round in every direction.

"Has he gone?" quoth he.

"Gone? Who?"

"He, the man with the red head, the giant man."

"Yes," said Alleyne, "he hath gone."

"And comes not back?"

"No."

"The better for him!" cried the little man, with a long sigh of relief. "Mon Dieu! What! am I not the champion of the Bishop of Montaubon? Ah, could I have descended, could I have come down, ere he fled! Then you would have seen. You would have beheld a spectacle then. There would have been one rascal the less upon earth. Ma foi, yes!"

"Good master Pelligny," said the landlord, "these gentlemen have not gone very fast, and I have a horse in the stable at your disposal, for I would rather have such bloody doings as you threaten outside the four walls of mine auberge."

"I hurt my leg and cannot ride," quoth the bishop's champion. "I strained a sinew on the day that I slew the three men at Castelnau."

"God save you, master Pelligny!" cried the landlord. "It must be an awesome thing to have so much blood upon one's soul. And yet I do not wish to see so valiant a man mishandled, and so I will, for friendship's sake, ride after this Englishman and bring him back to you."

"You shall not stir," cried the champion, seizing the inn-keeper in a convulsive grasp. "I have a love for you, Gaston, and I would not bring your house into ill repute, nor do such scath to these walls and chattels as must befall if two such men as this Englishman and I fall to work here."

"Nay, think not of me!" cried the inn-keeper. "What are my walls when set against the honor of Francois Poursuivant d'Amour Pelligny, champion of the Bishop of Montaubon. My horse, Andre!"

"By the saints, no! Gaston, I will not have it! You have said truly that it is an awesome thing to have such rough work upon one's soul. I am but a rude soldier, yet I have a mind. Mon Dieu! I reflect, I weigh, I balance. Shall I not meet this man again? Shall I not bear him in mind? Shall I not know him by his great paws and his red head? Ma foi, yes!"

"And may I ask, sir," said Alleyne, "why it is that you call yourself champion of the Bishop of Montaubon?"

"You may ask aught which it is becoming to me to answer. The bishop hath need of a champion, because, if any cause be set to test of combat, it would scarce become his office to go down into the lists with leather and shield and cudgel to exchange blows with any varlet. He looks around him then for some tried fighting man, some honest smiter who can give a blow or take one. It is not for me to say how far he hath succeeded, but it is sooth that he who thinks that he hath but to do with the Bishop of Montaubon, finds himself face to face with Francois Poursuivant d'Amour Pelligny."

At this moment there was a clatter of hoofs upon the road, and a varlet by the door cried out that one of the Englishmen was coming back. The champion looked wildly about for some corner of safety, and was clambering up towards the window, when Ford's voice sounded from without, calling upon Alleyne to hasten, or he might scarce find his way. Bidding adieu to landlord and to champion, therefore, he set off at a gallop, and soon overtook the two archers.

"A pretty thing this, John," said he. "Thou wilt have holy Church upon you if you hang her champions upon iron hooks in an inn kitchen."

"It was done without thinking," he answered apologetically, while Aylward burst into a shout of laughter.

"By my hilt! mon petit," said he, "you would have laughed also could you have seen it. For this man was so swollen with pride that he would neither drink with us, nor sit at the same table with us, nor as much as answer a question, but must needs talk to the varlet all the time that it was well there was peace, and that he had slain more Englishmen than there were tags to his doublet. Our good old John could scarce lay his tongue to French enough to answer him, so he must needs reach out his great hand to him and place him very gently where you saw him. But we must on, for I can scarce hear their hoofs upon the road."

"I think that I can see them yet," said Ford, peering down the moonlit road.

"Pardieu! yes. Now they ride forth from the shadow. And yonder dark clump is the Castle of Villefranche. En avant camarades! or Sir Nigel may reach the gates before us. But hark, mes amis, what sound is that?"

As he spoke the hoarse blast of a horn was heard from some woods upon the right. An answering call rung forth upon their left, and hard upon it two others from behind them.

"They are the horns of swine-herds," quoth Aylward. "Though why they blow them so late I cannot tell."

"Let us on, then," said Ford, and the whole party, setting their spurs to their horses, soon found themselves at the Castle of Villefranche, where the drawbridge had already been lowered and the portcullis raised in response to the summons of Du Guesclin.

XXIX

How the Blessed Hour of Sight Came to the Lady Tiphaine

Sir Tristram de Rochefort, Seneschal of Auvergne and Lord of Villefranche, was a fierce and renowned soldier who had grown gray in the English wars. As lord of the marches and guardian of an exposed country-side, there was little rest for him even in times of so-called peace, and his whole life was spent in raids and outfalls upon the Brabanters, late-comers, flayers, free companions, and roving archers who wandered over his province. At times he would come back in triumph, and a dozen corpses swinging from the summit of his keep would warn evil-doers that there was still a law in the land. At others his ventures were not so happy, and he and his troop would spur it over the drawbridge with clatter of hoofs hard at their heels and whistle of arrows about their ears. Hard he was of hand and harder of heart, hated by his foes, and yet not loved by those whom he protected, for twice he had been taken prisoner, and twice his ransom had been wrung by dint of blows and tortures out of the starving peasants and ruined farmers. Wolves or watch-dogs, it was hard to say from which the sheep had most to fear.

The Castle of Villefranche was harsh and stern as its master. A broad moat, a high outer wall turreted at the corners, with a great black keep towering above all—so it lay before them in the moonlight. By the light of two flambeaux, protruded through the narrow slit-shaped openings at either side of the ponderous gate, they caught a glimpse of the glitter of fierce eyes and of the gleam of the weapons of the guard. The sight of the two-headed eagle of Du Guesclin, however, was a passport into any fortalice in France, and ere they had passed the gate the old border knight came running forwards with hands out-thrown to greet his famous countryman. Nor was he less glad to see Sir Nigel, when the Englishman's errand was explained to him, for these archers had been a sore thorn in his side and had routed two expeditions which he had sent against them. A happy day it would be for the Seneschal of Auvergne when they should learn that the last yew bow was over the marches.

The material for a feast was ever at hand in days when, if there was grim want in the cottage, there was at least rude plenty in the castle.

Within an hour the guests were seated around a board which creaked under the great pasties and joints of meat, varied by those more dainty dishes in which the French excelled, the spiced ortolan and the truffled beccaficoes. The Lady Rochefort, a bright and laughter-loving dame, sat upon the left of her warlike spouse, with Lady Tiphaine upon the right. Beneath sat Du Guesclin and Sir Nigel, with Sir Amory Monticourt, of the order of the Hospitallers, and Sir Otto Harnit, a wandering knight from the kingdom of Bohemia. These with Alleyne and Ford, four French squires, and the castle chaplain, made the company who sat together that night and made good cheer in the Castle of Villefranche. The great fire crackled in the grate, the hooded hawks slept upon their perches, the rough deer-hounds with expectant eyes crouched upon the tiled floor; close at the elbows of the guests stood the dapper little lilac-coated pages; the laugh and jest circled round and all was harmony and comfort. Little they recked of the brushwood men who crouched in their rags along the fringe of the forest and looked with wild and haggard eyes at the rich, warm glow which shot a golden bar of light from the high arched windows of the castle.

Supper over, the tables dormant were cleared away as by magic and trestles and bancals arranged around the blazing fire, for there was a bitter nip in the air. The Lady Tiphaine had sunk back in her cushioned chair, and her long dark lashes drooped low over her sparkling eyes. Alleyne, glancing at her, noted that her breath came quick and short, and that her cheeks had blanched to a lily white. Du Guesclin eyed her keenly from time to time, and passed his broad brown fingers through his crisp, curly black hair with the air of a man who is perplexed in his mind.

"These folk here," said the knight of Bohemia, "they do not seem too well fed."

"Ah, canaille!" cried the Lord of Villefranche. "You would scarce credit it, and yet it is sooth that when I was taken at Poictiers it was all that my wife and foster-brother could do to raise the money from them for my ransom. The sulky dogs would rather have three twists of a rack, or the thumbikins for an hour, than pay out a denier for their own feudal father and liege lord. Yet there is not one of them but hath an old stocking full of gold pieces hid away in a snug corner."

"Why do they not buy food then?" asked Sir Nigel. "By St. Paul! it seemed to me their bones were breaking through their skin."

"It is their grutching and grumbling which makes them thin. We have a saying here, Sir Nigel, that if you pummel Jacques Bonhomme he will pat you, but if you pat him he will pummel you. Doubtless you find it so in England."

"Ma foi, no!" said Sir Nigel. "I have two Englishmen of this class in my train, who are at this instant, I make little doubt, as full of your wine as any cask in your cellar. He who pummelled them might come by such a pat as he would be likely to remember."

"I cannot understand it," quoth the seneschal, "for the English knights and nobles whom I have met were not men to brook the insolence of the base born."

"Perchance, my fair lord, the poor folk are sweeter and of a better countenance in England," laughed the Lady Rochefort. "Mon Dieu! you cannot conceive to yourself how ugly they are! Without hair, without teeth, all twisted and bent; for me, I cannot think how the good God ever came to make such people. I cannot bear it, I, and so my trusty Raoul goes ever before me with a cudgel to drive them from my path."

"Yet they have souls, fair lady, they have souls!" murmured the chaplain, a white-haired man with a weary, patient face.

"So I have heard you tell them," said the lord of the castle; "and for myself, father, though I am a true son of holy Church, yet I think that you were better employed in saying your mass and in teaching the children of my men-at-arms, than in going over the country-side to put ideas in these folks' heads which would never have been there but for you. I have heard that you have said to them that their souls are as good as ours, and that it is likely that in another life they may stand as high as the oldest blood of Auvergne. For my part, I believe that there are so many worthy knights and gallant gentlemen in heaven who know how such things should be arranged, that there is little fear that we shall find ourselves mixed up with base roturiers and swine-herds. Tell your beads, father, and con your psalter, but do not come between me and those whom the king has given to me!"

"God help them!" cried the old priest. "A higher King than yours has given them to me, and I tell you here in your own castle hall, Sir Tristram de Rochefort, that you have sinned deeply in your dealings with these poor folk, and that the hour will come, and may even now be at hand, when God's hand will be heavy upon you for what you have done." He rose as he spoke, and walked slowly from the room.

"Pest take him!" cried the French knight. "Now, what is a man to do with a priest, Sir Bertrand?—for one can neither fight him like a man nor coax him like a woman."

"Ah, Sir Bertrand knows, the naughty one!" cried the Lady Rochefort. "Have we not all heard how he went to Avignon and squeezed fifty thousand crowns out of the Pope."

"Ma foi!" said Sir Nigel, looking with a mixture of horror and admiration at Du Guesclin. "Did not your heart sink within you? Were you not smitten with fears? Have you not felt a curse hang over you?"

"I have not observed it," said the Frenchman carelessly. "But by Saint Ives! Tristram, this chaplain of yours seems to me to be a worthy man, and you should give heed to his words, for though I care nothing for the curse of a bad pope, it would be a grief to me to have aught but a blessing from a good priest."

"Hark to that, my fair lord," cried the Lady Rochefort. "Take heed, I pray thee, for I do not wish to have a blight cast over me, nor a palsy of the limbs. I remember that once before you angered Father Stephen, and my tire-woman said that I lost more hair in seven days than ever before in a month."

"If that be sign of sin, then, by Saint Paul! I have much upon my soul," said Sir Nigel, amid a general laugh. "But in very truth, Sir Tristram, if I may venture a word of counsel, I should advise that you make your peace with this good man."

"He shall have four silver candlesticks," said the seneschal moodily. "And yet I would that he would leave the folk alone. You cannot conceive in your mind how stubborn and brainless they are. Mules and pigs are full of reason beside them. God He knows that I have had great patience with them. It was but last week that, having to raise some money, I called up to the castle Jean Goubert, who, as all men know, has a casketful of gold pieces hidden away in some hollow tree. I give you my word that I did not so much as lay a stripe upon his fool's back, but after speaking with him, and telling him how needful the money was to me, I left him for the night to think over the matter in my dungeon. What think you that the dog did? Why, in the morning we found that he had made a rope from strips of his leathern jerkin, and had hung himself to the bar of the window."

"For me, I cannot conceive such wickedness!" cried the lady.

"And there was Gertrude Le Boeuf, as fair a maiden as eye could see, but as bad and bitter as the rest of them. When young Amory de Valance was here last Lammastide he looked kindly upon the girl, and even spoke of taking her into his service. What does she do, with her dog of a father? Why, they tie themselves together and leap into the

Linden Pool, where the water is five spears'-lengths deep. I give you my word that it was a great grief to young Amory, and it was days ere he could cast it from his mind. But how can one serve people who are so foolish and so ungrateful?"

Whilst the Seneschal of Villefranche had been detailing the evil doings of his tenants, Alleyne had been unable to take his eyes from the face of Lady Tiphaine. She had lain back in her chair, with drooping eyelids and bloodless face, so that he had feared at first her journey had weighed heavily upon her, and that the strength was ebbing out of her. Of a sudden, however, there came a change, for a dash of bright color flickered up on to either cheek, and her lids were slowly raised again upon eyes which sparkled with such lustre as Alleyne had never seen in human eyes before, while their gaze was fixed intently, not on the company, but on the dark tapestry which draped the wall. So transformed and so ethereal was her expression, that Alleyne, in his loftiest dream of archangel or of seraph, had never pictured so sweet, so womanly, and yet so wise a face. Glancing at Du Guesclin, Alleyne saw that he also was watching his wife closely, and from the twitching of his features, and the beads upon his brick-colored brow, it was easy to see that he was deeply agitated by the change which he marked in her.

"How is it with you, lady?" he asked at last, in a tremulous voice.

Her eyes remained fixed intently upon the wall, and there was a long pause ere she answered him. Her voice, too, which had been so clear and ringing, was now low and muffled as that of one who speaks from a distance.

"All is very well with me, Bertrand," said she. "The blessed hour of sight has come round to me again."

"I could see it come! I could see it come!" he exclaimed, passing his fingers through his hair with the same perplexed expression as before.

"This is untoward, Sir Tristram," he said at last. "And I scarce know in what words to make it clear to you, and to your fair wife, and to Sir Nigel Loring, and to these other stranger knights. My tongue is a blunt one, and fitter to shout word of command than to clear up such a matter as this, of which I can myself understand little. This, however, I know, that my wife is come of a very sainted race, whom God hath in His wisdom endowed with wondrous powers, so that Tiphaine Raquenel was known throughout Brittany ere ever I first saw her at Dinan. Yet these powers are ever used for good, and they are the gift of God and not of the devil, which is the difference betwixt white magic and black."

"Perchance it would be as well that we should send for Father Stephen," said Sir Tristram.

"It would be best that he should come," cried the Hospitaller.

"And bring with him a flask of holy water," added the knight of Bohemia.

"Not so, gentlemen," answered Sir Bertrand. "It is not needful that this priest should be called, and it is in my mind that in asking for this ye cast some slight shadow or slur upon the good name of my wife, as though it were still doubtful whether her power came to her from above or below. If ye have indeed such a doubt I pray that you will say so, that we may discuss the matter in a fitting way."

"For myself," said Sir Nigel, "I have heard such words fall from the lips of this lady that I am of the opinion that there is no woman, save only one, who can be in any way compared to her in beauty and in goodness. Should any gentleman think otherwise, I should deem it great honor to run a small course with him, or debate the matter in whatever way might be most pleasing to him."

"Nay, it would ill become me to cast a slur upon a lady who is both my guest and the wife of my comrade-in-arms," said the Seneschal of Villefranche. "I have perceived also that on her mantle there is marked a silver cross, which is surely sign enough that there is nought of evil in these strange powers which you say that she possesses."

This argument of the seneschal's appealed so powerfully to the Bohemian and to the Hospitaller that they at once intimated that their objections had been entirely overcome, while even the Lady Rochefort, who had sat shivering and crossing herself, ceased to cast glances at the door, and allowed her fears to turn to curiosity.

"Among the gifts which have been vouchsafed to my wife," said Du Guesclin, "there is the wondrous one of seeing into the future; but it comes very seldom upon her, and goes as quickly, for none can command it. The blessed hour of sight, as she hath named it, has come but twice since I have known her, and I can vouch for it that all that she hath told me was true, for on the evening of the Battle of Auray she said that the morrow would be an ill day for me and for Charles of Blois. Ere the sun had sunk again he was dead, and I the prisoner of Sir John Chandos. Yet it is not every question that she can answer, but only those——"

"Bertrand, Bertrand!" cried the lady in the same muttering far-away voice, "the blessed hour passes. Use it, Bertrand, while you may."

"I will, my sweet. Tell me, then, what fortune comes upon me?"

"Danger, Bertrand—deadly, pressing danger—which creeps upon you and you know it not."

The French soldier burst into a thunderous laugh, and his green eyes twinkled with amusement. "At what time during these twenty years would not that have been a true word?" he cried. "Danger is in the air that I breathe. But is this so very close, Tiphaine?"

"Here—now—close upon you!" The words came out in broken, strenuous speech, while the lady's fair face was writhed and drawn like that of one who looks upon a horror which strikes the words from her lips. Du Guesclin gazed round the tapestried room, at the screens, the tables, the abace, the credence, the buffet with its silver salver, and the half-circle of friendly, wondering faces. There was an utter stillness, save for the sharp breathing of the Lady Tiphaine and for the gentle soughing of the wind outside, which wafted to their ears the distant call upon a swine-herd's horn.

"The danger may bide," said he, shrugging his broad shoulders. "And now, Tiphaine, tell us what will come of this war in Spain."

"I can see little," she answered, straining her eyes and puckering her brow, as one who would fain clear her sight. "There are mountains, and dry plains, and flash of arms and shouting of battle-cries. Yet it is whispered to me that by failure you will succeed."

"Ha! Sir Nigel, how like you that?" quoth Bertrand, shaking his head. "It is like mead and vinegar, half sweet, half sour. And is there no question which you would ask my lady?"

"Certes there is. I would fain know, fair lady, how all things are at Twynham Castle, and above all how my sweet lady employs herself."

"To answer this I would fain lay hand upon one whose thoughts turn strongly to this castle which you have named. Nay, my Lord Loring, it is whispered to me that there is another here who hath thought more deeply of it than you."

"Thought more of mine own home?" cried Sir Nigel. "Lady, I fear that in this matter at least you are mistaken."

"Not so, Sir Nigel. Come hither, young man, young English squire with the gray eyes! Now give me your hand, and place it here across my brow, that I may see that which you have seen. What is this that rises before me? Mist, mist, rolling mist with a square black tower above it. See it shreds out, it thins, it rises, and there lies a castle in green plain, with the sea beneath it, and a great church within a bow-shot. There are two rivers which run through the meadows, and between them lie the tents of the besiegers."

"The besiegers!" cried Alleyne, Ford, and Sir Nigel, all three in a breath.

"Yes, truly, and they press hard upon the castle, for they are an exceeding multitude and full of courage. See how they storm and rage against the gate, while some rear ladders, and others, line after line, sweep the walls with their arrows. There are many leaders who shout and beckon, and one, a tall man with a golden beard, who stands before the gate stamping his foot and hallooing them on, as a pricker doth the hounds. But those in the castle fight bravely. There is a woman, two women, who stand upon the walls, and give heart to the men-at-arms. They shower down arrows, darts and great stones. Ah! they have struck down the tall leader, and the others give back. The mist thickens and I can see no more."

"By Saint Paul!" said Sir Nigel, "I do not think that there can be any such doings at Christchurch, and I am very easy of the fortalice so long as my sweet wife hangs the key of the outer bailey at the head of her bed. Yet I will not deny that you have pictured the castle as well as I could have done myself, and I am full of wonderment at all that I have heard and seen."

"I would, Lady Tiphaine," cried the Lady Rochefort, "that you would use your power to tell me what hath befallen my golden bracelet which I wore when hawking upon the second Sunday of Advent, and have never set eyes upon since."

"Nay, lady," said du Guesclin, "it does not befit so great and wondrous a power to pry and search and play the varlet even to the beautiful chatelaine of Villefranche. Ask a worthy question, and, with the blessing of God, you shall have a worthy answer."

"Then I would fain ask," cried one of the French squires, "as to which may hope to conquer in these wars betwixt the English and ourselves."

"Both will conquer and each will hold its own," answered the Lady Tiphaine.

"Then we shall still hold Gascony and Guienne?" cried Sir Nigel.

The lady shook her head. "French land, French blood, French speech," she answered. "They are French, and France shall have them."

"But not Bordeaux?" cried Sir Nigel excitedly.

"Bordeaux also is for France."

"But Calais?"

"Calais too."

"Woe worth me then, and ill hail to these evil words! If Bordeaux and Calais be gone, then what is left for England?"

"It seems indeed that there are evil times coming upon your country," said Du Guesclin. "In our fondest hopes we never thought to hold Bordeaux. By Saint Ives! this news hath warmed the heart within me. Our dear country will then be very great in the future, Tiphaine?"

"Great, and rich, and beautiful," she cried. "Far down the course of time I can see her still leading the nations, a wayward queen among the peoples, great in war, but greater in peace, quick in thought, deft in action, with her people's will for her sole monarch, from the sands of Calais to the blue seas of the south."

"Ha!" cried Du Guesclin, with his eyes flashing in triumph, "you hear her, Sir Nigel?—and she never yet said word which was not sooth."

The English knight shook his head moodily. "What of my own poor country?" said he. "I fear, lady, that what you have said bodes but small good for her."

The lady sat with parted lips, and her breath came quick and fast. "My God!" she cried, "what is this that is shown me? Whence come they, these peoples, these lordly nations, these mighty countries which rise up before me? I look beyond, and others rise, and yet others, far and farther to the shores of the uttermost waters. They crowd! They swarm! The world is given to them, and it resounds with the clang of their hammers and the ringing of their church bells. They call them many names, and they rule them this way or that but they are all English, for I can hear the voices of the people. On I go, and onwards over seas where man hath never yet sailed, and I see a great land under new stars and a stranger sky, and still the land is England. Where have her children not gone? What have they not done? Her banner is planted on ice. Her banner is scorched in the sun. She lies athwart the lands, and her shadow is over the seas. Bertrand, Bertrand! we are undone for the buds of her bud are even as our choicest flower!" Her voice rose into a wild cry, and throwing up her arms she sank back white and nerveless into the deep oaken chair.

"It is over," said Du Guesclin moodily, as he raised her drooping head with his strong brown hand. "Wine for the lady, squire! The blessed hour of sight hath passed."

XXX

How the Brushwood Men Came to the Chateau of Villefranche

It was late ere Alleyne Edricson, having carried Sir Nigel the goblet of spiced wine which it was his custom to drink after the curling of his hair, was able at last to seek his chamber. It was a stone-flagged room upon the second floor, with a bed in a recess for him, and two smaller pallets on the other side, on which Aylward and Hordle John were already snoring. Alleyne had knelt down to his evening orisons, when there came a tap at his door, and Ford entered with a small lamp in his hand. His face was deadly pale, and his hand shook until the shadows flickered up and down the wall.

"What is it, Ford?" cried Alleyne, springing to his feet.

"I can scarce tell you," said he, sitting down on the side of the couch, and resting his chin upon his hand. "I know not what to say or what to think."

"Has aught befallen you, then?"

"Yes, or I have been slave to my own fancy. I tell you, lad, that I am all undone, like a fretted bow-string. Hark hither, Alleyne! it cannot be that you have forgotten little Tita, the daughter of the old glass-stainer at Bordeaux?"

"I remember her well."

"She and I, Alleyne, broke the lucky groat together ere we parted, and she wears my ring upon her finger. 'Caro mio,' quoth she when last we parted, 'I shall be near thee in the wars, and thy danger will be my danger.' Alleyne, as God is my help, as I came up the stairs this night I saw her stand before me, her face in tears, her hands out as though in warning—I saw it, Alleyne, even as I see those two archers upon their couches. Our very finger-tips seemed to meet, ere she thinned away like a mist in the sunshine."

"I would not give overmuch thought to it," answered Alleyne. "Our minds will play us strange pranks, and bethink you that these words of the Lady Tiphaine Du Guesclin have wrought upon us and shaken us."

Ford shook his head. "I saw little Tita as clearly as though I were back at the Rue des Apotres at Bordeaux," said he. "But the hour is late, and I must go."

"Where do you sleep, then?"

"In the chamber above you. May the saints be with us all!" He rose from the couch and left the chamber, while Alleyne could hear his feet sounding upon the winding stair. The young squire walked across to the window and gazed out at the moonlit landscape, his mind absorbed by the thought of the Lady Tiphaine, and of the strange words that she had spoken as to what was going forward at Castle Twynham. Leaning his elbows upon the stonework, he was deeply plunged in reverie, when in a moment his thoughts were brought back to Villefranche and to the scene before him.

The window at which he stood was in the second floor of that portion of the castle which was nearest to the keep. In front lay the broad moat, with the moon lying upon its surface, now clear and round, now drawn lengthwise as the breeze stirred the waters. Beyond, the plain sloped down to a thick wood, while further to the left a second wood shut out the view. Between the two an open glade stretched, silvered in the moonshine, with the river curving across the lower end of it.

As he gazed, he saw of a sudden a man steal forth from the wood into the open clearing. He walked with his head sunk, his shoulders curved, and his knees bent, as one who strives hard to remain unseen. Ten paces from the fringe of trees he glanced around, and waving his hand he crouched down, and was lost to sight among a belt of furze-bushes. After him there came a second man, and after him a third, a fourth, and a fifth stealing across the narrow open space and darting into the shelter of the brushwood. Nine-and-seventy Alleyne counted of these dark figures flitting across the line of the moonlight. Many bore huge burdens upon their backs, though what it was that they carried he could not tell at the distance. Out of the one wood and into the other they passed, all with the same crouching, furtive gait, until the black bristle of trees had swallowed up the last of them.

For a moment Alleyne stood in the window, still staring down at the silent forest, uncertain as to what he should think of these midnight walkers. Then he bethought him that there was one beside him who was fitter to judge on such a matter. His fingers had scarce rested upon Aylward's shoulder ere the bowman was on his feet, with his hand outstretched to his sword.

"Qui va?" he cried. "Hola! mon petit. By my hilt! I thought there had been a camisade. What then, mon gar.?"

"Come hither by the window, Aylward," said Alleyne. "I have seen four-score men pass from yonder shaw across the glade, and nigh every man of them had a great burden on his back. What think you of it?"

"I think nothing of it, mon camarade! There are as many masterless folk in this country as there are rabbits on Cowdray Down, and there are many who show their faces by night but would dance in a hempen collar if they stirred forth in the day. On all the French marches are droves of outcasts, reivers, spoilers, and draw-latches, of whom I judge that these are some, though I marvel that they should dare to come so nigh to the castle of the seneschal. All seems very quiet now," he added, peering out of the window.

"They are in the further wood," said Alleyne.

"And there they may bide. Back to rest, mon petit; for, by my hilt! each day now will bring its own work. Yet it would be well to shoot the bolt in yonder door when one is in strange quarters. So!" He threw himself down upon his pallet and in an instant was fast asleep.

It might have been about three o'clock in the morning when Alleyne was aroused from a troubled sleep by a low cry or exclamation. He listened, but, as he heard no more, he set it down as the challenge of the guard upon the walls, and dropped off to sleep once more. A few minutes later he was disturbed by a gentle creaking of his own door, as though some one were pushing cautiously against it, and immediately afterwards he heard the soft thud of cautious footsteps upon the stair which led to the room above, followed by a confused noise and a muffled groan. Alleyne sat up on his couch with all his nerves in a tingle, uncertain whether these sounds might come from a simple cause—some sick archer and visiting leech perhaps—or whether they might have a more sinister meaning. But what danger could threaten them here in this strong castle, under the care of famous warriors, with high walls and a broad moat around them? Who was there that could injure them? He had well-nigh persuaded himself that his fears were a foolish fancy, when his eyes fell upon that which sent the blood cold to his heart and left him gasping, with hands clutching at the counterpane.

Right in front of him was the broad window of the chamber, with the moon shining brightly through it. For an instant something had obscured the light, and now a head was bobbing up and down outside, the face looking in at him, and swinging slowly from one side of the window to the other. Even in that dim light there could be no mistaking those features. Drawn, distorted and blood-stained, they were still those of the young fellow-squire who had sat so recently upon his own couch. With a cry of horror Alleyne sprang from his bed and rushed to the casement, while the two archers, aroused by the sound, seized their weapons and stared about them in bewilderment. One glance was enough to show Edricson that his fears were but too true. Foully murdered, with a score of wounds upon him and a rope round his neck, his poor friend had been cast from the upper window and swung slowly in the night wind, his body rasping against the wall and his disfigured face upon a level with the casement.

"My God!" cried Alleyne, shaking in every limb. "What has come upon us? What devil's deed is this?"

"Here is flint and steel," said John stolidly. "The lamp, Aylward! This moonshine softens a man's heart. Now we may use the eyes which God hath given us."

"By my hilt!" cried Aylward, as the yellow flame flickered up, "it is indeed young master Ford, and I think that this seneschal is a black villain, who dare not face us in the day but would murther us in our sleep. By the twang of string! if I do not soak a goose's feather with his heart's blood, it will be no fault of Samkin Aylward of the White Company."

"But, Aylward, think of the men whom I saw yesternight," said Alleyne. "It may not be the seneschal. It may be that others have come into the castle. I must to Sir Nigel ere it be too late. Let me go, Aylward, for my place is by his side."

"One moment, mon gar. Put that steel head-piece on the end of my yew-stave. So! I will put it first through the door; for it is ill to come out when you can neither see nor guard yourself. Now, camarades, out swords and stand ready! Hola, by my hilt! it is time that we were stirring!"

As he spoke, a sudden shouting broke forth in the castle, with the scream of a woman and the rush of many feet. Then came the sharp clink of clashing steel, and a roar like that of an angry lion—"Notre Dame Du Guesclin! St. Ives! St. Ives!" The bow-man pulled back the bolt of the door, and thrust out the headpiece at the end of the bow. A clash, the clatter of the steel-cap upon the ground, and, ere the man who struck could heave up for another blow, the archer had passed his sword through his body. "On, camarades, on!" he cried; and, breaking fiercely past two men who threw themselves in his way, he sped down the broad corridor in the direction of the shouting.

A sharp turning, and then a second one, brought them to the head of a short stair, from which they looked straight down upon the scene of the uproar. A square oak-floored hall lay beneath them, from which opened the doors of the principal guest-chambers. This hall was as light as day, for torches burned in numerous sconces upon the walls, throwing strange shadows from the tusked or antlered heads which ornamented them. At the very foot of the stair, close to the open door of their chamber, lay the seneschal and his wife: she with her head shorn from her shoulders, he thrust through with a sharpened stake, which still protruded from either side of his body. Three servants of the castle lay dead beside them, all torn and draggled, as though a pack of wolves had been upon them. In front of the central guest-chamber stood Du Guesclin and Sir Nigel, half-clad and unarmored, with the mad joy of battle gleaming in their eyes. Their heads were thrown back, their lips compressed, their blood-stained swords poised over their right shoulders, and their left feet thrown out. Three dead men lay huddled together in front of them: while a fourth, with the blood squirting from a severed vessel, lay back with updrawn knees, breathing in wheezy gasps. Further back—all panting together, like the wind in a tree—there stood a group of fierce, wild creatures, bare-armed and bare-legged, gaunt, unshaven, with deep-set murderous eyes and wild beast faces. With their flashing teeth, their bristling hair, their mad leapings and screamings, they seemed to Alleyne more like fiends from the pit than men of flesh and blood. Even as he looked, they broke into a hoarse yell and dashed once more upon the two knights, hurling themselves madly upon their sword-points; clutching, scrambling, biting, tearing, careless of wounds if they could but drag the two soldiers to earth. Sir Nigel was thrown down by the sheer weight of them, and Sir Bertrand with his thunderous war-cry was swinging round his heavy sword to clear a space for him to rise, when the whistle of two long English arrows, and the rush of the squire and the two English archers down the stairs, turned the tide of the combat. The assailants gave back, the knights rushed forward, and in a very few moments the hall was cleared, and Hordle John had hurled the last of the wild men down the steep steps which led from the end of it.

"Do not follow them," cried Du Guesclin. "We are lost if we scatter. For myself I care not a denier, though it is a poor thing to meet one's end at the hands of such scum; but I have my dear lady here, who must by no means be risked. We have breathing-space now, and I would ask you, Sir Nigel, what it is that you would counsel?"

"By St. Paul!" answered Sir Nigel, "I can by no means understand what hath befallen us, save that I have been woken up by your battle-cry, and, rushing forth, found myself in the midst of this small bickering. Harrow and alas for the lady and the seneschal! What dogs are they who have done this bloody deed?"

"They are the Jacks, the men of the brushwood. They have the castle, though I know not how it hath come to pass. Look from this window into the bailey."

"By heaven!" cried Sir Nigel, "it is as bright as day with the torches. The gates stand open, and there are three thousand of them within the walls. See how they rush and scream and wave! What is it that they thrust out through the postern door? My God! it is a man-at-arms, and they pluck him limb from limb like hounds on a wolf. Now another, and yet another. They hold the whole castle, for I see their faces at the windows. See, there are some with great bundles on their backs."

"It is dried wood from the forest. They pile them against the walls and set them in a blaze. Who is this who tries to check them? By St. Ives! it is the good priest who spake for them in the hall. He kneels, he prays, he implores! What! villains, would ye raise hands against those who have befriended you? Ah, the butcher has struck him! He is down! They stamp him under their feet! They tear off his gown and wave it in the air! See now, how the flames lick up the walls! Are there none left to rally round us? With a hundred men we might hold our own."

"Oh, for my Company!" cried Sir Nigel. "But where is Ford, Alleyne?"

"He is foully murdered, my fair lord."

"The saints receive him! May he rest in peace! But here come some at last who may give us counsel, for amid these passages it is ill to stir without a guide."

As he spoke, a French squire and the Bohemian knight came rushing down the steps, the latter bleeding from a slash across his forehead.

"All is lost!" he cried. "The castle is taken and on fire, the seneschal is slain, and there is nought left for us."

"On the contrary," quoth Sir Nigel, "there is much left to us, for there is a very honorable contention before us, and a fair lady for whom to give our lives. There are many ways in which a man might die, but none better than this."

"You can tell us, Godfrey," said Du Guesclin to the French squire: "how came these men into the castle, and what succors can we count upon? By St. Ives! if we come not quickly to some counsel we shall be burned like young rooks in a nest."

The squire, a dark, slender stripling, spoke firmly and quickly, as one who was trained to swift action. "There is a passage under the earth into the castle," said he, "and through it some of the Jacks made their way, casting open the gates for the others. They have had help from within the walls, and the men-at-arms were heavy with wine: they must have been slain in their beds, for these devils crept from room to room with soft step and ready knife. Sir Amory the Hospitaller was struck down with an axe as he rushed before us from his sleeping-chamber. Save only ourselves, I do not think that there are any left alive."

"What, then, would you counsel?"

"That we make for the keep. It is unused, save in time of war, and the key hangs from my poor lord and master's belt."

"There are two keys there."

"It is the larger. Once there, we might hold the narrow stair; and at least, as the walls are of a greater thickness, it would be longer ere they could burn them. Could we but carry the lady across the bailey, all might be well with us."

"Nay; the lady hath seen something of the work of war," said Tiphaine coming forth, as white, as grave, and as unmoved as ever. "I would not be a hamper to you, my dear spouse and gallant friend. Rest assured of this, that if all else fail I have always a safeguard here"—drawing a small silver-hilted poniard from her bosom—"which sets me beyond the fear of these vile and blood-stained wretches."

"Tiphaine," cried Du Guesclin, "I have always loved you; and now, by Our Lady of Rennes! I love you more than ever. Did I not know that your hand will be as ready as your words I would myself turn my last blow upon you, ere you should fall into their hands. Lead on, Godfrey! A new golden pyx will shine in the minster of Dinan if we come safely through with it."

The attention of the insurgents had been drawn away from murder to plunder, and all over the castle might be heard their cries and whoops of delight as they dragged forth the rich tapestries, the silver flagons, and the carved furniture. Down in the courtyard half-clad wretches, their bare limbs all mottled with blood-stains, strutted about with plumed helmets upon their heads, or with the Lady Rochefort's silken gowns girt round their loins and trailing on the ground behind them. Casks of choice wine had been rolled out from the cellars, and starving peasants squatted, goblet in hand, draining off vintages which De Rochefort had set aside for noble and royal guests. Others, with slabs of bacon and joints of dried meat upon the ends of their pikes, held them up to the blaze or tore at them ravenously with their teeth. Yet all order had not been lost amongst them, for some hundreds of the better armed stood together in a silent group, leaning upon their rude weapons and looking up at the fire, which had spread so rapidly as to involve one whole side of the castle. Already Alleyne could hear the crackling and roaring of the flames, while the air was heavy with heat and full of the pungent whiff of burning wood.

XXXI

How Five Men Held the Keep of Villefranche

Under the guidance of the French squire the party passed down two narrow corridors. The first was empty, but at the head of the second stood a peasant sentry, who started off at the sight of them, yelling loudly to his comrades. "Stop him, or we are undone!" cried Du Guesclin, and had started to run, when Aylward's great war-bow twanged like a harp-string, and the man fell forward upon his face, with twitching limbs and clutching fingers. Within five paces of where he lay a narrow and little-used door led out into the bailey. From beyond it came such a Babel of hooting and screaming, horrible oaths and yet more horrible laughter, that the stoutest heart might have shrunk from casting down the frail barrier which faced them.

"Make straight for the keep!" said Du Guesclin, in a sharp, stern whisper. "The two archers in front, the lady in the centre, a squire on either side, while we three knights shall bide behind and beat back those who press upon us. So! Now open the door, and God have us in his holy keeping!"

For a few moments it seemed that their object would be attained without danger, so swift and so silent had been their movements. They were half-way across the bailey ere the frantic, howling peasants made a movement to stop them. The few who threw themselves in their way were overpowered or brushed aside, while the pursuers were beaten back by the ready weapons of the three cavaliers. Unscathed they fought their way to the door of the keep, and faced round upon the swarming mob, while the squire thrust the great key into the lock.

"My God!" he cried, "it is the wrong key."

"The wrong key!"

"Dolt, fool that I am! This is the key of the castle gate; the other opens the keep. I must back for it!" He turned, with some wild intention of retracing his steps, but at the instant a great jagged rock, hurled by a brawny peasant, struck him full upon the ear, and he dropped senseless to the ground.

"This is key enough for me!" quoth Hordle John, picking up the huge stone, and hurling it against the door with all the strength of his enormous body. The lock shivered, the wood smashed, the stone flew into five pieces, but the iron clamps still held the door in its position. Bending down, he thrust his great fingers under it, and with a heave raised the whole mass of wood and iron from its hinges. For a moment it tottered and swayed, and then, falling outward, buried him in its ruin, while his comrades rushed into the dark archway which led to safety.

"Up the steps, Tiphaine!" cried Du Guesclin. "Now round, friends, and beat them back!" The mob of peasants had surged in upon their heels, but the two trustiest blades in Europe gleamed upon that narrow stair, and four of their number dropped upon the threshold. The others gave back, and gathered in a half circle round the open door, gnashing their teeth and shaking their clenched hands at the defenders. The body of the French squire had been dragged out by them and hacked to pieces. Three or four others had pulled John from under the door, when he suddenly bounded to his feet, and clutching one in either hand dashed them together with such force that they fell senseless across each other upon the ground. With a kick and a blow he freed himself from two others who clung to him, and in a moment he was within the portal with his comrades.

Yet their position was a desperate one. The peasants from far and near had been assembled for this deed of vengeance, and not less than six thousand were within or around the walls of the Chateau of Villefranche. Ill armed and half starved, they were still desperate men, to whom danger had lost all fears: for what was death that they should shun it to cling to such a life as theirs? The castle was theirs, and the roaring flames were spurting through the windows and flickering high above the turrets on two sides of the quadrangle. From either side they were sweeping down from room to room and from bastion to bastion in the direction of the keep. Faced by an army, and girt in by fire, were six men and one woman; but some of them were men so trained to danger and so wise in war that even now the combat was less unequal than it seemed. Courage and resource were penned in by desperation and numbers, while the great yellow sheets of flame threw their lurid glare over the scene of death.

"There is but space for two upon a step to give free play to our sword-arms," said Du Guesclin. "Do you stand with me, Nigel, upon the lowest. France and England will fight together this night. Sir Otto, I pray you to stand behind us with this young squire. The archers may go higher yet and shoot over our heads. I would that we had our harness, Nigel."

"Often have I heard my dear Sir John Chandos say that a knight should never, even when a guest, be parted from it. Yet it will be more honor to us if we come well out of it. We have a vantage, since we see them against the light and they can scarce see us. It seems to me that they muster for an onslaught."

"If we can but keep them in play," said the Bohemian, "it is likely that these flames may bring us succor if there be any true men in the country."

"Bethink you, my fair lord," said Alleyne to Sir Nigel, "that we have never injured these men, nor have we cause of quarrel against them. Would it not be well, if but for the lady's sake, to speak them fair and see if we may not come to honorable terms with them?"

"Not so, by St. Paul!" cried Sir Nigel. "It does not accord with mine honor, nor shall it ever be said that I, a knight of England, was ready to hold parley with men who have slain a fair lady and a holy priest."

"As well hold parley with a pack of ravening wolves," said the French captain. "Ha! Notre Dame Du Guesclin! Saint Ives! Saint Ives!"

As he thundered forth his war-cry, the Jacks who had been gathering before the black arch of the gateway rushed in madly in a desperate effort to carry the staircase. Their leaders were a small man, dark in the face, with his beard done up in two plaits, and another larger man, very bowed in the shoulders, with a huge club studded with sharp nails in his hand. The first had not taken three steps ere an arrow from Aylward's bow struck him full in the chest, and he fell coughing and spluttering across the threshold. The other rushed onwards, and breaking between Du Guesclin and Sir Nigel he dashed out the brains of the Bohemian with a single blow of his clumsy weapon. With three swords through him he still struggled on, and had almost won his way through them ere he fell dead upon the stair. Close at his heels came a hundred furious peasants, who flung themselves again and again against the five swords which confronted them. It was cut and parry and stab as quick as eye could see or hand act. The door was piled with bodies, and the stone floor was slippery with blood. The deep shout of Du Guesclin, the hard, hissing breath of the pressing multitude, the clatter of steel, the thud of falling bodies, and the screams of the stricken, made up such a medley as came often in after years to break upon Alleyne's sleep. Slowly and sullenly at last the throng drew off, with many a fierce backward glance, while eleven of their number lay huddled in front of the stair which they had failed to win.

"The dogs have had enough," said Du Guesclin.

"By Saint Paul! there appear to be some very worthy and valiant persons among them," observed Sir Nigel. "They are men from whom, had they been of better birth, much honor and advancement might be gained. Even as it is, it is a great pleasure to have seen them. But what is this that they are bringing forward?"

"It is as I feared," growled Du Guesclin. "They will burn us out, since they cannot win their way past us. Shoot straight and hard, archers; for, by St. Ives! our good swords are of little use to us."

As he spoke, a dozen men rushed forward, each screening himself behind a huge fardel of brushwood. Hurling their burdens in one vast heap within the portal, they threw burning torches upon the top of it. The wood had been soaked in oil, for in an instant it was ablaze, and a long, hissing, yellow flame licked over the heads of the defenders, and drove them further up to the first floor of the keep. They had scarce reached it, however, ere they found that the wooden joists and planks of the flooring were already on fire. Dry and worm-eaten, a spark upon them became a smoulder, and a smoulder a blaze. A choking smoke filled the air, and the five could scarce grope their way to the staircase which led up to the very summit of the square tower.

Strange was the scene which met their eyes from this eminence. Beneath them on every side stretched the long sweep of peaceful country, rolling plain, and tangled wood, all softened and mellowed in the silver moonshine. No light, nor movement, nor any sign of human aid could be seen, but far away the hoarse clangor of a heavy bell rose and fell upon the wintry air. Beneath and around them blazed the huge fire, roaring and crackling on every side of the bailey, and even as they looked the two corner turrets fell in with a deafening crash, and the whole castle was but a shapeless mass, spouting flames and smoke from every window and embrasure. The great black tower upon which they stood rose like a last island of refuge amid this sea of fire but the ominous crackling and roaring below showed that it would not be long ere it was engulfed also in the common ruin. At their very feet was the square courtyard, crowded with the howling and dancing peasants, their fierce faces upturned, their clenched hands waving, all drunk with bloodshed and with vengeance. A yell of execration and a scream of hideous laughter burst from the vast throng, as they saw the faces of the last survivors of their enemies peering down at them from the height of the keep. They still piled the brushwood round the base of the tower, and gambolled hand in hand around the blaze, screaming out the doggerel lines which had long been the watchword of the Jacquerie:

Cessez, cessez, gens d'armes et pietons,
De piller et manger le bonhomme
Qui de longtemps Jacques Bonhomme
Se nomme.

Their thin, shrill voices rose high above the roar of the flames and the crash of the masonry, like the yelping of a pack of wolves who see their quarry before them and know that they have well-nigh run him down.

"By my hilt!" said Aylward to John, "it is in my mind that we shall not see Spain this journey. It is a great joy to me that I have placed my feather-bed and other things of price with that worthy woman at Lyndhurst, who will now have the use of them. I have thirteen arrows yet, and if one of them fly unfleshed, then, by the twang of string! I shall deserve my doom. First at him who flaunts with my lady's silken frock. Clap in the clout, by God! though a hand's-breadth lower than I had meant. Now for the rogue with the head upon his pike. Ha! to the inch, John. When my eye is true, I am better at rovers than at long-butts or hoyles. A good shoot for you also, John! The villain hath fallen forward into the fire. But I pray you, John, to loose gently, and not to pluck with the drawing-hand, for it is a trick that hath marred many a fine bowman."

Whilst the two archers were keeping up a brisk fire upon the mob beneath them, Du Guesclin and his lady were consulting with Sir Nigel upon their desperate situation.

"'Tis a strange end for one who has seen so many stricken fields," said the French chieftain. "For me one death is as another, but it is the thought of my sweet lady which goes to my heart."

"Nay, Bertrand, I fear it as little as you," said she. "Had I my dearest wish, it would be that we should go together."

"Well answered, fair lady!" cried Sir Nigel. "And very sure I am that my own sweet wife would have said the same. If the end be now come, I have had great good fortune in having lived in times when so much glory was to be won, and in knowing so many valiant gentlemen and knights. But why do you pluck my sleeve, Alleyne?"

"If it please you, my fair lord, there are in this corner two great tubes of iron, with many heavy balls, which may perchance be those bombards and shot of which I have heard."

"By Saint Ives! it is true," cried Sir Bertrand, striding across to the recess where the ungainly, funnel-shaped, thick-ribbed engines were standing. "Bombards they are, and of good size. We may shoot down upon them."

"Shoot with them, quotha?" cried Aylward in high disdain, for pressing danger is the great leveller of classes. "How is a man to take aim with these fool's toys, and how can he hope to do scath with them?"

"I will show you," answered Sir Nigel; "for here is the great box of powder, and if you will raise it for me, John, I will show you how it may be used. Come hither, where the folk are thickest round the fire. Now, Aylward, crane thy neck and see what would have been deemed an old wife's tale when we first turned our faces to the wars. Throw back the lid, John, and drop the box into the fire!"

A deafening roar, a fluff of bluish light, and the great square tower rocked and trembled from its very foundations, swaying this way and that like a reed in the wind. Amazed and dizzy, the defenders, clutching at the cracking parapets for support, saw great stones, burning beams of wood, and mangled bodies hurtling past them through the air. When they staggered to their feet once more, the whole keep had settled down upon one side, so that they could scarce keep their footing upon the sloping platform. Gazing over the edge, they looked down upon the horrible destruction which had been caused by the explosion. For forty yards round the portal the ground was black with writhing, screaming figures, who struggled up and hurled themselves down again, tossing this way and that, sightless, scorched, with fire bursting from their tattered clothing. Beyond this circle of death their comrades, bewildered and amazed, cowered away from this black tower and from these invincible men, who were most to be dreaded when hope was furthest from their hearts.

"A sally, Du Guesclin, a sally!" cried Sir Nigel. "By Saint Paul! they are in two minds, and a bold rush may turn them." He drew his sword as he spoke and darted down the winding stairs, closely followed by his four comrades. Ere he was at the first floor, however, he threw up his arms and stopped. "Mon Dieu!" he said, "we are lost men!"

"What then?" cried those behind him.

"The wall hath fallen in, the stair is blocked, and the fire still rages below. By Saint Paul! friends, we have fought a very honorable fight, and may say in all humbleness that we have done our devoir, but I think that we may now go back to the Lady Tiphaine and say our orisons, for we have played our parts in this world, and it is time that we made ready for another."

The narrow pass was blocked by huge stones littered in wild confusion over each other, with the blue choking smoke reeking up through the crevices. The explosion had blown in the wall and cut off the only path by which they could descend. Pent in, a hundred feet from earth, with a furnace raging under them and a ravening multitude all round who thirsted for their blood, it seemed indeed as though no men had ever come through such peril with their lives. Slowly they made their way back to the summit, but as they came out upon it the Lady Tiphaine darted forward and caught her husband by the wrist.

"Bertrand," said she, "hush and listen! I have heard the voices of men all singing together in a strange tongue."

Breathless they stood and silent, but no sound came up to them, save the roar of the flames and the clamor of their enemies.

"It cannot be, lady," said Du Guesclin. "This night hath over wrought you, and your senses play you false. What men are there in this country who would sing in a strange tongue?"

"Hola!" yelled Aylward, leaping suddenly into the air with waving hands and joyous face. "I thought I heard it ere we went down, and now I hear it again. We are saved, comrades! By these ten finger-bones, we are saved! It is the marching song of the White Company. Hush!"

With upraised forefinger and slanting head, he stood listening. Suddenly there came swelling up a deep-voiced, rollicking chorus from somewhere out of the darkness. Never did choice or dainty ditty of Provence or Languedoc sound more sweetly in the ears than did the rough-tongued Saxon to the six who strained their ears from the blazing keep:

We'll drink all together
To the gray goose feather
And the land where the gray goose flew.

"Ha, by my hilt!" shouted Aylward, "it is the dear old bow song of the Company. Here come two hundred as tight lads as ever twirled a shaft over their thumbnails. Hark to the dogs, how lustily they sing!"

Nearer and clearer, swelling up out of the night, came the gay marching lilt:

What of the bow?
The bow was made in England.
Of true wood, of yew wood,
The wood of English bows;
For men who are free
Love the old yew-tree
And the land where the yew tree grows.

What of the men?
The men were bred in England,
The bowmen, the yeomen,
The lads of the dale and fell,
Here's to you and to you,
To the hearts that are true,
And the land where the true hearts dwell.

"They sing very joyfully," said Du Guesclin, "as though they were going to a festival."

"It is their wont when there is work to be done."

"By Saint Paul!" quoth Sir Nigel, "it is in my mind that they come too late, for I cannot see how we are to come down from this tower."

"There they come, the hearts of gold!" cried Aylward. "See, they move out from the shadow. Now they cross the meadow. They are on the further side of the moat. Hola camarades, hola! Johnston, Eccles, Cooke, Harward, Bligh! Would ye see a fair lady and two gallant knights done foully to death?"

"Who is there?" shouted a deep voice from below. "Who is this who speaks with an English tongue?"

"It is I, old lad. It is Sam Aylward of the Company; and here is your captain, Sir Nigel Loring, and four others, all laid out to be grilled like an Easterling's herrings."

"Curse me if I did not think that it was the style of speech of old Samkin Aylward," said the voice, amid a buzz from the ranks. "Wherever there are knocks going there is Sammy in the heart of it. But who are these ill-faced rogues who block the path? To your kennels, canaille! What! you dare look us in the eyes? Out swords, lads, and give them the flat of them! Waste not your shafts upon such runagate knaves."

There was little fight left in the peasants, however, still dazed by the explosion, amazed at their own losses and disheartened by the arrival of the disciplined archers. In a very few minutes they were in full flight for their brushwood homes, leaving the morning sun to rise upon a blackened and blood-stained ruin, where it had left the night before the magnificent castle of the Seneschal of Auvergne. Already the white lines in the east were deepening into pink as the archers gathered round the keep and took counsel how to rescue the survivors.

"Had we a rope," said Alleyne, "there is one side which is not yet on fire, down which we might slip."

"But how to get a rope?"

"It is an old trick," quoth Aylward. "Hola! Johnston, cast me up a rope, even as you did at Maupertuis in the war time."

The grizzled archer thus addressed took several lengths of rope from his comrades, and knotting them firmly together, he stretched them out in the long shadow which the rising sun threw from the frowning keep. Then he fixed the yew-stave of his bow upon end and measured the long, thin, black line which it threw upon the turf.

"A six-foot stave throws a twelve-foot shadow," he muttered. "The keep throws a shadow of sixty paces. Thirty paces of rope will be enow and to spare. Another strand, Watkin! Now pull at the end that all may be safe. So! It is ready for them."

"But how are they to reach it?" asked the young archer beside him.

"Watch and see, young fool's-head," growled the old bowman. He took a long string from his pouch and fastened one end to an arrow.

"All ready, Samkin?"

"Ready, camarade."

"Close to your hand then." With an easy pull he sent the shaft flickering gently up, falling upon the stonework within a foot of where Aylward was standing. The other end was secured to the rope, so that in a minute a good strong cord was dangling from the only sound side of the blazing and shattered tower. The Lady Tiphaine was lowered with a noose drawn fast under the arms, and the other five slid swiftly down, amid the cheers and joyous outcry of their rescuers.

XXXII

How the Company Took Counsel Round the Fallen Tree

"Where is Sir Claude Latour?" asked Sir Nigel, as his feet touched ground.

"He is in camp, near Montpezat, two hours' march from here, my fair lord," said Johnston, the grizzled bowman who commanded the archers.

"Then we shall march thither, for I would fain have you all back at Dax in time to be in the prince's vanguard."

"My lord," cried Alleyne, joyfully, "here are our chargers in the field, and I see your harness amid the plunder which these rogues have left behind them."

"By Saint Ives! you speak sooth, young squire," said Du Guesclin. "There is my horse and my lady's jennet. The knaves led them from the stables, but fled without them. Now, Nigel, it is great joy to me to have seen one of whom I have often heard. Yet we must leave you now, for I must be with the King of Spain ere your army crosses the mountains."

"I had thought that you were in Spain with the valiant Henry of Trastamare."

"I have been there, but I came to France to raise succor for him. I shall ride back, Nigel, with four thousand of the best lances of France at my back, so that your prince may find he hath a task which is worthy of him. God be with you, friend, and may we meet again in better times!"

"I do not think," said Sir Nigel, as he stood by Alleyne's side looking after the French knight and his lady, "that in all Christendom you will meet with a more stout-hearted man or a fairer and sweeter dame. But your face is pale and sad, Alleyne! Have you perchance met with some hurt during the ruffle?"

"Nay, my fair lord, I was but thinking of my friend Ford, and how he sat upon my couch no later than yesternight."

Sir Nigel shook his head sadly. "Two brave squires have I lost," said he. "I know not why the young shoots should be plucked, and an old weed left standing, yet certes there must be some good reason, since God hath so planned it. Did you not note, Alleyne, that the Lady Tiphaine did give us warning last night that danger was coming upon us?"

"She did, my lord."

"By Saint Paul! my mind misgives me as to what she saw at Twynham Castle. And yet I cannot think that any Scottish or French rovers could land in such force as to beleaguer the fortalice. Call the Company together, Aylward; and let us on, for it will be shame to us if we are not at Dax upon the trysting day."

The archers had spread themselves over the ruins, but a blast upon a bugle brought them all back to muster, with such booty as they could bear with them stuffed into their pouches or slung over their shoulders. As they formed into ranks, each man dropping silently into his place, Sir Nigel ran a questioning eye over them, and a smile of pleasure played over his face. Tall and sinewy, and brown, clear-eyed, hard-featured, with the stern and prompt bearing of experienced soldiers, it would be hard indeed for a leader to seek for a choicer following. Here and there in the ranks were old soldiers of the French wars, grizzled and lean, with fierce, puckered features and shaggy, bristling brows. The most, however, were young and dandy archers, with fresh English faces, their beards combed out, their hair curling from under their close steel hufkens, with gold or jewelled earrings gleaming in their ears, while their gold-spangled baldrics, their silken belts, and the chains which many of them wore round their thick brown necks, all spoke of the brave times which they had had as free companions. Each had a yew or hazel stave slung over his shoulder, plain and serviceable with the older men, but gaudily painted and carved at either end with the others. Steel caps, mail brigandines, white surcoats with the red lion of St. George, and sword or battle-axe swinging from their belts, completed this equipment, while in some cases the murderous maule or five-foot mallet was hung across the bowstave, being fastened to their leathern shoulder-belt by a hook in the centre of the handle. Sir Nigel's heart beat high as he looked upon their free bearing and fearless faces.

For two hours they marched through forest and marshland, along the left bank of the river Aveyron; Sir Nigel riding behind his Company, with Alleyne at his right hand, and Johnston, the old master bowman, walking by his left stirrup. Ere they had reached their journey's end the knight had learned all that he would know of his men, their doings and their intentions. Once, as they marched, they saw upon the further bank of the river a body of French men-at-arms, riding very swiftly in the direction of Villefranche.

"It is the Seneschal of Toulouse, with his following," said Johnston, shading his eyes with his hand. "Had he been on this side of the water he might have attempted something upon us."

"I think that it would be well that we should cross," said Sir Nigel. "It were pity to balk this worthy seneschal, should he desire to try some small feat of arms."

"Nay, there is no ford nearer than Tourville," answered the old archer. "He is on his way to Villefranche, and short will be the shrift of any Jacks who come into his hands, for he is a man of short speech. It was he and the Seneschal of Beaucaire who hung Peter Wilkins, of the Company, last Lammastide; for which, by the black rood of Waltham! they shall hang themselves, if ever they come into our power. But here are our comrades, Sir Nigel, and here is our camp."

As he spoke, the forest pathway along which they marched opened out into a green glade, which sloped down towards the river. High, leafless trees girt it in on three sides, with a thick undergrowth of holly between their trunks. At the farther end of this forest clearing there stood forty or fifty huts, built very neatly from wood and clay, with the blue smoke curling out from the roofs. A dozen tethered horses and mules grazed around the encampment, while a number of archers lounged about: some shooting at marks, while others built up great wooden fires in the open, and hung their cooking kettles above them. At the sight of their returning comrades there was a shout of welcome, and a horseman, who had been exercising his charger behind the camp, came cantering down to them. He was a dapper, brisk man, very richly clad, with a round, clean-shaven face, and very bright black eyes, which danced and sparkled with excitement.

"Sir Nigel!" he cried. "Sir Nigel Loring, at last! By my soul we have awaited you this month past. Right welcome, Sir Nigel! You have had my letter?"

"It was that which brought me here," said Sir Nigel. "But indeed, Sir Claude Latour, it is a great wonder to me that you did not yourself lead these bowmen, for surely they could have found no better leader?"

"None, none, by the Virgin of L'Esparre!" he cried, speaking in the strange, thick Gascon speech which turns every *v* into a *b*. "But you know what these islanders of yours are, Sir Nigel. They will not be led by any save their own blood and race. There is no persuading them. Not even I, Claude Latour Seigneur of Montchateau, master of the high justice, the middle and the low, could gain their favor. They must needs hold a council and put their two hundred thick heads together, and then there comes this fellow Aylward and another, as their spokesmen, to say that they will disband unless an Englishman of good name be set over them. There are many of them, as I understand, who come from some great forest which lies in Hampi, or Hampti—I cannot lay my tongue to the name. Your dwelling is in those parts, and so their thoughts turned to you as their leader. But we had hoped that you would bring a hundred men with you."

"They are already at Dax, where we shall join them," said Sir Nigel. "But let the men break their fast, and we shall then take counsel what to do."

"Come into my hut," said Sir Claude. "It is but poor fare that I can lay before you—milk, cheese, wine, and bacon—yet your squire and yourself will doubtless excuse it. This is my house where the pennon flies before the door—a small residence to contain the Lord of Montchateau."

Sir Nigel sat silent and distrait at his meal, while Alleyne hearkened to the clattering tongue of the Gascon, and to his talk of the glories of his own estate, his successes in love, and his triumphs in war.

"And now that you are here, Sir Nigel," he said at last, "I have many fine ventures all ready for us. I have heard that Montpezat is of no great strength, and that there are two hundred thousand crowns in the castle. At Castelnau also there is a cobbler who is in my pay, and who will throw us a rope any dark night from his house by the town wall. I promise you that you shall thrust your arms elbow-deep among good silver pieces ere the nights are moonless again; for on every hand of us are fair women, rich wine, and good plunder, as much as heart could wish."

"I have other plans," answered Sir Nigel curtly; "for I have come hither to lead these bowmen to the help of the prince, our master, who may have sore need of them ere he set Pedro upon the throne of Spain. It is my purpose to start this very day for Dax upon the Adour, where he hath now pitched his camp."

The face of the Gascon darkened, and his eyes flashed with resentment. "For me," he said, "I care little for this war, and I find the life which I lead a very joyous and pleasant one. I will not go to Dax."

"Nay, think again, Sir Claude," said Sir Nigel gently; "for you have ever had the name of a true and loyal knight. Surely you will not hold back now when your master hath need of you."

"I will not go to Dax," the other shouted.

"But your devoir—your oath of fealty?"

"I say that I will not go."

"Then, Sir Claude, I must lead the Company without you."

"If they will follow," cried the Gascon with a sneer. "These are not hired slaves, but free companions, who will do nothing save by their own good wills. In very sooth, my Lord Loring, they are ill men to trifle with, and it were easier to pluck a bone from a hungry bear than to lead a bowman out of a land of plenty and of pleasure."

"Then I pray you to gather them together," said Sir Nigel, "and I will tell them what is in my mind; for if I am their leader they must to Dax, and if I am not then I know not what I am doing in Auvergne. Have my horse ready, Alleyne; for, by St. Paul! come what may, I must be upon the homeward road ere mid-day."

A blast upon the bugle summoned the bowmen to counsel, and they gathered in little knots and groups around a great fallen tree which lay athwart the glade. Sir Nigel sprang lightly upon the trunk, and stood with blinking eye and firm lips looking down at the ring of upturned warlike faces.

"They tell me, bowmen," said he, "that ye have grown so fond of ease and plunder and high living that ye are not to be moved from this pleasant country. But, by Saint Paul! I will believe no such thing of you, for I can readily see that you are all very valiant men, who would scorn to live here in peace when your prince hath so great a venture before him. Ye have chosen me as a leader, and a leader I will be if ye come with me to Spain; and I vow to you that my pennon of the five roses shall, if God give me strength and life, be ever where there is most honor to be gained. But if it be your wish to loll and loiter in these glades, bartering glory and renown for vile gold and ill-gotten riches, then ye must find another leader; for I have lived in honor, and in honor I trust that I shall die. If there be forest men or Hampshire men amongst ye, I call upon them to say whether they will follow the banner of Loring."

"Here's a Romsey man for you!" cried a young bowman with a sprig of evergreen set in his helmet.

"And a lad from Alresford!" shouted another.

"And from Milton!"

"And from Burley!"

"And from Lymington!"

"And a little one from Brockenhurst!" shouted a huge-limbed fellow who sprawled beneath a tree.

"By my hilt! lads," cried Aylward, jumping upon the fallen trunk, "I think that we could not look the girls in the eyes if we let the prince cross the mountains and did not pull string to clear a path for him. It is very well in time of peace to lead such a life as we have had together, but now the war-banner is in the wind once more, and, by these ten finger-bones! if he go alone, old Samkin Aylward will walk beside it."

These words from a man as popular as Aylward decided many of the waverers, and a shout of approval burst from his audience.

"Far be it from me," said Sir Claude Latour suavely, "to persuade you against this worthy archer, or against Sir Nigel Loring; yet we have been together in many ventures, and perchance it may not be amiss if I say to you what I think upon the matter."

"Peace for the little Gascon!" cried the archers. "Let every man have his word. Shoot straight for the mark, lad, and fair play for all."

"Bethink you, then," said Sir Claude, "that you go under a hard rule, with neither freedom nor pleasure—and for what? For sixpence a day, at the most; while now you may walk across the country and stretch out either hand to gather in whatever you have a mind for. What do we not hear of our comrades who have gone with Sir John Hawkwood to Italy? In one night they have held to ransom six hundred of the richest noblemen of Mantua. They camp before a great city, and the base burghers come forth with the keys, and then they make great spoil; or, if it please them better, they take so many horse-loads of silver as a composition; and so they journey on from state to state, rich and free and feared by all. Now, is not that the proper life for a soldier?"

"The proper life for a robber!" roared Hordle John, in his thundering voice.

"And yet there is much in what the Gascon says," said a swarthy fellow in a weather-stained doublet; "and I for one would rather prosper in Italy than starve in Spain."

"You were always a cur and a traitor, Mark Shaw," cried Aylward. "By my hilt! if you will stand forth and draw your sword I will warrant you that you will see neither one nor the other."

"Nay, Aylward," said Sir Nigel, "we cannot mend the matter by broiling. Sir Claude, I think that what you have said does you little honor, and if my words aggrieve you I am ever ready to go deeper into the matter with you. But you shall have such men as will follow you, and you may go where you will, so that you come not with us. Let all who love their prince and country stand fast, while those who think more of a well-lined purse step forth upon the farther side."

Thirteen bowmen, with hung heads and sheepish faces, stepped forward with Mark Shaw and ranged themselves behind Sir Claude. Amid the hootings and hissings of their comrades, they marched off together to the Gascon's hut, while the main body broke up their meeting and set cheerily to work packing their possessions, furbishing their weapons, and preparing for the march which lay before them. Over the Tarn and the Garonne, through the vast quagmires of Armagnac, past the swift-flowing Losse, and so down the long valley of the Adour, there was many a long league to be crossed ere they could join themselves to that dark war-cloud which was drifting slowly southwards to the line of the snowy peaks, beyond which the banner of England had never yet been seen.

XXXIII

How the Army Made the Passage of Roncesvalles

The whole vast plain of Gascony and of Languedoc is an arid and profitless expanse in winter save where the swift-flowing Adour and her snow-fed tributaries, the Louts, the Oloron and the Pau, run down to the sea of Biscay. South of the Adour the jagged line of mountains which fringe the sky-line send out long granite claws, running down into the lowlands and dividing them into "gaves" or stretches of valley. Hillocks grow into hills, and hills into mountains, each range overlying its neighbor, until they soar up in the giant chain which raises its spotless and untrodden peaks, white and dazzling, against the pale blue wintry sky.

A quiet land is this—a land where the slow-moving Basque, with his flat biretta-cap, his red sash and his hempen sandals, tills his scanty farm or drives his lean flock to their hill-side pastures. It is the country of the wolf and the isard, of the brown bear and the mountain-goat, a land of bare rock and of rushing water. Yet here it was that the will of a great prince had now assembled a gallant army; so that from the Adour to the passes of Navarre the barren valleys and wind-swept wastes were populous with soldiers and loud with the shouting of orders and the neighing of horses. For the banners of war had been flung to the wind once more, and over those glistening peaks was the highway along which Honor pointed in an age when men had chosen her as their guide.

And now all was ready for the enterprise. From Dax to St. Jean Pied-du-Port the country was mottled with the white tents of Gascons, Aquitanians and English, all eager for the advance. From all sides the free companions had trooped in, until not less than twelve thousand of these veteran troops were cantoned along the frontiers of Navarre. From England had arrived the prince's brother, the Duke of Lancaster, with four hundred knights in his train and a strong company of archers. Above all, an heir to the throne had been born in Bordeaux, and the prince might leave his spouse with an easy mind, for all was well with mother and with child.

The keys of the mountain passes still lay in the hands of the shifty and ignoble Charles of Navarre, who had chaffered and bargained both with the English and with the Spanish, taking money from the one side to hold them open and from the other to keep them sealed. The mallet hand of Edward, however, had shattered all the schemes and wiles of the plotter. Neither entreaty nor courtly remonstrance came from the English prince; but Sir Hugh Calverley passed silently over the border with his company, and the blazing walls of the two cities of Miranda and Puenta de la Reyna warned the unfaithful monarch that there were other metals besides gold, and that he was dealing with a man to whom it was unsafe to lie. His price was paid, his objections silenced, and the mountain gorges lay open to the invaders. From the Feast of the Epiphany there was mustering and massing, until, in the first week of February—three days after the White Company joined the army—the word was given for a general advance through the defile of Roncesvalles. At five in the cold winter's morning the bugles were blowing in the hamlet of St. Jean Pied-du-Port, and by six Sir Nigel's Company, three hundred strong, were on their way for the defile, pushing swiftly in the dim light up the steep curving road; for it was the prince's order that they should be the first to pass through, and that they should remain on guard at the further end until the whole army had emerged from the mountains. Day was already breaking in the east, and the summits of the great peaks had turned rosy red, while the valleys still lay in the shadow, when they found themselves with the cliffs on either hand and the long, rugged pass stretching away before them.

Sir Nigel rode his great black war-horse at the head of his archers, dressed in full armor, with Black Simon bearing his banner behind him, while Alleyne at his bridle-arm carried his blazoned shield and his well-steeled ashen spear. A proud and happy man was the knight, and many a time he turned in his saddle to look at the long column of bowmen who swung swiftly along behind him.

"By Saint Paul! Alleyne," said he, "this pass is a very perilous place, and I would that the King of Navarre had held it against us, for it would have been a very honorable venture had it fallen to us to win a passage. I have heard the minstrels sing of one Sir Roland who was slain by the infidels in these very parts."

"If it please you, my fair lord," said Black Simon, "I know something of these parts, for I have twice served a term with the King of Navarre. There is a hospice of monks yonder, where you may see the roof among the trees, and there it was that Sir Roland was slain. The village upon the left is Orbaiceta, and I know a house therein where the right wine of Jurancon is to be bought, if it would please you to quaff a morning cup."

"There is smoke yonder upon the right."

"That is a village named Les Aldudes, and I know a hostel there also where the wine is of the best. It is said that the inn-keeper hath a buried treasure, and I doubt not, my fair lord, that if you grant me leave I could prevail upon him to tell us where he hath hid it."

"Nay, nay, Simon," said Sir Nigel curtly, "I pray you to forget these free companion tricks. Ha! Edricson, I see that you stare about you, and in good sooth these mountains must seem wondrous indeed to one who hath but seen Butser or the Portsdown hill."

The broken and rugged road had wound along the crests of low hills, with wooded ridges on either side of it over which peeped the loftier mountains, the distant Peak of the South and the vast Altabisca, which towered high above them and cast its black shadow from left to right across the valley. From where they now stood they could look forward down a long vista of beech woods and jagged rock-strewn wilderness, all white with snow, to where the pass opened out upon the uplands beyond. Behind them they could still catch a glimpse of the gray plains of Gascony, and could see her rivers gleaming like coils of silver in the sunshine. As far as eye could see from among the rocky gorges and the bristles of the pine woods there came the quick twinkle and glitter of steel, while the wind brought with it sudden distant bursts of martial music from the great host which rolled by every road and by-path towards the narrow pass of Roncesvalles. On the cliffs on either side might also be seen the flash of arms and the waving of pennons where the force of Navarre looked down upon the army of strangers who passed through their territories.

"By Saint Paul!" said Sir Nigel, blinking up at them, "I think that we have much to hope for from these cavaliers, for they cluster very thickly upon our flanks. Pass word to the men, Aylward, that they unsling their bows, for I have no doubt that there are some very worthy gentlemen yonder who may give us some opportunity for honorable advancement."

"I hear that the prince hath the King of Navarre as hostage," said Alleyne, "and it is said that he hath sworn to put him to death if there be any attack upon us."

"It was not so that war was made when good King Edward first turned his hand to it," said Sir Nigel sadly. "Ah! Alleyne, I fear that you will never live to see such things, for the minds of men are more set upon money and gain than of old. By Saint Paul! it was a noble sight when two great armies would draw together upon a certain day, and all who had a vow would ride forth to discharge themselves of it. What noble spear-runnings have I not seen, and even in an humble way had a part in, when cavaliers would run a course for the easing of their souls and for the love of their ladies! Never a bad word have I for the French, for, though I have ridden twenty times up to their array, I have never yet failed to find some very gentle and worthy knight or squire who was willing to do what he might to enable me to attempt some small feat of arms. Then, when all cavaliers had been satisfied, the two armies would come to hand-strokes, and fight right merrily until one or other had the vantage. By Saint Paul! it was not our wont in those days to pay gold for the opening of passes, nor would we hold a king as hostage lest his people come to thrusts with us. In good sooth, if the war is to be carried out in such a fashion, then it is grief to me that I ever came away from Castle Twynham, for I would not have left my sweet lady had I not thought that there were deeds of arms to be done."

"But surely, my fair lord," said Alleyne, "you have done some great feats of arms since we left the Lady Loring."

"I cannot call any to mind," answered Sir Nigel.

"There was the taking of the sea-rovers, and the holding of the keep against the Jacks."

"Nay, nay," said the knight, "these were not feats of arms, but mere wayside ventures and the chances of travel. By Saint Paul! if it were not that these hills are over-steep for Pommers, I would ride to these cavaliers of Navarre and see if there were not some among them who would help me to take this patch from mine eye. It is a sad sight to see this very fine pass, which my own Company here could hold against an army, and yet to ride through it with as little profit as though it were the lane from my kennels to the Avon."

All morning Sir Nigel rode in a very ill-humor, with his Company tramping behind him. It was a toilsome march over broken ground and through snow, which came often as high as the knee, yet ere the sun had begun to sink they had reached the spot where the gorge opens out on to the uplands of Navarre, and could see the towers of Pampeluna jutting up against the southern sky-line. Here the Company were quartered in a scattered mountain hamlet, and Alleyne spent the day looking down upon the swarming army which poured with gleam of spears and flaunt of standards through the narrow pass.

"Hola, mon gar.," said Aylward, seating himself upon a boulder by his side. "This is indeed a fine sight upon which it is good to look, and a man might go far ere he would see so many brave men and fine horses. By my hilt! our little lord is wroth because we have come peacefully through the passes, but I will warrant him that we have fighting enow ere we turn our faces northward again. It is said that there are four-score thousand men behind the King of Spain, with Du Guesclin and all the best lances of France, who have sworn to shed their heart's blood ere this Pedro come again to the throne."

"Yet our own army is a great one," said Alleyne.

"Nay, there are but seven-and-twenty thousand men. Chandos hath persuaded the prince to leave many behind, and indeed I think that he is right, for there is little food and less water in these parts for which we are bound. A man without his meat or a horse without his fodder is like a wet bow-string, fit for little. But voila, mon petit, here comes Chandos and his company, and there is many a pensil and banderole among yonder squadrons which show that the best blood of England is riding under his banners."

Whilst Aylward had been speaking, a strong column of archers had defiled through the pass beneath them. They were followed by a banner-bearer who held high the scarlet wedge upon a silver field which proclaimed the presence of the famous warrior. He rode himself within a spear's-length of his standard, clad from neck to foot in steel, but draped in the long linen gown or parement which was destined to be the cause of his death. His plumed helmet was carried behind him by his body-squire, and his head was covered by a small purple cap, from under which his snow-white hair curled downwards to his shoulders. With his long beak-like nose and his single gleaming eye, which shone brightly from under a thick tuft of grizzled brow, he seemed to Alleyne to have something of the look of some fierce old bird of prey. For a moment he smiled, as his eye lit upon the banner of the five roses waving from the hamlet; but his course lay for Pampeluna, and he rode on after the archers.

Close at his heels came sixteen squires, all chosen from the highest families, and behind them rode twelve hundred English knights, with gleam of steel and tossing of plumes, their harness jingling, their long straight swords clanking against their stirrup-irons, and the beat of their chargers' hoofs like the low deep roar of the sea upon the shore. Behind them marched six hundred Cheshire and Lancashire archers, bearing the badge of the Audleys, followed by the famous Lord Audley himself, with the four valiant squires, Dutton of Dutton, Delves of Doddington, Fowlehurst of Crewe, and Hawkestone of Wainehill, who had all won such glory at Poictiers. Two hundred heavily-armed cavalry rode behind the Audley standard, while close at their heels came the Duke of Lancaster with a glittering train, heralds tabarded with the royal arms riding three deep upon cream-colored chargers in front of him. On either side of the young prince rode the two seneschals of Aquitaine, Sir Guiscard d'Angle and Sir Stephen Cossington, the one bearing the banner of the province and the other that of Saint George. Away behind him as far as eye could reach rolled the far-stretching, unbroken river of steel—rank after rank and column after column, with waving of plumes, glitter of arms, tossing of guidons, and flash and flutter of countless armorial devices. All day Alleyne looked down upon the changing scene, and all day the old bowman stood by his elbow, pointing out the crests of famous warriors and the arms of noble houses. Here were the gold mullets of the Pakingtons, the sable and ermine of the Mackworths, the scarlet bars of the Wakes, the gold and blue of the Grosvenors, the cinque-foils of the Cliftons, the annulets of the Musgraves, the silver pinions of the Beauchamps, the crosses of the Molineaux, the bloody chevron of the Woodhouses, the red and silver of the Worsleys, the swords of the Clarks, the boars'-heads of the Lucies, the crescents of the Boyntons, and the wolf and dagger of the Lipscombs. So through the sunny winter day the chivalry of England poured down through the dark pass of Roncesvalles to the plains of Spain.

It was on a Monday that the Duke of Lancaster's division passed safely through the Pyrenees. On the Tuesday there was a bitter frost, and the ground rung like iron beneath the feet of the horses; yet ere evening the prince himself, with the main battle of his army, had passed the gorge and united with his vanguard at Pampeluna. With him rode the King of Majorca, the hostage King of Navarre, and the fierce Don Pedro of Spain, whose pale blue eyes gleamed with a sinister light as they rested once more upon the distant peaks of the land which had disowned him. Under the royal banners rode many a bold Gascon baron and many a hot-blooded islander. Here were the high stewards of Aquitaine, of Saintonge, of La Rochelle, of Quercy, of Limousin, of Agenois, of Poitou, and of Bigorre, with the banners and musters of their provinces. Here also were the valiant Earl of Angus, Sir Thomas Banaster with his garter over his greave, Sir Nele Loring, second cousin to Sir Nigel, and a long column of Welsh footmen who marched under the red banner of Merlin. From dawn to sundown the long train wound through the pass, their breath reeking up upon the frosty air like the steam from a cauldron.

The weather was less keen upon the Wednesday, and the rear-guard made good their passage, with the bombards and the wagon-train. Free companions and Gascons made up this portion of the army to the number of ten thousand men. The fierce Sir Hugh Calverley, with his yellow mane, and the rugged Sir Robert Knolles, with their war-hardened and veteran companies of English bowmen, headed the long column; while behind them came the turbulent bands of the Bastard of Breteuil, Nandon de Bagerant, one-eyed Camus, Black Ortingo, La Nuit and others whose very names seem to smack of hard hands and ruthless deeds. With them also were the pick of the Gascon chivalry—the old Duc d'Armagnac, his nephew Lord d'Albret, brooding and scowling over his wrongs, the giant Oliver de Clisson, the Captal de Buch, pink of knighthood, the sprightly Sir Perducas d'Albret, the red-bearded Lord d'Esparre, and a long train of needy and grasping border nobles, with long pedigrees and short purses, who had come down from their hill-side strongholds, all hungering for the spoils and the ransoms of Spain. By the Thursday morning the whole army was encamped in the Vale of Pampeluna, and the prince had called his council to meet him in the old palace of the ancient city of Navarre.

XXXIV

How the Company Made Sport in the Vale of Pampeluna

Whilst the council was sitting in Pampeluna the White Company, having encamped in a neighboring valley, close to the companies of La Nuit and of Black Ortingo, were amusing themselves with sword-play, wrestling, and shooting at the shields, which they had placed upon the hillside to serve them as butts. The younger archers, with their coats of mail thrown aside, their brown or flaxen hair tossing in the wind, and their jerkins turned back to give free play to their brawny chests and arms, stood in lines, each loosing his shaft in turn, while Johnston, Aylward, Black Simon, and half-a-score of the elders lounged up and down with critical eyes, and a word of rough praise or of curt censure for the marksmen. Behind stood knots of Gascon and Brabant crossbowmen from the companies of Ortingo and of La Nuit, leaning upon their unsightly weapons and watching the practice of the Englishmen.

"A good shot, Hewett, a good shot!" said old Johnston to a young bowman, who stood with his bow in his left hand, gazing with parted lips after his flying shaft. "You see, she finds the ring, as I knew she would from the moment that your string twanged."

"Loose it easy, steady, and yet sharp," said Aylward. "By my hilt! mon gar., it is very well when you do but shoot at a shield, but when there is a man behind the shield, and he rides at you with wave of sword and glint of eyes from behind his vizor, you may find him a less easy mark."

"It is a mark that I have found before now," answered the young bowman.

"And shall again, camarade, I doubt not. But hola! Johnston, who is this who holds his bow like a crow-keeper?"

"It is Silas Peterson, of Horsham. Do not wink with one eye and look with the other, Silas, and do not hop and dance after you shoot, with your tongue out, for that will not speed it upon its way. Stand straight and firm, as God made you. Move not the bow arm, and steady with the drawing hand!"

"I' faith," said Black Simon, "I am a spearman myself, and am more fitted for hand-strokes than for such work as this. Yet I have spent my days among bowmen, and I have seen many a brave shaft sped. I will not say but that we have some good marksmen here, and that this Company would be accounted a fine body of archers at any time or place. Yet I do not see any men who bend so strong a bow or shoot as true a shaft as those whom I have known."

"You say sooth," said Johnston, turning his seamed and grizzled face upon the man-at-arms. "See yonder," he added, pointing to a bombard which lay within the camp: "there is what hath done scath to good bowmanship, with its filthy soot and foolish roaring mouth. I wonder that a true knight, like our prince, should carry such a scurvy thing in his train. Robin, thou red-headed lurden, how oft must I tell thee not to shoot straight with a quarter-wind blowing across the mark?"

"By these ten finger-bones! there were some fine bowmen at the intaking of Calais," said Aylward. "I well remember that, on occasion of an outfall, a Genoan raised his arm over his mantlet, and shook it at us, a hundred paces from our line. There were twenty who loosed shafts at him, and when the man was afterwards slain it was found that he had taken eighteen through his forearm."

"And I can call to mind," remarked Johnston, "that when the great cog 'Christopher,' which the French had taken from us, was moored two hundred paces from the shore, two archers, little Robin Withstaff and Elias Baddlesmere, in four shots each cut every strand of her hempen anchor-cord, so that she well-nigh came upon the rocks."

"Good shooting, i' faith rare shooting!" said Black Simon. "But I have seen you, Johnston, and you, Samkin Aylward, and one or two others who are still with us, shoot as well as the best. Was it not you, Johnston, who took the fat ox at Finsbury butts against the pick of London town?"

A sunburnt and black-eyed Brabanter had stood near the old archers, leaning upon a large crossbow and listening to their talk, which had been carried on in that hybrid camp dialect which both nations could understand. He was a squat, bull-necked man, clad in the iron helmet, mail tunic, and woollen gambesson of his class. A jacket with hanging sleeves, slashed with velvet at the neck and wrists, showed that he was a man of some consideration, an under-officer, or file-leader of his company.

"I cannot think," said he, "why you English should be so fond of your six-foot stick. If it amuse you to bend it, well and good; but why should I strain and pull, when my little moulinet will do all for me, and better than I can do it for myself?"

"I have seen good shooting with the prod and with the latch," said Aylward, "but, by my hilt! camarade, with all respect to you and to your bow, I think that is but a woman's weapon, which a woman can point and loose as easily as a man."

"I know not about that," answered the Brabanter, "but this I know, that though I have served for fourteen years, I have never yet seen an Englishman do aught with the long-bow which I could not do better with my arbalest. By the three kings! I would even go further, and say that I have done things with my arbalest which no Englishman could do with his long-bow."

"Well said, mon gar.," cried Aylward. "A good cock has ever a brave call. Now, I have shot little of late, but there is Johnston here who will try a round with you for the honor of the Company."

"And I will lay a gallon of Jurancon wine upon the long-bow," said Black Simon, "though I had rather, for my own drinking, that it were a quart of Twynham ale."

"I take both your challenge and your wager," said the man of Brabant, throwing off his jacket and glancing keenly about him with his black, twinkling eyes. "I cannot see any fitting mark, for I care not to waste a bolt upon these shields, which a drunken boor could not miss at a village kermesse."

"This is a perilous man," whispered an English man-at-arms, plucking at Aylward's sleeve. "He is the best marksman of all the crossbow companies and it was he who brought down the Constable de Bourbon at Brignais. I fear that your man will come by little honor with him."

"Yet I have seen Johnston shoot these twenty years, and I will not flinch from it. How say you, old war-hound, will you not have a flight shot or two with this springald?"

"Tut, tut, Aylward," said the old bowman. "My day is past, and it is for the younger ones to hold what we have gained. I take it unkindly of thee, Samkin, that thou shouldst call all eyes thus upon a broken bowman who could once shoot a fair shaft. Let me feel that bow, Wilkins! It is a Scotch bow, I see, for the upper nock is without and the lower within. By the black rood! it is a good piece of yew, well nocked, well strung, well waxed, and very joyful to the feel. I think even now that I might hit any large and goodly mark with a bow like this. Turn thy quiver to me, Aylward. I love an ash arrow pierced with cornel-wood for a roving shaft."

"By my hilt! and so do I," cried Aylward. "These three gander-winged shafts are such."

"So I see, comrade. It has been my wont to choose a saddle-backed feather for a dead shaft, and a swine-backed for a smooth flier. I will take the two of them. Ah! Samkin, lad, the eye grows dim and the hand less firm as the years pass."

"Come then, are you not ready?" said the Brabanter, who had watched with ill-concealed impatience the slow and methodic movements of his antagonist.

"I will venture a rover with you, or try long-butts or hoyles," said old Johnston. "To my mind the long-bow is a better weapon than the arbalest, but it may be ill for me to prove it."

"So I think," quoth the other with a sneer. He drew his moulinet from his girdle, and fixing it to the windlass, he drew back the powerful double cord until it had clicked into the catch. Then from his quiver he drew a short, thick quarrel, which he placed with the utmost care upon the groove. Word had spread of what was going forward, and the rivals were already surrounded, not only by the English archers of the Company, but by hundreds of arbalestiers and men-at-arms from the bands of Ortingo and La Nuit, to the latter of which the Brabanter belonged.

"There is a mark yonder on the hill," said he; "mayhap you can discern it."

"I see something," answered Johnston, shading his eyes with his hand; "but it is a very long shoot."

"A fair shoot—a fair shoot! Stand aside, Arnaud, lest you find a bolt through your gizzard. Now, comrade, I take no flight shot, and I give you the vantage of watching my shaft."

As he spoke he raised his arbalest to his shoulder and was about to pull the trigger, when a large gray stork flapped heavily into view skimming over the brow of the hill, and then soaring up into the air to pass the valley. Its shrill and piercing cries drew all eyes upon it, and, as it came nearer, a dark spot which circled above it resolved itself into a peregrine falcon, which hovered over its head, poising itself from time to time, and watching its chance of closing with its clumsy quarry. Nearer and nearer came the two birds, all absorbed in their own contest, the stork wheeling upwards, the hawk still fluttering above it, until they were not a hundred paces from the camp. The Brabanter raised his weapon to the sky, and there came the short, deep twang of his powerful string. His bolt struck the stork just where its wing meets the body, and the bird whirled aloft in a last convulsive flutter before falling wounded and flapping to the earth. A roar of applause burst from the crossbowmen; but at the instant that the bolt struck its mark old

Johnston, who had stood listlessly with arrow on string, bent his bow and sped a shaft through the body of the falcon. Whipping the other from his belt, he sent it skimming some few feet from the earth with so true an aim that it struck and transfixed the stork for the second time ere it could reach the ground. A deep-chested shout of delight burst from the archers at the sight of this double feat, and Aylward, dancing with joy, threw his arms round the old marksman and embraced him with such vigor that their mail tunics clanged again.

"Ah! camarade," he cried, "you shall have a stoup with me for this! What then, old dog, would not the hawk please thee, but thou must have the stork as well. Oh, to my heart again!"

"It is a pretty piece of yew, and well strung," said Johnston with a twinkle in his deep-set gray eyes. "Even an old broken bowman might find the clout with a bow like this."

"You have done very well," remarked the Brabanter in a surly voice. "But it seems to me that you have not yet shown yourself to be a better marksman than I, for I have struck that at which I aimed, and, by the three kings! no man can do more."

"It would ill beseem me to claim to be a better marksman," answered Johnston, "for I have heard great things of your skill. I did but wish to show that the long-bow could do that which an arbalest could not do, for you could not with your moulinet have your string ready to speed another shaft ere the bird drop to the earth."

"In that you have vantage," said the crossbowman. "By Saint James! it is now my turn to show you where my weapon has the better of you. I pray you to draw a flight shaft with all your strength down the valley, that we may see the length of your shoot."

"That is a very strong prod of yours," said Johnston, shaking his grizzled head as he glanced at the thick arch and powerful strings of his rival's arbalest. "I have little doubt that you can overshoot me, and yet I have seen bowmen who could send a cloth-yard arrow further than you could speed a quarrel."

"So I have heard," remarked the Brabanter; "and yet it is a strange thing that these wondrous bowmen are never where I chance to be. Pace out the distances with a wand at every five score, and do you, Arnaud, stand at the fifth wand to carry back my bolts to me."

A line was measured down the valley, and Johnston, drawing an arrow to the very head, sent it whistling over the row of wands.

"Bravely drawn! A rare shoot!" shouted the bystanders.

"It is well up to the fourth mark."

"By my hilt! it is over it," cried Aylward. "I can see where they have stooped to gather up the shaft."

"We shall hear anon," said Johnston quietly, and presently a young archer came running to say that the arrow had fallen twenty paces beyond the fourth wand.

"Four hundred paces and a score," cried Black Simon. "I' faith, it is a very long flight. Yet wood and steel may do more than flesh and blood."

The Brabanter stepped forward with a smile of conscious triumph, and loosed the cord of his weapon. A shout burst from his comrades as they watched the swift and lofty flight of the heavy bolt.

"Over the fourth!" groaned Aylward. "By my hilt! I think that it is well up to the fifth."

"It is over the fifth!" cried a Gascon loudly, and a comrade came running with waving arms to say that the bolt had pitched eight paces beyond the mark of the five hundred.

"Which weapon hath the vantage now?" cried the Brabanter, strutting proudly about with shouldered arbalest, amid the applause of his companions.

"You can overshoot me," said Johnston gently.

"Or any other man who ever bent a long-bow," cried his victorious adversary.

"Nay, not so fast," said a huge archer, whose mighty shoulders and red head towered high above the throng of his comrades. "I must have a word with you ere you crow so loudly. Where is my little popper? By sainted Dick of Hampole! it will be a strange thing if I cannot outshoot that thing of thine, which to my eyes is more like a rat-trap than a bow. Will you try another flight, or do you stand by your last?"

"Five hundred and eight paces will serve my turn," answered the Brabanter, looking askance at this new opponent.

"Tut, John," whispered Aylward, "you never were a marksman. Why must you thrust your spoon into this dish?"

"Easy and slow, Aylward. There are very many things which I cannot do, but there are also one or two which I have the trick of. It is in my mind that I can beat this shoot, if my bow will but hold together."

"Go on, old babe of the woods!" "Have at it, Hampshire!" cried the archers laughing.

"By my soul! you may grin," cried John. "But I learned how to make the long shoot from old Hob Miller of Milford." He took up a great black bow, as he spoke, and sitting down upon the ground he placed his two feet on either end of the stave. With an arrow fitted, he then pulled the string towards him with both hands until the head of the shaft was level with the wood. The great bow creaked and groaned and the cord vibrated with the tension.

"Who is this fool's-head who stands in the way of my shoot?" said he, craning up his neck from the ground.

"He stands on the further side of my mark," answered the Brabanter, "so he has little to fear from you."

"Well, the saints assoil him!" cried John. "Though I think he is over-near to be scathed." As he spoke he raised his two feet, with the bow-stave upon their soles, and his cord twanged with a deep rich hum which might be heard across the valley. The measurer in the distance fell flat upon his face, and then jumping up again, he began to run in the opposite direction.

"Well shot, old lad! It is indeed over his head," cried the bowmen.

"Mon Dieu!" exclaimed the Brabanter, "who ever saw such a shoot?"

"It is but a trick," quoth John. "Many a time have I won a gallon of ale by covering a mile in three flights down Wilverley Chase."

"It fell a hundred and thirty paces beyond the fifth mark," shouted an archer in the distance.

"Six hundred and thirty paces! Mon Dieu! but that is a shoot! And yet it says nothing for your weapon, mon gros camarade, for it was by turning yourself into a crossbow that you did it."

"By my hilt! there is truth in that," cried Aylward. "And now, friend, I will myself show you a vantage of the long-bow. I pray you to speed a bolt against yonder shield with all your force. It is an inch of elm with bull's hide over it."

"I scarce shot as many shafts at Brignais," growled the man of Brabant; "though I found a better mark there than a cantle of bull's hide. But what is this, Englishman? The shield hangs not one hundred paces from me, and a blind man could strike it." He screwed up his string to the furthest pitch, and shot his quarrel at the dangling shield. Aylward, who had drawn an arrow from his quiver, carefully greased the head of it, and sped it at the same mark.

"Run, Wilkins," quoth he, "and fetch me the shield."

Long were the faces of the Englishmen and broad the laugh of the crossbowmen as the heavy mantlet was carried towards them, for there in the centre was the thick Brabant bolt driven deeply into the wood, while there was neither sign nor trace of the cloth-yard shaft.

"By the three kings!" cried the Brabanter, "this time at least there is no gainsaying which is the better weapon, or which the truer hand that held it. You have missed the shield, Englishman."

"Tarry a bit! tarry a bit, mon gar.!" quoth Aylward, and turning round the shield he showed a round clear hole in the wood at the back of it. "My shaft has passed through it, camarade, and I trow the one which goes through is more to be feared than that which bides on the way."

The Brabanter stamped his foot with mortification, and was about to make some angry reply, when Alleyne Edricson came riding up to the crowds of archers.

"Sir Nigel will be here anon," said he, "and it is his wish to speak with the Company."

In an instant order and method took the place of general confusion. Bows, steel caps, and jacks were caught up from the grass. A long cordon cleared the camp of all strangers, while the main body fell into four lines with under-officers and file-leaders in front and on either flank. So they stood, silent and motionless, when their leader came riding towards them, his face shining and his whole small figure swelling with the news which he bore.

"Great honor has been done to us, men," cried he: "for, of all the army, the prince has chosen us out that we should ride onwards into the lands of Spain to spy upon our enemies. Yet, as there are many of us, and as the service may not be to the liking of all, I pray that those will step forward from the ranks who have the will to follow me."

There was a rustle among the bowmen, but when Sir Nigel looked up at them no man stood forward from his fellows, but the four lines of men stretched unbroken as before. Sir Nigel blinked at them in amazement, and a look of the deepest sorrow shadowed his face.

"That I should live to see the day!" he cried. "What! not one——"

"My fair lord," whispered Alleyne, "they have all stepped forward."

"Ah, by Saint Paul! I see how it is with them. I could not think that they would desert me. We start at dawn to-morrow, and ye are to have the horses of Sir Robert Cheney's company. Be ready, I pray ye, at early cock-crow."

A buzz of delight burst from the archers, as they broke their ranks and ran hither and thither, whooping and cheering like boys who have news of a holiday. Sir Nigel gazed after them with a smiling face, when a heavy hand fell upon his shoulder.

"What ho! my knight-errant of Twynham!" said a voice, "You are off to Ebro, I hear; and, by the holy fish of Tobias! you must take me under your banner."

"What! Sir Oliver Buttesthorn!" cried Sir Nigel. "I had heard that you were come into camp, and had hoped to see you. Glad and proud shall I be to have you with me."

"I have a most particular and weighty reason for wishing to go," said the sturdy knight.

"I can well believe it," returned Sir Nigel; "I have met no man who is quicker to follow where honor leads."

"Nay, it is not for honor that I go, Nigel."

"For what then?"

"For pullets."

"Pullets?"

"Yes, for the rascal vanguard have cleared every hen from the countryside. It was this very morning that Norbury, my squire, lamed his horse in riding round in quest of one, for we have a bag of truffles, and nought to eat with them. Never have I seen such locusts as this vanguard of ours. Not a pullet shall we see until we are in front of them; so I shall leave my Winchester runagates to the care of the provost-marshal, and I shall hie south with you, Nigel, with my truffles at my saddle-bow."

"Oliver, Oliver, I know you over-well," said Sir Nigel, shaking his head, and the two old soldiers rode off together to their pavilion.

XXXV

How Sir Nigel Hawked at an Eagle

To the south of Pampeluna in the kingdom of Navarre there stretched a high table-land, rising into bare, sterile hills, brown or gray in color, and strewn with huge boulders of granite. On the Gascon side of the great mountains there had been running streams, meadows, forests, and little nestling villages. Here, on the contrary, were nothing but naked rocks, poor pasture, and savage, stone-strewn wastes. Gloomy defiles or barrancas intersected this wild country with mountain torrents dashing and foaming between their rugged sides. The clatter of waters, the scream of the eagle, and the howling of wolves the only sounds which broke upon the silence in that dreary and inhospitable region.

Through this wild country it was that Sir Nigel and his Company pushed their way, riding at times through vast defiles where the brown, gnarled cliffs shot up on either side of them, and the sky was but a long winding blue slit between the clustering lines of box which fringed the lips of the precipices; or, again leading their horses along the narrow and rocky paths worn by the muleteers upon the edges of the chasm, where under their very elbows they could see the white streak which marked the *gave* which foamed a thousand feet below them. So for two days they pushed their way through the wild places of Navarre, past Fuente, over the rapid Ega, through Estella, until upon a winter's evening the mountains fell away from in front of them, and they saw the broad blue Ebro curving betwixt its double line of homesteads and of villages. The fishers of Viana were aroused that night by rough voices speaking in a strange tongue, and ere morning Sir Nigel and his men had ferried the river and were safe upon the land of Spain.

All the next day they lay in a pine wood near to the town of Logrono, resting their horses and taking counsel as to what they should do. Sir Nigel had with him Sir William Felton, Sir Oliver Buttesthorn, stout old Sir Simon Burley, the Scotch knight-errant, the Earl of Angus, and Sir Richard Causton, all accounted among the bravest knights in the army, together with sixty veteran men-at-arms, and three hundred and twenty archers. Spies had been sent out in the morning, and returned after nightfall to say that the King of Spain was encamped some fourteen miles off in the direction of Burgos, having with him twenty thousand horse and forty-five thousand foot.

A dry-wood fire had been lit, and round this the leaders crouched, the glare beating upon their rugged faces, while the hardy archers lounged and chatted amid the tethered horses, while they munched their scanty provisions.

"For my part," said Sir Simon Burley, "I am of opinion that we have already done that which we have come for. For do we not now know where the king is, and how great a following he hath, which was the end of our journey."

"True," answered Sir William Felton, "but I have come on this venture because it is a long time since I have broken a spear in war, and, certes, I shall not go back until I have run a course with some cavalier of Spain. Let those go back who will, but I must see more of these Spaniards ere I turn."

"I will not leave you, Sir William," returned Sir Simon Burley; "and yet, as an old soldier and one who hath seen much of war, I cannot but think that it is an ill thing for four hundred men to find themselves between an army of sixty thousand on the one side and a broad river on the other."

"Yet," said Sir Richard Causton, "we cannot for the honor of England go back without a blow struck."

"Nor for the honor of Scotland either," cried the Earl of Angus. "By Saint Andrew! I wish that I may never set eyes upon the water of Leith again, if I pluck my horse's bridle ere I have seen this camp of theirs."

"By Saint Paul! you have spoken very well," said Sir Nigel, "and I have always heard that there were very worthy gentlemen among the Scots, and fine skirmishing to be had upon their border. Bethink you, Sir Simon, that we have this news from the lips of common spies, who can scarce tell us as much of the enemy and of his forces as the prince would wish to hear."

"You are the leader in this venture, Sir Nigel," the other answered, "and I do but ride under your banner."

"Yet I would fain have your rede and counsel, Sir Simon. But, touching what you say of the river, we can take heed that we shall not have it at the back of us, for the prince hath now advanced to Salvatierra, and thence to Vittoria, so that if we come upon their camp from the further side we can make good our retreat."

"What then would you propose?" asked Sir Simon, shaking his grizzled head as one who is but half convinced.

"That we ride forward ere the news reach them that we have crossed the river. In this way we may have sight of their army, and perchance even find occasion for some small deed against them."

"So be it, then," said Sir Simon Burley; and the rest of the council having approved, a scanty meal was hurriedly snatched, and the advance resumed under the cover of the darkness. All night they led their horses, stumbling and groping through wild defiles and rugged valleys, following the guidance of a frightened peasant who was strapped by the wrist to Black Simon's stirrup-leather. With the early dawn they found themselves in a black ravine, with others sloping away from it on either side, and the bare brown crags rising in long bleak terraces all round them.

"If it please you, fair lord," said Black Simon, "this man hath misled us, and since there is no tree upon which we may hang him, it might be well to hurl him over yonder cliff."

The peasant, reading the soldier's meaning in his fierce eyes and harsh accents dropped upon his knees, screaming loudly for mercy.

"How comes it, dog?" asked Sir William Felton in Spanish. "Where is this camp to which you swore that you would lead us?"

"By the sweet Virgin! By the blessed Mother of God!" cried the trembling peasant, "I swear to you that in the darkness I have myself lost the path."

"Over the cliff with him!" shouted half a dozen voices; but ere the archers could drag him from the rocks to which he clung Sir Nigel had ridden up and called upon them to stop.

"How is this, sirs?" said he. "As long as the prince doth me the honor to entrust this venture to me, it is for me only to give orders; and, by Saint Paul! I shall be right blithe to go very deeply into the matter with any one to whom my words may give offence. How say you, Sir William? Or you, my Lord of Angus? Or you, Sir Richard?"

"Nay, nay, Nigel!" cried Sir William. "This base peasant is too small a matter for old comrades to quarrel over. But he hath betrayed us, and certes he hath merited a dog's death."

"Hark ye, fellow," said Sir Nigel. "We give you one more chance to find the path. We are about to gain much honor, Sir William, in this enterprise, and it would be a sorry thing if the first blood shed were that of an unworthy boor. Let us say our morning orisons, and it may chance that ere we finish he may strike upon the track."

With bowed heads and steel caps in hand, the archers stood at their horse's heads, while Sir Simon Burley repeated the Pater, the Ave, and the Credo. Long did Alleyne bear the scene in mind—the knot of knights in their dull leaden-hued armor, the ruddy visage of Sir Oliver, the craggy features of the Scottish earl, the shining scalp of Sir Nigel, with the dense ring of hard, bearded faces and the long brown heads of the horses, all topped and circled by the beetling cliffs. Scarce had the last deep "amen" broken from the Company, when, in an instant, there rose the scream of a hundred bugles, with the deep rolling of drums and the clashing of cymbals, all sounding together in one deafening uproar. Knights and archers sprang to arms, convinced that some great host was upon them; but the guide dropped upon his knees and thanked Heaven for its mercies.

"We have found them, caballeros!" he cried. "This is their morning call. If ye will but deign to follow me, I will set them before you ere a man might tell his beads."

As he spoke he scrambled down one of the narrow ravines, and, climbing over a low ridge at the further end, he led them into a short valley with a stream purling down the centre of it and a very thick growth of elder and of box upon either side. Pushing their way through the dense brushwood, they looked out upon a scene which made their hearts beat harder and their breath come faster.

In front of them there lay a broad plain, watered by two winding streams and covered with grass, stretching away to where, in the furthest distance, the towers of Burgos bristled up against the light blue morning sky. Over all this vast meadow there lay a great city of tents—thousands upon thousands of them, laid out in streets and in squares like a well-ordered town. High silken pavilions or colored marquees, shooting up from among the crowd of meaner dwellings, marked where the great lords and barons of Leon and Castile displayed their standards, while over the white roofs, as far as eye could reach, the waving of ancients, pavons, pensils, and banderoles, with flash of gold and glow of colors, proclaimed that all the chivalry of Iberia were mustered in the plain beneath them. Far off, in the centre of the camp, a huge palace of red and white silk, with the royal arms of Castile waiving from the summit, announced that the gallant Henry lay there in the midst of his warriors.

As the English adventurers, peeping out from behind their brushwood screen, looked down upon this wondrous sight they could see that the vast army in front of them was already afoot. The first pink light of the rising sun glittered upon the steel caps and breastplates of dense masses of slingers and of crossbowmen, who drilled and marched in the spaces which had been left for their exercise. A thousand columns of smoke reeked up into the pure morning air where the faggots were piled and the camp-kettles already simmering. In the open plain clouds of light horse galloped and swooped with swaying bodies and waving javelins, after the fashion which the Spanish had adopted from their Moorish enemies. All along by the sedgy banks of the rivers long lines of pages led their masters' chargers down to water, while the knights themselves lounged in gayly-dressed groups about the doors of their pavilions, or rode out, with their falcons upon their wrists and their greyhounds behind them, in quest of quail or of leveret.

"By my hilt! mon gar.!" whispered Aylward to Alleyne, as the young squire stood with parted lips and wondering eyes, gazing down at the novel scene before him, "we have been seeking them all night, but now that we have found them I know not what we are to do with them."

"You say sooth, Samkin," quoth old Johnston. "I would that we were upon the far side of Ebro again, for there is neither honor nor profit to be gained here. What say you, Simon?"

"By the rood!" cried the fierce man-at-arms, "I will see the color of their blood ere I turn my mare's head for the mountains. Am I a child, that I should ride for three days and nought but words at the end of it?"

"Well said, my sweet honeysuckle!" cried Hordle John. "I am with you, like hilt to blade. Could I but lay hands upon one of those gay prancers yonder, I doubt not that I should have ransom enough from him to buy my mother a new cow."

"A cow!" said Aylward. "Say rather ten acres and a homestead on the banks of Avon."

"Say you so? Then, by our Lady! here is for yonder one in the red jerkin!"

He was about to push recklessly forward into the open, when Sir Nigel himself darted in front of him, with his hand upon his breast.

"Back!" said he. "Our time is not yet come, and we must lie here until evening. Throw off your jacks and headpieces, least their eyes catch the shine, and tether the horses among the rocks."

The order was swiftly obeyed, and in ten minutes the archers were stretched along by the side of the brook, munching the bread and the bacon which they had brought in their bags, and craning their necks to watch the ever-changing scene beneath them. Very quiet and still they lay, save for a muttered jest or whispered order, for twice during the long morning they heard bugle-calls from amid the hills on either side of them, which showed that they had thrust themselves in between the outposts of the enemy. The leaders sat amongst the box-wood, and took counsel together as to what they should do; while from below there surged up the buzz of voices, the shouting, the neighing of horses, and all the uproar of a great camp.

"What boots it to wait?" said Sir William Felton. "Let us ride down upon their camp ere they discover us."

"And so say I," cried the Scottish earl; "for they do not know that there is any enemy within thirty long leagues of them."

"For my part," said Sir Simon Burley, "I think that it is madness, for you cannot hope to rout this great army; and where are you to go and what are you to do when they have turned upon you? How say you, Sir Oliver Buttesthorn?"

"By the apple of Eve!" cried the fat knight, "it appears to me that this wind brings a very savory smell of garlic and of onions from their cooking-kettles. I am in favor of riding down upon them at once, if my old friend and comrade here is of the same mind."

"Nay," said Sir Nigel, "I have a plan by which we may attempt some small deed upon them, and yet, by the help of God, may be able to draw off again; which, as Sir Simon Burley hath said, would be scarce possible in any other way."

"How then, Sir Nigel?" asked several voices.

"We shall lie here all day; for amid this brushwood it is ill for them to see us. Then when evening comes we shall sally out upon them and see if we may not gain some honorable advancement from them."

"But why then rather than now?"

"Because we shall have nightfall to cover us when we draw off, so that we may make our way back through the mountains. I would station a score of archers here in the pass, with all our pennons jutting forth from the rocks, and as many nakirs and drums and bugles as we have with us, so that those who follow us in the fading light may think that the whole army of the prince is upon them, and fear to go further. What think you of my plan, Sir Simon?"

"By my troth! I think very well of it," cried the prudent old commander. "If four hundred men must needs run a tilt against sixty thousand, I cannot see how they can do it better or more safely."

"And so say I," cried Felton, heartily. "But I wish the day were over, for it will be an ill thing for us if they chance to light upon us."

The words were scarce out of his mouth when there came a clatter of loose stones, the sharp clink of trotting hoofs, and a dark-faced cavalier, mounted upon a white horse, burst through the bushes and rode swiftly down the valley from the end which was farthest from the Spanish camp. Lightly armed, with his vizor open and a hawk perched upon his left wrist, he looked about him with the careless air of a man who is bent wholly upon pleasure, and unconscious of the possibility of danger. Suddenly, however, his eyes lit upon the fierce faces which glared out at him from the brushwood. With a cry of terror, he thrust his spurs into his horse's sides and dashed for the narrow opening of the gorge. For a moment it seemed as though he would have reached it, for he had trampled over or dashed aside the archers who threw themselves in his way; but Hordle John seized him by the foot in his grasp of iron and dragged him from the saddle, while two others caught the frightened horse.

"Ho, ho!" roared the great archer. "How many cows wilt buy my mother, if I set thee free?"

"Hush that bull's bellowing!" cried Sir Nigel impatiently. "Bring the man here. By St. Paul! it is not the first time that we have met; for, if I mistake not, it is Don Diego Alvarez, who was once at the prince's court."

"It is indeed I," said the Spanish knight, speaking in the French tongue, "and I pray you to pass your sword through my heart, for how can I live—I, a caballero of Castile—after being dragged from my horse by the base hands of a common archer?"

"Fret not for that," answered Sir Nigel. "For, in sooth, had he not pulled you down, a dozen cloth-yard shafts had crossed each other in your body."

"By St. James! it were better so than to be polluted by his touch," answered the Spaniard, with his black eyes sparkling with rage and hatred. "I trust that I am now the prisoner of some honorable knight or gentleman."

"You are the prisoner of the man who took you, Sir Diego," answered Sir Nigel. "And I may tell you that better men than either you or I have found themselves before now prisoners in the hands of archers of England."

"What ransom, then, does he demand?" asked the Spaniard.

Big John scratched his red head and grinned in high delight when the question was propounded to him. "Tell him," said he, "that I shall have ten cows and a bull too, if it be but a little one. Also a dress of blue sendall for mother and a red one for Joan; with five acres of pasture-land, two scythes, and a fine new grindstone. Likewise a small house, with stalls for the cows, and thirty-six gallons of beer for the thirsty weather."

"Tut, tut!" cried Sir Nigel, laughing. "All these things may be had for money; and I think, Don Diego, that five thousand crowns is not too much for so renowned a knight."

"It shall be duly paid him."

"For some days we must keep you with us; and I must crave leave also to use your shield, your armor, and your horse."

"My harness is yours by the law of arms," said the Spaniard, gloomily.

"I do but ask the loan of it. I have need of it this day, but it shall be duly returned to you. Set guards, Aylward, with arrow on string, at either end of the pass; for it may happen that some other cavaliers may visit us ere the time be come." All day the little band of Englishmen lay in the sheltered gorge, looking down upon the vast host of their unconscious enemies. Shortly after mid-day, a great uproar of shouting and cheering broke out in the camp, with mustering of men and calling of bugles. Clambering up among the rocks, the companions saw a long rolling cloud of dust along the whole eastern sky-line, with the glint of spears and the flutter of pennons, which announced the approach of a large body of cavalry. For a moment a wild hope came upon them that perhaps the prince had moved more swiftly than had been planned, that he had crossed the Ebro, and that this was his vanguard sweeping to the attack.

"Surely I see the red pile of Chandos at the head of yonder squadron!" cried Sir Richard Causton, shading his eyes with his hand.

"Not so," answered Sir Simon Burley, who had watched the approaching host with a darkening face. "It is even as I feared. That is the double eagle of Du Guesclin."

"You say very truly," cried the Earl of Angus. "These are the levies of France, for I can see the ensigns of the Marshal d'Andreghen, with that of the Lord of Antoing and of Briseuil, and of many another from Brittany and Anjou."

"By St. Paul! I am very glad of it," said Sir Nigel. "Of these Spaniards I know nothing; but the French are very worthy gentlemen, and will do what they can for our advancement."

"There are at the least four thousand of them, and all men-at-arms," cried Sir William Felton. "See, there is Bertrand himself, beside his banner, and there is King Henry, who rides to welcome him. Now they all turn and come into the camp together."

As he spoke, the vast throng of Spaniards and of Frenchmen trooped across the plain, with brandished arms and tossing banners. All day long the sound of revelry and of rejoicing from the crowded camp swelled up to the ears of the Englishmen, and they could see the soldiers of the two nations throwing themselves into each other's arms and dancing hand-in-hand round the blazing fires. The sun had sunk behind a cloud-bank in the west before Sir Nigel at last gave word that the men should resume their arms and have their horses ready. He had himself thrown off his armor, and had dressed himself from head to foot in the harness of the captured Spaniard.

"Sir William," said he, "it is my intention to attempt a small deed, and I ask you therefore that you will lead this outfall upon the camp. For me, I will ride into their camp with my squire and two archers. I pray you to watch me, and to ride forth when I am come among the tents. You will leave twenty men behind here, as we planned this morning, and you will ride back here after you have ventured as far as seems good to you."

"I will do as you order, Nigel; but what is it that you propose to do?"

"You will see anon, and indeed it is but a trifling matter. Alleyne, you will come with me, and lead a spare horse by the bridle. I will have the two archers who rode with us through France, for they are trusty men and of stout heart. Let them ride behind us, and let them leave their bows here among the bushes for it is not my wish that they should know that we are Englishmen. Say no word to any whom we may meet, and, if any speak to you, pass on as though you heard them not. Are you ready?"

"I am ready, my fair lord," said Alleyne.

"And I," "And I," cried Aylward and John.

"Then the rest I leave to your wisdom, Sir William; and if God sends us fortune we shall meet you again in this gorge ere it be dark."

So saying, Sir Nigel mounted the white horse of the Spanish cavalier, and rode quietly forth from his concealment with his three companions behind him, Alleyne leading his master's own steed by the bridle. So many small parties of French and Spanish horse were sweeping hither and thither that the small band attracted little notice, and making its way at a gentle trot across the plain, they came as far as the camp without challenge or hindrance. On and on they pushed past the endless lines of tents, amid the dense swarms of horsemen and of footmen, until the huge royal pavilion stretched in front of them. They were close upon it when of a sudden there broke out a wild hubbub from a distant portion of the camp, with screams and war-cries and all the wild tumult of battle. At the sound soldiers came rushing from their tents, knights shouted loudly for their squires, and there was mad turmoil on every hand of bewildered men and plunging horses. At the royal tent a crowd of gorgeously dressed servants ran hither and thither in helpless panic for the guard of soldiers who were stationed there had already ridden off in the direction of the alarm. A man-at-arms on either side of the doorway were the sole protectors of the royal dwelling.

"I have come for the king," whispered Sir Nigel; "and, by Saint Paul! he must back with us or I must bide here."

Alleyne and Aylward sprang from their horses, and flew at the two sentries, who were disarmed and beaten down in an instant by so furious and unexpected an attack. Sir Nigel dashed into the royal tent, and was followed by Hordle John as soon as the horses had been secured. From within came wild screamings and the clash of steel, and then the two emerged once more, their swords and forearms reddened with blood, while John bore over his shoulder the senseless body of a man whose gay surcoat, adorned with the lions and towers of Castile, proclaimed him to belong to the royal house. A crowd of white-faced sewers and pages swarmed at their heels, those behind pushing forwards, while the foremost shrank back from the fierce faces and reeking weapons of the adventurers. The senseless body was thrown across the spare horse, the four sprang to their saddles, and away they thundered with loose reins and busy spurs through the swarming camp.

But confusion and disorder still reigned among the Spaniards for Sir William Felton and his men had swept through half their camp, leaving a long litter of the dead and the dying to mark their course. Uncertain who were their attackers, and unable to tell their English enemies from their newly-arrived Breton allies, the Spanish knights rode wildly hither and thither in aimless fury. The mad turmoil, the mixture of races, and the fading light, were all in favor of the four who alone knew their own purpose among the vast uncertain multitude. Twice ere they reached open ground they had to break their way through small bodies of horses, and once there came a whistle of arrows and singing of stones about their ears; but, still dashing onwards, they shot out from among the tents and found their own comrades retreating for the mountains at no very great distance from them. Another five minutes of wild galloping over the plain, and they were all back in their gorge, while their pursuers fell back before the rolling of drums and blare of trumpets, which seemed to proclaim that the whole army of the prince was about to emerge from the mountain passes.

"By my soul! Nigel," cried Sir Oliver, waving a great boiled ham over his head, "I have come by something which I may eat with my truffles! I had a hard fight for it, for there were three of them with their mouths open and the knives in their hands, all sitting agape round the table, when I rushed in upon them. How say you, Sir William, will you not try the smack of the famed Spanish swine, though we have but the brook water to wash it down?"

"Later, Sir Oliver," answered the old soldier, wiping his grimed face. "We must further into the mountains ere we be in safety. But what have we here, Nigel?"

"It is a prisoner whom I have taken, and in sooth, as he came from the royal tent and wears the royal arms upon his jupon, I trust that he is the King of Spain."

"The King of Spain!" cried the companions, crowding round in amazement.

"Nay, Sir Nigel," said Felton, peering at the prisoner through the uncertain light, "I have twice seen Henry of Transtamare, and certes this man in no way resembles him."

"Then, by the light of heaven! I will ride back for him," cried Sir Nigel.

"Nay, nay, the camp is in arms, and it would be rank madness. Who are you, fellow?" he added in Spanish, "and how is it that you dare to wear the arms of Castile?"

The prisoner was bent recovering the consciousness which had been squeezed from him by the grip of Hordle John. "If it please you," he answered, "I and nine others are the body-squires of the king, and must ever wear his arms, so as to shield him from even such perils as have threatened him this night. The king is at the tent of the brave Du Guesclin, where he will sup to night. But I am a caballero of Aragon, Don Sancho Penelosa, and, though I be no king, I am yet ready to pay a fitting price for my ransom."

"By Saint Paul! I will not touch your gold," cried Sir Nigel. "Go back to your master and give him greeting from Sir Nigel Loring of Twynham Castle, telling him that I had hoped to make his better acquaintance this night, and that, if I have disordered his tent, it was but in my eagerness to know so famed and courteous a knight. Spur on, comrades! for we must cover many a league ere we can venture to light fire or to loosen girth. I had hoped to ride without this patch to-night, but it seems that I must carry it yet a little longer."

XXXVI

How Sir Nigel Took the Patch From His Eye

It was a cold, bleak morning in the beginning of March, and the mist was drifting in dense rolling clouds through the passes of the Cantabrian mountains. The Company, who had passed the night in a sheltered gully, were already astir, some crowding round the blazing fires and others romping or leaping over each other's backs for their limbs were chilled and the air biting. Here and there, through the dense haze which surrounded them, there loomed out huge pinnacles and jutting boulders of rock: while high above the sea of vapor there towered up one gigantic peak, with the pink glow of the early sunshine upon its snow-capped head. The ground was wet, the rocks dripping, the grass and ever-greens sparkling with beads of moisture; yet the camp was loud with laughter and merriment, for a messenger had ridden in from the prince with words of heart-stirring praise for what they had done, and with orders that they should still abide in the forefront of the army.

Round one of the fires were clustered four or five of the leading men of the archers, cleaning the rust from their weapons, and glancing impatiently from time to time at a great pot which smoked over the blaze. There was Aylward squatting cross-legged in his shirt, while he scrubbed away at his chain-mail brigandine, whistling loudly the while. On one side of him sat old Johnston, who was busy in trimming the feathers of some arrows to his liking; and on the other Hordle John, who lay with his great limbs all asprawl, and his headpiece balanced upon his uplifted foot. Black Simon of Norwich crouched amid the rocks, crooning an Eastland ballad to himself, while he whetted his sword upon a flat stone which lay across his knees; while beside him sat Alleyne Edricson, and Norbury, the silent squire of Sir Oliver, holding out their chilled hands towards the crackling faggots.

"Cast on another culpon, John, and stir the broth with thy sword-sheath," growled Johnston, looking anxiously for the twentieth time at the reeking pot.

"By my hilt!" cried Aylward, "now that John hath come by this great ransom, he will scarce abide the fare of poor archer lads. How say you, camarade? When you see Hordle once more, there will be no penny ale and fat bacon, but Gascon wines and baked meats every day of the seven."

"I know not about that," said John, kicking his helmet up into the air and catching it in his hand. "I do but know that whether the broth be ready or no, I am about to dip this into it."

"It simmers and it boils," cried Johnston, pushing his hard-lined face through the smoke. In an instant the pot had been plucked from the blaze, and its contents had been scooped up in half a dozen steel head-pieces, which were balanced betwixt their owners' knees, while, with spoon and gobbet of bread, they devoured their morning meal.

"It is ill weather for bows," remarked John at last, when, with a long sigh, he drained the last drop from his helmet. "My strings are as limp as a cow's tail this morning."

"You should rub them with water glue," quoth Johnston. "You remember, Samkin, that it was wetter than this on the morning of Crecy, and yet I cannot call to mind that there was aught amiss with our strings."

"It is in my thoughts," said Black Simon, still pensively grinding his sword, "that we may have need of your strings ere sundown. I dreamed of the red cow last night."

"And what is this red cow, Simon?" asked Alleyne.

"I know not, young sir; but I can only say that on the eve of Cadsand, and on the eve of Crecy, and on the eve of Nogent, I dreamed of a red cow; and now the dream has come upon me again, so I am now setting a very keen edge to my blade."

"Well said, old war-dog!" cried Aylward. "By my hilt! I pray that your dream may come true, for the prince hath not set us out here to drink broth or to gather whortle-berries. One more fight, and I am ready to hang up my bow, marry a wife, and take to the fire corner. But how now, Robin? Whom is it that you seek?"

"The Lord Loring craves your attendance in his tent," said a young archer to Alleyne.

The squire rose and proceeded to the pavilion, where he found the knight seated upon a cushion, with his legs crossed in front of him and a broad ribbon of parchment laid across his knees, over which he was poring with frowning brows and pursed lips.

"It came this morning by the prince's messenger," said he, "and was brought from England by Sir John Fallislee, who is new come from Sussex. What make you of this upon the outer side?"

"It is fairly and clearly written," Alleyne answered, "and it signifies To Sir Nigel Loring, Knight Constable of Twynham Castle, by the hand of Christopher, the servant of God at the Priory of Christchurch."

"So I read it," said Sir Nigel. "Now I pray you to read what is set forth within."

Alleyne turned to the letter, and, as his eyes rested upon it, his face turned pale and a cry of surprise and grief burst from his lips.

"What then?" asked the knight, peering up at him anxiously. "There is nought amiss with the Lady Mary or with the Lady Maude?"

"It is my brother—my poor unhappy brother!" cried Alleyne, with his hand to his brow. "He is dead."

"By Saint Paul! I have never heard that he had shown so much love for you that you should mourn him so."

"Yet he was my brother—the only kith or kin that I had upon earth. Mayhap he had cause to be bitter against me, for his land was given to the abbey for my upbringing. Alas! alas! and I raised my staff against him when last we met! He has been slain—and slain, I fear, amidst crime and violence."

"Ha!" said Sir Nigel. "Read on, I pray you."

"'God be with thee, my honored lord, and have thee in his holy keeping. The Lady Loring hath asked me to set down in writing what hath befallen at Twynham, and all that concerns the death of thy ill neighbor the Socman of Minstead. For when ye had left us, this evil man gathered around him all outlaws, villeins, and masterless men, until they were come to such a force that they slew and scattered the king's men who went against them. Then, coming forth from the woods, they laid siege to thy castle, and for two days they girt us in and shot hard against us, with such numbers as were a marvel to see. Yet the Lady Loring held the place stoutly, and on the second day the Socman was slain—by his own men, as some think—so that we were delivered from their hands; for which praise be to all the saints, and more especially to the holy Anselm, upon whose feast it came to pass. The Lady Loring, and the Lady Maude, thy fair daughter, are in good health; and so also am I, save for an imposthume of the toe-joint, which hath been sent me for my sins. May all the saints preserve thee!'"

"It was the vision of the Lady Tiphaine," said Sir Nigel, after a pause. "Marked you not how she said that the leader was one with a yellow beard, and how he fell before the gate. But how came it, Alleyne, that this woman, to whom all things are as crystal, and who hath not said one word which has not come to pass, was yet so led astray as to say that your thoughts turned to Twynham Castle even more than my own?"

"My fair lord," said Alleyne, with a flush on his weather-stained cheeks, "the Lady Tiphaine may have spoken sooth when she said it; for Twynham Castle is in my heart by day and in my dreams by night."

"Ha!" cried Sir Nigel, with a sidelong glance.

"Yes, my fair lord; for indeed I love your daughter, the Lady Maude; and, unworthy as I am, I would give my heart's blood to serve her."

"By St. Paul! Edricson," said the knight coldly, arching his eyebrows, "you aim high in this matter. Our blood is very old."

"And mine also is very old," answered the squire.

"And the Lady Maude is our single child. All our name and lands centre upon her."

"Alas! that I should say it, but I also am now the only Edricson."

"And why have I not heard this from you before, Alleyne? In sooth, I think that you have used me ill."

"Nay, my fair lord, say not so; for I know not whether your daughter loves me, and there is no pledge between us."

Sir Nigel pondered for a few moments, and then burst out a-laughing. "By St. Paul!" said he, "I know not why I should mix in the matter; for I have ever found that the Lady Maud was very well able to look to her own affairs. Since first she could stamp her little foot, she hath ever been able to get that for which she craved; and if she set her heart on thee, Alleyne, and thou on her, I do not think that this Spanish king, with his three-score thousand men, could hold you apart. Yet this I will say, that I would see you a full knight ere you go to my daughter with words of love. I have ever said that a brave lance should wed her; and, by my soul! Edricson, if God spare you, I think that you will acquit yourself well. But enough of such trifles, for we have our work before us, and it will be time to speak of this matter when we see the white cliffs of England once more. Go to Sir William Felton, I pray you, and ask him to come hither, for it is time that we were marching. There is no pass at the further end of the valley, and it is a perilous place should an enemy come upon us."

Alleyne delivered his message, and then wandered forth from the camp, for his mind was all in a whirl with this unexpected news, and with his talk with Sir Nigel. Sitting upon a rock, with his burning brow resting upon his hands, he thought of his brother, of their quarrel, of the Lady Maude in her bedraggled riding-dress, of the gray old castle, of the proud pale face in the armory, and of the last fiery words with which she had sped him on his way. Then he was but a penniless, monk-bred lad, unknown and unfriended. Now he was himself Socman of Minstead, the head of an old stock, and the lord of an estate which, if reduced from its former size, was still ample to preserve the dignity of his family. Further, he had become a man of experience, was counted brave among brave men, had won the esteem and confidence of her father, and, above all, had been listened to by him when he told him the secret of his love. As to the gaining of knighthood, in such stirring times it was no great matter for a brave squire of gentle birth to aspire to that honor. He would leave his bones among these Spanish ravines, or he would do some deed which would call the eyes of men upon him.

Alleyne was still seated on the rock, his griefs and his joys drifting swiftly over his mind like the shadow of clouds upon a sunlit meadow, when of a sudden he became conscious of a low, deep sound which came booming up to him through the fog. Close behind him he could hear the murmur of the bowmen, the occasional bursts of hoarse laughter, and the champing and stamping of their horses. Behind it all, however, came that low-pitched, deep-toned hum, which seemed to come from every quarter and to fill the whole air. In the old monastic days he remembered to have heard such a sound when he had walked out one windy night at Bucklershard, and had listened to the long waves breaking upon the shingly shore. Here, however, was neither wind nor sea, and yet the dull murmur rose ever louder and stronger out of the heart of the rolling sea of vapor. He turned and ran to the camp, shouting an alarm at the top of his voice.

It was but a hundred paces, and yet ere he had crossed it every bowman was ready at his horse's head, and the group of knights were out and listening intently to the ominous sound.

"It is a great body of horse," said Sir William Felton, "and they are riding very swiftly hitherwards."

"Yet they must be from the prince's army," remarked Sir Richard Causton, "for they come from the north."

"Nay," said the Earl of Angus, "it is not so certain; for the peasant with whom we spoke last night said that it was rumored that Don Tello, the Spanish king's brother, had ridden with six thousand chosen men to beat up the prince's camp. It may be that on their backward road they have come this way."

"By St. Paul!" cried Sir Nigel, "I think that it is even as you say, for that same peasant had a sour face and a shifting eye, as one who bore us little good will. I doubt not that he has brought these cavaliers upon us."

"But the mist covers us," said Sir Simon Burley. "We have yet time to ride through the further end of the pass."

"Were we a troop of mountain goats we might do so," answered Sir William Felton, "but it is not to be passed by a company of horsemen. If these be indeed Don Tello and his men, then we must bide where we are, and do what we can to make them rue the day that they found us in their path."

"Well spoken, William!" cried Sir Nigel, in high delight. "If there be so many as has been said, then there will be much honor to be gained from them and every hope of advancement. But the sound has ceased, and I fear that they have gone some other way."

"Or mayhap they have come to the mouth of the gorge, and are marshalling their ranks. Hush and hearken! for they are no great way from us."

The Company stood peering into the dense fog-wreath, amidst a silence so profound that the dripping of the water from the rocks and the breathing of the horses grew loud upon the ear. Suddenly from out the sea of mist came the shrill sound of a neigh, followed by a long blast upon a bugle.

"It is a Spanish call, my fair lord," said Black Simon. "It is used by their prickers and huntsmen when the beast hath not fled, but is still in its lair."

"By my faith!" said Sir Nigel, smiling, "if they are in a humor for venerie we may promise them some sport ere they sound the mort over us. But there is a hill in the centre of the gorge on which we might take our stand."

"I marked it yester-night," said Felton, "and no better spot could be found for our purpose, for it is very steep at the back. It is but a bow-shot to the left, and, indeed, I can see the shadow of it."

The whole Company, leading their horses, passed across to the small hill which loomed in front of them out of the mist. It was indeed admirably designed for defence, for it sloped down in front, all jagged and boulder-strewn, while it fell away in a sheer cliff of a hundred feet or more. On the summit was a small uneven plateau, with a stretch across of a hundred paces, and a depth of half as much again.

"Unloose the horses!" said Sir Nigel. "We have no space for them, and if we hold our own we shall have horses and to spare when this day's work is done. Nay, keep yours, my fair sirs, for we may have work for them. Aylward, Johnston, let your men form a harrow on either side of the ridge. Sir Oliver and you, my Lord Angus, I give you the right wing, and the left to you, Sir Simon, and to you, Sir Richard Causton. I and Sir William Felton will hold the centre with our men-at-arms. Now order the ranks, and fling wide the banners, for our souls are God's and our bodies the king's, and our swords for Saint George and for England!"

Sir Nigel had scarcely spoken when the mist seemed to thin in the valley, and to shred away into long ragged clouds which trailed from the edges of the cliffs. The gorge in which they had camped was a mere wedge-shaped cleft among the hills, three-quarters of a mile deep, with the small rugged rising upon which they stood at the further end, and the brown crags walling it in on three sides. As the mist parted, and the sun broke through, it gleamed and shimmered with dazzling brightness upon the armor and headpieces of a vast body of horsemen who stretched across the barranca from one cliff to the other, and extended backwards until their rear guard were far out upon the plain beyond. Line after line, and rank after rank, they choked the neck of the valley with a long vista of tossing pennons, twinkling lances, waving plumes and streaming banderoles, while the curvets and gambades of the chargers lent a constant motion and shimmer to the glittering, many-colored mass. A yell of exultation, and a forest of waving steel through the length and breadth of their column, announced that they could at last see their entrapped enemies, while the swelling notes of a hundred bugles and drums, mixed with the clash of Moorish cymbals, broke forth into a proud peal of martial triumph. Strange it was to these gallant and sparkling cavaliers of Spain to look upon this handful of men upon the hill, the thin lines of bowmen, the knots of knights and men-at-arms with armor rusted and discolored from long service, and to learn that these were indeed the soldiers whose fame and prowess had been the camp-fire talk of every army in Christendom. Very still and silent they stood, leaning upon their bows, while their leaders took counsel together in front of them. No clang of bugle rose from their stern ranks, but in the centre waved the leopards of England, on the right the ensign of their Company with the roses of Loring, and on the left, over three score of Welsh bowmen, there floated the red banner of Merlin with the boars'-heads of the Buttesthorns. Gravely and sedately they stood beneath the morning sun waiting for the onslaught of their foemen.

"By Saint Paul!" said Sir Nigel, gazing with puckered eye down the valley, "there appear to be some very worthy people among them. What is this golden banner which waves upon the left?"

"It is the ensign of the Knights of Calatrava," answered Felton.

"And the other upon the right?"

"It marks the Knights of Santiago, and I see by his flag that their grand-master rides at their head. There too is the banner of Castile amid yonder sparkling squadron which heads the main battle. There are six thousand men-at-arms with ten squadrons of slingers as far as I may judge their numbers."

"There are Frenchmen among them, my fair lord," remarked Black Simon. "I can see the pennons of De Couvette, De Brieux, Saint Pol, and many others who struck in against us for Charles of Blois."

"You are right," said Sir William, "for I can also see them. There is much Spanish blazonry also, if I could but read it. Don Diego, you know the arms of your own land. Who are they who have done us this honor?"

The Spanish prisoner looked with exultant eyes upon the deep and serried ranks of his countrymen.

"By Saint James!" said he, "if ye fall this day ye fall by no mean hands, for the flower of the knighthood of Castile ride under the banner of Don Tello, with the chivalry of Asturias, Toledo, Leon, Cordova, Galicia, and Seville. I see the guidons of Albornez, Cacorla, Rodriguez, Tavora, with the two great orders, and the knights of France and of Aragon. If you will take my rede you will come to a composition with them, for they will give you such terms as you have given me."

"Nay, by Saint Paul! it were pity if so many brave men were drawn together, and no little deed of arms to come of it. Ha! William, they advance upon us; and, by my soul! it is a sight that is worth coming over the seas to see."

As he spoke, the two wings of the Spanish host, consisting of the Knights of Calatrava on the one side and of Santiago upon the other, came swooping swiftly down the valley, while the main body followed more slowly behind. Five hundred paces from the English the two great bodies of horse crossed each other, and, sweeping round in a curve, retired in feigned confusion towards their centre. Often in bygone wars had the Moors tempted the hot-blooded Spaniards from their places of strength by such pretended flights, but there were men upon the hill to whom every ruse and trick of war were as their daily trade and practice. Again and even nearer came the rallying Spaniards, and again with cry of fear and stooping bodies they swerved off to right and left, but the English still stood stolid and observant among their rocks. The vanguard halted a long bow shot from the hill, and with waving spears and vaunting shouts challenged their enemies to come forth, while two cavaliers, pricking forward from the glittering ranks, walked their horses slowly between the two arrays with targets braced and lances in rest like the challengers in a tourney.

"By Saint Paul!" cried Sir Nigel, with his one eye glowing like an ember, "these appear to be two very worthy and debonair gentlemen. I do not call to mind when I have seen any people who seemed of so great a heart and so high of enterprise. We have our horses, Sir William: shall we not relieve them of any vow which they may have upon their souls?"

Felton's reply was to bound upon his charger, and to urge it down the slope, while Sir Nigel followed not three spears'-lengths behind him. It was a rugged course, rocky and uneven, yet the two knights, choosing their men, dashed onwards at the top of their speed, while the gallant Spaniards flew as swiftly to meet them. The one to whom Felton found himself opposed was a tall stripling with a stag's head upon his shield, while Sir Nigel's man was broad and squat with plain steel harness, and a pink and white torse bound round his helmet. The first struck Felton on the target with such force as to split it from side to side, but Sir William's lance crashed through the camail which shielded the Spaniard's throat, and he fell, screaming hoarsely, to the ground. Carried away by the heat and madness of fight, the English knight never drew rein, but charged straight on into the array of the knights of Calatrava. Long time the silent ranks upon the hill could see a swirl and eddy deep down in the heart of the Spanish column, with a circle of rearing chargers and flashing blades. Here and there tossed the white plume of the English helmet, rising and falling like the foam upon a wave, with the fierce gleam and sparkle ever circling round it until at last it had sunk from view, and another brave man had turned from war to peace.

Sir Nigel, meanwhile, had found a foeman worthy of his steel for his opponent was none other than Sebastian Gomez, the picked lance of the monkish Knights of Santiago, who had won fame in a hundred bloody combats with the Moors of Andalusia. So fierce was their meeting that their spears shivered up to the very grasp, and the horses reared backwards until it seemed that they must crash down upon their riders. Yet with consummate horsemanship they both swung round in a long curvet, and then plucking out their swords they lashed at each other like two lusty smiths hammering upon an anvil. The chargers spun round each other, biting and striking, while the two blades wheeled and whizzed and circled in gleams of dazzling light. Cut, parry, and thrust followed so swiftly upon each other that the eye could not follow them, until at last coming thigh to thigh, they cast their arms around each other and rolled off their saddles to the ground. The heavier Spaniard threw himself upon his enemy, and pinning him down beneath him raised his sword to slay him, while a shout of triumph rose from the ranks of his countrymen. But the fatal blow never fell, for even as his arm quivered before descending, the Spaniard gave a shudder, and stiffening himself rolled heavily over upon his side, with the blood gushing from his armpit and from the slit of his vizor. Sir Nigel sprang to his feet with his bloody dagger in his left hand and gazed down upon his adversary, but that fatal and sudden stab in the vital spot, which the Spaniard had exposed by raising his arm, had proved instantly mortal. The Englishman leaped upon his horse and made for the hill, at the very instant that a yell of rage from a thousand voices and the clang of a score of bugles announced the Spanish onset.

But the islanders were ready and eager for the encounter. With feet firmly planted, their sleeves rolled back to give free play to their muscles, their long yellow bow-staves in their left hands, and their quivers slung to the front, they had waited in the four-deep harrow formation which gave strength to their array, and yet permitted every man to draw his arrow freely without harm to those in front. Aylward and Johnston had been engaged in throwing light tufts of grass into the air to gauge the wind force, and a hoarse whisper passed down the ranks from the file-leaders to the men, with scraps of advice and admonition.

"Do not shoot outside the fifteen-score paces," cried Johnston. "We may need all our shafts ere we have done with them."

"Better to overshoot than to undershoot," added Aylward. "Better to strike the rear guard than to feather a shaft in the earth."

"Loose quick and sharp when they come," added another. "Let it be the eye to the string, the string to the shaft, and the shaft to the mark. By Our Lady! their banners advance, and we must hold our ground now if ever we are to see Southampton Water again."

Alleyne, standing with his sword drawn amidst the archers, saw a long toss and heave of the glittering squadrons. Then the front ranks began to surge slowly forward, to trot, to canter, to gallop, and in an instant the whole vast array was hurtling onward, line after line, the air full of the thunder of their cries, the ground shaking with the beat of their hoofs, the valley choked with the rushing torrent of steel, topped by the waving plumes, the slanting spears and the fluttering banderoles. On they swept over the level and up to the slope, ere they met the blinding storm of the English arrows. Down went the whole ranks in a whirl of mad confusion, horses plunging and kicking, bewildered men falling, rising, staggering on or back, while ever new lines of horsemen came spurring through the gaps and urged their chargers up the fatal slope. All around him Alleyne could hear the stern, short orders of the master-bowmen, while the air was filled with the keen twanging of the strings and the swish and patter of the shafts. Right across the foot of the hill there had sprung up a long wall of struggling horses and stricken men, which ever grew and heightened as fresh squadrons poured on the attack. One young knight on a gray jennet leaped over his fallen comrades and galloped swiftly up the hill, shrieking loudly upon Saint James, ere he fell within a spear-length of the English line, with the feathers of arrows thrusting out from every crevice and joint of his armor. So for five long minutes the gallant horsemen of Spain and of France strove ever and again to force a passage, until the wailing note of a bugle called them back, and they rode slowly out of bow-shot, leaving their best and their bravest in the ghastly, blood-mottled heap behind them.

But there was little rest for the victors. Whilst the knights had charged them in front the slingers had crept round upon either flank and had gained a footing upon the cliffs and behind the outlying rocks. A storm of stones broke suddenly upon the defenders, who, drawn up in lines upon the exposed summit, offered a fair mark to their hidden foes. Johnston, the old archer, was struck upon the temple and fell dead without a groan, while fifteen of his bowmen and six of the men-at-arms were struck down at the same moment. The others lay on their faces to avoid the deadly hail, while at each side of the plateau a fringe of bowmen exchanged shots with the slingers and crossbowmen among the rocks, aiming mainly at those who had swarmed up the cliffs, and bursting into laughter and cheers when a well-aimed shaft brought one of their opponents toppling down from his lofty perch.

"I think, Nigel," said Sir Oliver, striding across to the little knight, "that we should all acquit ourselves better had we our none-meat, for the sun is high in the heaven."

"By Saint Paul!" quoth Sir Nigel, plucking the patch from his eye, "I think that I am now clear of my vow, for this Spanish knight was a person from whom much honor might be won. Indeed, he was a very worthy gentleman, of good courage, and great hardiness, and it grieves me that he should have come by such a hurt. As to what you say of food, Oliver, it is not to be thought of, for we have nothing with us upon the hill."

"Nigel!" cried Sir Simon Burley, hurrying up with consternation upon his face, "Aylward tells me that there are not ten-score arrows left in all their sheaves. See! they are springing from their horses, and cutting their sollerets that they may rush upon us. Might we not even now make a retreat?"

"My soul will retreat from my body first!" cried the little knight. "Here I am, and here I bide, while God gives me strength to lift a sword."

"And so say I!" shouted Sir Oliver, throwing his mace high into the air and catching it again by the handle.

"To your arms, men!" roared Sir Nigel. "Shoot while you may, and then out sword, and let us live or die together!"

XXXVII

How the White Company Came to Be Disbanded

Then up rose from the hill in the rugged Cantabrian valley a sound such as had not been heard in those parts before, nor was again, until the streams which rippled amid the rocks had been frozen by over four hundred winters and thawed by as many returning springs. Deep and full and strong it thundered down the ravine, the fierce battle-call of a warrior race, the last stern welcome to whoso should join with them in that world-old game where the stake is death. Thrice it swelled forth and thrice it sank away, echoing and reverberating amidst the crags. Then, with set faces, the Company rose up among the storm of stones, and looked down upon the thousands who sped swiftly up the slope against them. Horse and spear had been set aside, but on foot, with sword and battle-axe, their broad shields slung in front of them, the chivalry of Spain rushed to the attack.

And now arose a struggle so fell, so long, so evenly sustained, that even now the memory of it is handed down amongst the Cantabrian mountaineers and the ill-omened knoll is still pointed out by fathers to their children as the "Altura de los Inglesos," where the men from across the sea fought the great fight with the knights of the south. The last arrow was quickly shot, nor could the slingers hurl their stones, so close were friend and foe. From side to side stretched the thin line of the English, lightly armed and quick-footed, while against it stormed and raged the pressing throng of fiery Spaniards and of gallant Bretons. The clink of crossing sword-blades, the dull thudding of heavy blows, the panting and gasping of weary and wounded men, all rose together in a wild, long-drawn note, which swelled upwards to the ears of the wondering peasants who looked down from the edges of the cliffs upon the swaying turmoil of the battle beneath them. Back and forward reeled the leopard banner, now borne up the slope by the rush and weight of the onslaught, now pushing downwards again as Sir Nigel, Burley, and Black Simon with their veteran men-at arms, flung themselves madly into the fray. Alleyne, at his lord's right hand, found himself swept hither and thither in the desperate struggle, exchanging savage thrusts one instant with a Spanish cavalier, and the next torn away by the whirl of men and dashed up against some new antagonist. To the right Sir Oliver, Aylward, Hordle John, and the bowmen of the Company fought furiously against the monkish Knights of Santiago, who were led up the hill by their prior—a great, deep-chested man, who wore a brown monastic habit over his suit of mail. Three archers he slew in three giant strokes, but Sir Oliver flung his arms round him, and the two, staggering and straining, reeled backwards and fell, locked in each other's grasp, over the edge of the steep cliff which flanked the hill. In vain his knights stormed and raved against the thin line which barred their path: the sword of Aylward and the great axe of John gleamed in the forefront of the battle and huge jagged pieces of rock, hurled by the strong arms of the bowmen, crashed and hurtled amid their ranks. Slowly they gave back down the hill, the archers still hanging upon their skirts, with a long litter of writhing and twisted figures to mark the course which they had taken. At the same instant the Welshmen upon the left, led on by the Scotch earl, had charged out from among the rocks which sheltered them, and by the fury of their outfall had driven the Spaniards in front of them in headlong flight down the hill. In the centre only things seemed to be going ill with the defenders. Black Simon was down—dying, as he would wish to have died, like a grim old wolf in its lair with a ring of his slain around him. Twice Sir Nigel had been overborne, and twice Alleyne had fought over him until he had staggered to his feet once more. Burley lay senseless, stunned by a blow from a mace, and half of the men-at-arms lay littered upon the ground around him. Sir Nigel's shield was broken, his crest shorn, his armor cut and smashed, and the vizor torn from his helmet; yet he sprang hither and thither with light foot and ready hand, engaging two Bretons and a Spaniard at the same instant—thrusting, stooping, dashing in, springing out—while Alleyne still fought by his side, stemming with a handful of men the fierce tide which surged up against them. Yet it would have fared ill with them had not the archers from either side closed in upon the flanks of the attackers, and pressed them very slowly and foot by foot down the long slope, until they were on the plain once more, where their fellows were already rallying for a fresh assault.

But terrible indeed was the cost at which the last had been repelled. Of the three hundred and seventy men who had held the crest, one hundred and seventy-two were left standing, many of whom were sorely wounded and weak from loss of blood. Sir Oliver Buttesthorn, Sir Richard Causton, Sir Simon Burley, Black Simon, Johnston, a hundred and fifty archers, and forty-seven men-at-arms had fallen, while the pitiless hail of stones was already whizzing and piping once more about their ears, threatening every instant to further reduce their numbers.

Sir Nigel looked about him at his shattered ranks, and his face flushed with a soldier's pride.

"By St. Paul!" he cried, "I have fought in many a little bickering, but never one that I would be more loth to have missed than this. But you are wounded, Alleyne?"

"It is nought," answered his squire, stanching the blood which dripped from a sword-cut across his forehead.

"These gentlemen of Spain seem to be most courteous and worthy people. I see that they are already forming to continue this debate with us. Form up the bowmen two deep instead of four. By my faith! some very brave men have gone from among us. Aylward, you are a trusty soldier, for all that your shoulder has never felt accolade, nor your heels worn the gold spurs. Do you take charge of the right; I will hold the centre, and you, my Lord of Angus, the left."

"Ho! for Sir Samkin Aylward!" cried a rough voice among the archers, and a roar of laughter greeted their new leader.

"By my hilt!" said the old bowman, "I never thought to lead a wing in a stricken field. Stand close, camarades, for, by these finger-bones! we must play the man this day."

"Come hither, Alleyne," said Sir Nigel, walking back to the edge of the cliff which formed the rear of their position. "And you, Norbury," he continued, beckoning to the squire of Sir Oliver, "do you also come here."

The two squires hurried across to him, and the three stood looking down into the rocky ravine which lay a hundred and fifty feet beneath them.

"The prince must hear of how things are with us," said the knight. "Another onfall we may withstand, but they are many and we are few, so that the time must come when we can no longer form line across the hill. Yet if help were brought us we might hold the crest until it comes. See yonder horses which stray among the rocks beneath us?"

"I see them, my fair lord."

"And see yonder path which winds along the hill upon the further end of the valley?"

"I see it."

"Were you on those horses, and riding up yonder track, steep and rough as it is, I think that ye might gain the valley beyond. Then on to the prince, and tell him how we fare."

"But, my fair lord, how can we hope to reach the horses?" asked Norbury.

"Ye cannot go round to them, for they would be upon ye ere ye could come to them. Think ye that ye have heart enough to clamber down this cliff?"

"Had we but a rope."

"There is one here. It is but one hundred feet long, and for the rest ye must trust to God and to your fingers. Can you try it, Alleyne?"

"With all my heart, my dear lord, but how can I leave you in such a strait?"

"Nay, it is to serve me that ye go. And you, Norbury?"

The silent squire said nothing, but he took up the rope, and, having examined it, he tied one end firmly round a projecting rock. Then he cast off his breast-plate, thigh pieces, and greaves, while Alleyne followed his example.

"Tell Chandos, or Calverley, or Knolles, should the prince have gone forward," cried Sir Nigel. "Now may God speed ye, for ye are brave and worthy men."

It was, indeed, a task which might make the heart of the bravest sink within him. The thin cord dangling down the face of the brown cliff seemed from above to reach little more than half-way down it. Beyond stretched the rugged rock, wet and shining, with a green tuft here and there thrusting out from it, but little sign of ridge or foothold. Far below the jagged points of the boulders bristled up, dark and menacing. Norbury tugged thrice with all his strength upon the cord, and then lowered himself over the edge, while a hundred anxious faces peered over at him as he slowly clambered downwards to the end of the rope. Twice he stretched out his foot, and twice he failed to reach the point at which he aimed, but even as he swung himself for a third effort a stone from a sling buzzed like a wasp from amid the rocks and struck him full upon the side of his head. His grasp relaxed, his feet slipped, and in an instant he was a crushed and mangled corpse upon the sharp ridges beneath him.

"If I have no better fortune," said Alleyne, leading Sir Nigel aside. "I pray you, my dear lord, that you will give my humble service to the

Lady Maude, and say to her that I was ever her true servant and most unworthy cavalier."

The old knight said no word, but he put a hand on either shoulder, and kissed his squire, with the tears shining in his eyes. Alleyne sprang to the rope, and sliding swiftly down, soon found himself at its extremity. From above it seemed as though rope and cliff were well-nigh touching, but now, when swinging a hundred feet down, the squire found that he could scarce reach the face of the rock with his foot, and that it was as smooth as glass, with no resting-place where a mouse could stand. Some three feet lower, however, his eye lit upon a long jagged crack which slanted downwards, and this he must reach if he would save not only his own poor life, but that of the eight-score men above him. Yet it were madness to spring for that narrow slit with nought but the wet, smooth rock to cling to. He swung for a moment, full of thought, and even as he hung there another of the hellish stones sang through his curls, and struck a chip from the face of the cliff. Up he clambered a few feet, drew up the loose end after him, unslung his belt, held on with knee and with elbow while he spliced the long, tough leathern belt to the end of the cord: then lowering himself as far as he could go, he swung backwards and forwards until his hand reached the crack, when he left the rope and clung to the face of the cliff. Another stone struck him on the side, and he heard a sound like a breaking stick, with a keen stabbing pain which shot through his chest. Yet it was no time now to think of pain or ache. There was his lord and his eight-score comrades, and they must be plucked from the jaws of death. On he clambered, with his hand shuffling down the long sloping crack, sometimes bearing all his weight upon his arms, at others finding some small shelf or tuft on which to rest his foot. Would he never pass over that fifty feet? He dared not look down and could but grope slowly onwards, his face to the cliff, his fingers clutching, his feet scraping and feeling for a support. Every vein and crack and mottling of that face of rock remained forever stamped upon his memory. At last, however, his foot came upon a broad resting-place and he ventured to cast a glance downwards. Thank God! he had reached the highest of those fatal pinnacles upon which his comrade had fallen. Quickly now he sprang from rock to rock until his feet were on the ground, and he had his hand stretched out for the horse's rein, when a sling-stone struck him on the head, and he dropped senseless upon the ground.

An evil blow it was for Alleyne, but a worse one still for him who struck it. The Spanish slinger, seeing the youth lie slain, and judging from his dress that he was no common man, rushed forward to plunder him, knowing well that the bowmen above him had expended their last shaft. He was still three paces, however, from his victim's side when John upon the cliff above plucked up a huge boulder, and, poising it for an instant, dropped it with fatal aim upon the slinger beneath him. It struck upon his shoulder, and hurled him, crushed and screaming, to the ground, while Alleyne, recalled to his senses by these shrill cries in his very ear, staggered on to his feet, and gazed wildly about him. His eyes fell upon the horses, grazing upon the scanty pasture, and in an instant all had come back to him—his mission, his comrades, the need for haste. He was dizzy, sick, faint, but he must not die, and he must not tarry, for his life meant many lives that day. In an instant he was in his saddle and spurring down the valley. Loud rang the swift charger's hoofs over rock and reef, while the fire flew from the stroke of iron, and the loose stones showered up behind him. But his head was whirling round, the blood was gushing from his brow, his temple, his mouth. Ever keener and sharper was the deadly pain which shot like a red-hot arrow through his side. He felt that his eye was glazing, his senses slipping from him, his grasp upon the reins relaxing. Then with one mighty effort, he called up all his strength for a single minute. Stooping down, he loosened the stirrup-straps, bound his knees tightly to his saddle-flaps, twisted his hands in the bridle, and then, putting the gallant horse's head for the mountain path, he dashed the spurs in and fell forward fainting with his face buried in the coarse, black mane.

Little could he ever remember of that wild ride. Half conscious, but ever with the one thought beating in his mind, he goaded the horse onwards, rushing swiftly down steep ravines over huge boulders, along the edges of black abysses. Dim memories he had of beetling cliffs, of a group of huts with wondering faces at the doors, of foaming, clattering water, and of a bristle of mountain beeches. Once, ere he had ridden far, he heard behind him three deep, sullen shouts, which told him that his comrades had set their faces to the foe once more. Then all was blank, until he woke to find kindly blue English eyes peering down upon him and to hear the blessed sound of his country's speech. They were but a foraging party—a hundred archers and as many men-at-arms—but their leader was Sir Hugh Calverley, and he was not a man to bide idle when good blows were to be had not three leagues from him. A scout was sent flying with a message to the camp, and Sir Hugh, with his two hundred men, thundered off to the rescue. With them went Alleyne, still bound to his saddle, still dripping with blood, and swooning and recovering, and swooning once again. On they rode, and on, until, at last, topping a ridge, they looked down upon the fateful valley. Alas! and alas! for the sight that met their eyes.

There, beneath them, was the blood-bathed hill, and from the highest pinnacle there flaunted the yellow and white banner with the lions and the towers of the royal house of Castile. Up the long slope rushed ranks and ranks of men exultant, shouting, with waving pennons and brandished arms. Over the whole summit were dense throngs of knights, with no enemy that could be seen to face them, save only that at one corner of the plateau an eddy and swirl amid the crowded mass seemed to show that all resistance was not yet at an end. At the sight a deep groan of rage and of despair went up from the baffled rescuers, and, spurring on their horses, they clattered down the long and winding path which led to the valley beneath.

But they were too late to avenge, as they had been too late to save. Long ere they could gain the level ground, the Spaniards, seeing them riding swiftly amid the rocks, and being ignorant of their numbers, drew off from the captured hill, and, having secured their few prisoners, rode slowly in a long column, with drum-beating and cymbal-clashing, out of the valley. Their rear ranks were already passing out of sight ere the new-comers were urging their panting, foaming horses up the slope which had been the scene of that long drawn and bloody fight.

And a fearsome sight it was that met their eyes! Across the lower end lay the dense heap of men and horses where the first arrow-storm had burst. Above, the bodies of the dead and the dying—French, Spanish, and Aragonese—lay thick and thicker, until they covered the whole ground two and three deep in one dreadful tangle of slaughter. Above them lay the Englishmen in their lines, even as they had stood, and higher yet upon the plateau a wild medley of the dead of all nations, where the last deadly grapple had left them. In the further corner, under the shadow of a great rock, there crouched seven bowmen, with great John in the centre of them—all wounded, weary, and in sorry case, but still unconquered, with their blood-stained weapons waving and their voices ringing a welcome to their countrymen. Alleyne rode across to John, while Sir Hugh Calverley followed close behind him.

"By Saint George!" cried Sir Hugh, "I have never seen signs of so stern a fight, and I am right glad that we have been in time to save you."

"You have saved more than us," said John, pointing to the banner which leaned against the rock behind him.

"You have done nobly," cried the old free companion, gazing with a soldier's admiration at the huge frame and bold face of the archer. "But why is it, my good fellow, that you sit upon this man."

"By the rood! I had forgot him," John answered, rising and dragging from under him no less a person than the Spanish caballero, Don Diego Alvarez. "This man, my fair lord, means to me a new house, ten cows, one bull—if it be but a little one—a grindstone, and I know not what besides; so that I thought it well to sit upon him, lest he should take a fancy to leave me."

"Tell me, John," cried Alleyne faintly: "where is my dear lord, Sir Nigel Loring?"

"He is dead, I fear. I saw them throw his body across a horse and ride away with it, but I fear the life had gone from him."

"Now woe worth me! And where is Aylward?"

"He sprang upon a riderless horse and rode after Sir Nigel to save him. I saw them throng around him, and he is either taken or slain."

"Blow the bugles!" cried Sir Hugh, with a scowling brow. "We must back to camp, and ere three days I trust that we may sec these Spaniards again. I would fain have ye all in my company."

"We are of the White Company, my fair lord," said John.

"Nay, the White Company is here disbanded," answered Sir Hugh solemnly, looking round him at the lines of silent figures. "Look to the brave squire, for I fear that he will never see the sun rise again."

XXXVIII

Of the Home-coming to Hampshire

It was a bright July morning four months after that fatal fight in the Spanish barranca. A blue heaven stretched above, a green rolling plain undulated below, intersected with hedge-rows and flecked with grazing sheep. The sun was yet low in the heaven, and the red cows stood in the long shadow of the elms, chewing the cud and gazing with great vacant eyes at two horsemen who were spurring it down the long white road which dipped and curved away back to where the towers and pinnacles beneath the flat-topped hill marked the old town of Winchester.

Of the riders one was young, graceful, and fair, clad in plain doublet and hosen of blue Brussels cloth, which served to show his active and well-knit figure. A flat velvet cap was drawn forward to keep the glare from his eyes, and he rode with lips compressed and anxious face, as one who has much care upon his mind. Young as he was, and peaceful as was his dress, the dainty golden spurs which twinkled upon his heels proclaimed his knighthood, while a long seam upon his brow and a scar upon his temple gave a manly grace to his refined and delicate countenance. His comrade was a large, red-headed man upon a great black horse, with a huge canvas bag slung from his saddle-bow, which jingled and clinked with every movement of his steed. His broad, brown face was lighted up by a continual smile, and he looked slowly from side to side with eyes which twinkled and shone with delight. Well might John rejoice, for was he not back in his native Hampshire, had he not Don Diego's five thousand crowns rasping against his knee, and above all was he not himself squire now to Sir Alleyne Edricson, the young Socman of Minstead lately knighted by the sword of the Black Prince himself, and esteemed by the whole army as one of the most rising of the soldiers of England.

For the last stand of the Company had been told throughout Christendom wherever a brave deed of arms was loved, and honors had flowed in upon the few who had survived it. For two months Alleyne had wavered betwixt death and life, with a broken rib and a shattered head; yet youth and strength and a cleanly life were all upon his side, and he awoke from his long delirium to find that the war was over, that the Spaniards and their allies had been crushed at Navaretta, and that the prince had himself heard the tale of his ride for succor and had come in person to his bedside to touch his shoulder with his sword and to insure that so brave and true a man should die, if he could not live, within the order of chivalry. The instant that he could set foot to ground Alleyne had started in search of his lord, but no word could he hear of him, dead or alive, and he had come home now sad-hearted, in the hope of raising money upon his estates and so starting upon his quest once more. Landing at London, he had hurried on with a mind full of care, for he had heard no word from Hampshire since the short note which had announced his brother's death.

"By the rood!" cried John, looking around him exultantly, "where have we seen since we left such noble cows, such fleecy sheep, grass so green, or a man so drunk as yonder rogue who lies in the gap of the hedge?"

"Ah, John," Alleyne answered wearily, "it is well for you, but I never thought that my home-coming would be so sad a one. My heart is heavy for my dear lord and for Aylward, and I know not how I may break the news to the Lady Mary and to the Lady Maude, if they have not yet had tidings of it."

John gave a groan which made the horses shy. "It is indeed a black business," said he. "But be not sad, for I shall give half these crowns to my old mother, and half will I add to the money which you may have, and so we shall buy that yellow cog wherein we sailed to Bordeaux, and in it we shall go forth and seek Sir Nigel."

Alleyne smiled, but shook his head. "Were he alive we should have had word of him ere now," said he. "But what is this town before us?"

"Why, it is Romsey!" cried John. "See the tower of the old gray church, and the long stretch of the nunnery. But here sits a very holy man, and I shall give him a crown for his prayers."

Three large stones formed a rough cot by the roadside, and beside it, basking in the sun, sat the hermit, with clay-colored face, dull eyes, and long withered hands. With crossed ankles and sunken head, he sat as though all his life had passed out of him, with the beads slipping slowly through his thin, yellow fingers. Behind him lay the narrow cell, clay-floored and damp, comfortless, profitless and sordid. Beyond it there lay amid the trees the wattle-and-daub hut of a laborer, the door open, and the single room exposed to the view. The man ruddy and yellow-haired, stood leaning upon the spade wherewith he had been at work upon the garden patch. From behind him came the ripple of a happy woman's laughter, and two young urchins darted forth from the hut, bare-legged and towsy, while the mother, stepping out, laid her hand upon her husband's arm and watched the gambols of the children. The hermit frowned at the untoward noise which broke upon his prayers, but his brow relaxed as he looked upon the broad silver piece which John held out to him.

"There lies the image of our past and of our future," cried Alleyne, as they rode on upon their way. "Now, which is better, to till God's earth, to have happy faces round one's knee, and to love and be loved, or to sit forever moaning over one's own soul, like a mother over a sick babe?"

"I know not about that," said John, "for it casts a great cloud over me when I think of such matters. But I know that my crown was well spent, for the man had the look of a very holy person. As to the other, there was nought holy about him that I could see, and it would be cheaper for me to pray for myself than to give a crown to one who spent his days in digging for lettuces."

Ere Alleyne could answer there swung round the curve of the road a lady's carriage drawn by three horses abreast with a postilion upon the outer one. Very fine and rich it was, with beams painted and gilt, wheels and spokes carved in strange figures, and over all an arched cover of red and white tapestry. Beneath its shade there sat a stout and elderly lady in a pink cote-hardie, leaning back among a pile of cushions, and plucking out her eyebrows with a small pair of silver tweezers. None could seem more safe and secure and at her ease than this lady, yet here also was a symbol of human life, for in an instant, even as Alleyne reined aside to let the carriage pass, a wheel flew out from among its fellows, and over it all toppled—carving, tapestry and gilt—in one wild heap, with the horses plunging, the postilion shouting, and the lady screaming from within. In an instant Alleyne and John were on foot, and had lifted her forth all in a shake with fear, but little the worse for her mischance.

"Now woe worth me!" she cried, "and ill fall on Michael Easover of Romsey! for I told him that the pin was loose, and yet he must needs gainsay me, like the foolish daffe that he is."

"I trust that you have taken no hurt, my fair lady," said Alleyne, conducting her to the bank, upon which John had already placed a cushion.

"Nay, I have had no scath, though I have lost my silver tweezers. Now, lack-a-day! did God ever put breath into such a fool as Michael Easover of Romsey? But I am much beholden to you, gentle sirs. Soldiers ye are, as one may readily see. I am myself a soldier's daughter," she added, casting a somewhat languishing glance at John, "and my heart ever goes out to a brave man."

"We are indeed fresh from Spain," quoth Alleyne.

"From Spain, say you? Ah! it was an ill and sorry thing that so many should throw away the lives that Heaven gave them. In sooth, it is bad for those who fall, but worse for those who bide behind. I have but now bid farewell to one who hath lost all in this cruel war."

"And how that, lady?"

"She is a young damsel of these parts, and she goes now into a nunnery. Alack! it is not a year since she was the fairest maid from Avon to Itchen, and now it was more than I could abide to wait at Romsey Nunnery to see her put the white veil upon her face, for she was made for a wife and not for the cloister. Did you ever, gentle sir, hear of a body of men called 'The White Company' over yonder?"

"Surely so," cried both the comrades.

"Her father was the leader of it, and her lover served under him as squire. News hath come that not one of the Company was left alive, and so, poor lamb, she hath——"

"Lady!" cried Alleyne, with catching breath, "is it the Lady Maude Loring of whom you speak?"

"It is, in sooth."

"Maude! And in a nunnery! Did, then, the thought of her father's death so move her?"

"Her father!" cried the lady, smiling. "Nay; Maude is a good daughter, but I think it was this young golden-haired squire of whom I have heard who has made her turn her back upon the world."

"And I stand talking here!" cried Alleyne wildly. "Come, John, come!"

Rushing to his horse, he swung himself into the saddle, and was off down the road in a rolling cloud of dust as fast as his good steed could bear him.

Great had been the rejoicing amid the Romsey nuns when the Lady Maude Loring had craved admission into their order—for was she not sole child and heiress of the old knight, with farms and fiefs which she could bring to the great nunnery? Long and earnest had been the talks of the gaunt lady abbess, in which she had conjured the young novice to turn forever from the world, and to rest her bruised heart under the broad and peaceful shelter of the church. And now, when all was settled, and when abbess and lady superior had had their will, it was but fitting that some pomp and show should mark the glad occasion. Hence was it that the good burghers of Romsey were all in the streets, that gay flags and flowers brightened the path from the nunnery to the church, and that a long procession wound up to the old arched door leading up the bride to these spiritual nuptials. There was lay-sister Agatha with the high gold crucifix, and the three incense-bearers, and the two-and-twenty garbed in white, who cast flowers upon either side of them and sang sweetly the while. Then, with four attendants, came the novice, her drooping head wreathed with white blossoms, and, behind, the abbess and her council of older nuns, who were already counting in their minds whether their own bailiff could manage the farms of Twynham, or whether a reeve would be needed beneath him, to draw the utmost from these new possessions which this young novice was about to bring them.

But alas! for plots and plans when love and youth and nature, and above all, fortune are arrayed against them. Who is this travel-stained youth who dares to ride so madly through the lines of staring burghers? Why does he fling himself from his horse and stare so strangely about him? See how he has rushed through the incense-bearers, thrust aside lay-sister Agatha, scattered the two-and-twenty damosels who sang so sweetly—and he stands before the novice with his hands out-stretched, and his face shining, and the light of love in his gray eyes. Her foot is on the very lintel of the church, and yet he bars the way—and she, she thinks no more of the wise words and holy rede of the lady abbess, but she hath given a sobbing cry and hath fallen forward with his arms around her drooping body and her wet cheek upon his breast. A sorry sight this for the gaunt abbess, an ill lesson too for the stainless two-and-twenty who have ever been taught that the way of nature is the way of sin. But Maude and Alleyne care little for this. A dank, cold air comes out from the black arch before them. Without, the sun shines bright and the birds are singing amid the ivy on the drooping beeches. Their choice is made, and they turn away hand-in-hand, with their backs to the darkness and their faces to the light.

Very quiet was the wedding in the old priory church at Christchurch, where Father Christopher read the service, and there were few to see save the Lady Loring and John, and a dozen bowmen from the castle. The Lady of Twynham had drooped and pined for weary months, so that her face was harsher and less comely than before, yet she still hoped on, for her lord had come through so many dangers that she could scarce believe that he might be stricken down at last. It had been her wish to start for Spain and to search for him, but Alleyne had persuaded her to let him go in her place. There was much to look after, now that the lands of Minstead were joined to those of Twynham, and Alleyne had promised her that if she would but bide with his wife he would never come back to Hampshire again until he had gained some news, good or ill, of her lord and lover.

The yellow cog had been engaged, with Goodwin Hawtayne in command, and a month after the wedding Alleyne rode down to Bucklershard to see if she had come round yet from Southampton. On the way he passed the fishing village of Pitt's Deep, and marked that a little creyer or brig was tacking off the land, as though about to anchor there. On his way back, as he rode towards the village, he saw that she had indeed anchored, and that many boats were round her, bearing cargo to the shore.

A bow-shot from Pitt's Deep there was an inn a little back from the road, very large and wide-spread, with a great green bush hung upon a pole from one of the upper windows. At this window he marked, as he rode up, that a man was seated who appeared to be craning his neck in his direction. Alleyne was still looking up at him, when a woman came rushing from the open door of the inn, and made as though she would climb a tree, looking back the while with a laughing face. Wondering what these doings might mean, Alleyne tied his horse to a tree, and was walking amid the trunks towards the inn, when there shot from the entrance a second woman who made also for the trees. Close at her heels came a burly, brown-faced man, who leaned against the door-post and laughed loudly with his hand to his side, "Ah, mes belles!" he cried, "and is it thus you treat me? Ah, mes petites! I swear by these finger-bones that I would not hurt a hair of your pretty heads; but I have been among the black paynim, and, by my hilt! it does me good to look at your English cheeks. Come, drink a stoup of muscadine with me, mes anges, for my heart is warm to be among ye again."

At the sight of the man Alleyne had stood staring, but at the sound of his voice such a thrill of joy bubbled up in his heart that he had to bite his lip to keep himself from shouting outright. But a deeper pleasure yet was in store. Even as he looked, the window above was pushed outwards, and the voice of the man whom he had seen there came out from it. "Aylward," cried the voice, "I have seen just now a very worthy person come down the road, though my eyes could scarce discern whether he carried coat-armor. I pray you to wait upon him and tell him that a very humble knight of England abides here, so that if he be in need of advancement, or have any small vow upon his soul, or desire to exalt his lady, I may help him to accomplish it."

Aylward at this order came shuffling forward amid the trees, and in an instant the two men were clinging in each other's arms, laughing and shouting and patting each other in their delight; while old Sir Nigel came running with his sword, under the impression that some small bickering had broken out, only to embrace and be embraced himself, until all three were hoarse with their questions and outcries and congratulations.

On their journey home through the woods Alleyne learnt their wondrous story: how, when Sir Nigel came to his senses, he with his fellow-captive had been hurried to the coast, and conveyed by sea to their captor's castle; how upon the way they had been taken by a Barbary rover, and how they exchanged their light captivity for a seat on a galley bench and hard labor at the pirate's oars; how, in the port at Barbary, Sir Nigel had slain the Moorish captain, and had swum with Aylward to a small coaster which they had taken, and so made their way to England with a rich cargo to reward them for their toils. All this Alleyne listened to, until the dark keep of Twynham towered above them in the gloaming, and they saw the red sun lying athwart the rippling Avon. No need to speak of the glad hearts at Twynham Castle that night, nor of the rich offerings from out that Moorish cargo which found their way to the chapel of Father Christopher.

Sir Nigel Loring lived for many years, full of honor and laden with every blessing. He rode no more to the wars, but he found his way to every jousting within thirty miles; and the Hampshire youth treasured it as the highest honor when a word of praise fell from him as to their management of their horses, or their breaking of their lances. So he lived and so he died, the most revered and the happiest man in all his native shire.

For Sir Alleyne Edricson and for his beautiful bride the future had also naught but what was good. Twice he fought in France, and came back each time laden with honors. A high place at court was given to him, and he spent many years at Windsor under the second Richard and the fourth Henry—where he received the honor of the Garter, and won the name of being a brave soldier, a true-hearted gentleman, and a great lover and patron of every art and science which refines or ennobles life.

As to John, he took unto himself a village maid, and settled in Lyndhurst, where his five thousand crowns made him the richest franklin for many miles around. For many years he drank his ale every night at the "Pied Merlin," which was now kept by his friend Aylward, who had wedded the good widow to whom he had committed his plunder. The strong men and the bowmen of the country round used to drop in there of an evening to wrestle a fall with John or to shoot a round with Aylward; but, though a silver shilling was to be the prize of the victory, it has never been reported that any man earned much money in that fashion. So they lived, these men, in their own lusty, cheery fashion—rude and rough, but honest, kindly and true. Let us thank God if we have outgrown their vices. Let us pray to God that we may ever hold their virtues. The sky may darken, and the clouds may gather, and again the day may come when Britain may have sore need of her children, on whatever shore of the sea they be found. Shall they not muster at her call?

A Note About the Author

Sir Arthur Conan Doyle (1859–1930) was a Scottish author best known for his classic detective fiction, although he wrote in many other genres including dramatic work, plays, and poetry. He began writing stories while studying medicine and published his first story in 1887. His Sherlock Holmes character is one of the most popular inventions of English literature, and has inspired films, stage adaptions, and literary adaptations for over 100 years.

A Note from the Publisher